The Collected Stories of Sean O'Faolain

Volume 2

By the same author

*Novels*

A Nest of Simple Folk
Bird Alone
Come Back to Erin
And Again?

*Biography*

Constance Markievicz
King of the Beggars
The Great O'Neill
Newman's Way

*Autobiography*

Vive Moi!

*Travel*

An Irish Journey
A Summer in Italy
An Autumn in Italy

*Miscellaneous*

The Short Story
The Vanishing Hero
She Had to Do Something
The Silver Branch
The Irish

# The Collected Stories of Sean O'Faolain

Volume 2

Constable London

First published in Great Britain 1981
by Constable and Company Limited
10 Orange Street, London WC2H 7EG
Copyright © 1949, 1953, 1954, 1956, 1957,
1958, 1959, 1961, 1963, 1965, 1966, 1981
ISBN 0 09 464210 9
Set in 9pt Pilgrim by Coats Dataprint, Inverness
Printed in Great Britain by
REDWOOD BURN LIMITED
Trowbridge

# Contents

6   *Contents*

# Childybawn

When Benjy Spillane's mother got a letter signed 'A True Friend' informing her that Benjy had been 'carrying on' for years with a young lady in the bank she at once sank beneath all the appropriate maternal emotions. She saw her treasure looted, her future imperilled, her love deceived. She saw her poor, foolish child beguiled, his innocence undermined, his sanity destroyed. At this time Benjy was just turned forty-one, a cheerful man-about-town with a winy face like a Halloween turnip with a candle inside it, a pair of merry bull's eyes, a hint of grey at his temples, and his overcoat hung down straight from his paunch as if he was going to have a baby. He was an accountant at the bank, his rank and his cubicle next to the manager's.

For two weeks Benjy could not go out for a walk or open a letter at the breakfast table without evoking long, anxious, secretive looks from his mother. At last she could stand it no longer, and put the question point-blank to him.

'Benjy, lovey, is it true what I heard? That you're thinking of getting married? Not, of course, childybawn, that anything would give me more joy than to see you settled down. But, of course, you have time enough, too, and I'd like to see you happy. It isn't a thing you'd rush into, you know.'

Benjy's eyes were normally *à fleur de tête*. At this they protruded as if he had goitre. His little mouth was open like a toy fish. Then he hooted loudly.

'Me? Married? In the name of God where did you get that yarn?'

'I dunno now what put it into my head,' she said, her heart beginning to glow with relief and joy. 'I wonder could it be something that ould jade Ma Looney said to me the other night at the chapel? About how I'd soon be losing you, or something like that. She was always a bad-minded ould rip.'

'Well, you can tell her from me she's talking through her left leg. I know, Mammy, when I'm well off,' and he slapped her knee. 'Aren't

you better to me than any wife? And amn't I as good as a second husband to you?'

Which, natural functions apart, was quite true; for, like all Irish mothers, she had him fastened to her with hoops of comfort, and he was so devoted to her that his young lady at the bank once told him that it made her sick to see the pair of them together. So she thought no more about it, beyond petting and spoiling him worse than ever, until she got another letter, this time signed 'A Well Wisher', a few days after he came home from his Easter holidays, informing her that the young lady at the bank had gone with him to Paris and Cannes. At this she began to steam open his correspondence. Since Benjy and his ladylove were at the same bank it was over a month before she was rewarded. She was scarlet before she finished the first sentence: 'Darling Benjy Wenjy, Your poor little Angela is in bed with the flu, and isn't it a shame, a show and a scandal that 'tis only the flu I'm in bed with. . . .' As she watched Benjy reading the letter that evening over dinner, with a foolish smile on his fat face, she wished that his Angela would get double pneumonia and never rise from her bed again.

The first thing she did was to toddle off to her father confessor. He annoyed her exceedingly by advising her to pray for her son's early marriage. She thanked him. She said she would. But she had no intention of doing anything of the kind; firstly because it was the last thing she wanted herself, and secondly because she had to face the fact that it was the last thing Benjy wanted either. She thought up a much more satisfying plan. She had always had an intense devotion to Saint Monica, the mother of Saint Augustine, and she now started to make a novena to the pair of them. She hung up their pictures in Benjy's bedroom. One day she went so far as to borrow a copy of *The Confessions of Saint Augustine* from the free library, and laid it casually under the *Sporting Chronicle* on Benjy's armchair. It was the night he usually took her to the pictures, so when she said she was a bit tired and would rather stay at home he naturally sat down on the book.

'Hello!' he said, lugging it out. 'Where did you get this?'

'That?' she said, peering at it over her specs. 'Wisha, I dunno now where did I get that? Ah, yes, I remember now I got it in the free library. I suppose 'tis edifying, but . . . Anyway, the old print is too small for my poor eyes.'

'Would you like me to read a bit of it for you?' said Benjy, who used sometimes to read aloud to her on their nights at home.

'If you like,' she said without enthusiasm.

He humoured her, but after a few minutes he began to ruffle the pages.

'Why doesn't he come to the point?' he asked impatiently. 'This is all crawthumping stuff. There's not as much as a bottle of stout in it yet. I mean, what did he do anyway after all his old guff?'

'Not much, then,' she said, and gazed sadly into the fire. 'God help the poor creature!' she sighed. 'That's all I have to say – God help her!'

'God help who?' said Benjy. 'Oh, but you're right, didn't he go off with a woman or something?' – and he began to turn the pages more hopefully.

'I'm referring to Monica,' said his mother severely. 'He broke his poor mother's heart. But,' she said cheerfully, 'he mended it again, God bless him and protect him. When he turned from his bad ways! Ah, that was a lovely scene, the two of them sitting in the window, and the sun going down over the sea. Hand in hand. Mother and son. Lovely! Ah! Lovely! Lovely!'

'You seem to have the book off by heart. We didn't come to that at all yet.'

'Yerrah, what book, childybawn? I don't need any book. Amn't I going to the special anniversary sermon on him every year for the last forty years down in Saint Augustine's? And that was another lovely scene, the day in the orchard. When the poor boy was feeling down in the dumps. His conscience at him, I suppose. And the voice said, *Tolle lege, tolle lege*. And there and then he took up the book, and what did he read in the first line?' She fixed her eye on Benjy, who was looking at her in astonishment out of his cheerful, ruddy, turnip face, and she let him have it full blast: '*Not in rioting nor in wantonness, not in chambering nor in drunkenness, but put ye on the garment of the Lord Jesus Christ.*' She said it so dramatically that Benjy thought she was going to begin the next sentence with 'Dearly beloved brethren.' 'Aha!' she went on. 'That was when the arrow struck him. As it strikes each and every one of us sooner or later. Even the hardest hearted amongst us. *I come*, says the Lord, *like a thief in the night, seeking whom I may devour!*'

Benjy looked at her sourly.

'There was a great preacher lost in you,' he said, and went on looking for the spicy bit.

She was silent for a while. He had succeeded in finding a not-too-bad description of what he took to be a bullfight, so he did not see the sharp looks she was giving him. Then he heard her say, lightly, to nobody in particular:

'I was at confession today.'

Benjy grunted. That was nothing new.

'Father Benignus I went to. Over at the Capuchins.'

Benjy was now deeply interested in the bullfight, so he said nothing to this either.

'He says he knows you.'

At this Benjy looked up.

'Me? I never laid eyes on him.' And he looked down again.

'He laid eyes on you, then. He says he knows you as well as a bad ha'penny.'

Benjy laid down the book. The crawthumping stuff had begun again.

'Oho? So ye were talking about me?' with an ominous note in his voice which she nervously observed and dared to ignore.

'No, no! Sure, amn't I telling you it was inside in confession? 'Twas only just how we were talking about poor Saint Augustine.'

'Is that so?' says Benjy, giving her a long look. 'Tell me! Is there, by any chance, any other priest who knows me like that?'

'Father Semple at the South Chapel told me he often saw you at the bank. And Father Milvey up in the Lough Chapel says you have a great future if you'll only mind your *p*'s and *q*'s.'

At that Benjy flared:

'I see you have me well bell-a-ragged around the town! I suppose you're telling them all that I'm a trial and a torment to you?'

'Oh! Benjy! What a dreadful thing you're after saying! All I ever said to anyone, and I'd say it to the Pope himself, is that you're the best son ever trod shoe leather. As you are! So far as I know!' A hurt came into her voice as she added, 'What do I know about your affairs? Only what you tell me.' A long pause. 'Your life is your own.' A still longer pause. 'To make or to mar.'

There was a long silence between them after that.

'I think,' said Benjy, 'I'll take the ould dog out for a walk.'

He got no farther than the local, where he had a couple of brooding drinks. He needed them. So did she, and had them. For it was one of her little habits – which she never mentioned to Benjy; it would be only troubling the poor boy – to have a nip of brandy every night, or if the poor heart was weak, or over-excited, maybe two. She felt so much better after them that she was able to put on her specs again and have a look in the *Sporting Chronicle* for tomorrow's starters at Leopardstown; an old County Kildare woman, she had never lost her interest in the nags.

The Monica regimen went on for about three months. During all that time she never said a single word of reproach to him. Every morning she said good-bye to him with a sad smile. She welcomed him home every evening with a fond, pathetic kiss, going down then on her knees, in spite of all his protests, to remove his galoshes. He was never so well looked after. She used to heat the seat of his trousers by the fire every morning before letting him put them on. But she stopped going to the pictures. She said she had no heart for them. Instead she would sit opposite him saying the Rosary. If he said anything cheerful she would let out a deep sigh. He found it hard to concentrate on the *Sporting Chronicle*.

After about three months of this both their nerves were so shaken that when he was going to Biarritz for his summer holidays he gave himself away to her by assuring her three times that he was going alone. She decided to call in the help of the bank manager.

'But, my dear Mrs Spillane', he said to her, when she had finished her extraordinary story, 'what on earth can I do? The private lives of my staff are no concern of mine – provided, of course, that there isn't any public scandal, and that it doesn't interfere with the affairs of the bank. I can assure you that your son is an exemplary official. In fact, what you tell me astonishes me. Have you any proof of it?'

She couldn't mention that she had been opening his letters, so she side-stepped that one. What she did say was:

'Amn't I his mother? And let me tell you that if you're astonished I'm more astonished to think you'd allow lassies like that one to be working in a respectable bank like this. 'Tis against nature to have women in banks. 'Tis against God! Banks, indeed! I know another name some people would give them with straps like that one waiting to put their claws into the first poor innocent boy they can capture!'

This rattled him. He had married a lady bank clerk himself and had lived to regret it.

'Mrs Spillane, your son is not a boy. He's a grown man. And you're doing him no good at all with this kind of talk. Your son will probably become a manager himself one day, but it's unlikely unless he gets married. Now, wouldn't the very best solution to all this be if your *boy* were to marry this young lady?'

She rose up before him to her full height, a small, humpty-dumpty old woman, and with misery in her pale-blue eyes and hatred in her voice she said:

'I'd rather see him in his pools of blood at my feet than see him married to that Jezebel!'

The day after he came back from Biarritz he fell down at her feet spouting blood from a burst ulcer, and was rushed off to hospital. Before they started to operate they brought in the priest to him, and by then Benjy was in no state – moral, physical, or strategical – to resist his administrations. It was a close shave; they barely pulled him through; and by the time he was recuperating he was a changed man. The day Mrs Spillane passed a bold-looking strap on the stairs of the nursing home, her eyes as red as her painted lips from crying, and walked in to find Benjy reading *The Life of the Curé d'Ars* of his own free will, she knew that mother love had triumphed at last.

After that Benjy developed a great regard for Saint Augustine. Every evening, now, side by side, he and his mother sat in the bay window of their little villa watching the sun slowly draw its light away from the bay. He never went out of evenings except on works of charity with the Saint Vincent de Pauls. He gave up the liquor. He banned the *Sporting Chronicle*. The only visitors were other fellows from the S. V. de P.'s, or Father Benignus from the Capuchin priory, or Father Semple from the South Chapel, or the curate who had salvaged him in the nursing home. One night when he saw his mother reading a novel called *Her Scarlet Lover* he got up, went to his shelves, and with a sad little smile he handed her a new biography of a Peruvian Jesuit who used to flagellate himself with whips made of old safety-razor blades. There was an embarrassing moment another night when he came home a bit early from his charitable rounds, moved a cushion, found a half-empty bottle of Hennessy's Three Star, and got a definite smell of brandy in the air. Not that he said anything. Nor did he a few evenings later when, with a wry memory of his past follies, he took up that morning's paper to have a look at the racing page and found that day's starters at Hurst Park all checked off pro and con in pencil, with the odds written in beside them. But he began to remember things; he even began to brood – the steak that night had been a bit tough and she had brought him Bordeaux instead of Burgundy. He remembered how, about a year back, he had come one morning on a little heap of coloured betting slips behind D'Alton's six-volume *History of Ireland* on his bookshelves, and hastily and fearfully burned them as his own. He became aware that she was backbiting Ma Looney:

'God forgive me,' she was saying, 'I ran into that ould jade Ma Looney this morning after Mass, and it didn't do me a hap'orth of good. That one is always detracting and backbiting. Oh, an envious jade! Do you remember the time she wanted to persuade me, right or wrong, that you were getting married? Pure jealousy, that's what it was! She's eaten up with it. Do you know now what that one is...'

In his years of wickedness Benjy would have listened to her with an indulgent smile. She saw him looking at her now as coldly as if she were a strange woman in a bus. She faltered, shuffled, petered out, and suggested humbly to him that he might like to take the dog for a walk. He did. She profited by his absence: two quick ones. The next night he profited by hers when she toddled off to confession: he rooted the house upside down. He found two empty brandy bottles, eight more betting tickets, her grocer's bills with several incriminating items, and the three anonymous letters. With a sad heart he put them all back where he found them.

'The poor old divil,' he was saying to himself. 'What a lousy, lonely, empty life I've driven her to! God! I've been a bastard to her!'

That night when she came home he had a new bottle of Three Star ready for her. She took a great deal of persuading before she would accept a teeny, little nightcap. She took less and less persuading every night after, but always she took the nip from him humbly, cringingly. He began to collect racing tips for her at the bank.

'You should put a bob on, now and again,' he would say, with his cheery hoot of laughter. 'There's no harm in it, Mammy! 'Twill only amuse you.'

After that it was a joy to him to see her handing out her shilling to him every morning with a cackle of laughter at her own folly – until the day she won at ten to one on an outsider. In her excitement she let out a wail:

'Oh, what misfortune I had that I didn't put ten bob on him!'

With a shock he thought that maybe she always used to put half a crown on her fancy before. He cursed his meanness.

'Never mind,' he comforted her. 'Sure, 'tis only fun. I mean, what do you want the money for?'

'Oho, then, and oho, then,' she said fretfully, 'we could all do with the money. 'Tis all right for you; you don't have to worry about it. Housekeeping isn't what it was when you were a boy.'

'Mammy, are the accounts a worry to you? Would you prefer me to take them off your chest?'

'No, no, no!' she cried at once. 'No worry at all! What would the worry be? Chuchuchu! For goodness' sake, what worry?'

All the same he dropped in to the grocer the next morning on his way to the bank. He came out trembling. Not a bill paid for six months. The butcher had the same story for him. All that morning at the bank he was distracted by misery at the thought of the poor old creature crimping for money while he had been gallivanting with her ladyship in Paris and Biarritz and Cannes. At his lunch hour he went sadly into Joe Rosenberg's betting office to put her shilling on a horse called Silver Lining. It was Joe who took the bob. He looked at it, looked at Benjy, and said:

'Mr Spillane, could I have a word with you for a minute?'

Much surprised at being addressed by name, Benjy passed the lifted lid of the counter to where Joe's big fat hand was already slowly turning the pages of a ledger. Benjy's stomach was slowly turning over with it. Sure enough, when Joe had smoothened out a page with his big fingers that looked as if they had been worn flat by delving in his money satchel, Benjy saw her name at the top of the page. His eye raced down to the foot of the page. A total, in the red, of £125.17.6.

'I thought you didn't know,' said Joe, seeing the look in his face. Then, slowly tapping out 'The Dead March' with his fingers across the total: 'I suppose my money is safe with you?'

'You'll get it,' said Benjy, knowing well that Joe knew well that it was as much as his job was worth to plead the Gaming Act and disown it. He saw that there was no bet under two pounds, several for a fiver, and there was one wild splurge of a tenner.

'What did she back that day?' he asked. Joe had to laugh.

'Do you remember that old four-year-old mare of Billy Morgan's at Punchestown last year?'

'Jasus!' Benjy moaned. 'Sure they're looking for her yet. You'll have to take it in instalments, Joe. Give her no more credit.'

When he got back to the bank he had to sit down. When he saw Angela's legs as she sailed down the aisle, the seam of her black nylons as straight and swelling as the line of a yacht, he thought his ulcer was going to burst all over again. Twice during that afternoon he caught her flirting gaily with the teller in the next cubicle and he got so dizzy that he had to hold on to the desk.

That night as he ate his dinner opposite his mother the silence lay heavy between them like a gramophone record that has not been started. He waited until they were by the fire to let it go.

'Mammy,' he said, leading with his left and ready with the right for her answer, 'would it upset you very much if I got married?'

She turned joyfully to him.

'Oh, Benjy! Isn't that great news? Who is the lucky girl?'

'A young lady I know at the bank,' said Benjy, giving her the right, and waiting with the left for the knockout. 'Her name is Angela.'

He found his two hands being grasped and kissed.

'Childybawn, I'm simply delighted. How soon will it be?'

'You seem,' he said, taken aback, 'to be bloody anxious to get rid of me?'

'No! No, Benjy love! No!' And she began to sniffle. 'Only you've been so cross with me this last six months. There's no pleasing you.'

'Cross?' he roared. 'Cross? Am I hearing things? Was I cross about the brandy? Was I cross about the grocer's bills? Or about the butcher? And what about your hundred and twenty-five pounds, seventeen shillings and sixpence that you owe Joe Rosenberg?'

She crouched down in her chair, her two withered hands clasped before her, and stared at him in horror.

'Oh, Benjy!' she fluttered. 'Is that all you found out?'

You could have counted out one hundred and twenty-five pounds, seventeen shillings, and six pennies before Benjy could close his mouth and control his wandering paws.

'Sacred Heart!' he whispered at last. 'What else is there?'

Her snuffle rose into a wail:

'There's the bloody old money lenders!'

As Benjy sank back into his armchair and gazed at the ceiling, as helpless as a man in a barber's chair, her wail sirened up into a bawl.

'I only wish to God. You got married years and years ago. Ever since you took to. That old piety of yours. You've made my life a misery. Giving me thimblefuls of brandy like a baby. Making me bet in measly ould bobs. Picking and prying at me. From morning to night. Watching every penny I spend. Go on!' she bawled. 'Go on, and get married! And torment some other misfortunate woman. The way you're tormenting *me*!'

Benjy's eyes roved patiently all over the ceiling as if he were in search of the answer to the mystery of life. Not finding it in any part of the ceiling he looked out at the sky. He sought for it in the grass of the garden. At last he sought for it in her face, at the sight of which, all puckered up comically like a baby with the gripes, he burst into laughter. He laughed and he laughed.

'Honest to God, Mammy,' he howled, 'you ought to be put in the budget. You bloody ould rip of hell you!'

She clutched his two hands and drew him towards her.

'Oh, childybawn, they're the first natural words you've said to me in six months!'

He detached himself from her, got up, and looked down at her, flooding with pity at the thought of what the two of them had been through since the Easter before. He patted her hand and said:

'I'm going for a walk.'

He was back in ten minutes with a new bottle of Hennessy. He got out the tumblers and slapped out two hard ones. He put one in her fist, sat on the arm of her chair, put his arm around her shoulder, and made her clink glasses. She was beginning to protest when his look stopped her. The two of them were soon laughing like children or lovers, and discussing his wedding like any natural mother and son the world over.

An hour later, well fortified, he put on his hat and coat and went down to Angela's digs. She was in slacks, and shapely in them, and only that he was not too sure of his ground he would have loved to squeeze the life out of her. Instead she led him into the back parlour, closed the door, walked over to him, and slapped his face. She called him a creeping rat, a cringing worm, a bloody mammy's darling. She asked him did he think she could be picked up and dropped again at his own sweet will. She told him she wouldn't marry him if he was the last man on earth. She asked him did he think she was a common trollop. She asked him why didn't he go and marry his mother since he was so bloody fond of her. To none of this was Benjy in a position to give a truthful, or indeed any, answer. She slapped his face once more. Then she burst into floods of tears on his shoulder. At a quarter to two in the morning the landlady came down in her dressing-gown and threw him out, battered, exhausted, but affianced.

When his old mother died, about five years later, he did marry Angela. As he said when a bachelor pal teased him at the wedding for marrying so young:

'That's all very fine, but, damn it all, I mean to say, a fellow has to have *some* regard for his mother!'

# Lovers of the Lake

'They might wear whites,' she had said, as she stood sipping her tea and looking down at the suburban tennis players in the square. And then, turning her head in that swift movement that always reminded him of a jackdaw: 'By the way, Bobby, will you drive me up to Lough Derg next week?'

He replied amiably from the lazy deeps of her armchair.

'Certainly! What part? Killaloe? But is there a good hotel there?'

'I mean the other Lough Derg. I want to do the pilgrimage.'

For a second he looked at her in surprise and then burst into laughter; then he looked at her peeringly.

'Jenny! Are you serious?'

'Of course.'

'Do you mean that place with the island where they go around on their bare feet on sharp stones, and starve for days, and sit up all night ologroaning and ologoaning?' He got out of the chair, went over to the cigarette box on the bookshelves, and, with his back to her, said coldly, 'Are you going religious on me?'

She walked over to him swiftly, turned him about, smiled her smile that was whiter than the whites of her eyes, and lowered her head appealingly on one side. When this produced no effect she said:

'Bobby! I'm always praising you to my friends as a man who takes things as they come. So few men do. Never looking beyond the day. Doing things on the spur of the moment. It's why I like you so much. Other men are always weighing up, and considering and arguing. I've built you up as a sort of magnificent, wild, brainless tomcat. Are you going to let me down now?'

After a while he had looked at his watch and said:

'All right, then. I'll try and fix up a few days free next week. I must drop into the hospital now. But I warn you, Jenny, I've noticed this Holy Joe streak in you before. You'll do it once too often.'

She patted his cheek, kissed him sedately, said, 'You are a good boy,' and saw him out with a loving smile.

They enjoyed that swift morning drive to the Shannon's shore. He suspected nothing when she refused to join him in a drink at Carrick. Leaning on the counter they had joked with the barmaid like any husband and wife off on a motoring holiday. As they rolled smoothly around the northern shore of Lough Gill he had suddenly felt so happy that he had stroked her purple glove and winked at her. The lough was vacant under the midday sun, its vast expanse of stillness broken only by a jumping fish or by its eyelash fringe of reeds. He did not suspect anything when she sent him off to lunch by himself in Sligo, saying that she had to visit an old nun she knew in the convent. So far the journey had been to him no more than one of her caprices; until a yellow signpost marked TO BUNDORAN made them aware that her destination and their parting was near, for she said:

'What are you proposing to do until Wednesday?'

'I hadn't given it a thought.'

'Don't go off and forget all about me, darling. You know you're to pick me up on Wednesday about midday?'

After a silence he grumbled:

'You're making me feel a hell of a bastard, Jenny.'

'Why on earth?'

'All this penitential stuff is because of me, isn't it?'

'Don't be silly. It's just something I thought up all by myself out of my own clever little head.'

He drove on for several miles without speaking. She looked sideways, with amusement, at his ruddy, healthy, hockey-player face glummering under the peak of his checked cap. The brushes at his temples were getting white. Everything about him bespoke the distinguished Dublin surgeon on holiday: his pale-green shirt, his darker-green tie, his double-breasted waistcoat, his driving gloves with the palms made of woven cord. She looked pensively towards the sea. He growled:

'I may as well tell you this much, Jenny, if you were my wife I wouldn't stand for any of this nonsense.'

So their minds had travelled to the same thought? But if she were his wife the question would never have arisen. She knew by the sudden rise of speed that he was in one of his tempers, so that when he pulled into the grass verge, switched off, and turned towards her she was not taken by surprise. A sea gull moaned high overhead. She lifted her grey eyes to his, and smiled, waiting for the attack.

'Jenny, would you mind telling me exactly what all this is about? I mean, why are you doing this fal-lal at this particular time?'

'I always wanted to do this pilgrimage. So it naturally follows that I would do it sometime, doesn't it?'

'Perhaps. But why, for instance, this month and not last month?'

'The island wasn't open to pilgrims last month.'

'Why didn't you go last year instead of this year?'

'You know we went to Austria last year.'

'Why not the year before last?'

'I don't know. And stop bullying me. It is just a thing that everybody wants to do sometime. It is a special sort of Irish thing, like Lourdes, or Fatima, or Lisieux. Everybody who knows about it feels drawn to it. If you were a practising Catholic you'd understand.'

'I understand quite well,' he snapped. 'I know perfectly well that people go on pilgrimages all over the world. Spain. France. Mexico. I shouldn't be surprised if they go on them in Russia. What I am asking you is what has cropped up to produce this extra-special performance just *now*?'

'And I tell you I don't know. The impulse came over me suddenly last Sunday looking at those boys and girls playing tennis. For no reason. It just came. I said to myself, "All right, go now!" I felt that if I didn't do it on the impulse I'd never do it at all. Are you asking me for a rational explanation? I haven't got one. I'm not clever and intelligent like you, darling.'

'You're as clever as a bag of cats.'

She laughed at him.

'I do love you, Bobby, when you are cross. Like a small boy.'

'Why didn't you ask George to drive you?'

She sat up straight.

'I don't want my husband to know anything whatever about this. Please don't mention a word of it to him.'

He grinned at his small victory, considered the scythe of her jawbone, looked at the shining darkness of her hair, and restarted the car.

'All the same,' he said after a mile, 'there must be some reason. Or call it a cause if you don't like the word reason. And I'd give a lot to know what it is.'

After another mile:

'Of course, I might as well be talking to that old dolmen over there as be asking a woman why she does anything. And if she knew she wouldn't tell you.'

After another mile:

'Mind you, I believe all this is just a symptom of something else. Never forget, my girl, that I'm a doctor. I'm trained to interpret symptoms. If a woman comes to me with a pain...'

'Oh, yes, if a woman comes to Surgeon Robert James Flannery with a pain he says to her, "Never mind, that's only a pain." My God! If a woman has a pain she has a bloody pain!'

He said quietly:

'Have you a pain?'

'Oh, do shut up! The only pain I have is in my tummy. I'm ravenous.'

'I'm sorry. Didn't they give you a good lunch at the convent?'

'I took no lunch; you have to arrive at the island fasting. That's the rule.'

'Do you mean to say you've had nothing at all to eat since breakfast?'

'I had no breakfast.'

'What will you get to eat when you arrive on the island?'

'Nothing. Or next to nothing. Everybody has to fast on the island the whole time. Sometime before night I might get a cup of black tea, or hot water with pepper and salt in it. I believe it's one of their lighthearted jokes to call it soup.'

Their speed shot up at once to sixty-five. He drove through Bundoran's siesta hour like the chariot of the Apocalypse. Nearing Ballyshannon they slowed down to a pleasant, humming fifty.

'Jenny!'

'Yes?'

'Are you tired of me?'

'Is this more of you and your symptoms?'

He stopped the car again.

'Please answer my question.'

She laid her purple-gloved hand on his clenched fist.

'Look, darling! We've known one another for six years. You know that like any good little Catholic girl I go to my duties every Easter and every Christmas. Once or twice I've told you so. You've growled and grumbled a bit, but you never made any fuss about it. What are you suddenly worrying about now?'

'Because all that was just routine. Like the French or the Italians. Good Lord, I'm not bigoted. There's no harm in going to church now and again. I do it myself on state occasions, or if I'm staying in some house where they'd be upset if I didn't. But this sort of lunacy isn't routine!'

She slewed her head swiftly away from his angry eyes. A child in a pink pinafore with shoulder frills was driving two black cows through a gap.

'It was never routine. It's the one thing I have to hang on to in an otherwise meaningless existence. No children. A husband I'm not in love with. And I can't marry you.'

She slewed back to him. He slewed away to look up the long empty road before them. He slewed back; he made as if to speak; he slewed away impatiently again.

'No?' she interpreted. 'It isn't any use, is it? It's my problem, not yours. Or if it is yours you've solved it long ago by saying it's all a lot of damned nonsense.'

'And how have you solved it?' he asked sardonically.

'Have you any cause to complain of how I've solved it? Oh, I'm not defending myself. I'm a fraud, I'm a crook, I admit it. You are more honest than I am. You don't believe in anything. But it's the truth that all I have is you and . . .'

'And what?'

'It sounds so blasphemous I can't say it.'

'Say it!'

'All I have is you, and God.'

He took out his cigarette case and took one. She took one. When he lit hers their eyes met. He said, very softly, looking up the empty road:

'Poor Jenny! I wish you'd talked like this to me before. It is, after all, as you say, your own affair. But what I can't get over is that this thing you're doing is so utterly extravagant. To go off to an island, in the middle of a lake, in the mountains, with a lot of Crawthumpers of every age and sex, and no sex, and peel off your stockings and your shoes, and go limping about on your bare feet on a lot of sharp stones, and kneel in the mud, psalming and beating your breast like a criminal, and drink nothing for three days but salt water . . . it's not like you. It's a side of you I've never known before. The only possible explanation for it must be that something is happening inside in you that I've never seen happen before!'

She spread her hands in despair. He chucked away his cigarette and restarted the car. They drove on in silence. A mist began to speckle the windscreen. They turned off the main road into sunless hills, all brown as hay. The next time he glanced at her she was making up her face; her mouth rolling the lipstick into her lips; her eyes rolling around the mirror. He said:

'You're going to have a nice picnic if the weather breaks.'

She glanced out apprehensively.

'It won't be fun.'

A sudden flog of rain lashed into the windscreen. The sky had turned its bucket upside down. He said:

'Even if it's raining do you still have to keep walking around on those damn stones?'

'Yes.'

'You'll get double pneumonia.'

'Don't worry, darling. It's called Saint Patrick's Purgatory. He will look after me.'

That remark started a squabble that lasted until they drew up beside the lake. Other cars stood about like stranded boats. Other pilgrims stood by the boat slip, waiting for the ferry, their backs hunched to the wind, their clothes ruffled like the fur of cattle. She looked out across the lough at the creeping worms of foam.

He looked about him sullenly at the waiting pilgrims, a green bus, two taxi-loads of people waiting for the rain to stop. They were not his kind of people at all, and he said so.

'That,' she smiled, 'is what comes of being a surgeon. You don't meet people, you meet organs. Didn't you once tell me that when you are operating you never look at the patient's face?'

He grunted. Confused and hairy-looking clouds combed themselves on the ridges of the hills. The lake was crumpled and grey, except for those yellow worms of foam blown across it in parallel lines. To the south a cold patch of light made it all look far more dreary. She stared out towards the island and said:

'It's not at all like what I expected.'

'And what the hell did you expect? Capri?'

'I thought of an old island, with old grey ruins, and old holly trees and rhododendrons down to the water, a place where old monks would live.'

They saw tall buildings like modern hotels rising by the island's shore, an octagonal basilica big enough for a city, four or five bare, slated houses, a long shed like a ballroom. There was one tree. Another bus drew up beside them and people peered out through the wiped glass.

'Oh, God!' she groaned. 'I hope this isn't going to be like Lourdes.'

'And what, pray, is wrong with Lourdes when it's at home?'

'Commercialized. I simply can't believe that this island was the most famous pilgrimage of the Middle Ages. On the rim of the known world. It must have been like going off to Jerusalem or coming home brown from the sun with a cockle in your hat from Galilee.'

He put on a vulgar Yukon voice:

'Thar's gold somewhere in them thar hills. It looks to me like a damn good financial proposition for somebody.'

She glared at him. The downpour had slackened. Soon it almost ceased. Gurgles of streams. A sound of pervasive drip. From the back seat she took a small red canvas bag marked T.W.A.

'You will collect me on Wednesday about noon, won't you?'

He looked at her grimly. She looked every one of her forty-one years. The skin of her neck was corrugated. In five years' time she would begin to have jowls.

'Have a good time,' he said, and slammed in the gears, and drove away.

The big, lumbering ferryboat was approaching, its prow slapping the corrugated waves. There were three men to each oar. It began to spit rain again. With about a hundred and fifty men and women, of every age and, so far as she could see, of every class, she clambered aboard. They pushed out and slowly they made the crossing, huddling together from the wind and rain. The boat nosed into its cleft and unloaded. She had a sensation of dark water, wet cement, houses, and a great number of people; and that she would have given gold for a cup of hot tea. Beyond the four or five white-washed houses – she guessed that they had been the only buildings on the island before trains and buses made the pilgrimage popular – and beyond the cement paths, she came on the remains of the natural island: a knoll, some warm grass, the tree, and the roots of the old hermits' cells across whose teeth of stone barefooted pilgrims were already treading on one another's heels. Most of these barefooted people wore mackintoshes. They not only stumbled on one another's heels; they kneeled on one another's toes and tails; for the island was crowded – she thought there must be nearly two thousand people on it. They were packed between the two modern hostels and the big church. She saw a priest in sou'wester and gum boots. A nun waiting for the new arrivals at the door of the women's hostel took her name and address, and gave her the number of her cubicle. She went upstairs to it, laid her red bag on the cot, sat beside it, unfastened her garters, took off her shoes, unpeeled her nylons, and without transition became yet another anonymous pilgrim. As she went out among the pilgrims already praying in the rain she felt only a sense of shame as if she were specially singled out under the microscope of the sky. The wet ground was cold.

A fat old woman in black, rich-breasted, grey-haired, took her kindly by the arm and said in a warm, Kerry voice: 'You're shivering, you poor creature! Hould hard now. Sure, when we have the first station done they'll be giving us the ould cup of black tay.'

And laughed at the folly of this longing for the tea. She winced when she stepped on the gritty concrete of the terrace surrounding the basilica, built out on piles over the lake. A young man smiled sympathetically, seeing that she was a delicate subject for the rigours before her: he was dressed like a clerk, with three pens in his breast pocket, and he wore a Total Abstinence badge.

'Saint's Island they call it,' he smiled. 'Some people think it should be called Divil's Island.'

She disliked his kindness – she had never in her life asked for pity from anybody, but she soon found that the island floated on kindness. Everything and everybody about her seemed to say, 'We are all sinners here, wretched creatures barely worthy of mercy.' She felt the abasement of the doomed. She was among people who had surrendered all personal identity, all pride. It was like being in a concentration camp.

The fat old Kerrywoman was explaining to her what the routine was, and as she listened she realized how long her stay would really be. In prospect it had seemed so short: come on Monday afternoon, leave on Wednesday at noon; it had seemed no more than one complete day and two bits of nights. She had not foreseen that immediately after arriving she must remain out of doors until the darkness fell, walking the rounds of the stones, praying, kneeling, for about five hours. And even then she would get no respite, for she must stay awake all night praying in the basilica. It was then that she would begin the second long day, as long and slow as the night; and on the third day she would still be walking those rounds until mid-day. She would be without food, even when she would have left the island, until the midnight of that third day.

'Yerrah, but sure,' the old woman cackled happily, 'they say that fasting is good for the stomach.'

She began to think of 'they'.

They had thought all this up. They had seen how much could be done with simple prayers. For when she began to tot up the number of Paternosters and Aves that she must say she had to stop at the two thousandth. And these reiterated prayers must be said while walking on the stones, or kneeling in the mud, or standing upright with her two arms extended. This was the posture she disliked most. Every time she came to do it, her face to the lake, her arms spread, the queue listening to her renouncing her sins, she had to force herself to the posture and the words. The first time she did it, with the mist blowing into her eyes, her arms out like a crucifix, her lips said the words but her heart cursed herself for coming so unprepared, for coming at all. Before she had completed her first circuit – four times around each one of six cells – one ankle and one toe was bleeding. She was then permitted to ask for the cup of black tea. She received it sullenly, as a prisoner might receive his bread and water.

She wished after that first circuit to start again and complete a second – the six cells, and the seven other ordeals at other points of the island – and so be done for the day. But she found that 'they' had invented something else: she must merge with the whole anonymous mass of pilgrims for mass prayer in the church.

A slur of wet feet; patter of rain on leaded windows; smells of bog water and damp clothing; the thousand voices responding to the incantations. At her right a young girl of about seventeen was uttering heartfelt responses. On her left an old man in his sixties gave them out loudly. On all sides, before her, behind her, the same passionate exchange of energy, while all she felt was a crust hardening about her heart, and she thought, in despair, 'I have no more feeling than a stone!' And she thought, looking about her, that tonight this vigil would go on for hour after hour until the dark, leaded windows coloured again in the morning light. She leaned her face in her palms and whispered, 'O God, please let me out of myself!' The waves of voices beat and rumbled in her ears as in an empty shell.

She was carried out on the general sliding whispering of the bare feet into the last gleanings of the daylight to begin her second circuit. In the porch she cowered back from the rain. It was settling into a filthy night. She was thrust forward by the crowd, flowed with its force to the iron cross by the shingle's edge. She took her place in the queue and then with the night wind pasting her hair across her face she raised her arms and once again renounced the world, the flesh, and the Devil. She did four circles of the church on the gritty concrete. She circled the first cell's stones. She completed the second circle. Her prayers were become numb by now. She stumbled, muttering them, up and down the third steeply sloped cell, or bed. She was a drowned cat and one knee was bleeding. At the fourth cell she saw him.

He was standing about six yards away looking at her. He wore a white raincoat buttoned tight about his throat. His feet were bare. His hair was streaked down his forehead as if he had been swimming. She stumbled towards him and dragged him by the arm down to the edge of the boat slip.

'What are you doing here?' she cried furiously. 'Why did you follow me?'

He looked down at her calmly:

'Why shouldn't I be here?'

'Because you don't believe in it! You've just followed me to sneer at me, to mock at me! Or from sheer vulgar curiosity!'

'No,' he said, without raising his voice. 'I've come to see just what it is that you believe in. I want to know all about you. I want to know why you came here. I don't want you to do anything or have anything that I can't do or can't know. And as for believing – we all believe in something.'

Dusk was closing in on the island and the lake. She had to peer into his face to catch his expression.

'But I've known you for years and you've never shown any sign of believing in anything but microscopes and microbes and symptoms. It's absurd, you couldn't be serious about anything like this. I'm beginning to hate you!'

'Are you?' he said, so softly that she had to lean near him to hear him over the slapping of the waves against the boat slip. A slow rift in the clouds let down a star; by its light she saw his smile.

'Yes!' she cried, so loudly that he swept out a hand and gripped her by the arm. Then he took her other arm and said gently:

'I don't think you should have come here, Jenny. You're only tearing yourself to bits. There are some places where some people should never go, things some people should never try to do – however good they may be for others. I know why you came here. You feel you ought to get rid of me, but you haven't the guts to do it, so you come up here into the mountains to get your druids to work it by magic. All right! I'm going to ask them to help you.'

He laughed and let her go, giving her a slight impulse away from him.

'Ask? You will *ask*? Do you mean to tell me that you have said as much as one single, solitary prayer on this island?'

'Yes,' he said casually, 'I have.'

She scorned him.

'Are you trying to tell me, Bobby, that you are doing this pilgrimage?'

'I haven't fasted. I didn't know about that. And, anyway, I probably won't. I've got my pockets stuffed with two pounds of the best chocolates I could buy in Bundoran. I don't suppose I'll even stay up all night like the rest of you. The place is so crowded that I don't suppose anybody will notice me if I curl up in some corner of the boathouse. I heard somebody saying that people had to sleep there last night. But you never know – I might – I just might stay awake. If I do, it will remind me of going to midnight Mass with my father when I was a kid. Or going to retreats, when we used all hold up a lighted candle and renounce the Devil.

'It was a queer sensation standing up there by the lake and saying those words all over again. Do you know, I thought I'd completely forgotten them!'

'The next thing you're going to say is that you believe in the Devil! You fraud!'

'Oh, there's no trouble about believing in that old gentleman. There isn't a doctor in the world who doesn't, though he will give him another name. And on a wet night, in a place like this, you could believe in a lot of things. No, my girl, what I find it hard to believe in is the flesh and the world. They are good things. Do you think I'm ever going to believe that your body and my body are evil? And you don't either! And you are certainly never going to renounce the world, because you are tied to it hand and foot!'

'That's not true!'

His voice cut her like a whip:

'Then why do you go on living with your husband?'

She stammered feebly. He cut at her again:

'You do it because he's rich, and you like comfort, and you like being a "somebody".'

With a switch of her head she brushed past him. She did not see him again that night.

The night world turned imperceptibly. In the church, for hour after hour, the voices obstinately beat back the responses. She sank under the hum of the prayer wheel, the lust for sleep, her own despairs. Was he among the crowd? Or asleep in a corner of the boatshed? She saw his flatly domed fingers, a surgeon's hand, so strong, so sensitive. She gasped at the sensual image she had evoked.

The moon touched a black window with colour. After an age it had stolen to another. Heads drooped. Neighbours poked one another awake with a smile. Many of them had risen from the benches in order to keep themselves awake and were circling the aisles in a loose procession of slurring feet, responding as they moved. Exhaustion began to work on her mind. Objects began to disconnect, become isolated each within its own outline – now it was the pulpit, now a statue, now a crucifix. Each object took on the vividness of a hallucination. The crucifix detached itself from the wall and leaned towards her, and for a long while she saw nothing but the heavy pendent body, the staring eyes, so that when the old man at her side let his head sink over on her shoulder and then woke up with a start she felt him no more than if they were two fishes touching in the sea. Bit by bit the incantations drew her in; sounds came from her mouth; prayers flowed between her and those troubled eyes that fixed hers. She swam into an ecstasy as rare as one of those perfect dances of her youth when she used to swing in a whirl of music, a swirl of bodies, a circling of lights, floated out of her mortal frame, alone in the arms that embraced her.

Suddenly it all exploded. One of the four respites of the night had halted the prayers. The massed pilgrims relaxed. She looked blearily about her, no longer disjunct. Her guts rumbled. She looked at the old man beside her. She smiled at him and he at her.

'My poor old knees are crucified,' he grinned.

'You should have the skirts,' she grinned back.

They were all going out to stretch in the cool, and now dry, air, or to snatch a smoke. The amber windows of the church shivered in a pool of water. A hearty-voiced young woman leaning on the balustrade lit a match for her. The match hissed into the invisible lake lapping below.

'The ould fag,' said the young woman, dragging deep on her cigarette, 'is a great comfort. 'Tis as good as a man.'

'I wonder,' she said, 'what would Saint Patrick think if he saw women smoking on his island?'

'He'd beat the living lights out of the lot of us.'

She laughed aloud. She must tell him that . . . . She began to wander through the dark crowds in search of him. He had said something that wasn't true and she would answer him. She went through the crowds down to the boat slip. He was standing there, looking out into the dark as if he had not stirred since she saw him there before midnight. For a moment she regarded him, frightened by the force of the love that gushed into her. Then she approached him.

'Well, Mr Worldly Wiseman? Enjoying your boathouse bed?'

'I'm doing the vigil,' he said smugly.

'You sound almighty pleased with yourself.'

He spoke eagerly now:

'Jenny, we mustn't quarrel. We must understand one another. And understand this place. I'm just beginning to. An island. In a remote lake. Among the mountains. Nighttime. No sleep. Hunger. The conditions of the desert. I was right in what I said to you. Can't you see how the old hermits who used to live here could swim off into a trance in which nothing existed but themselves and their visions? I told you a man can renounce what he calls the Devil, but not the flesh, not the world. They thought, like you, that they could throw away the flesh and the world, but they were using the flesh to achieve one of the rarest experiences in the world! Don't you see it?'

'Experiences! The next thing you'll be talking about is symptoms.'

'Well, surely, you must have observed?' He peered at the luminous dial of his watch. 'I should say that about four o'clock we will probably begin to experience a definite sense of dissociation. After that a positive alienation . . .'

She turned furiously from him. She came back to say:

'I would much prefer, Bobby, if you would have the decency to go away in the morning. I can find my own way home. I hope we don't meet again on this island. Or out of it!'

'The magic working?' he laughed.

After that she made a deliberate effort of the mind to mean and to feel every separate word of the prayers – which is a great foolishness since prayers are not poems to be read or even understood; they are an instinct; to dance would be as wise. She thought that if she could not feel what she said how could she mean it, and so she tried to savour every word, and, from trying to mean each word, lagged behind the rest, sank into herself, and ceased to pray. After the second respite she prayed only to keep awake. As the first cold pallor of morning came into the windows her heart rose again. But the eastern hills are high here and the morning holds off stubbornly. It is the worst hour of the vigil, when the body ebbs, the prayers sink to a drone, and the night seems to have begun all over again.

At the last respite she emerged to see pale tents of blue on the hills. The slow cumulus clouds cast a sheen on the water. There is no sound. No birds sing. At this hour the pilgrims are too awed or too exhausted to speak, so that the island reverts to its ancient silence in spite of the crowds.

By the end of the last bout she was calm like the morning lake. She longed for the cup of black tea. She was unaware of her companions. She did not think of him. She was unaware of herself. She no more thought of God than a slave thinks of his master, and after she had drunk her tea she sat in the morning sun outside the women's hostel like an old blind woman who has nothing in life to wait for but sleep.

The long day expired as dimly as the vapour rising from the water. The heat became morbid. One is said to be free on this second day to converse, to think, to write, to read, to do anything at all that one pleases except the one thing everybody wants to do – to sleep. She did nothing but watch the clouds, or listen to the gentle muttering of the lake. Before noon she heard some departing pilgrims singing a hymn as the great ferryboats pushed off. She heard their voices without longing;

she did not even desire food. When she met him she was without rancour.

'Still here?' she said, and when he nodded: 'Sleepy?'

'Sleepy.'

'Too many chocolates, probably.'

'I didn't eat them. I took them out of my pockets one by one as I leaned over the balustrade and guessed what centre each had – coffee, marshmallow, nut, toffee, cream – and dropped it in with a little splash to the holy fishes.'

She looked up at him gravely.

'Are you really trying to join in this pilgrimage?'

'Botching it. I'm behindhand with my rounds. I have to do five circuits between today and tomorrow. I may never get them done. Still, something is better than nothing.'

'You dear fool!'

If he had not walked away then she would have had to; such a gush of affection came over her at the thought of what he was doing, and why he was doing it – stupidly, just like a man; sceptically, just like a man; not admitting it to himself, just like a man; for all sorts of damn-fool rational reasons, just like a man; and not at all for the only reason that she knew was his real reason: because she was doing it, which meant that he loved her. She sat back, and closed her eyes, and the tears of chagrin oozed between her lids as she felt her womb stir with desire of him.

When they met again it was late afternoon.

'Done four rounds,' he said so cheerfully that he maddened her.

'It's not golf, Bobby, damn you!'

'I should jolly well think not. I may tell you my feet are in such a condition I won't be able to play golf for a week. Look!'

She did not look. She took his arm and led him to the quietest corner she could find.

'Bobby, I am going to confess something to you. I've been thinking about it all day trying to get it clear. I know now why I came here. I came because I know inside in me that some day our apple will have to fall off the tree. I'm forty. You are nearly fifty. It will have to happen. I came here because I thought it right to admit that some day, if it has to be, I am willing to give you up.'

He began to shake all over with laughter.

'What the hell are you laughing at?' she moaned.

'When women begin to reason! Listen, wasn't there a chap one time who said, "O God, please make me chaste, but not just yet"?'

'What I am saying is "now," if it has to be, if it can be, if I can make it be. I suppose,' she said wildly, 'I'm really asking for a miracle, that my husband would die, or that you'd die, or something like that that would make it all come right!'

He burst into such a peal of laughter that she looked around her apprehensively. A few people near them also happened to be laughing over something and looked at them indulgently.

'Do you realize, Bobby, that when I go to confession here I will have to tell all about us, and I will have to promise to give you up?'

'Yes, darling, and you won't mean a single word of it.'

'But I always mean it!'

He stared at her as if he were pushing curtains aside in her.

'Always? Do you mean you've been saying it for six years?'

'I mean it when I say it. Then I get weak. I can't help it, Bobby. You know that!' She saw the contempt in his eyes and began to talk rapidly, twisting her marriage ring madly around her finger. He kept staring into her eyes like a man staring down the long perspective of a railway line waiting for the engine to appear. 'So you see why there wasn't any sense in asking me yesterday why I come now and not at some other time, because with me there isn't any other time, it's always *now*, I meet you *now*, and I love you *now*, and I think it's not right *now*, and then I think, "No, not *now*," and then I say I'll give you up *now*, and I mean it every time until we meet again, and it begins all over again, and there's never any end to it until some day I can say, "Yes, I used to know him once, but not now," and then it will be a *now* where there won't be any other *now* any more because there'll be nothing to live for.'

The tears were leaking down her face. He sighed:

'Dear me! You have got yourself into a mess, haven't you?'

'O God, the promises and the promises! I wish the world would end tonight and we'd both die together!'

He gave her his big damp handkerchief. She wiped her eyes and blew her nose and said:

'You don't mean to go to confession, do you?'

He chuckled sourly.

'And promise? I must go and finish a round of pious golf. I'm afraid, old girl, you just want to get me into the same mess as yourself. No, thank you. You must solve your own problems in your own way, and I in mine.'

That was the last time she spoke to him that day.

She went back to the balustrade where she had smoked with the hearty girl in the early hours of the morning. She was there again. She wore a scarlet beret. She was smoking again. She began to talk, and the talk flowed from her without stop. She had fine broad shoulders, a big mobile mouth, and a pair of wild goat's eyes. After a while it became clear that the woman was beside herself with terror. She suddenly let it all out in a gush of exhaled smoke.

'Do you know why I'm hanging around here? Because I ought to go into confession and I'm in dread of it. He'll tear me alive. He'll murdher me. It's not easy for a girl like me, I can promise you!'

'You must have terrible sins to tell?' she smiled comfortingly.

'He'll slaughter me, I'm telling you.'

'What is it? Boys?'

The two goat's eyes dilated with fear and joy. Her hands shook like a drunkard's.

'I can't keep away from them. I wish to God I never came here.'

'But how silly! It's only a human thing. I'm sure half the people here have the same tale to tell. It's an old story, child, the priests are sick of hearing it.'

'Oh, don't be talking! Let me alone! I'm criminal, I tell yeh! And there are things you can't explain to a priest. My God, you can hardly explain 'em to a doctor!'

'You're married?' – looking at her ring.

'Poor Tom! I have him wore out. He took me to a doctor one time to know would anything cure me. The old foolah took me temperature and gave me a book like a bus guide about when it's safe and when it isn't safe to make love, the ould eedjut! I was pregnant again before Christmas. Six years married and I have six kids; nobody could stand that gait o' going. And I'm only twenty-four. Am I to have a baby every year of my life? I'd give me right hand this minute for a double whiskey.'

'Look, you poor child! We are all in the same old ferryboat here. What about me?'

'You?'

'It's not men with me, it's worse.'

'Worse? In God's name, what's worse than men?'

The girl looked all over her, followed her arm down to her hand, to her third finger.

'One man.'

The tawny eyes swivelled back to her face and immediately understood.

'Are you very fond of him?' she asked gently, and taking the unspoken answer said, still more pityingly, 'You can't give him up?'

'It's six years now and I haven't been able to give him up.'

The girl's eyes roved sadly over the lake as if she were surveying a lake of human unhappiness. Then she threw her butt into the water and her red beret disappeared into the maw of the church porch.

She saw him twice before the dusk thickened and the day grew cold again with the early sunset. He was sitting directly opposite her before the men's hostel, smoking, staring at the ground between his legs. They sat facing one another. They were separated by their identities, joined by their love. She glimpsed him only once after that, at the hour when the sky and the hills merge, an outline passing across the lake. Soon after she had permission to go to her cubicle. Immediately she lay down she spiralled to the bottom of a deep lake of sleep.

She awoke refreshed and unburthened. She had received the island's gift: its sense of remoteness from the world, almost a sensation of the world's death. It is the source of the island's kindness. Nobody is just matter, poor to be exploited by rich, weak to be exploited by the strong; in mutual generosity each recognizes the other only as a form of soul; it is a brief, harsh Utopia of equality in nakedness. The bare feet are a symbol of that nakedness unknown in the world they have left.

The happiness to which she awoke was dimmed a little by a conversation she had with an Englishman over breakfast – the usual black tea and a piece of oaten bread. He was a city man who had arrived the day before, been up all night while she slept. He had not yet shaved; he was about sixty-two or three; small and tubby, his eyes perpetually wide and unfocusing behind pince-nez glasses.

'That's right,' he said, answering her question. 'I'm from England. Liverpool. I cross by the night boat and get here the next afternoon. Quite convenient, really. I've come here every year for the last twenty-two years, apart from the war years. I come on account of my wife.'

'Is she ill?'

'She died twenty-two years ago. No, it's not what you might think – I'm not praying for her. She was a good woman, but, well, you see, I wasn't very kind to her. I don't mean I quarrelled with her, or drank, or was unfaithful. I never gambled. I've never smoked in my life.' His hands made a faint movement that was meant to express a whole life, all the confusion and trouble of his soul. 'It's just that I wasn't kind. I didn't make her happy.'

'Isn't that,' she said, to comfort him, 'a very private feeling? I mean, it's not in the Ten Commandments that thou shalt make thy wife happy.'

He did not smile. He made the same faint movement with his fingers.

'Oh, I don't know! What's love if it doesn't do that? I mean to say, it is something godly to love another human being, isn't it? I mean, what does "godly" mean if it doesn't mean giving up everything for another? It isn't human to love, you know. It's foolish, it's a folly, a divine folly. It's beyond all reason, all limits. I didn't rise to it,' he concluded sadly.

She looked at him, and thought, 'A little fat man, a clerk in some Liverpool office all his life, married to some mousy little woman, thinking about love as if he were some sort of Greek mystic.'

'It's often,' she said lamely, 'more difficult to love one's husband, or one's wife, as the case may be, than to love one's neighbour.'

'Oh, much!' he agreed without a smile. 'Much! Much more difficult!'

At which she was overcome by the thought that inside ourselves we have no room without a secret door; no solid self that has not a ghost inside it trying to escape. If I leave Bobby I still have George. If I leave George I still have myself, and whatever I find in myself. She patted the little man's hand and left him, fearing that if she let him talk on even his one little piece of sincerity would prove to be a fantasy, and in the room that he had found behind his own room she would open other doors leading to other obsessions. He had told her something true about her own imperfection, and about the nature of love, and she wanted to share it while it was still true. But she could not find him, and there was still one more circuit to do before the ferryboat left. She did meet Goat's Eyes. The girl clutched her with tears magnifying her yellow-and-green irises and gasped joyously:

'I found a lamb of a priest. A saint anointed! He was as gentle! "What's your husband earning?" says he. "Four pounds ten a week, Father," says I. "And six children?" says he. "You poor woman," says he, "you don't need to come here at all. Your Purgatory is at home." He laid all the blame on poor Tom. And, God forgive me, I let him do it. "Bring him here to me," says he, "and I'll cool him for you." God bless the poor innocent priest, I wish I knew as little about marriage as he does. But,' and here she broke into a wail, 'sure he has me ruined altogether now. He's after making me so fond of poor Tommy I think I'll never get home soon enough to go to bed with him.' And in a vast flood of tears of joy, of relief, and of fresh misery: 'I wish I was a bloomin' nun!'

It was not until they were all waiting at the ferryboat that she saw him. She managed to sit beside him in the boat. He touched her hand and winked. She smiled back at him. The bugler blew his bugle. A tardy traveller came racing out of the men's hostel. The boatload cheered him, the bugler helped him aboard with a joke about people who can't be persuaded to stop praying, and there was a general chaff about people who have a lot to pray about, and then somebody raised the parting hymn, and the rowers began to push the heavy oars, and singing they were slowly rowed across the summer lake back to the world.

They were driving back out of the hills by the road they had come, both silent. At last she could hold in her question no longer:

'Did you go, Bobby?'

Meaning: had he, after all his years of silence, of rebellion, of disbelief, made his peace with God at the price of a compact against her. He replied gently:

'Did I probe your secrets all these years?'

She took the rebuke humbly, and for several miles they drove on in silence. They were close, their shoulders touched, but between them there stood that impenetrable wall of identity that segregates every human being in a private world of self. Feeling it she realized at last that it is only in places like the lake-island that the barriers of self break down. The tubby little clerk from Liverpool had been right. Only when love desires nothing but renunciation, total surrender, does self surpass self. Everybody who ever entered the island left the world of self behind for a few hours, exchanged it for what the little man had called a divine folly. It was possible only for a few hours – unless one had the courage, or the folly, to renounce the world altogether. Then another thought came to her. In the world there might also be escape from the world.

'Do you think, Bobby, that when people are in love they can give up everything for one another?'

'No,' he said flatly. 'Except perhaps in the first raptures?'

'If I had a child I think I could sacrifice anything for it. Even my life.'

'Yes,' he agreed. 'It has been known to happen.'

And she looked at him sadly, knowing that they would never be able to marry, and even if she did that she would never have children. And yet, if they could have married, there was a lake . . .

'Do you know what I'm planning at this moment?' he asked breezily.

She asked without interest what it was.

'Well, I'm simply planning the meal we're going to eat tonight in Galway, at midnight.'

'At midnight? Then we're going on with this pilgrimage? Are we?'

'Don't *you* want to? It was your idea in the beginning.'

'All right. And what are we going to do until midnight? I've never known time to be so long.'

'I'm going to spend the day fishing behind Glencar. That will kill the hungry day. After that, until midnight, we'll take the longest possible road around Connemara. Then would you have any objections to mountain trout cooked in milk, stuffed roast kid with fresh peas and spuds in their jackets, apple pie and whipped cream, with a cool Pouilly Fuissé, a cosy 1929 claret, West of Ireland Pont l'Évêque, finishing up with Gaelic coffee and two Otards? Much more in your line, if I know anything about you, than your silly old black tea and hot salt water.'

'I admit I like the things of the flesh.'

'You live for them!'

He had said it so gently, so affectionately that, half in dismay, half with amusement, she could not help remembering Goat's Eyes, racing home as fast as the bus would carry her to make love to her Tommy. After that they hardly spoke at all, and then only of casual things such as a castle beside the road, the sun on the edging sea, a tinker's caravan, an opening view. It was early afternoon as they entered the deep valley

at Glencar and he probed in second gear for an attractive length of
stream, found one and started eagerly to put his rod together. He began
to walk up against the dazzling bubble of water and within an hour was
out of sight. She stretched herself out on a rug on the bank and fell
sound asleep.

It was nearly four o'clock before she woke up, stiff and thirsty. She
drank from a pool in the stream, and for an hour she sat alone by the
pool, looking into its peat-brown depth, as vacantly contented as a
tinker's wife to live for the moment, to let time wind and unwind
everything. It was five o'clock before she saw him approaching,
plodding in his flopping waders, with four trout on a rush stalk. He
threw the fish at her feet and himself beside them.

'I nearly ate them raw,' he said.

'Let's cook them and eat them,' she said fiercely.

He looked at her for a moment, then got up and began to gather dry
twigs, found Monday's newspaper in the car – it looked like a paper of
years ago – and started the fire. She watched while he fed it. When it
was big enough in its fall to have made a hot bed of embers he roasted
two of the trout across the hook of his gaff, and she smelled the crisping
flesh and sighed. At last he laid them, browned and crackly, on the
grass by her hand. She took one by its crusted tail, smelled it, looked
at him, and slung it furiously into the heart of the fire. He gave a
sniff-laugh and did the same with his.

'Copy cat!' she said.

'Let's get the hell out of here,' he said, jumping up. 'Carry the kit,
will you?'

She rose, collected the gear, and followed him saying:

'I feel like an Arab wife. "Carry the pack. Go here. Go there."'

They climbed out of the glens on to the flat moorland of the Easky
peninsula where the evening light was a cold ochre gleaming across
green bogland that was streaked with all the weedy colours of a strand
at ebb. At Ballina she suggested that they should have tea.

'It will be a pleasant change of diet!' he said.

When they had found a café and she was ordering the tea he said to
the waitress:

'And bring lots of hot buttered toast.'

'This,' she said, as she poured out the tea and held up the milk jug
questioningly, 'is a new technique of seduction. Milk?'

'Are you having milk?'

'No.'

'No, then.'

'Some nice hot buttered toast?'

'Are you having toast?' he demanded.

'Why the bloody hell should it be up to me to decide?'

'I asked you a polite question,' he said rudely.

'No.'

'No!'

They looked at one another as they sipped the black tea like two people who are falling head over heels into hatred of one another.

'Could you possibly tell me,' he said presently, 'why I bother my head with a fool of a woman like you?'

'I can only suppose, Bobby, that it is because we are in love with one another.'

'I can only suppose so,' he growled. 'Let's get on!'

They took the longest way round he could find on the map, west into County Mayo, across between the lake at Pontoon, over the level bogland to Castlebar. Here the mountains walled in the bogland plain with cobalt air – in the fading light the land was losing all solidity. Clouds like soapsuds rose and rose over the edges of the mountains until they glowed as if there was a fire of embers behind the blue ranges. In Castlebar he pulled up by the post office and telephoned to the hotel at Salthill for dinner and two rooms. When he came out he saw a poster in a shop window and said:

'Why don't we go to the pictures? It will kill a couple of hours.'

'By rights,' she said, 'you ought to be driving me home to Dublin.'

'If you wish me to I will.'

'Would you if I asked you?'

'Do you want me to?'

'I suppose it's rather late now, isn't it?'

'Not at all. Fast going we could be there about one o'clock. Shall we?'

'It wouldn't help. George is away. I'd have to bring you in and give you something to eat, and ... Let's go to the blasted movies!'

The film was *Charley's Aunt*. They watched its slapstick gloomily. When they came out, after nine o'clock, there was still a vestigial light in the sky. They drove on and on, westward still, prolonging the light, prolonging the drive, holding off the night's decision. Before Killary they paused at a black-faced lake, got out, and stood beside its quarried beauty. Nothing along its stony beach but a few wind-torn rushes.

'I could eat you,' he said.

She replied that only lovers and cannibals talk like that.

They dawdled past the long fiord of Killary where young people on holiday sat outside the hotel, their drinks on the trestled tables. In Clifden the street was empty, people already climbing to bed, as the lights in the upper windows showed. They branched off on the long coastal road where the sparse whitewashed cottages were whiter than the foam of waves that barely suggested sea. At another darker strand they halted, but now they saw no foam at all and divined the sea only by its invisible whispering, or when a star touched a wave. Midnight was now only an hour away.

Their headlights sent rocks and rabbits into movement. The heather streamed past them like kangaroos. It was well past eleven as they poured along the lonely land by Galway Bay. Neither of them had spoken for an hour. As they drove into Salthill there was nobody abroad. Galway was dark. Only the porch light of the hotel showed that it was alive. When he turned off the engine the only sound at first was the crinkle of contracting metal as the engine began to cool. Then to their right they heard the lisping bay. The panel button lit the dashboard clock.

'A quarter to,' he said, leaning back. She neither spoke nor stirred. 'Jenny!' he said sharply.

She turned her head slowly and by the dashboard light he saw her white smile.

'Yes, darling?'

'Worn out?' he asked, and patted her knee.

She vibrated her whole body so that the seat shook, and stretched her arms about her head, and lowering them let her head fall on his shoulder, and sighed happily, and said:

'What I want is a good long drink of anything on earth except tea.'

These homing twelve o'clockers from Lough Derg are well known in every hotel all over the west of Ireland. Revelry is the reward of penance. The porter welcomed them as if they were heroes returned from a war. As he led them to their rooms he praised them, he sympathized with them, he patted them up and he patted them down, he assured them that the ritual grill was at that moment sizzling over the fire, he proffered them hot baths, and he told them where to discover the bar. 'Ye will discover it . . . ' was his phrase. The wording was exact, for the bar's gaiety was muffled by dim lighting, drawn blinds, locked doors. In the overheated room he took off his jacket and loosened his tie. They had to win a corner of the counter, and his order was for two highballs with ice in them. Within two minutes they were at home with the crowd. The island might never have existed if the barmaid, who knew where they had come from, had not laughed: 'I suppose ye'll ate like lions?'

After supper they relished the bar once more, sipping slowly now, so refreshed that they could have started on the road again without distaste or regret. As they sipped they gradually became aware of a soft strumming and drumming near at hand, and were told that there was a dance on in the hotel next door. He raised his eyebrows to her. She laughed and nodded.

They gave it up at three o'clock and walked out into the warm-cool of the early summer morning. Gently tipsy, gently tired they walked to the little promenade. They leaned on the railing and he put his arm about her waist, and she put hers around his, and they gazed at the moon silently raking its path across the sea towards Aran. They had come, she knew, to the decisive moment. He said:

'They have a fine night for it tonight on the island.'

'A better night than we had,' she said tremulously.

After another spell of wave fall and silence he said:

'Do you know what I'm thinking, Jenny? I'm thinking that I wouldn't mind going back there again next year. Maybe I might do it properly the next time?'

'The next time?' she whispered, and all her body began to dissolve and, closing her eyes, she leaned against him. He, too, closed his eyes, and all his body became as rigid as a steel girder that flutters in a storm. Slowly they opened their love-drunk eyes, and stood looking long over the brightness and blackness of the sea. Then, gently, ever so gently, with a gentleness that terrified her he said:

'Shall we go in, my sweet?'

She did not stir. She did not speak. Slowly turning to him she lifted her eyes to him pleadingly.

'No, Bobby, please, not yet.'

'Not yet?'

'Not tonight!'

He looked down at her, and drew his arms about her. They kissed passionately. She knew what that kiss implied. Their mouths parted. Hand in hand they walked slowly back to the hotel, to their separate rooms.

# The Fur Coat

When Maguire became Parliamentary Secretary to the Minister for Roads and Railways his wife wound her arms around his neck, lifted herself on her toes, gazed into his eyes and said, adoringly:

'Now, Paddy, I must have a fur coat.'

'Of course, of course, me dear,' Maguire cried, holding her out from him admiringly; for she was a handsome little woman still, in spite of the greying hair and the first hint of a stoop. 'Get two fur coats! Switzer's will give us any amount of tick from now on.'

Molly sat back into her chair with her fingers clasped between her knees and said, chidingly:

'You think I'm extravagant!'

'Indeed, then, I do not. We've had some thin times together and it's about time we had a bit of comfort in our old age. I'd like to see my wife in a fur coat. I'd love to see my wife take a shine out of some of those straps in Grafton Street – painted jades that never lifted a finger for God or man, not to as much as mention the word *Ireland*. By all means get a fur coat. Go down to Switzer's tomorrow morning,' he cried with all the innocence of a warm-hearted, inexperienced man, 'and order the best fur coat that money can buy.'

Molly Maguire looked at him with affection and irritation. The years had polished her hard – politics, revolution, husband in and out of prison, children reared with the help of relatives and Prisoners' Dependents' funds. You could see the years on her finger tips, too pink, too coarse, and in her diamond-bright eyes.

'Paddy, you big fool, do you know what you'd pay for a mink coat? Not to mention a sable? And not as much as to whisper the word broadtail?'

'Say a hundred quid,' said Paddy, manfully. 'What's a hundred quid? I'll be handling millions of public money from now on. I have to think big.'

She replied in her warm Limerick singsong; sedately and proudly as befitted a woman who had often, in her father's country store, handled thousands of pound notes.

'Do you know, Paddy Maguire, what a really bang-up fur coat could cost you? It could cost you a thousand guineas, and more.'

'One thousand guineas? For a coat? Sure, that's a whole year's salary.'

'It is.'

Paddy drew into himself. 'And,' he said, in a cautious voice, 'is that the kind of coat you had in mind?'

She laughed, satisfied at having taken him off his perch.

'Yerrah, not at all. I thought I might pick up a nice little coat for, maybe, thirty or forty or, at the outside, fifty quid. Would that be too much?'

'Go down to Switzer's in the morning and bring it home on your back.'

But, even there, she thought she detected a touch of the bravo, as if he was still feeling himself a great fellow. She let it pass. She said she might have a look around. There was no hurry. She did not bring up the matter again for quite fifteen minutes.

'Paddy! About that fur coat. I sincerely hope you don't think I'm being *vulgar*?'

'How could you be vulgar?'

'Oh, sort of *nouveau riche*. I don't want a fur coat for show-off.' She leaned forward eagerly. 'Do you know the reason why I want a fur coat?'

'To keep you warm. What else?'

'Oh, well, that too, I suppose, yes,' she agreed shortly. 'But you must realize that from this on we'll be getting asked out to parties and receptions and so forth. And – well – I haven't a rag to wear!'

'I see,' Paddy agreed; but she knew that he did not see.

'Look,' she explained, 'what I want is something I can wear any old time. I don't want a fur coat for grandeur.' (This very scornfully.) 'I want to be able to throw it on and go off and be as well dressed as anybody. You see, you can wear any old thing under a fur coat.'

'That sounds a good idea.' He considered the matter as judiciously as if he were considering a memorandum for a projected bypass. She leaned back, contented, with the air of a woman who has successfully laid her conscience to rest.

Then he spoiled it all by asking, 'But, tell me, what do all the women do who haven't fur coats?'

'They dress.'

'Dress? Don't ye all dress?'

'Paddy, don't be silly. They think of nothing else but dress. I have no time for dressing. I'm a busy housewife and, anyway, dressing costs a lot of money.' (Here she caught a flicker in his eye which obviously meant that forty quid isn't to be sniffed at either.) 'I mean they have costumes that cost twenty-five pounds. Half a dozen of 'em. They spend a lot of time and thought over it. They live for it. If you were married to one of 'em you'd soon know what it means to dress. The beauty of a fur coat is that you can just throw it on and you're as good as the best of them.'

'Well, that's fine! Get the ould coat.'

He was evidently no longer enthusiastic. A fur coat, he had learned, is not a grand thing – it is just a useful thing. He drew his brief case towards him. There was that pier down in Kerry to be looked at. 'Mind you,' he added, 'it'd be nice and warm, too. Keep you from getting a cold.'

'Oh, grand, yes, naturally, cosy, yes, all that, yes, yes!'

And she crashed out and banged the door after her and put the children to bed as if she were throwing sacks of turf into a cellar. When she came back he was poring over maps and specifications. She began to patch one of the boy's pyjamas. After a while she held it up and looked at it in despair. She let it sink into her lap and looked at the pile of mending beside her.

'I suppose when I'm dead and gone they'll invent plastic pyjamas that you can wash with a dishcloth and mend with a lump of glue.'

She looked into the heart of the turf fire. A dozen pyjamas ... underwear for the whole house ...

'Paddy!'

'Huh?'

'The last thing that I want anybody to start thinking is that I, by any possible chance, could be getting grand notions.'

She watched him hopefully. He was lost in his plans.

'I can assure you, Paddy, that I loathe – I simply loathe all this modern show-off.'

'That's right.'

'Those wives that think they haven't climbed the social ladder until they've got a fur coat!'

He grunted at the map of the pier.

'Because I don't care what you or anybody else says, Paddy, there *is* something vulgar about a fur coat. There's no shape to them. Especially musquash. What I was thinking of was black Indian lamb. Of course, the real thing would be ocelot. But they're much too dear. The real ones. And I wouldn't be seen dead in an imitation ocelot.'

He glanced sideways from the table. 'You seem to know a lot about fur.' He leaned back and smiled benevolently. 'I never knew you were hankering all this time after a fur coat.'

'Who said I'm hankering! I am *not*. What do you mean? Don't be silly. I just want something decent to wear when we go out to a show, or to wear over a dance frock, that's all. What do you mean – hankering?'

'Well, what's wrong with that thing you have with the fur on the sleeves? The shiny thing with the what-do-you-call-'ems – sequins, is it?'

'*That*! Do you mean *that*? For heaven's sake, don't be talking about what you don't know anything about. I've had *that* for fourteen years. It's like something me grandmother wore at her own funeral.'

He laughed. 'You used to like it.'

'Of course, I liked it when I got it. Honestly, Paddy Maguire, there are times when . . .'

'Sorry, sorry, sorry. I was only trying to be helpful. How much is an ocelot?'

'Eighty-five or ninety – at the least.'

'Well, why not?'

'Paddy, tell me honestly. Honestly, now! Do you seriously think that I could put eighty-five pounds on my back?'

With his pencil Maguire frugally drew a line on the map, reducing the pier by five yards, and wondered would the county surveyor let him get away with it.

'Well, the question is: will you be satisfied with the Indian lamb? What colour did you say it is? Black? That's a very queer lamb.'

Irritably he rubbed out the line. The wretched thing would be too shallow at low water if he cut five yards off it.

'It's dyed. You could get it brown, too,' she cried. 'You could get all sorts of lamb. Broadtail is the fur of unborn Persian lambs.'

That woke him up: the good farmer stock in him was shocked.

'Unborn lambs!' he cried. 'Do you mean to say that they . . .'

'Yes, isn't it awful? Honest to Heaven, Paddy, anyone that'd wear broadtail ought to be put in prison. Paddy, I've made up my mind. I just couldn't buy a fur coat. I just won't buy it. That's the end of it.'

She picked up the pyjamas again and looked at them with moist eyes. He turned to devote his full attention to her problem.

'Molly, darling, I'm afraid I don't understand what you're after. I mean, do you or do you not want a fur coat? I mean, supposing you didn't buy a fur coat, what else could you do?'

'Just exactly what do you mean?' – very coldly.

'I mean, it isn't apparently necessary that you should buy a fur coat. I mean, not if you don't really want to. There must be some other way of dressing besides fur coats? If you have a scunner against fur coats, why not buy something else just as good? There's hundreds of millions of other women in the world and they all haven't fur coats.'

'I've told you before that they dress! And I've no time to dress. I've explained all that to you.'

Maguire got up. He put his back to the fire, his hands behind him, a judicial look on him. He addressed the room.

'All the other women in the world can't all have time to dress. There must be some way out of it. For example, next month there'll be a garden party up at the President's house. How many of all these women will be wearing fur coats?' He addressed the armchair. 'Has Mrs de Valera time to dress?' He turned and leaned over the turf basket. 'Has Mrs General Mulcahy time to dress? There's ways and means of doing everything.' (He shot a quick glance at the map of the pier; you could always knock a couple of feet off the width of it.) 'After all, you've told me yourself that you could purchase a black costume for twenty-five guineas. Is that or is that not a fact? Very well then,' triumphantly, 'why not buy a black costume for twenty-five guineas?'

'Because, you big fathead, I'd have to have shoes and a blouse and hat and gloves and a fur and a purse and everything to match it, and I'd spend far more in the heel of the hunt, and I haven't time for that sort of thing and I'd have to have two or three costumes – Heaven above, I can't appear day after day in the same old rig, can I?'

'Good! Good! That's settled. Now, the question is: shall we or shall we not purchase a fur coat? Now! What is to be said for a fur coat?' He marked off the points on his fingers. 'Number one: it is warm. Number two: it will keep you from getting a cold. Number three . . .'

Molly jumped up, let a scream out of her, and hurled the basket of mending at him.

'Stop it! I told you I don't want a fur coat! And you don't want me to get a fur coat! You're too mean, that's what it is! And, like all the Irish, you have the peasant streak in you. You're all alike, every bloody wan of ye. Keep your rotten fur coat. I never wanted it . . .'

And she ran from the room sobbing with fury and disappointment.

'Mean?' gasped Maguire to himself. 'To think that anybody could say that I . . . Mean!'

She burst open the door to sob:

'I'll go to the garden party in a mackintosh. And I hope that'll satisfy you!' and ran out again.

He sat miserably at his table, cold with anger. He murmured the hateful word over and over, and wondered could there be any truth in it. He added ten yards to the pier. He reduced the ten to five, and then, seeing what he had done, swept the whole thing off the table.

It took them three days to make it up. She had hit him below the belt and they both knew it. On the fourth morning she found a cheque for a hundred and fifty pounds on her dressing table. For a moment her heart leaped. The next moment it died in her. She went down and put her arms about his neck and laid the cheque, torn in four, into his hand.

'I'm sorry, Paddy,' she begged, crying like a kid. 'You're not mean. You never were. It's me that's mean.'

'You! Mean?' he said, fondly holding her in his arms.

'No, I'm not mean. It's not that. I just haven't the heart, Paddy. It was knocked out of me donkeys' years ago.' He looked at her sadly. 'You know what I'm trying to say?'

He nodded. But she saw that he didn't. She was not sure that she knew herself. He took a deep, resolving breath, held her out from him by the shoulders, and looked her straight in the eyes. 'Molly, tell me the truth. You want this coat?'

'I do. O God, I do!'

'Then go out and buy it.'

'I couldn't, Paddy. I just couldn't.'

He looked at her for a long time. Then he asked:

'Why?'

She looked straight at him and, shaking her head sadly, she said in a little sobbing voice:

'I don't know.'

# Up the Bare Stairs

*A pity beyond all telling is hid in the heart of love.*

All the way from Dublin my travelling companion had not spoken a dozen words. After a casual interest in the countryside as we left Kingsbridge he had wrapped a rug about his legs, settled into his corner, and dozed.

He was a bull-shouldered man, about sixty, with coarse, sallow skin stippled with pores, furrowed by deep lines on either side of his mouth: I could imagine him dragging these little dikes open when shaving. He was dressed so conventionally that he might be a judge, a diplomat, a shopwalker, a shipowner, or an old-time Shakespearian actor: black coat, striped trousers, grey spats, white slip inside his waistcoat, butterfly collar folded deeply, and a black cravat held by a gold clasp with a tiny diamond.

The backs of his fingers were hairy: he wore an amethyst ring almost as big as a bishop's. His temples were greying and brushed up in two sweeping wings – wherefore the suggestion of the actor. On the rack over his head was a leather hat case with the initials F.J.N. in Gothic lettering. He was obviously an Englishman who had crossed the night before. Even when the steam of the train lifted to show the black January clouds sweeping across the Galtees, and a splash of sleet hit the window by his ear, he did not waken. Just then the ticket checker came in from the corridor and tipped his shoulder. As he received back his ticket he asked, 'What time do we arrive in Cork?' He said the word *Cork* as only a Corkman can say it, giving the *r* its distinctively delicate palatal trill, not saying 'Corrrk,' or 'Cohk.' He was unmistakably a Corkonian.

At Mallow I came back from tea to find him stretching his legs on the platform and taking notice. He had bought the evening paper and was tapping his thigh with it as he watched, with a quizzical smile, two tipsy old countrymen in amiable dispute, nose to nose, outside the bar. A fine man on his feet; at least six foot two. I bought a paper, also, at the bookstall and as we went on our way we both read.

My eye floated from a heading about a licensing case – the usual long verbatim report, two men found hiding under the stairs, six men with bottles in the stable, much laughter in court, and so on – to a headline beside it: CORKMAN IN BIRTHDAY HONOURS LIST. The paragraph referred to 'Francis James Nugent, Baronet: for War Services.' I looked across at him.

'Did you say something?' he asked.

'No, no! Or, rather, I don't think so.'

'Pretty cold,' he said, in a friendly way. 'Though I will say one thing for the G.S.R., they do heat their trains.'

'Yes, it's nice and warm today. They're not, of course, the G.S.R. now, you know. They're called Corus Iompair Eireann.'

'What's that? Irish for G.S.R.?'

'More or less.'

We talked a bit about the revival of the language. Not that he was interested; but he was tolerant, or perhaps the right word is indifferent. After a bit I said:

'I see there's a Corkman in the new honours list.'

'Oh?'

I glanced up at the rack and said, with a grin:

'I see the initials on your hatbox.'

He chuckled, pleased.

'I suppose I'd better plead guilty.'

'Congratulations.'

'Thank you.'

'What does it feel like?'

He glanced out at the wheeling fields, with their lochs of water and cowering cattle, and then looked back at me with a cynical smile.

'It doesn't feel any different. By the time you get it you've pretty well enjoyed everything it stands for. Still, it helps.'

'I see from the paper that you went to the same school as myself.'

'Are you the old Red and Green, too?'

'Up the Abbey!'

He laughed, pleased again.

'Does all that go on just the same as before?'

'It goes on. Perhaps not just the same as before.'

We talked of West Abbey. I knew none of the men he knew, but he thawed out remembering them.

'Are all the old photographs still in the main hall? Chaps in the

Indian Civil, the Canadian Mounted, the Navy, the Indian Police? God, I used to stare at them when I was a kid.'

'They're gone. They've been replaced by Confirmation groups all wearing holy medals.'

He made a bored face.

'I suppose in those days you little thought you'd be coming back to Cork one day as Sir Francis Nugent.'

He peered at me through his cigarette smoke and nodded sagely.

'I knew.'

'You did!'

'I shouldn't have said that. I couldn't know. But I had a pretty good idea.'

Then he leaned forward and let down all his reserves. As he began my heart sank. He was at the favourite theme of every successful man: 'How I Began.' But as he went on I felt mean and rebuked. I doubt if he had ever told anyone, and before he finished I could only guess why he chose to tell me now.

'You know, it's extraordinary the things that set a fellow going. I always knew I'd get somewhere. Not merely that, but I can tell you the very day, the very hour, I made up my mind I was going to get there. I don't think I was more than fourteen or fifteen at the time. Certainly not more than fifteen. It was as simple as that' – clicking his fingers. 'It was all on account of a little man named Angelo – one of the monks who was teaching us. He's gone to God by now. There was a time when I thought he was the nicest little man in the whole school. Very handsome. Cheeks as red as a girl's, black bristly hair, blue eyes, and the most perfect teeth I've ever seen between a man's lips. He was absolutely full of life, bursting with it. He was really just a big boy and that's probably why we got on so well with him. I've seen him get as much fun out of solving a quadratic equation or a problem in Euclid as a kid with a new toy. He had a marvellous trick of flinging his *cappa* over one shoulder, shoving his two wrists out of his sleeves like a conjurer, snapping up a bit of chalk and saying, "Watch what I'm going to do now," that used to make us sit bolt upright in our desks as if . . . well, as if he was going to do a conjuring trick. And if you could only have seen the way he'd kick ball with us in the yard – you know, the old yard at the back of West Abbey – all we had was a lump of paper tied with twine – shouting and racing like any of us. He really was a good chap. We were very fond of him.

'Too fond of him, I've often thought. He knew it, you see, and it made him put too much of himself into everything we did. And the result was that we were next door to helpless without him. He made us depend on him too much. Perhaps he wasn't the best kind of teacher; perhaps he was too good a teacher – I don't know – have it whichever way you like. If he was tired, or had a headache, or sagged, we sagged. If he was away sick and somebody else had to take charge of us we were a set of duffers. They could be just as cross as he was – he was very severe, he'd take no excuses from anybody – or they could be as merry as he was: it just wasn't the same thing. They had a job to do, and they did the best they could, but with him it wasn't a job, it was his life, it was his joy and his pleasure. You could tell how much the fellows liked him by the way they'd crowd around him at play hour, or at the end of the holidays to say good-bye.

'One particularly nice thing about him was that he had no favourites, no pets, as we used to call them. Did you call them that in your time? But he was – what shall I say? – more than a little partial to me. And for a very, if you like to call it, silly reason. In those days, you see, politics were very hot in Cork city; very hot, very passionate. Of course, they were the old Irish Party days, long before your time, when politics were taken much more seriously than I've ever seen them taken anywhere else. John Redmond had one party called the Molly Maguires, and William O'Brien had another party called the All for Irelanders. Mind you, if you asked me now what it was all about I'd find it very hard to tell you, because they were all the one party at Westminster, and they were all agreed about home rule, but once it came to election time they tore one another to pieces. Fights in the street every night, baton charges, clashes between rival bands, instruments smashed on the pavements. One night, with my own eyes. I saw a big six-foot countryman take a running jump down the grand parade and land right on top of a big drum.

'Well, Angelo was a Molly, and I needn't tell you he was just as excited about politics as he was about everything else, and I was also a Molly and a very hot one. Not that I understood anything at all about it, but just that my father was one of the hottest Redmondites in the city of Cork. And, of course, nothing would do Angelo but to bring politics into class. He'd divide the class into Mollies and All Fors and when we'd be doing Euclid or reciting poetry he'd set one team against the other, and he'd work up the excitement until the fellows would be clambering across the desks, and if any fellow let down his side we'd glare at him until he'd want to creep away out of sight, and if he scored a point we'd cheer him as if he'd kicked a goal in an All Ireland Final.

'It was on one of these days that it happened. We were at the Eighth Problem. The Mollies wanted one point to pull even. I was the last man in – and I muffed it. And no wonder, with Angelo shouting at me like a bull, "Come on, now, Frankie. If A.B. be placed on C.D. . . . . Up the Mollies! Go on, Frankie. Go on. If A.B. . . . ."

'The All Fors won. Angelo laughed it off with, "Very good, very good, back to yeer places now. Work is work. This isn't the Old Market Place. Now for tomorrow," and so on.

'But he kept me in after school. There I sat, alone in the empty classroom upstairs – you know the one, near the ball alley – with the crows outside in the yard picking up the crusts, and the dusk falling over the city, and Angelo, never speaking a word, walking up and down the end of the room reading his office. As a rule we were let out at three. He kept me there until five o'clock rang. Then he told me to go home and went off himself up to the monastery.

'I walked out of the yard behind him, and at that moment if I had had a revolver in my hand I'd have shot him. I wouldn't have cared if he'd beaten me black and blue. I wouldn't have cared if he'd given me extra work to do at home. He deliberately got me into trouble with my father and mother, and what that meant he understood exactly. Perhaps you don't. You don't know my background as he knew it. When I tell you that my father was a tailor and my mother was a seamstress I needn't tell you any more. When a kid's mother has to work as hard as his father to push him through school you can guess the whole picture. I don't seem to remember an hour, except for Sundays, when one or other, or both, of these machines wasn't whirring in that little room where we lived, down by the distillery, sometimes until twelve or one o'clock at night. I remember that day as I walked home I kept saying to myself over and over again, "If only my mummy wasn't sick." All the way. Past the distillery. Around by the tannery. You possibly know the little terrace of houses. They've been there since the eighteenth century. Dark. We had only two rooms. In the hall. I can still get that stuffy smell that had been locked up there for a hundred and fifty years – up the bare stairs. On the landing there was a tap dripping into an old leaden trough that had been there since the year dot. I could hear the machine whirring. I remember I stopped at the window and picked a dead leaf from the geraniums. I went up the last few steps and I lifted the latch. My father was bent over the machine; specs on his forehead, black skeins of thread around his neck, bare arms. My mother was wrapped in shawls in the old basket chair before the fire. I could draw that room; the two machines, my bed in one corner, my dinner waiting on the table, the tailor's goose heating on the grate. The machine stopped.

"'In the name of God what happened to you, boy?" says my father. "Is there anything wrong? What kept you? Your poor mother there is out of her head worrying about you."

"'Ah, I was just kept in, sir," says I, passing it off as airily as I could. "How are you, Mummy?"

'The old man caught me by the arm.

"'Kept in?" says he, and the way he said it you'd think I was after coming out of the lockup. "Why were you kept in?"

"'Ah, 'twas just a bit of Euclid I didn't know, that's all."

'It was only then I noticed that the mother was asleep. I put my hand to my lips begging him not to waken her. He let a roar out of him.

"'A nice disgrace! Kept in because you didn't know your Euclid!"

"'What is it, what is it, Frankie?" she says, waking up in a fright. "What did they do to you, boy?"

"''Twas nothing at all, Mummy, just that I didn't know a bit of Euclid. I had to stay back to learn it."

"'A nice how d'ye do! And why didn't you know your Euclid?" – and he had me up against the wall and his fist raised.

"'It wasn't really Euclid at all, Father. It was all Angelo's fault. It was all politics. He divided the class into All Fors and Mollies and because the All Fors won he kept me in out of spite. Honestly, that's all it was, Mummy, there was nothing else to it."

"'Holy God," whispers the old man. "So it wasn't only the Euclid, but lettin' down John Redmond in front of the whole class. That's what you did, is it?"

"'Oh, for God's sake, Billy," says the mother, "don't mind John Redmond. 'Tis little John Redmond or any other John Redmond cares about us, but 'tis the work, the work. What are we slaving for, boy, day and night, and all the rest of it? There's your poor father working himself to the bone to send you through school. And so on. Nothing matters, boy, but the work! The work!"

"'Tisn't only the work," says the old man. "'Tisn't only the work," and he was sobbing over it. "But to think of poor John Redmond fighting night after night for Ireland, standing up there in the House of Commons, and you – you brat – couldn't even do a sum in Euclid to stand by him! In your own school! Before everybody! Look at him," he wails, with his arm up to the picture of John Redmond on the wall, with his hooked nose and his jowls like an old countrywoman. "Look at the dacent gentleman. A man that never let down his side. A gentleman to the tips of his toes if there ever was one. And you couldn't do a simple sum in Euclid to help him! Th'other fellows could do it. The All Fors could do it. But my son couldn't do it!"

'And with that he gave me a crack that nearly sent me into the fire.

'The end of it was that I was on my knees with my head on the mother's lap, blubbering, and the old man with his two hands up to John Redmond, and the tears flowing down his face like rain, and the mother wailing, "Won't you promise, Frankie, won't you promise to work, boy?" and I promising and promising anything if she'd only stop crying.

'That was the moment that I swore to myself to get on. But wait! You won't understand why until I've finished.

'The next day Angelo took the same problem, at the same hour, and he asked me to do it again. Now, kids are no fools. I knew by the look on his face why he asked me to do it. He wanted to make friends with me, to have everything the same as if yesterday had never happened. But he didn't know what had happened inside in me the night before. I went through the problem, step by step – I knew it perfectly – down to the Q.E.D.

'"Now, isn't it a pity, Frankie," he says, smiling at me, "that you wouldn't do that yesterday?"

'"Oh," I said, in a very lordly, tired voice, "I just didn't feel like it."

'I knew what was coming to me, and I wanted it, and to make sure that I got it I gave him that sort of insolent smile that drives grownups mad with children. I've seen that smile on my own children's faces now and again, and when I see it I have to go outside the door for fear I'd knock them the length of the room. That is what Angelo did to me. I got up off the floor and I sat back in my place and I had the same insolent smile on my face.

'"Now, if you please," says Angelo, reaching for his cane, and he was as white as his teeth, "will you kindly do the next problem?"

'I did it, step by step, calm as a breeze, down to the Q.E.D. I'd prepared it the night before.

'"Right," says Angelo, and his voice was trembling with rage. "Do the next problem."

'I had him where I wanted him. He was acting unfairly, and he knew it, and the class knew it. I had that problem prepared too. Just to tease him I made a couple of slips, but just as he'd be reaching for the cane I'd correct them. I was a beast, but he'd made me a beast. I did it, down to the Q.E.D., and I smiled at him, and he looked at me. We both knew that from that moment it was war to the knife.

'I worked that night until twelve o'clock; and I worked every night until I left school until twelve o'clock. I never gave him a chance. I had to, because until the day I left that place he followed me. He followed me into the fifth form. And into the sixth. He made several efforts to make it up with me, but I wouldn't let him. He was too useful to me the other way. I sat for the Civil Service and I got first place in the British Isles in three subjects out of five, geometry, chemistry, and history, third in mathematics, fifth in German. I did worst in German because I didn't have Angelo for German. I think I can say without arrogance that I was the most brilliant student that ever passed out of West Abbey School.'

Sir Francis leaned back.

'You must have worked like a black.'

'I did.'

'Well, it was worth it!'

He looked out over the fields which were now becoming colourless in the falling dusk and his voice sank to a murmur, as if he were thinking aloud.

'I don't know. For me? Yes, perhaps. I had no youth. For them? I don't know. I didn't work to get on, I worked to get out. I didn't work to please my mother or my father. I hated my mother and I hated my father from the day they made me cry. They did the one thing to me that I couldn't stand up against. They did what that little cur Angelo planned they'd do. They broke my spirit with pity. They made me cry with pity. Oh, I needn't say I didn't go on hating them. A boy doesn't nourish hatred. He has his life before him. I was too sorry for them. But that's where they lost everything. A boy can be sorry for people who are weak and pitiable, but he can't respect them. And you can't love people if you don't respect them. I pitied them and I despised them. That's the truth.'

He leaned back again.

'You don't look like a man whose spirit was ever broken,' I laughed, a little embarrassed.

'The spirit is always broken by pity. Oh, I patched it up pretty well. I made a man of myself. Or, rather,' he said with passion, 'with what was left of myself after they'd robbed me of my youth that I spent slaving to get away from them.'

'You'd have slaved anyway. You were full of ambition.'

'If I did I'd have done it for ambition alone. I tell you I did it for pity and hate and pride and contempt and God knows what other reason. No. They broke my spirit all right. I know it. The thing I've put in its place is a very different thing. I know it. I've met plenty of men who've got along on ambition and they're whole men. I know it. I'm full of what they put into me – pity and hate and rage and pride and contempt for the weak and anger against all bullying, but, above all, pity, chock-a-block with it. I know it. Pity is the most disintegrating of all human emotions. It's the most disgusting of all human emotions. I know it.'

'What happened to Angelo?'

'I don't know. Nor care. Died, I suppose.'

'And . . . your father?'

'Fifteen years after I left Cork he died. I never saw him. I brought my mother to live with me in London.'

'That was good. You were fond of her.'

'I was sorry for her. That's what she asked me for when I was a boy. I've been sorry for her all my life. Ah!'

His eyes lit up. I looked sideways to see what had arrested him. It was the first lights of Cork, and, mingling with the smoke over the roofs, the January night. Behind the violet hills the last cinder of the sun made a saffron horizon. As the train roared into the tunnel we could see children playing in the streets below the steep embankment, and he was staring at them thirstily, and I must have imagined that I heard their happy shouts. Then the tunnel opened and swallowed us.

There were no lights in the carriage. All I could see was the occasional glow of his cigarette. Presently the glow moved and my knee was touched. His voice said:

'She's with me on this train. My mother. I'm bringing her back to Cork.'

'Will she like that?'

'She's dead.'

The train roared on through the tunnel. As we passed under the first tunnel vent a drip of water fell on the roof. The tiny glow swelled and ebbed softly.

'I'm very sorry.'

His voice said, in the darkness:

'I meant to bury her in London. But I couldn't do it. Silly, wasn't it?'

After a while another drip of water splashed on the roof. The windows were grey.

'You did the kind thing.'

His voice was so low that I barely heard it.

'Kind!'

In a few more minutes we were drawing up in steam alongside the lighted platform. He was standing up, leaning over his hatbox. From it he lifted a silk topper and a dark scarf. He put on his black frock coat. 'Good-bye,' he said politely, and beckoned for a porter.

From the platform I watched him walk down towards the luggage van where a tiny group already stood waiting. They were all poor people. There was a bent old woman there in a black shawl, and three or four humble-looking men in bowler hats and caps. As I watched him bow to them and doff his hat to the old woman and introduce himself, the yellow pine-and-brass of the coffin was already emerging from the van and the undertaker's men in their brass-buttoned coats were taking it from the porters. Among his poor relations he walked reverently, bareheaded, out into the dark stationyard.

They slid the coffin into the motor hearse; he showed his relatives into the carriages, and, stooping, he went in after them. Then the little procession moved slowly out into the streets on its way to whatever chapel would take her for the night into its mortuary.

# One True Friend

The lonely woman was as big a . . . No! I won't say it. 'T wasn't a very kind thing I was going to say. And I suppose that's the way God made her. And, as the old joker said, we're all as God made us – and some of us worse. But I will say this about her, and her own sons often said it – and 'twas they gave her the name of the lonely woman – she was (if you will pardon my saying so) a damn nuisance. Mind you, she was a good soul – a good, pious, kindly, Christian soul. But she was a nuisance. Her trouble was that she really was lonely, and she was always complaining about how lonely she was, but she would never do anything about it because, so I firmly believe, she liked being lonely.

Where she lived, of course, was no fit place for any Christian to live. She lived in her old rooky-rawky of a house over a tinsmith's shop, where she'd lived since she was first married, and where she'd brought up her family, and where her husband was carried out on the flat of his back, but where now – for she had let her extra rooms, one by one, to the tinsmith downstairs – you heard nothing all day long but the tinny hammering, a *tic-tac-too, tic-tac-too* that would drive anybody mad. And what kind of a house was it, where you smelled nothing but boiling solder from morning to night?

Her sons were always at her to leave it and she'd say, 'I know I ought to leave it. I know it's no place for a lonely woman like me. Nobody to hand me as much as a drop of cold water if I got a stitch in the middle of the night, or maybe an appendicitis. But sure where can I go?'

'But,' they'd say then, 'Mother, come and live with us!'

'Oh, no!' she'd say then. 'Oh, no! Is it go and live with a daughter-in-law? Ha! Cock 'em up with comfort. Tisn't mother-in-laws they want. Oh, no! Nobody wants a poor lonely old woman like me.'

And then her sons would persuade her, and their wives would persuade her, and perhaps, after a lot of persuading, she would agree, and they would go home and get a room ready for her. She would change her mind during the night. Not that they blamed her. Her little kitchen was her palace, and she was the queen of it. She had her cup and her saucer, and her knife and her fork, and she could come when she liked and go when she liked. And if it was a bit silent there at night, when there wasn't a sound from the city, and not a sound in the house but the mice scrabbling downstairs in the dustbin, or the tap dripping, well, she had other things. She had company of her own kind. She would sit looking into the fire in the range, her eyes lost in the great distance of her love for her dead husband, her dead sisters, or the saints. Her sons had each, at one time or another, seen her like that, and as they would look about them at their childhood home picked to the bone, they would find that even in the middle of the day the busy, hammering house would cease to exist, and the little city streets would drop away. Looking at her, and hearing her gentle sigh, how could anyone say to her then, as they so often said on other occasions, 'Mother, why the blazes don't you try to make some friends?' – not seeing her glance up with a smile at Saint Francis, and Saint Francis smiling back.

Then one day, one August second, to be precise, out of the blue, lo and behold, she wrote to one of her sons that she had just met a very nice woman. It had apparently happened when she was doing the Ins and Outs. The Ins and Outs is a devotion where you pay as many visits as possible to a church on the feast called Portiuncula. You go in one door, and say a prayer, and come out another, and that counts as a visit. Then you go back, say another prayer, come out, and that is a second visit, and so on until weariness defeats the pious heart. Mrs Moore was doing this, very contentedly, when she suddenly noticed a young girl in a red beret passing quietly from one Station of the Cross to another. She smiled happily, and went on with her prayers. The church was warm with imprisoned sunlight and the candles on the altar drank in the air. The hot gladioli consumed themselves among the consuming lights. Peace and comfort fell on the old lady, and when the girl slipped in beside her on the bench she was about to put out her hand to stroke the child's head when she saw the girl's fingers creep along the bench, take her purse, and disappear. The next thing was the girl running up the aisle. Mrs Moore ran after her. The girl ran faster. The old woman called on her to stop. The worshippers stood up and looked at them. The girl dropped the purse in the hall and ran across the street – where she was nearly killed by a bus – and the lonely woman fainted. When she woke up she was in the sacristy, and a lady whom she had often seen before was giving her a glass of water.

'You're all right now, Mrs Moore,' said the lady.

'How well you know my name,' she whispered.

'Oh, sure, we all know Mrs Moore,' said the lady. 'Is there a church in the city that doesn't know you? Sure, you live in the churches.'

'It's my only company,' she sighed.

'A holy woman,' said the lady. 'We know you as well as we know the priests. My name is Mrs Calvert.'

'What a shocking thing to happen!'

'Frightful,' said Mrs Calvert. 'Especially when you think the girl was so young. Think of the condition of her soul!'

'We must do something about it,' said the lonely woman.

At once the two old ladies became as friendly in that common cause as if they had been friends all their lives. They toddled across the street to the dairy where Mrs Calvert lived, and each had a glass of milk. If anybody had looked in through the open door and seen them or if anybody had heard them, he would have said that they were sisters. It turned out that they were alike in everything except what didn't matter. They were both widows. Their families were scattered. They both lived alone. Each was the kind of woman who tells the time by the tolling of the church bells. Mrs Moore hated the noise of the tinsmith. Mrs Calvert was waked every morning by the clank of churns. And if the smell of boiling solder is not nice, neither is the smell of sour milk and cow manure. Nothing distinguished them except that, as they laughingly said, one of them swore by Saint Francis and the other swore by Saint Peter in Chains. After a while, when they were getting up to go, it was a case of:

'And now, Mrs Moore, that we know each other, won't you pray for me?'

'Oh, Mrs Calvert, how can you say that? It is you who must pray for me.'

'Now, now, Mrs Moore, you know you're a saint anointed.'

'Ah, Mrs Calvert, that's all you know. I'm a sinner. A wicked sinner. But when I look at you, I say to myself, "If there was ever a soul with the mark of salvation on her, it's Mrs Calvert."'

'Now, Mrs Moore, it's not kind of you to flatter a wicked person. You must pray for me every day. I need it badly.'

'Mrs Calvert, we'll pray for one another.'

When she had come home from this happy adventure the lonely woman met a strange man on her doorstep.

'Am I speaking to Mrs Moore?' he said politely.

'How well you know my name,' she said.

'Oh,' he smiled, 'sure, we all know Mrs Moore.'

'Really?' she said, very pleased, very grand, but very humble. 'A poor lonely woman like me that I thought nobody knew!'

He laughed at that.

'Now,' he said, 'I believe you had a purse snatched from you this morning?'

'Oh? And who told you that?'

'A friend of yours.'

'A friend of mine? Who on earth can that be?'

'She gave her name as Mrs Calvert. She rang up the police station a quarter of an hour ago. I'm a police detective, and I must investigate the matter. We've had a lot of these complaints recently. Mrs Calvert said you'd recognize this girl. Is that right?'

'You mean would I know her again? I'd know her painted.'

'Fine! Now, I'll tell you what I'll do. If I have a motor car here at your very door, tomorrow morning, will you come down to the Bridewell, and if we have that girl there will you recognize her?'

'O-o-oh, n-o-o-o!' said Mrs Moore. 'I couldn't do *that*!'

And she began a long, long rigmarole that went on for half an hour about how she never went out except to go to the church, and how she could never go down there, behind the old-clothes' market, to the Bridewell, where all the drunks are put every night, and how she really never did go anywhere, and how her sons were always at her to go out more and make friends, and what a lonely life she had, and how it would be far better if she did go out, and all about how she used to go out long ago with her husband, and all about her sisters, and her daughters-in-law, and he listened with the endless curiosity of the born detective, and the endless patience of a man whose spirit is broken from dealing with women, and he kept on talking about that motor car, and how she would drive across the city, and be driven back again, until, gradually, his tempting began to win out. She began to see herself in the car. She thought how she would tell her sons about it. She yielded. Off he went, wiping his brow, exhausted but victorious.

But she did not yield in her mind. At the back of her head, there was a feeling that everything was not quite right. However, her sons had always told her that she was much too suspicious, and that she would make many more friends if she were less suspicious, so she shoved it down and tried to forget all about it.

The following morning she went to the Bridewell in the car, and though her old heart began thumping at the sight of the room the detective took her to, and the handcuffs hanging up, and all the police with their collars open, she did exactly as she was told. She went in and looked at the line-up and came out and said, 'Yes. She was there. The fifth girl from the end, in the red beret.' She was so happy at having done this that she did not pay a great deal of attention to what else they told her, and she was home, after a ride again in the car, before it dawned on her what exactly they had told her. Then she realized that she would have to go to the district court, and get up, before everybody, in the witness box and swear that this was the girl. At that she sat down and shook all over. The girl's relatives would see her. Rough lane people. Her father, her brother, her mother would accost her in the street and abuse her.

'Oh!' she gasped. 'The clever woman! She knew that she might be called on to identify the girl. That was why she sent the detective to me. Oh, the guile! The guile and cleverness of some people! And me, a poor, lonely old woman! What a thing to do to a poor, simple old woman the like of me!'

Whereupon she clapped her hat on her head, and with her white hair flying in the wind she went back to the Bridewell, and sought out the detective and said to him:

'I made a mistake. It was the wrong girl. I remember now. My head is getting addled. I'm so old I don't know what I do be saying. You must forget all about it.'

And even though that man was a patient man, and knew how to handle women, he could not budge her; not with pleading, begging, imploring, even threatening, not even when he sat down on one of the iron-legged stools and growled at her like a tiger.

'Oh, no!' said the lonely woman. 'I'm not able for the world at all. I'm all alone by myself, and I can't be up to the clever and calculating people that are in it. Let the wise and clever Mrs Calvert do it this time – the brave and gallant Mrs Calvert with her Saint Peter in Chains, and her "Pray for me, Mrs Moore!"'

And she told him about her lonely life, and her sisters, and her dead husband, and her sons, and her daughters-in-law, and he listened, and then he said:

'You know! Mrs Calvert *is* going to identify the girl for us. She promised me today that she would. You're wronging her. It's just that she wants you to keep her company. As she says herself, she is of a very nervous disposition and a melancholy turn of mind.'

'Nervous?' cried Mrs Moore. 'I'm five and forty times as nervous as her! What right has she to be nervous and she living over a dairy? Not like a poor, wretched, abandoned creature like me, living with a hammering in my ears all day long – a boozing and a woozing would addle a saint.'

And off she went again about her sons and her sisters and her husband and her daughters-in-law, but it was all to blind herself against the fact that she *had* been wronging Mrs Calvert, and that her suspicious mind – against which her sons so often warned her – had led her astray. At the same time, the detective, in his ingratiating country brogue, kept talking about the car and the drive, and once more, before she rightly knew what she was doing, she yielded, and before she could change her mind, he fled from her and took two double whiskeys at his own expense.

Next morning there was Mrs Calvert smiling sweetly down at her, as if it was *her* bag that was snatched, and as if it was *she* owned the car, and as if the detective was *her* chauffeur, and as if it was *she* who had planned it all. They started off, and the two old ladies chatted the whole way. They enjoyed the sun, and the crowds, and the traffic, and whenever they saw anybody they knew walking along the streets they waved whether the people saw them or not. They said they were doing the right thing, and the girl would be thankful in the end, and the church would be thankful, and the city ought to be thankful, and by the time they had said all that, they were being ushered together into the room with the handcuffs hanging on the wall and the bare stools and the policemen with their collars open as always.

They went in together. Side by side, very pale, Mrs Moore and Mrs Calvert walked up and down before the row of suspects, and sure enough, they saw the bag snatcher staring up at them as bold as brass. They said nothing; they were not supposed to until they came out; but when they came out they said nothing either. At this, the detective, very much surprised, challenged them:

'Well? Ye *did* recognize her! I saw ye did!'

The two pious old ladies gave one another short glances, and the lonely woman whispered:

'What would you say, Mrs Calvert?'

'Did *you* recognize her, Mrs Moore?' murmured the other, shaking from head to foot, and with her mouth in a twisty smile like a woman with palsy.

'I was wondering, Mrs Calvert, what *you* would say,' the lonely woman replied, her two little fists tightly clutched.

'Look here!' put in the detective. 'After all my trouble, don't tell me ye're going to let me down again?'

'Oho! You can't be up to the cleverness of the world nowadays!' said the lonely woman.

'*You* have been very nice about everything,' Mrs Calvert said, turning to him. 'It was a lovely motor drive. I enjoyed it very much.'

The detective gazed at them, first the one shut mouth, and then the other. He saw them looking at him pityingly.

He let them walk home. It was a hot day, and the two ladies were soon tired. They did not speak to each other as they walked across the city. They were so exhausted that they passed two churches without stopping to go in. At last, they came to their own parish church, and at the entrance they separated, bowing to each other without a look or a word. They went into the cool dimness of the church, each to her separate corner, and presently the two grey heads were drooping piously and the familiar beads of prayer dropped from their lips. The lonely woman looked up at Saint Francis, and the other looked up at Saint Peter in Chains. Cautiously, now and again, each looked across the nave when the other was not looking, and then she would turn back, with a sigh of trust and happiness, to look up again at her one true friend.

# Persecution Mania

There are two types of Irishman I cannot stand. The first is always trying to behave the way he thinks the English behave. The second is always trying to behave the way he thinks the Irish behave. That sort is a roaring bore. Ike Dignam is like that. He believes that the Irish are witty, so he is forever making laborious jokes. He has a notion that the Irish have a gift for fantasy, so he is constantly talking fey. He also has a notion that the Irish have a magnificent gift for malice, mixed up with another idea of the Irish as great realists, so he loves to abuse everybody for not having more common sense. But as he also believes that the Irish are the most kind and charitable people in the world he ends up every tirade with, 'Ah, sure, God help us, maybe the poor fellow is good at heart.' The result is that you do not know, from one moment to the next, whom you are talking to – Ike the fey or Ike the realist, Ike the malicious or Ike the kind.

I am sure he has no clear idea of himself. He is a political journalist. I have seen him tear the vitals out of a man, and then, over a beer, say, with a shocked guffaw:

'I'm after doin' a terrible thing. Do you know what I said in my column this morning about Harry Lombard? I said, "There is no subject under the sun on which the eloquence does not pour from his lips with the thin fluidity of ass's milk." Honest to God, we're a terrible race. Of course, the man will never talk to me again.'

All as if right hand had no responsibility for left hand. But the exasperating thing is that his victims do talk to him again, and in the most friendly way, though why they do it I do not know considering some of the things he says and writes about them. He is the man who said of a certain woman who is in the habit of writing letters to the press in defense of the Department of Roads and Railways, 'Ah, sure, she wrote that with the minister's tongue in her cheek.' Yet the Minister for Roads and Railways is one of his best friends, and he says, 'Ike Dignam? Ah, sure! He's all right. The poor divil is good at heart.' And the cursed thing is that Ike *is* good at heart. I have long since given up trying to understand what this means. Something vaguely connected with hope, and consolation, and despair, and the endless mercy of God.

Ike naturally has as many enemies as friends, and this is something that *he* cannot understand. Somebody may say:

'But you're forgetting, Ike, what you said about him last year. You said every time he sings "Galway Bay" he turns it into a street puddle.'

Ike will laugh delightedly.

'That was only a bit o' fun. Who'd mind that?'

'How would you like to have things like that said about yourself?'

He will reply, valiantly:

'I wouldn't mind one bit. Not one bit in the world. I'd know 'twas all part of the game. I'd know the poor fellow was really good at heart.'

A few weeks ago he got a taste of his own medicine. He committed the folly of granting to his rivals the ancient wish of all rivals, 'That mine enemy would write a book.' The subject of his book – it was a pamphlet rather than a book – was *The Irish Horse in Irish History*, and it was savagely disembowelled in an anonymous review in one of the popular weeklies. The sentence that wounded him, as it was intended to do, said, 'Mr Dignam's knowledge of hunters is weak, of hacks most profound.'

That very afternoon I met him in Mooney's pub, on the quay. He was staring into the bog-hole deeps of a pint of porter. Seeing me he turned such a morose eye on me that I could tell he had been badly hit.

'You saw what the *Sun* said about my book?' he asked, and when I nodded: 'That's a low paper. A low rag. A vicious-minded rag. That's what it is. Full of venom and hate and the lust for power. And,' he added, slapping the counter, 'destruction!'

'Somebody getting his own back, I suppose?'

'What did I ever do to anybody? Only a bit of give and take. What's done every day of the week in journalism. Surely to Gawd, nobody takes me as seriously as all that!'

'Well, that's more or less all your reviewer did with your book.'

Again the indignant palm slapped the mahogany.

'That's exactly what I dislike about that review. The mean implication. The dirty innuendo. Why couldn't he come out and say it in the open like a man? It's the anonymity of the thing that's so despicable.' Here he fixed me with a cunning eye. 'Who do ye think wrote it?'

I spread my hands.

'I think,' he said sourly, 'that it was Mulvaney wrote it. I made a hare of him one time in my column. But I'm not sure. That's the curse of it. He hasn't enough brains to write it.' He gazed at me for a moment through his eyelashes. 'You didn't write it yourself by any chance?'

I laughed and told him I hadn't read his book. I'd bought it, of course (which I had not), and had every intention of reading it (which was also untrue).

'Or it could be that drunk Cassidy,' he said. 'That fellow has it in for me ever since I said that he spoke in the Dail with the greatest sobriety.' He laughed feebly. 'Everyone knew what I meant. Do you think it might be Cassidy?'

'Ikey, it might be a dozen people.'

'It could be anybody,' he snarled. 'Anybody! Damn it all, if I ever say a thing I say it straight out from the shoulder. Why can't they come into the open?' He leaned nearer and dropped to a whisper. 'I was thinking it might be that redheaded bastard from the All Souls Club. That fellow thinks I'm anticlerical. And,' he guffawed, 'I'm not! That's the joke of it, I'm not!'

'What in the name of all that's holy,' I asked crossly, 'has anti-clericalism got to do with horses?'

He scratched his head fiercely and moaned and shook it.

'Ye never know. The people in this country have as much sense when it comes to religion ... Tell me, did ye ever hear of a thing called Discovery of Documents?'

It was only then I fully realized how badly he had been hit.

'You're not being such an idiot as to be thinking of taking this thing to law?'

'Look't! I don't give one tinker's curse about what anybody says against me, but the one thing I *must* know is who wrote it! If I don't find out who wrote it I'll be suspecting my best friends for the rest of my born days.'

'Well,' I said, finishing my drink and leaving him, 'happy hunting to you.'

A couple of days later I saw him cruising towards me along O'Connell Street glowing like a sunrise.

'I'm on the track of that,' he shouted at me from fifteen yards off. 'I'm on the right scent,' he babbled, and I had time to remember what he was talking about while he explained how he had worked up a friendship with a girl in the office of the *Sun.* ''Tis none of the people I suspected at all. Do you know who I think wrote it now?'

'God knows, maybe you wrote it yourself.'

He shook with laughter.

''Twould be great publicity if I could say I did.' Then he glowered. 'They're entirely capable of saying I did. If they thought anybody would believe 'em. No!' He gripped my arm. ''Twas a woman did it. I should have guessed it from the word "Go."'

'Who is she?'

'I don't know,' he said, sadly.

'Then why did you say . . .?'

'I had a dhream about it. Didn't I see the long, lean, bony hand holding the pen, coming out like a snake from behind a red curtain? Didn't I see the gold bangle on the wrist and all?'

'Did you pull the curtain to see who it was?'

'I pulled and I pulled,' Ikey assured me enthusiastically. 'Dear Gawd, I was all the night pullin'!'

'And,' I suggested bitterly, 'I suppose the curtain was made of iron? You know, Ikey, you'll go crackers if you go on like this.'

With his two hands he dragged his hat down on his head as if he wanted to extinguish himself.

'I will!' he cried, so loudly that passers-by turned to look at the pair of us. 'I'll go stark, staring, roaring mad if I don't find out who wrote that dirty thing about me.'

'Look,' I pleaded. 'What does it all matter? The whole thing is gone completely out of everybody's head but your own. It's all over and done with. And even supposing you did find out who wrote it, what could you do then?'

He folded his arms and gazed down O'Connell Street like Napoleon looking over the Atlantic from St Helena.

'I'd write a Limerick on him. I'd *shrivel* him. I wouldn't leave a peck on his bones. As a matter of fact – cocking an eye on me – 'I've done it already. I wrote ten Limericks the other night on ten different people who might have written that review. I'm thinking of publishing the whole lot of 'em, and if the cap fits they can share it and wear it.'

And before I could stop him he recited to the sky four blistering quatrains on 'Irish Bards and Botch Reviewers'. I took his arm.

'Ikey, that'll be ten enemies you'll make instead of one! Come in here, Ikey, and let me talk to you like a father.'

We went across to Mooney's and I talked for half an hour. I told him we had all been through this sort of thing. I told him that no man who cannot grow an epidermis against malice should try to live in small countries like ours. I said that all that matters is a man's work. I assured him, Heaven forgive me, that he had written a masterly record of *The Irish Horse in Irish History* and that that was the main thing. I developed this soundly into the theory that everything is grist to the mill, and that instead of worrying about this silly review he should go home and write a comic piece about it for *Dublin Opinion*, which, indeed, he could do very well. I built him up as *Dignam solus contra mundum*. He agreed to every word of it. We parted cordially. He was in the happiest temper.

Three days later he came striding towards me, beaming. From afar he hailed my passing ship, roaring like a bosun:

'I found out that bastard! Mulvaney! A friend of mine charged him with it and he didn't deny it.'

'Good. You're satisfied now.'

'I am. I don't give a damn about it now. Sure that fellow's brains are all in his behind. Who'd mind anything he'd say?'

'The whole thing is of no importance.'

'None whatsoever.'

'Splendid. It's all over now.'

'Finished. And done with!'

'Grand!'

'I sent him a hell of a postcard!'

'No?'

'I did,' he chortled, 'I did. All I wrote on it was what I said to yourself: "Your second front is your behind." An open postcard. It was a terrible thing to do,' he beamed. 'Oh, shocking!'

His laughter gusted.

'And you put your name to that?'

'I did not. What a fool I'd be! That'll keep him guessing for a while. 'Twill do him no harm in the world. He's not a bad poor gom. Ah! Sure! The poor divil is good at heart.'

Off he went, striding along, as happy as a child. I went into

Mooney's. There at the counter was Mulvaney, sucking his empty pipe, staring in front of him, his bushy eyebrows as black as night. I wheeled quickly, but he caught the movement and called me. His hand strayed to his breast pocket.

'I'm after receiving a very myst-e-e-rious communication,' he said sombrely.

I did not hear what else he said. I realized that you could do nothing with these people. I realized that the only sensible thing to do was to write a satire on the whole lot of them. I began to wonder could I get any editor anywhere to publish it anonymously.

# The Judas Touch

'Mummy!' he screamed from the doorstep as she raced up the path for the bus.

'What is it?' she shouted back, halting, fumbling in her handbag to see if she had her compact. She heard the hum of the starting bus and raced again for the gate.

'Mummy!' he shouted again, and went racing up the path after her.

'Well?' she yelled, looking out the gate, and then looking back, and then looking out again and putting up her hand to stop the bus.

'Can't I go to *The Bandits of Sherwood Forest?*'

'No!' and she was out through the gate and the gate went *bang*!

He raced madly up the path and out after her, and clutched her skirt as the brakes whined and the driver glared at her.

'Mummy, you promised!'

She swept his hand away, furious at the public scene, and climbed on the bus. Then, remembering that she had promised and that she must make some excuse, she added from the step of the bus:

'It's Lent. Nobody goes to the pictures in Lent!'

And the bus went on its way. He raced, bawling, after it until her promise and his hopes were swept around the corner. The road was empty. He collapsed sobbing on the footpath. With the sobs his tummy went in and out like an engine. He tore penny-leaves from the wall. He said all the bad words he knew, which are the same bad words we all know only that he did not know what they meant. Lent was *foutu*! He had already given up sweets for Lent. Sweets were *foutus*! He had given them up to be a good little boy. Good little boys were all *foutus*! He dragged himself up and with one hand he played harp strings of misery along the wall back to the gate. He dragged his feet through the gravel of the path to make tram lines. He scraped with a rusty nail on the new paint of the door. Then he went slowly into the breakfast room, where the morning paper stood up like a tent. Upstairs the vacuum cleaner moaned. A sputter of March rain hit the windows briefly. He saw an aged fly make a smooth landing on the marmalade. His five fingers stole up over it and squashed it into the marmalade. He wiped his fingers all across the tablecloth. Then he surveyed the table in search of something else to do that he ought not to do. The maid stood at the door.

'Did she let you go?'

'No.'

'Did you do what I told you and ask God in your prayers last night to make her let you go?'

'No.'

'You couldn't have luck.' And she went off for the dustpan.

He waited until she had gone upstairs and he heard her *swish-swish*. Then he said, 'God is no blooming good!' with a quick look at the door to be sure that nobody heard that one. His eye caught the shine of the ould jug on the sideboard. His daddy always called it an ould jug; he would say to Mummy, 'I might as well be talking to that ould jug.' He surveyed the jug for a bit out of the corners of his eyes. Then he looked at the door again, up at the ceiling, back to the door, back to the ould jug. His heart thumped fiercely. He took down the jug – it was pink lustre outside, gold inside – and he put it on the chair. He flopped down on his knees before it, joined his two sweaty palms, and said, staring earnestly at the pink belly of the jug:

'O Jug, I adore thee and bless thee. Please, O my good Jug, send me to *The Bandits of Sherwood Forest* at the Plaza.'

He looked up at the ceiling and stuck out his tongue. He looked at the jug. He wagged his palms at it swiftly, a dozen times.

'Jug, gimme half a dollar.'

Not a sound but the upstairs *swish-swish*. He sat back on his heels and considered the jug. He put his nose up to the jug to see himself round and fat; and he blew out a big face to see himself twice as round and fat. Then he bethought himself and kneeled up reverently. He cocked his head on one side and said:

'Jug?'

Nothing happened. He grabbed it and shook it and shouted furiously:

'JUG!'

The next moment he had his fist in the jug, grubbing excitedly. He pulled out two raffle tickets, a bottle of red pills, a foreign coin, a champagne cork, and a half-crown piece. In two shakes of a lamb's tail he was in the hall, dragging on his blue gaberdine, and out the gate with his skullcap down over one eye, pelting up to the village. Billy Busher was there, floating a tin motorboat in a puddle of water. He yelled, 'Busher, I got half a dollar.' And he hunched up to him, swaggering the silver half crown forward guardedly in his palm. Busher's eyes became as big as half crowns and at once he shouted: '*Bandits of Sherwood Forest?*'

'No!'

The tin motorboat meant sea, and sand, and roundabouts, and ice cream, and swimming, and holidays.

'Busher, come on and we'll go down to the seaside.'

They marched off down the hill to the station. A cab driver's erect whip floated over his shoulder like a single strand of hair. The station was empty; there would not be a train for an hour and five minutes. They were content wandering about the platforms, watching a goods train shunting, its steam blowing about them, or they jumped up and down on the weighing machine, and they played with an idle truck. Their tickets cost tenpence each, which left tenpence for grub. They worked it out that they could spend fourpence on ice cream and sixpence on lemonade, cakes, and sweets. They tried to buy ice cream at the bookstall, but the woman gave them a sour look, pulled her scarf more tightly around her chest, and sold them a packet of cough lozenges for twopence: coffee-coloured things, hexagonal, flat, stamped *Mother Markey's Marvels*. They had a rotten taste, like bad liquorice. They stuck them with a quick suck to the windows of the carriage.

Long before they came within sight of the sea they said they could smell it – cool, damp, deep, salty, spumy, windy, roaring; the big green animal of the sea that opens up long white jaws to swallow you up with a swoosh and a roar, but you always run away from it just in time, jumping on the wet sand, shrieking and laughing, and then you run in after it until another long white mouth curls up its jaws to eat you up and spit you out and you run away shrieking again. In their joy and terror of the millions of long white mouths they climbed on the dusty seats of the carriage, and clawed the glass, and hunched their shoulders and hissed at one another like geese. They clung their cheeks sideways to the windows in order to be, each, the first one to shout, 'I see it!'

When the train stopped they were jolted on to the floor. They scrambled up and out, and galloped ahead of the only two other travellers, who drove off into the town on a sidecar, collars up. When they reached the embankment above the station they were blown back on their heels by the wind. They held on to their caps, coats flapping, bodies bumping, looking at the waves thundering on the groaning gravel, and the dust of the waves in the wind, and every cement-fronted villa boarded up and shiny in the spume and the sun.

'Come on away up to the merry-go-rounds,' he screamed, and they ran for the end of the prom and the hillock beyond it where the roundabouts always stood. All they found was a circle of cinders and big pools of water snaked with petrol. When his cap blew into one of those greasy pools he laughed loudly, and Busher laughed loudly, and for fun threw his own cap into another pool. At that they both laughed like mad.

'Come on away up to the ould Crystal Café,' Busher shouted into his ear, 'and we'll buy the ould lemonade.'

They raced one another around the broken wall and up the steps to the upper road, shoving, falling over one another. In the window of the café was a big yellow-and-black notice: TO LET. A rain squall blasted down on them out of the purple sky. For a while they hugged back into the shelter of the café porch. Then Busher said in a flat voice:

'It's all a blooming suck-in.'

When the rain stopped they went slowly to the big tin shelter beside the railway restaurant; it was wide open to the front so that halfway in across its concrete was wet with the rain. They bought one bottle of lemonade in the restaurant and took it out to the long bench of the shelter, and had every second slug out of the bottle. They got one laugh out of that, when the fizz choked Busher's nose. Every few seconds the tin roofs squeaked above the kettledrums of another downpour. At last Busher said:

'You and your shaggin' ould cough lozenges!'

Calvert did not say anything.

'If we had that tuppence now we could buy a cake.'

Calvert did not reply.

'You and your swimming!' Busher snarled. 'You and your merry-go-rounds! Why didn't you come to *The Bandits of Sherwood Forest* when I asked you?'

Calvert said nothing to that either.

'I'm going home,' said Busher and walked off to the station.

Calvert watched him go away. After a few minutes his heart rose – Busher was coming back.

'There's no train,' Busher started to wail, 'until nine o'clock. There's only two trains a day in the winter.' His wail broke into a shameless bawling. 'You're after getting me into a nice fix. My da will leather hell out of me when he catches me home.'

Calvert looked at him in silence.

'And where did you get that half dollar anyway?' Busher charged. 'I bet you stole it from your ma.'

Calvert told him. Busher stopped snivelling.

'Gawd! Calvert! You're after praying to the divil. You'll be damned for a-a-all E-eturnity!'

And he tore out his railway ticket and flung it in terror on the concrete and ran bawling out into the rain. He ran and ran, down into the streets of the town, where, taking thought in his desperation, he made his way to the bus stop, told a sad yarn to the driver and the conductor, and got carried home, gratis and in good time.

The rain hammered the convex roof; the wind rattled its bones; bits of paper went whispering around the corners like mice; the gutters spilled; the light faded. He heard the drums of the high tide pounding the beach. Twice he went out looking for Busher. He returned each time with his hair plastered down his forehead. At six o'clock the woman in charge of the restaurant came out, locked up, and saw him in the dim corner of the shelter. She came over to him, found him shivering, and told him to take shelter in the waiting room of the station.

Nobody had bothered to light the room. There was nothing there but a pine table, two benches, an empty grate, and a poster showing the Bay of Naples. It was so dark that he saw only the table and the poster whenever the eye of the lighthouse beam from Pitch Point looked in through the misted window. He sat there until nearly nine o'clock, not daring to stir, watching and watching for that peering eye.

When he got home his father rushed at him and shouted at him to know where the blazes he had been, and his mother was crying, but when they saw the cut of him they stopped. His mummy and the maid got a hot bath ready for him before the fire, and his da called him 'old man' and undressed him on the warm hearthrug, and his mummy brought him in hot chocolate, and for the first time that day he suddenly began to cry. As he sat in the hot bath and his mummy soaped him they asked him again what had happened to him, and they were so nice about it that he began to bawl and he told them all about the ould jug. His daddy, first, and then his mummy and the maid burst into peal upon peal of laughter, while he sat there in the hot water, holding his mug of chocolate, bawling at the cruelty of everything and everybody who ever had anything to do with him since the day he was born.

# The End of the Record

The news went around the poorhouse that there was a man with a recording van in the grounds. He was picking up old stories and songs.

'And they say that he would give you a five-shilling piece into your hand for two verses of an old song,' said Thomas Hunter, an old man from Coomacoppal, in West Kerry, forgetting that five-shilling pieces were no longer in fashion. 'Or for a story, if you have a good one.'

'What sort of stories would them be?' Michael Kivlehan asked sceptically. He was from the barony of Forth and Bargy, in County Wexford, and had been in the poorhouse for eleven years.

'Any story at all only it is to be an old story and a good story. A story about the fairies, or about ghosts, or about the way people lived long ago.'

'And what do he do with 'um when he have 'um?'

'Hasn't he a phonograph? And doesn't he give them out over the wireless? And doesn't everyone in Ireland be listening to them?'

'I wonder now,' said Michael Kivlehan, 'would he give me five shillings for the "Headless Horseman and the Coacha Bowr"?'

Thomas Hunter sighed.

'One time I had a grand story about Finn MacCool and the Scotch giant. But it is gone from me. And I'd be getting my fine five-shilling piece into my fist this minute if I could only announce it to him.'

The two old men sat on the sides of their beds and tried to remember stories. But it was other things they remembered and they forgot all about the man outside who had set them thinking of their childhood.

The doctor had taken the collector into the women's ward to meet Mary Creegan. She was sitting up in bed, alone in the long room; all the other women were out in the warm sun. As the two men walked up the bare floor the collector was trailing a long black cable from a microphone in his hand, and the doctor was telling him that she came from a place called Faill-a-ghleanna in West Cork.

'She should have lots of stories because her husband was famous for them. After he died she went a bit airy so they had to bring her to us. 'Twas a bit tough on her at first. Sixty years in the one cottage – and then to finish up here.' They stood beside her bed. 'I brought a visitor to see you, Mary,' he said in a loud voice.

She did not appear to see them. She was humming happily to herself. Her bony fingers were wound about an ancient rosary beads. Her white hair floated up above a face as tiny and as wrinkled as a forgotten crab apple. All her teeth were gone so that her face was as broad as it was long: it was as if the midwife had pressed the baby's chin and forehead between thumb and forefinger. The doctor gently laid his hand under the tiny chin and turned her face towards him. She smiled.

'Put down the kettle and wet the tay,' she ordered.

The doctor sat on the bed; so did the collector.

''Tis down, Mary, and two eggs in the pot. This poor man here is after coming a long way to talk to you. He's tired out.'

She turned and looked at the stranger. Encouraged by a brightening spark in the depths of her eyes he turned aside and murmured quietly into the microphone, 'Reggy? Recording ten seconds from . . . now.'

'It's a bad road,' she said. 'Ask Jamesy is he keeping that divil of a cow out of the cabbage.'

'She's all right,' the doctor cried into her ear. 'Jamesy is watching her. Be talking to us while we're waiting for the tay. You told me one time you saw a ghost. Is that true?'

She looked out of the window and her eyes opened and narrowed like a fish's gills as if they were sucking something in from the blue sky outside. The collector stealthily approached her chin with the microphone.

'Ghosts? Ayeh! Ha! My ould divil of a tailor is forever and always talkin' about 'um. But, sure, I wouldn't heed him. Bummin' and boashtin' he is from morning to night and never a needle to be shtuck in the shtuff. Where is he? Why don't you ask him to be talking to you about ghoshts?'

The doctor looked across the bed at the collector and raised his eyebrows.

'Maybe you don't believe in them yourself?' he mocked.

'I do *not* believe in 'um. But they're there. Didn't I hear tell of 'um from them that saw 'um? Aye, and often. And often! Aye' – still collecting her thoughts from the sky above the bakehouse chimney –

'wasn't it that way the night Father Regan died? Huh! They called him Father Regan, but he was not a right priest. He was silenced for some wrong thing he did when he was a young priest, and they sent him to Faill-a-ghleanna to be doing penance for it. When his time came to die it was a bad, shtormy night. And when he sent for the parish priest to hear his confession the priest said he could not come. And that was a hard thing to do, for no man should refuse the dying. And they sent another messenger for the priest, and still the priest could not come. "Oh," said Father Regan, "I'm lost now." So they sent a third messenger. And for the third time the priest could not come. And on his way back wasn't the messenger shtopped on the road by a woman? It was Father Regan's own mother. "Go back," says she, "and if the candles by his bed light up," says she, "of their own accord," says she, "he is saved." And the messenger went back, and Father Regan gave wan look at him and he closed his eyes for the last time. With that all the people went on their knees. And they began to pray. If they did, there were three candles at the head of the dead priest. And didn't the one beside the window light up? And after a little while the candle beside the fire clevy lit up. And they went on praying. And the wind and the shtorm screaming about the house, and they watching the wick of the last candle. And, bit by bit, the way you'd blow up a fire with a bellows, didn't the candle over the priest's head light up until the whole room was like broad daylight.'

The old woman's voice suddenly became bright and hard.

'Isn't that tay ready a-yet? Domn and blosht it, ye'll have them eggs like bullets.' She looked alertly at the two men. 'Where am I? Where's Jamesy? What are ye doing to me?'

The doctor held her wrist. Her eyes faded. She sank back heavily.

'I thought,' she wailed, 'that it was how I saw a great brightness.'

The collector spoke one word into the microphone. The old woman had fainted. Overcome with regrets he began to apologize, but the doctor waved his hand at him.

'Excited. I'll send up the sister to give her an injection. Sometimes she loves to talk about old times. It does her good.'

They went out of the empty ward, the cable trailing softly. They passed the male ward. Michael Kivlehan and Thomas Hunter were sitting on their beds. As the doctor led the way downstairs, he said, 'When that generation goes it will be all over. Wait for me outside. There are a couple more. You might get bits and scraps from them.'

The engineer put his head out of the van and said, in the gloomy voice of all engineers, 'That might come through all right.'

When the doctor came out again they sat with a middle-aged man from Wicklow, named Fenelon. He had been on the roads until arthritis crippled him. When he counted the years he spoke in Urdu. He had scraps of the tinker's language which is called Shelta. He said:

'I often walked from Dublin to Puck, and that's a hundred miles, without ever disturbing anything but a hare or a snipe. I'd make for Ross, and then cross to Callan, and by Slievenamon west to the Galtees.'

He did not see the microphone; he did not see his visitors; as the needle softly cut the disc he was seeing only the mountainy sheep that looked at him with slitted eyes, a thing as shaggy as themselves.

They moved on to an old woman who sang a love song for them in a cracked voice. She said she had learned it in Chicago. She gave them a poem of twelve verses about a voyage to the South Seas. They were finishing a disc with a very old man from Carlow when the sister came out and hastily beckoned to the doctor. As they folded up the cable he came back. He said, with a slow shake of the head:

'It's old Mary. I must leave ye. But ye have the best of them. The rest is only the shakings of the bag.'

When they had thanked him and were driving away, the collector said, eagerly:

'Pull up when we're out of the town. I want to play back those discs.'

They circled up and out of the town until its murmur was so faint that they could hear only the loudest cries of the playing children. There they played back the discs, and as they leaned towards the loud-speaker and the black record circled smoothly they could see, sideways through the window, the smoke of the hollow town. The last voice was Mary Creegan's.

' ... *and after a little while the candle beside the fire clevy lit up. And they went on praying. And the wind and the shtorm screaming about the house, and they watching the wick of the last candle. And, bit by bit, the way you'd blow up a fire with a bellows, didn't the candle over the priest's head light up until the whole room was like broad daylight. . . . Isn't that tay ready a-yet? Domn and blosht it, ye'll have them eggs like bullets. . . . Where am I? Where's Jamesy? What are ye doing to me? . . . I thought that it was how I saw a great brightness.'*

The listeners relaxed. Then from the record came a low, lonely cry. It was the fluting of a bittern over moorland. It fluted sadly once again, farther away; and for a third time, almost too faint to be heard. Many times the two men played back those last few inches of disc. Every time they heard the bittern wailing over the mountains.

It was dusk. They laid the voices in a black box and drove away. Then they topped the hill, and the antennae of their headlamps began to probe the winding descent to the next valley.

# Lord and Master

Every time Master Kennedy and his wife passed the gates of Carews-court House, and the round little gate lodge and smooth pond, he said that when he retired he would rent that cottage. The summer he retired he did rent it. He was sad that his wife had not lived to share it with him, but he was as happy, otherwise, as a Chinese philosopher, with his books, and his cat, and his tiny garden with its four standard roses, its six gooseberry bushes and its single pear tree.

Around Christmas he fell ill with a cold that nearly finished him, and it was as he lay in bed that he first noticed the patches of damp on the walls. He did not pay much attention until February, when his foot went through the floor of the front room and his boot sole came up green with mildew. He took his stick, put on his hat, and sought out Paddy Markham, the mason, whom he found plastering the base of the wall of Neville's pub in the Main Street.

'Paddy,' he said, 'I have a little job for you.'

Paddy had a hump and a squint and was half the height of the teacher. He had the trowel in one hand and the hawk in the other, and as he listened he kept mixing the bit of mortar on the hawk with the point of the trowel. In the end he chucked the trowel into the mortar and looked up at his old teacher.

'Masther! I'll tell you no lie. I've been tinkerin' with that ould cottage for the last thirty-five years. I made people spend hundreds of pounds on the cottage trying to get the damp out of it. And,' he said triumphantly, 'it's as soppin' as if they never spent a penny on it. I put a damp course under it. I waterproofed it. I plastered it with Pluvex and Supex and Pudlo and Cudlo and Dudlo and the divil knows whato. And you might as well be tryin' to plaster up th' Atlantic Ocean. Oh, mind you,' Paddy went on comfortingly as the master stared down gloomily at his enthusiastic, stupid face, 'It's a nate little house. The house is all right. 'Tis well built, 'tis solid as the Rock o'Gibraltar. But there's wan thing wrong with it.'

'And what the devil is that, pray?'

''Tis the pond that you have in front of you that's seeping onderneath your foundations. There'll be days, Masther, and if you were to take up a floor board in the front room you'd find a lake of wather onderneath it!'

'Oh, well, in that case,' cried the master happily, 'all I have to do is get rid of the pond!'

Paddy cocked his quizzical crooked eye up at him.

'How?' he asked.

'Where does the water in the pond come from?'

Paddy drew back and looked sideways at him.

'It comes in a stream from the big lake in front of Carewscourt House, where else? Or are you coddin' me? As if you didn't know! Do you mean to say you don't know the ould gully with the wooden dam beside Beechmount crossroads? Sure all the water in the town comes down there. Down through the channel from the River Villy that the Carews cut hundreds and hundreds of years ago.'

The master touched his beard.

'And flows into their lake? And out of the lake into my pond? And from my pond in front of all the cottages? And from . . .'

He stopped. He saw a small boy throwing stones into the stream that runs down the middle of the main street of Rathvilly between two low walls and two lines of lime trees. The child stood on the far pavement, which is three steps above the street on that side. The master looked down at the base of the wall that Paddy had been plastering.

'Then that stream must be seeping under every shop along this side of the street? And under every cottage back along the road? As well as under my cottage?'

'To be sure it does,' the mason agreed placidly.

'Then I have no job at all for you, Paddy. The County Council must wall up the dam at Beechmount crossroads.'

And off with the Master back down the street, past the last line of cabins, each with its own little wooden bridge, to his cottage by the pond. There he sat down and wrote a long letter to the secretary of the County Council requesting that the dam at Beechmount be permanently closed.

'But sure, my dear Michael,' laughed the county engineer, Corny Cosgrave, when he called on the master (who had taught him his first pothooks in the national school), 'if we did what you want us to do we'd dry up the bloody lake in Carewscourt.'

'And why not, Cornelius?' the master asked calmly.

'But, it's *their* lake!'

'Is that a fact, Cornelius?' The master smiled patiently. 'And who gave them the right, Cornelius, to deflect the water to make the lake? Did they ask permission of the town of Rathvilly to make the lake? Did they get permission from the County Council to make the lake?'

'You know damn well,' cried Corny testily, 'that there was no such a thing as asking permission in those days. Are ye daft? Sure, if there was even such a thing as a County Council in those days they *were* the County Council. And as for asking permission from the town, sure they made, owned, and ran the bloody town.'

'And do they still own the town, Cornelius?' asked the master, glaring at his pupil like Moses at a backsliding Israelite. 'Is this all our much-vaunted liberty has brought us? You,' persisted the master, in his slow Biblical voice, 'were one of the first young men in this county to take up arms for the independence of your country. You fought...'

Corny held the master's arm.

'Look, Master! For God's sake, leave politics out of this. You'd drag politics into the sale of a wheelbarrow. This question is not a political question. It is a legal question.'

'And is the law of Ireland,' asked the master fiercely, 'for the Saxon or is it for the Gael?'

'The law,' said Cornelius, throwing his arms as wide as possible as if to throw the whole matter as far away from himself as possible, 'is for everybody. Rich and poor. Gentle and simple. Christian and Jew. Young and old. Male and female. Without the slightest distinction of class *or* creed.'

The master smiled at his pupil. Then, as if he had a cane behind his back and was saying, 'Kindly tell me what is the capital of Arakan,' he said:

'Kindly tell me, Cornelius, what is the law in this matter?'

'That will be for the courts to decide.'

At that the master let such a roar out of him that Corny, from old habit, half raised a protective arm.

'So!' the master cried. 'Your decision is that I must go behind the County Council to the courts?'

Corny saw that he had fallen into a trap.

'Now! Now! Don't take me up on a word! How do I know what the council will decide to do?'

'You know damn well that you've decided already what you're going to tell them to do!'

Corny took the master by the arm again. He spoke like a fluting pigeon to him.

'Listen to me, Mr Kennedy.' (The old man did not fail to notice the change from 'My dear Michael' to 'Master' and from 'Master' to 'Mister,' together with the increasing amiability.) 'You and I were old campaigners together. You were a Fenian, and the son of a Fenian. You were the first man to open my eyes to the true facts of the national question. Sure, the way you taught Irish history was a marvel! A positive marvel! And you know that I'm as sound an Irishman as you'll get in the four quarters of Ireland. You know me. I know you. And the two of us understand one another's lingo. But what you forget, and a lot of other people forget, and I say this, now, with the greatest respect for you and in the highest possible regard, is that the people of Ireland can't be going back over old sores forever and ever. There are such things, you know, as what they call *fate accomplee*.' He slapped the master on the shoulder as if it were he who was the ex-teacher and the master the ex-pupil. 'I often heard of people wanting to turn back the clock, but this is the first time I heard of a man wanting to turn back a blooming river!'

The master listened sourly to his peals of laughter.

'Are you telling me, Mr Cosgrave, that you're not able to dam a little stream no bigger than a dog's piddle for the sake of the health of your own town?'

'My dear sir, give me one man with a shovel and I'll do it for you in five minutes.'

'Then why don't you do it in five minutes?'

'Because, dammit, certain people have certain rights, and that's why.'

'It's not by any chance because certain people are afraid of certain people, and that's why?'

Corny went pink. He seized his hat.

'I will make my report directly to the County Council,' he said coldly. He paused at the door. 'You were always a cantankerous ould divil.'

'And,' the master shouted after him, 'I never gave you enough of the stick on your backside when I had you!'

The clang of the motor-car door and the bang of the cottage door were simultaneous.

Within a week the master's pond had the whole town turned upside down. If a child's cap blew into the stream in the middle of the street, or if he got his feet wet beside the cottages, or if a woman as much as sneezed, or if some old fellow who had never done a day's work in his life got a twinge of rheumatism, somebody would start cursing the stream. He might even strike an attitude and say, 'Is it for this we bled and died?' There was nothing that couldn't be and wasn't connected with the stream. When the price of coal went up, somebody was heard to say:

'And timber galore in the demesne! How fair they wouldn't give it out to the poor? Oho no! All they ever gave us to warm us was their dirty ould wather!'

It wasn't only the Carews. Their relations all over the county came in for it, the Eustaces, the Brodricks, the Connollys, and the Suttons, until, as one of the opposition said, you'd think the stream had as many tributaries as the Ganges. And then there was an ex-soldier who told a whole pub how he once met an Englishman in Burma who said, 'Rathvilly? Isn't that the place where the river runs down the middle of the street?' Hammering the counter this traveller shouted, 'Are we to deshtroy a shtrame that have us made famous the world over?'

'I agree,' the doctor said in the lounge of the Royal Hibernian Hotel, 'that, ideally, the stream ought to be closed. But you know very well that if you close up the stream they'll simply throw their rubbish into the street. And if you block up the stream the cottages will have no running water to wash their clothes in.'

Nobody said anything to that. But the vet winked at the ceiling. They all knew that the doctor attended the Carews.

'Aesthetically speaking,' said the bank clerk, 'it would be a pity to dry up the stream. It's a very pleasant feature in the town. I grant you there's a bit of a niff off it in the summer, but . . .'

'Am I wrong,' the town's cryptosocialist said, 'in thinking that your bank handles the Carews' account?'

'Aha!' from the bank clerk. 'There's Russia talking! You don't mind having your own sister working as a parlourmaid in Carewscourt?'

'A perfect example,' the cryptosocialist cried, 'of the evil network of feudalism.'

'Why the hell's blazes,' said John Jo Sullivan, who owned the garage, and used to be a commandant of the I.R.A. thirty-two years ago, before he got paunchy and balding, 'don't we go out some night and settle the whole bloody thing with one good stick o' dynamite under the ould dam?'

'Well, why don't you, John Jo?' smiled the inspector of the guards, who used to be John Jo's adjutant in those good old days when every question was 'settled with one good stick of dynamite.'

'Because I don't trust you, you bastard,' said John Jo bitterly.

'There was a time when you'd have taken a chance, John Jo,' said the inspector easily. And he added, by way of no harm, from the depths of his armchair, 'By the way, did Carew order that new Humber Hawk from you yet?'

The master thus found support on all sides.

He was all the more dumbfounded when he got a letter a week later from Corny Cosgrave saying that 'in view of the enclosed document no action can be taken in the matter until the next meeting of the County Council.' The document was 'A Grand Petition,' pleading for the preservation of the stream, signed by 279 out of Rathvilly's total of 395 inhabitants. When he had read down the list of names he hurled the paper on the floor and cursed Rathvilly, man, woman, and child, lock, stock, and barrel, back to their seventy-seven generations, for a pack of cowards, liars, and cringing slaves.

Not that he did not know perfectly well the pressure that lay behind every signature on the list. The first name on it was Paddy Markham's. Paddy's brother worked in the Carewscourt sawmills. Every shopkeeper in the town was there: which meant that the Carews owed hundreds of pounds all over the place, and everybody knows there is only one way to treat creditors and that is to make them hop or they'll walk on you. As he examined the list he could find only two names that had not been extracted by force: they were two old women who, to his knowledge, were dead and buried for at least three years. When he saw the two names the master cursed Rathvilly more bitterly than ever.

'My god!' he ground out. 'All we've taught the Carews is how to beat us at our own game!'

It was three weeks to the next meeting of the council. He spent every day of it canvassing the members. Not one man of them refused him support, none promised it. What maddened him above all was the way somebody who had signed the 'Grand Petition' would accost him and congratulate him on the fight he was making.

'But,' he would say coldly, 'your own name is on the petition, signed there in black and white!'

The man would say something like:

'Yerrah, Master, what signify that? Sure all I told them was to throw me name on the ould paper if it gave them any satisfaction. I can assure you, Master, that I'm *one hundred per cent* with you for getting rid of that old stream. 'Tis destroying the health of the town. Fight them, Master! We're behind you to the last ditch.'

At the next meeting of the council he sat at the rear of the room. To his delight one man stood up to support him. He was the Labour member.

'I maintain, Mr Chairman,' the Labour member declared, 'that it would be a most progressive action, which, as well as giving much-needed employment to the town and borough, would benefit the health and sanitation of the working classes, if it was a thing that the stream at present pursuing its noxious course through the main street was to be filled up. It would, for one thing, widen the street.'

'That's right,' put in the Ratepayers' member. 'The unemployed could park their motor cars there.'

'That,' shouted the Labour member, 'is an unworthy remark, but no more than I would expect from the low quarter from whence it came.'

'Your own brother,' shouted the Ratepayers' member, 'signed the petition for to keep it.'

'The brother,' roared the Labour member, 'is as good an Irishman as anybody in this room. And he was never before the courts for keeping his pub open after hours!'

'No, nor for poaching salmon either, I suppose?' taunted the Ratepayers' member.

The chairman banged the table for three solid minutes, during which the two speakers investigated the history of their respective families between the years 1810 and 1952.

'May I ask,' he said, when he had restored order, 'where the sewage would go if we were to fill up the stream?'

'That, Mr Chairman,' declared the Labour member, 'is the whole point. It is high time that the sewage system of this town was put into a proper condition.'

'Aha!' the Farmers' member shouted. 'Now we're getting at it! And your own uncle a contractor!'

This time it took the chairman five minutes to restore order. He gave the floor to John Jo Sullivan, who, they all knew, was going to stand at the next general election for the Dail.

'Mr Chairman,' John Jo said, 'I do not think that I need to make any excuses for what I am going to say here today. I do not think I need to blow my own trumpet. I have no wish nor desire to boast of my national record, nor of those far-off days when Ireland lit a torch that shone around the world. Be that as it may, today, thanks be to God, we have a free country (all but the six northern counties, I hasten to say) in which every man is guaranteed his rights under a free constitution, equally approved by church and state. We have a country, moreover, where any man who may have any doubts as to his rights can have free recourse to the courts of law, where all such little disputes can be amicably settled in honesty and in friendship. Our people,' he intoned, 'have made themselves – and our dear little island – famous all over the world for their long fight down the ages for liberty, and for Christianity. In these dark and troubled days, Mr Chairman, that surround us, with the spectres of war . . .'

At the rear of the room the master rose and walked out so quietly that nobody noticed his going. On his way home he almost admired Carew Outnumbered four hundred to one he could still keep the rabble under his heels.

On the next morning he went into Limerick city to a solicitor. The solicitor listened to him patiently. Then he said, in the sad, tired voice of a man who is sick to death of all litigation:

'I'm afraid, Mr Kennedy, you have a case. I'm sorry to say I think you have a case.'

'Afraid? Sorry? What do you mean?'

'I mean that you'll go ahead with it. And you won't win it. I know Carew, Mr Kennedy. He is a determined man. If you beat him in the lower courts he'll take you up to the Four Courts, and he won't stop until he ruins you. And if you should, by some miracle, beat him in law he won't stop until he runs you out of the town. He'll fight you to the

last ditch, and beyond it. And I must confess, Mr Kennedy, I don't
blame him.'

The master rose in his chair.

'That's queer kind of talk to be going on with to your own client. Are
you on his side or are you on mine?'

'Sit down there and listen to me! I'm not on his side. But I can put
myself in his position. And if you could do the same you'd see that if
you were Lord Carew you'd do to him exactly what he is doing to you.
Tell the truth, Mr Kennedy. If somebody tried to take away from you
something that you and your people had owned for going on two
hundred and fifty years, something that you'd looked at every day of
your life, ever since you were a boy, something that all your memories
were wrapped up in, and your father's and your mother's before you,
and back behind them for the seven generations – something you were
very, very fond of, Mr Kennedy – wouldn't you fight that man down
to the last brass farthing you possessed?'

The master scattered the air with his hands.

'There's no sense nor meaning to this kind of talk! I'm not interested
in hypotheses. I'm not Lord Carew, and I don't want to be Lord Carew,
and I know nothing about Lord Carew, but I know this, that if I *was*
Lord Carew and I wanted to make a lake in front of my house I hope
I'd do it some other way than by draining my dirty water past every
cottage between my front gate and the gable wall of the chapel.' The
old man leaned halfway over the desk. His voice rose. 'If I wanted to
make a lake this minute in front of *my* house would I be allowed to run
away with half the river to do it? They stole the river!' he shouted. 'They
stole the river, and if there's justice in the country they should be made
to give it back to the people that owns it. Lord Carew? How could I be
. . . ' He laughed derisively. 'Do you know,' he ground out hatefully,
'what the Carews did to Rathvilly during the Rebellion of 1798? Do you
know that . . .'

The solicitor listened wearily. When the old man sank back, panting
and trembling, he said:

'Very well. You evidently feel strongly about it. And if your mind is
made up, your mind is made up. But I warn you that it's going to leave
a blister on you to the end of your days. It would be far cheaper for you
to leave the cottage altogether.'

'I will *not* leave the cottage. Ever since my wife, God rest her, saw
that cottage twenty-five years ago she wanted me to have it. I put the

best part of my life's savings into furnishing that cottage. I love the cottage.'

'So be it.'

The master calmed down.

'Why have I a case?'

'If the water is damaging your property somebody must be liable.'

'Good.'

'Mind you, it may not be Carew. It may be the County Council.'

'It *is* Carew. And I'll get him.'

'But Carew will get at the council, you know.'

'How?'

The solicitor parted the air gently with his hands.

All the way back in the train the old teacher kept remembering that gesture. It reminded him of the priest at Mass turning to the people to say *Dominus vobiscum*. He kept murmuring the words to the wet, wheeling fields. They recurred to him many times during the following days, which he spent, often late into the night, writing appealing letters to everybody of position whom he had ever even slightly known. During those nights when he would hear nothing but the swish of the willow outside, or an occasional car driving fast through the town, it seemed to him that, in some way, his desire to go on living in his cottage was linked with his wife's desire to possess it, and that those words, *Dominus vobiscum*, were words of encouragement from her to him. He would seize a new sheet then, and write another long angry letter, to a member of the Dail, to a priest, or to the bishop. He even wrote to the President of Eire. To not one of these letters did he ever receive a reply.

The lawyers were writing more letters. His solicitor quoted against the council a statute from the reign of King John about public waterways. The council's solicitor countered that the lake and its tributaries were Lord Carew's private property. The master's solicitor quoted this against Carew's solicitors. Carew's solicitors replied that they acknowledged responsibility as for the lake, but that once the stream left the demesne it became the public property of the people of Rathvilly. They were sparring all the winter.

Then one afternoon, in late April, the words *Dominus vobiscum* suddenly came to the master with a new meaning. As he murmured the words he looked out of his window. He saw a rainbow that seemed to leap directly from his pond across the sky to the spire on Chapel Hill, and he heard his wife's voice saying, as she had so often said, 'Ah, wisha, Patrick, why do you be always growling against the Church? 'Tis our only friend.' He took his hat and stick and stumped down into the town, and up Chapel Hill to the presbytery. Painfully he climbed the long steps. Puffed, he pulled the china handle of the bell and asked the housekeeper for the monsignor. She put him to wait in the small side parlour.

As he stood and looked over the woven reed of the half screen across the smoky thatch of the little town he saw something he had not noticed before: a big motor car below at the presbytery gate. It was the Carewscourt car.

At the same moment, across the hall, he became aware of a murmur of voices and the sound of somebody laughing. He opened his door a crack. It was the delicate laugh of the monsignor, and he could imagine the dainty little figure, the white hair, the rosy cheeks, the jigging hand, and the touches of red on his vest and his biretta. He felt his heart thrusting against his breastbones. The blood pumped up under his eyes. He crossed the hall and flung open the parlour door. There was Lord Carew, as sallow as an old spoon, long-faced, smiling; and the monsignor seated opposite him, with his pale-pink hand on the big ordnance map spread on the plush-covered table between them. The master lashed the table with his stick so that the papers flew.

'I knew it,' the old man whispered, glaring from one astonished face to the other. 'For forty-five years,' he gasped, 'I've taught in this town, and my poor wife with me. I served you' – he pointed his trembling stick at the monsignor – 'since I was a boy serving Mass at the altar, and now I find you conspiring against me with the gentry!' The monsignor had risen, fluttering his two palms. 'I hoped,' the master sobbed, 'I hoped to find the Church on my side and on the side of my poor wife. But the Church is against us! As the Church was always against us. Against the Fenians. The men of forty-eight. Parnell. Sinn Fein. In the fight for the Republic . . . .'

At that he collapsed. After they had partly revived him, they helped him out between them, down the long steps, and into Carew's car. The cries of the children at play did not pause.

On the way, Carew remembered that the old chap lived alone and instead of pausing at the lodge gates he went on into the avenue to his own front steps. There the butler, hearing him come, was already

waiting to open the door of the car. By this time the master had
recovered. He looked out at the butler, an old pupil of his, one Timsy
Twomey, realized where he was, and scrambled out in angry disdain.

'You'd better have a brandy, Mr Kennedy,' Carew suggested and
nodded to Twomey.

'I want nothing from you but the one thing,' the master began
haughtily, 'and that...'

He stopped. Behind the haze of fishing flies on Carew's tweed hat he
saw an oblong sheet of water burning below its low granite coping, fiery
in the sun that was sinking between a rosy scallop of clouds and the
flowing hills of Villy, now as hard as jewels in the cold April air. Its
long smooth glow was broken only by a row of cypresses at its far end,
the reflection of whose black plumes plunged into the burning pool to
spear the light again. Beneath them were two wrestling Tritons from
whose mouths two fountains rose, and crossed and fell with a soft
splash. Carew watched the old man's eyes for a moment or two. They
were a play of astonishment, delight, and hate.

'Well, Mr Kennedy, there's the cause of it all. And you're looking at
it, I think, for the first time? And, probably, for the last time.'

The master looked quickly at him, arrested by his tone.

'I mean,' Carew said, with a little crooked smile on his long sallow
face, 'the lake is going to be drained.'

'You're closing the dam?' the master asked, unbelievingly, and
looked back at the water which, already, was growing dark and cold.

'You may as well know, if it gives you any pleasure, I'm selling
Carewscourt. I've sold it to a teaching order of nuns. Good teachers,
I believe. Or so the monsignor tells me. One of the first things they're
going to do is to drain the lake. And I'm not much surprised, for it has
damn near drained me.'

And he began to explain how badly it had been constructed, with
somebody always having to empty it and mend the bottom, or grout
the sides, or repair the plumbing of the fountain, or dredge the channels
down through the town.

'The sisters are going to plant a sunken garden in it. I'm sorry, but
... Oh, well! They haven't sat here of summer evenings as I have,
watching the sun go down.'

The splash of the fountains had become more distinct. The hills were
dark when Twomey opened the glass doors behind them, and stood
waiting for his old teacher.

'It'll be a hard frost tonight,' said Carew. 'Do come in. We use the hall now for a dining room,' he said, and he and the master went up the three shallow steps into the house. Twomey held out the glasses on a salver. Each took one. 'I've emptied nearly every room in the house,' Carew said. 'I'll sell everything except those books.'

They walked across the hall to the big bookcase. The master looked into them with interest.

'Mostly Irish books,' Carew said. 'Family history. I'll keep these.'

'And where,' asked the master, speaking for the first time since he asked who would dam the lake, 'where are you going to live, Lord Carew?'

Carew tapped his chest.

'I haven't long to run.' He drained his brandy. 'Can I drive you as far as the gates?'

It took the master a long time to reply. Then he said:

'Thank you. I'd be obliged to you.'

They drove circuitously, around the far end of the lake. There Carew halted the car for a few seconds to look. One star shone greenly in the water. At the far end the hallway made a brief dagger of light. The house rose square, and straight and clear-cut in the last of the sun.

'It is a fine house,' said the master grudgingly.

'It was,' said Carew.

They drove on over the gravel to the gates, the cottage, and the pool.

'Good night, Mr Kennedy. Take care of yourself.'

'Good night, Lord Carew. I suppose the sisters will want this cottage?'

Carew lifted an uncertain hand, meshed his gears, drove away.

When the car lights vanished down the road the master walked towards his cottage. In his willow pool he saw the evening star. He stood looking at it for a long time, serene in the water. As he looked it began to fade. Clouds were coming across the sky. It gleamed again, more brilliantly than before. Then it went out.

He went into his cottage and closed the door. From where he sat inside he could hear the willow whispering to the water and the wall. He would miss his little pool.

# An Enduring Friendship

When Georgie Canty saw Louis Golden at the customs counter of the airport he muttered 'Bastard!' under his breath: which was what he hoped most people in Ireland thought of Mr Louis Bloody Well Golden, editor of the *Daily Crucifix*, 'Ireland's One and Only Catholic Daily' – and one too many at that!

Georgie's eyes closed, his mouth zipped tight. His duodenum walked slowly all round his waist with spiked boots. It stuck a redhot sword in through his navel. It pulled his liver out through his ribs. His eyes closed in agony. . . .

He lifted his lids and his eyes swivelled down the counter length at Golden – at his long neck like a heron, his little rabbit's puss with the two white teeth like a nutria, the hunched shoulders of a constipated stork, and the same soapy grin for the customs officer that he probably switched on whenever he'd be talking to a bishop. As he looked at him Georgie wondered if there ever had been a plane crash in which everybody was saved, except one man.

That night at the United Bankers! With himself and Golden, two of a platform of four, debating the motion *That the Irish Are the Most Tolerant Race in the World*. Three sentences. Three not too lengthy sentences about how silly it is for Irishmen to be chasing Freemasons as if they had four horns and two tails; and there he was, the next morning, crucified in the *Crucifix* under a three-column headline – BANKERS DEFEND MASONS – and, on page four, a leading article entitled, 'So This Is Holy Ireland?' signed *Louis Paul Golden*. Naturally he was barely inside the door of the bank before he was called into the parlour.

'I understand, Mr Canty,' old Plummer smiled at him across the carpet with teeth that would clip a hedge, 'I understand that you saw fit to defend Freemasonry in public last night? Is that correct?'

Now, of course every man in the bank knows perfectly well that there isn't a month that old Plumtree Gum doesn't toddle off to the Masonic

Hall with his little apron and all the rest of his regalia; and, for all anybody knows, he might be the great Mah Jong of Molesworth Street, he might be the Prince Mason of the Western World. So, what could Georgie do but rub his palms, smile a man-of-the-world smile, and utter these famous last words:

'Irishmen are in many ways absurd . . .'

They heard Plummer's roar outside in the Foreign Exchange Department. After that it was ding-dong bell for five minutes . . . . Who – would somebody please, *please*, tell him – who ever asked anybody to defend anybody in private or in public? And if, by any possible chance, however remote, anybody ever did happen to require the kind services of anybody why should anybody think that *his* brilliant services were what was specifically demanded by the occasion? And, furthermore, there were people in this city who were very well equipped to defend themselves for themselves. And, furthermore, he himself had lived in this city for fifty-odd years and he had never made any secret of the fact that he was a member of the Worshipful Grand Order, and if he was ever required to defend himself he could do it very well indeed thank you without anybody's assistance! And, further-more, and especially, he would be greatly obliged if people would have the goodness to remember that their job, first, foremost, and before all, was to consider the interests of the institution that paid them and made them, which would be a jolly sight better thing for all concerned than to be going out and opening their bloody gobs to make roaring asses of themselves in the bloody press, and he would be infinitely obliged to Mr Canty if he would remember *that*. And furthermore . . .

Not a peep out of Georgie. He sat dumb as a goldfish until he heard the voice of God Almighty bidding him good morning in a voice like a hangman's chaplain, followed by the words: 'I will consider later, Mr Canty, what disciplinary action may be most appropriate to the occasion.' As Georgie walked back over the two and a half miles of marble floor to his cubbyhole not a sound was heard, not a funeral note, except for some scut softly whistling 'Will Ye No' Come Back Again?' He had not done much work in his cubbyhole that day, waiting to be packed off to some back-of-beyond like Killorglin or Cahirciveen. After six weeks without one good night's sleep, he had applied for a week's leave of absence, on a doctor's certificate.

The loud-speaker retailed a female voice in Irish, of which he understood only the word *Gurrabbulluballoo*, which means, 'Thanks.'

He opened his eyes to see the queue trailing out. He was the last man on the plane. He took the last seat. He found himself sitting beside the last man in the world he had wanted to see again. Their safety belts got entangled. Golden looked up and at once shot out his paw.

'Georgie Canty, for all the world! Well, isn't this the real McCoy! This is great luck.'

Georgie shook his hand warmly.

'Louis Golden. Well, I'm delighted, simply delighted to see you. Travelling far?'

'Let me help you with that belt,' said Golden, and he tucked Canty in like a baby in its pram. Then he patted his thigh. 'How's tricks? I heard you weren't too well.'

'Not bad, not bad. And yourself? And the missus? All the care doing well?'

As they roared down the runway for the take-off Golden blessed himself piously. Canty thought it just as well to do a fiddle, also, around his third vest button.

'I suppose,' he said presently, trying to suggest (but only suggest) a faint sneer, 'you're off to some ecclesiastical conference?'

Golden leaned over with a confidential, crooked grin and nudged Canty.

'Mattherofact, d'ye know what I was doing the last time I was in Paris? I was touring an Australian Jesuit around the night clubs. He was very agreeably surprised.'

'In which sense?' asked Georgie, modulating between innocence and insinuation. Golden only laughed and waved a tolerant claw.

'Harmless. A bit of leg. Nothing more. The usual routine. We did about five or six of them. Folies Bergère. Bal Tabarin. Chin-Chin. Eve. The Blue Angel. Nothing at all to it.'

Georgie squinted sideways at him, thinking of the moths in the Bal Tabarin coming out in the altogether.

'Did *you* approve?' he inquired.

'It's not a question of approving.' When he said 'question' his two white teeth went bare. 'It's all a matter of atmosphere. When in Rome, and so on.'

He grabbed the hostess by the hip and ordered two double brandies. This, mind you, at nine-thirty in the morning!

'Morals,' he explained to Georgie, 'morals in the sense of *mores* are always affected by time and place. For example, would you walk down

O'Connell Street in the middle of the noonday with nothing on but a Lastex slip?'

'The Guards'd have me in the Bridewell in two ticks.'

'There was a fella walked down the Rue Royale last year with nothin' at all on. He was only fined five francs. Betty Grable could walk down the beach at Biarritz in a G-string and a smile and nobody would look twice at her.'

The brandy was going to Georgie's head. He leaned over and laughed.

'I believe Lady Godiva rode down Broadway wan time in her skin and everybody ran out in wild excitement to see the white horse. But if that be so what's this I hear about the bishops not wanting to see girls wearing cycling shorts?'

'Who would?' cackled Golden, and they went hard at it.

They were still arguing the toss over the Channel, and whether it was the six double brandies, or the elevating sensation of being up in the air, Georgie began, in spite of himself, to find the little runt almost bearable. It was not until the Eiffel Tower appeared out of the smoke that he brought down the question of Freemasons.

'You knew blooming well that night that I wasn't defending Freemasonry. But in spite of that, you bastard, you came out in your rotten rag and tore the guts out of me.'

'Editorial policy.' Blandly.

'Do you realize that you nearly cost me my job?' And he told him all about it.

'Ah! No!' cried Louis, genuinely distressed. 'For God's sake! Is that true? Well, now, doesn't that show ye what Freemasons are!'

All the same he stuck to his guns. Georgie had to grant him that he stuck to his guns.

They were still at it as they whirled around the Undying Flame in the bus; and as Georgie had not booked a hotel he went off with Louis; and by the time they were finishing lunch, and two bottles of Nuits Saint Georges, they had arrived at the Arian heresy – about which they both knew sweet damn-all – and were still at Homoiousian and Homoousian at half past four in front of two Otards and the Café de Paris in the blazing sun.

'Now, look, Louis, you flaming scoundrel,' Georgie was saying, 'your trouble is you're a moralist. All you want is an autocratic, oligarchic church laying down the law about everything from cremation to contraceptives. You're a Puritan! That's what you are!'

Louis leaned a gentle hand on Georgie's arm and breathed on him like a father confessor.

'Georgie! I'll tell you something. Here in Paris. As bloke to bloke. I have exactly the same pashuns as you have. But I *know* me pashuns! I *know* them – and they're dynamite! And what's more, the pashuns of every Irishman are dynamite! And double dynamite! And triple dynamite! And if the priests of Ireland are hard on their own people, it's because they know that if they once took the lid off the pashuns of Irish men and Irish women, aye and of Irish children, the country would *blow up*! Look at Saint Paul!'

Georgie looked and saw a smashing blonde. Louis dragged him ashore, and the pair of them took Saint Paul down to the Rue Donau where Golden knew a little bar called, of all things, *Le Crucifix*; and then they took Saint Augustine, who was a bloke Georgie said he never liked – and he didn't care *who* knew it! – across to a bar on the Quatre Septembre where they had four flat Guinnesses for ould Ireland's sake; and then they took the Manichees, and the Jansenists, and Pascal, up to the bar at the Gare du Nord; and then they went up to Sacré Coeur to say a prayer, and lean on the balustrade, and Louis explained all about Modernism to Georgie, and Georgie said it was his cup of tea, and to hell with the Council of Trent anyway for jiggering up everything; and then they had dinner near the old Pigalle, with two more bottles of Nuits Saint Georges; and then nothing would do Louis but to prove he wasn't a Puritan by going off to the Bal Tabarin, where they had two bottles of *champagne obligatoire* at three thousand francs a nose.

All Georgie could remember after that was seeing twelve girls coming out on the platform, with about as much on them, if it was all sewn together, as would make a fair-sized loincloth for one Zulu, and telling Louis, with his arm out to the twelve girls:

'There y'are! Janshenist'd shay thatsh shinful! And you – and you're a fellow I never liked, and I don't care what you think! – *you* agree with them!'

'No! Exhplain to ye! Nothing that God made is shinful. Couldn't be. Shin is in us. Those girls aren't even an occashun of shin. And why? 'Cos they don't bother us.'

'Bother me,' said Georgie. 'Bother me a helluva lot. That little wan with the green hair would bother Saint Augustine!'

'God's truth?' asked Louis.

'Struth,' said Georgie.

'Come on out,' said Louis, getting up.

'Sit down,' shouted Georgie, dragging him back.

'C'mout,' said Louis, getting up again.

'Down!' shouts Georgie, hauling him down again.

'Out!' shouts Louis.

'Be quiet!' shouts everybody, and your two men began to shout at everybody else, and to fight one another, and a table gets knocked over, and champagne gets spilled on a girl's dress, and the twelve girls pay no attention at all, only kicking away up in the air like galvanized geese, and the two of them get hauled out and slung out on their backs on the pavement. Like one man they rush back. Like one man they get slung out again. At that they get up and they look into one another's faces, their noses one inch apart.

'You dirty little Freemason!' says Golden, baring his two teeth, and his lips glistening in the moonlight.

'You rotten little Puritan!' says Georgie with the hate of hell in his voice.

At that the two of them stopped dead as if they were a pair of waxworks out of the Musée Grevin, horrified by the sight of the hate in one another's faces. They were so horrified that they burst into a wild fit of laughing. They rocked there in one another's arms, falling over one another with the bitterness of the laughing and the hatred and the shame.

A taxi drew up beside them. They tumbled into it. And the next place they were was in the square in front of Nôtre Dame because Georgie said he wanted to see if the moon could laugh at them as much as it laughed at the gargoyles. The square was empty – it was after one in the morning. The two of them linked arms and began to stroll along the river singing the saddest Irish dirges they knew. Georgie used to say afterwards that he often thought of the poor women inside in the Hôtel Dieu enduring the pangs of childbirth while the two of them were bawling away about their Wild Irish Rose, and wouldn't she come home again, Kathl-e-e-en!

For the rest of the week they were inseparable.

When Georgie and Louis meet nowadays in the street, they always greet one another warmly. They ask after one another's health. They send their regards to one another's wives. If a companion asks either of them, 'Who was that?' he will say the name, add, 'Not a bad sort of chap,' and feel the shame of that night burning in him all over again. For, of course, the truth of the whole matter is that once you go on a drunk with a fellow you're stuck with him for life; and in Ireland every bitter word we say has to be paid for sooner or later in shame, in pity, in kindness, and perhaps even in some queer sort of perverted love.

# I Remember! I Remember!

I believe that in every decisive moment of our lives the spur to action comes from that part of the memory where desire lies dozing, awaiting the call to arms. We say to ourselves, 'Now I have decided to do so-and-so,' and straightway we remember that for years and years we have been wanting to do this very thing. There it is, already fully created, clear on the horizon, our longed-for island, its palm tree waving, its white hut gleaming, a brown figure standing on the beach, smiling patiently.

I am remembering Sarah Cotter and her infallible memory. If she were not so childlike, so modest, so meekly and sweetly resigned, she could be a Great Bore, as oppressively looming as the Great Bear. She can remember every least thing she ever heard, down to the last detail, even to the hour of the day when it happened. She is a Domesday Book of total recall for the whole of the little town of Ardagh, where she has lived for some twenty-five years in, you might almost say, the same corner of the same room of the same house, ever since an accident to her spine imprisoned her in a Bath chair at the age of eleven. This accident absolved her from all but the simplest decisions: there was no far-off island for her to dream of. It also meant that all she can now know of the world outside is what she reads, or what she is told by her friends, so that if her friends have told her fibs their consciences should prick them when she trustingly retails something that did not happen, or not quite in that way.

She is a little hunched-up woman with a face like a bit of burnt cork, whose plainness, some might say whose ugliness, you forget immediately you notice her gentle expression, her fluent lips, her warm brown eyes. Remember that, because of her ailment, she is always looking upwards at you when you meet her, so that her eyes have the pleading look of a spaniel, as if she were excusing herself for so much as existing. Her only handsome feature, apart from her doggy eyes, is her hair, long and rich and fair, on which she spends hours every morning, brushing it down into her lap over her shoulder, then brushing and pinning it up in a soft cloud, so overflowing that it makes her agile monkey-face seem about the size of a hazelnut. She lives in almost constant pain. She never complains of it. I have met nobody who does not admire her, nobody who has the least fault to find with her, apart from her invulnerable memory, which all Ardagh both enjoys and fears, and whose insistence can kill like the sirocco.

The only grumbles ever heard from her are two, as constant and soft as the leaves of a bamboo grove. The first is that she wishes she could see more of her sister Mary, a tall, slim, pretty, volatile girl, who twelve years ago married an American businessman, Richard Carton, a Continental buyer for one of New York's biggest stores.

'Not,' she always adds, 'that I don't realize how lucky the pair of us are. We mightn't be seeing one another at all only for Richard having that wonderful job.'

Because of this job, a cablegram or a letter has come twice a year from Mary saying that Richard is off to Europe on another buying spree, which means that Mary will presently stop off at Shannon and drive over to Ardagh for a week of heavenly gossip. Sarah at once announces the news to the whole of Ardagh, with burning cheeks and sparkling eyes. Then she may murmur her other grumble:

'Imagine it! I've seen Richard only once in my life. If he wasn't so busy! If only he could come with Mary for a real long holiday! Then she wouldn't have to go away after one little week. But, of course, she's indispensable to him.'

What she does not know, and what Mary intends that she never shall know, though she fears sometimes that one or two people in Ardagh may know it, or at least suspect it – such as Joe Shorthall, who picks her up at Shannon in his taxi, or the postmistress, who has sent off an occasional telegram for her – is that for the last six years Richard and she have been living partly in New York and partly in their small, elegant house in Zurich, near which their three children are at an English boarding school – so that, all unknown to Sarah, her sister passes between Switzerland and New York about six times a year. As for being indispensable to Richard in his work, the only time she ever ventured to advise him was in Rome. He looked at the object, a large, handsome blue fruit dish, turned it over and showed her the mark of its Californian manufacturer. What keeps her from visiting Sarah more often is the tireless whisper of the Recording Angel's Dictaphone playing back every lightest word that has passed between the two of them since they could begin to talk. She once incautiously wailed to Richard about it:

'It's not just that it's disconcerting to be reminded about things you've said, or discarded or forgotten years and years ago. Oh, if it was only that! She brings out these bits and scraps of things I've forgotten since I was ten, like a dog digging up some old thing you've thrown out on the ash heap and laying it lovingly at your feet – grubby, pointless, silly, worn, stupid things – and she says, "That's you." And I don't recognize them. Or don't want to see them. Old toys, old hats, old buried bones. Sometimes she has to remind me and remind me before I can even know what she's talking about. And, anyway, by this time they're no longer bits of me, they're bits of her. She knows more about me than I know myself. I keep on wondering what else does she know about me that I don't know. What's she going to produce next? Isn't my life my own, goddammit, to keep or to lose or to throw away if I want to? Am I me? Or am I her? I sometimes think I'm possessed by that old Chucklepuss the way some people are possessed by the devil!'

Richard had laughed heartily, and she, remembering too late his first, famous, fatal and final session with Sarah, could have bitten her tongue off. She stuck it out at him. Remembering again, he laughed all the more. Because Richard's memory is just as unerring as Sarah's; and his interest in Mary's past just as avid, or it used to be during the first years of their marriage. He wanted to know everybody she ever knew before he met her, every single thing she had ever done, every thought she had ever thought, every place she had ever been. So, at that first and last meeting between him and Sarah, she had to sit listening, apprehensive or embarrassed, while those two laid out the days of her youth before them like precious things that a pair of antiquaries might love to display to one another but would never part with. As they went on and on she got more and more furious with them:

'Ye make me feel like baby's first shoe. Or a photograph of a First Communion group. Or me aunt's wedding veil. Ye make me feel ninety. Ye make me feel dead!'

Richard only laughed his jolly, buyer's laugh, hangjawed like a pelican – worth thousands to him in his job – and roared at her to go away and leave them to it.

'This Sally girl knows tons more than you ever told me.'

But how could she go? She was as fascinated as she was furious. She was also frightened. For, while Sarah did know, or remember, 'tons more', it was all untrue in the way that a police report is untrue, because it leaves out everything except the facts. As she listened, transfixed as a rabbit is by a dazzling light that hides anything behind it, she remembered a wonderful thing she had once read in Stendhal's diaries – that 'True feeling leaves no memory': meaning that every deep feeling is like a peach, to be eaten straight from the tree of life, not spoiled by pawing and pressing. She swore afterwards that she lost pounds in perspiration while listening to them. The worst sequence was when they started talking about Corney Canty:

'Sally!' she heard Richard saying suddenly. 'Tell me about this young Corney Canty of Mary's. She's told me a lot about that wild boyo. As a matter of fact, why don't we meet him?'

'But, darling,' Mary protested, 'I've told you a dozen times over all that there is . . .'

'Now, Mary! Now! Let Sally tell me. Go on, Sally! Mary's told me about how they used to go riding to hounds together. And all the other adventures they had. That must have been a wonderful day – As I recall, Mary, it was the May of nineteen-thirty-seven? – when the two of you, alone with three hounds, flushed a fox out of Ballycoole woods and ran him to the edge of Gaunt's Quarry. And the brave Corney – He must really be a marvellous horseman, Sally – just slid after him down the gravel face of that quarry without a moment's hesitation. And poor little Mary here – Look at her, she's pale again at the thought of it! – God, how I admire you, darling! – terrified out of her wits though she was, slid down after him. And they cornered the fox in that quarry! I'd really love to meet this fellow. Why don't we ask him in for a drink tonight?'

Sarah's eyes dropped.

'God rest him!' she murmured.

'Not dead? Killed on the hunting field? A fine young man like that killed in the prime of life! Did you know this, Mary?'

'Did you say "young," Richard?' Sarah soothed him. 'Sure when he died of the drink there a few years back he was seventy-two to the month.'

'Seventy-two?' – looking wide-eyed at Mary, who was crying out desperately:

'Sarah, you're thinking of Corney's uncle. Or his father. He wasn't a year over forty, and as limber as twenty-five. Of course,' gushing to

Richard, 'he was a great rascal, you couldn't trust a word he said, didn't I tell ye the time he deliberately made me fall off that grey mare of his, setting me to a stone wall he knew damn well she couldn't take, so that he could come around and kneel over me on the grass, feeling me here and feeling me there with "Does it hurt here, ducky?" and "Does it hurt there, ducky?," and me with the wind gone out of me so that I couldn't say a bloody worrrd!'

Richard laughed at the familiar story, one of his favourites that he liked to make her tell at every second party, because it brought out the brogue in her voice. Sarah was not to be silenced.

'He was,' she said primly, even a little severely, 'seventy-two years old to the month when he died. No more. No less. I myself witnessed his cross – he couldn't read or write – on the Old Age Pension form on December the first, nineteen hundred and forty-three. He was wearing that old red-flannel-lined raincoat your daddy gave him in thirty-seven when...'

'But,' Richard put in, 'that was the year of the quarry hunt.'

'That's right. "I have this coat," said Corney to me, "for six years, and your poor father had it for six years before that, and..."'

Mary could see by Richard's face – he could multiply 113 by 113 in his head – that he had already established for himself that 'young Corney' had been an old lad in his middle sixties when she knew him. Sure enough, when Sarah paused, there was a brief silence, suspenseful and decisive, and then he broke into a series of monster guffaws, beating his palms together with delight, relishing with loving malice his wife's scarlet embarrassment. Through his guffaws he managed to utter:

'Mary, you little divil, I always knew you exaggerate a bit, but this...'

Wildly she fought for her hour as she had lived it:

'I didn't exaggerate. That was typical of Corney to exaggerate his age to get the pension. He fooled you up to the eyes, Sarah; when we hunted that fox he was forty, forty-two at the very most, forty-two at the outside limit, not a minute over it.'

One glance from Richard's bubbling shoulders and wrinkled-up eyes to Sarah's prim mouth told her that the battle was hopeless. There Sarah sat, erect in her chair, too nice to contradict further, too honest to compound a felony, giving her head short little shakes that said as plainly as speech, 'Seventy-two. To the month. No more. No less.'

Neither then nor at any time after could Mary have understood that Richard was just as happy with her as a splendid Teller of Tales as he had been with her as his Wild Irish Girl. Blinded by love, he drew out the session for hour after hour. He only realized his folly that night, in the hour of tenderness, in bed.

'Dammit,' she said, as they lay side by side, in her parents' old room upstairs, the heavy mirror in the coffinlike wardrobe catching the last of the summer daylight, the faint baa-ing of sheep coming from the Fair Green, 'I did slide down that old quarry. I wasn't codding about it. And he wasn't an old man. And even if he was I think that makes it a hell of a sight more exciting than the sentimental way you want it. Handsome young Irish huntsman. Brave young Irish girl. It makes me sick the way you always want to romanticize everything about me.'

His hands behind his poll, he began to shake all over again until she started to hammer him with her fists on his chest, and he to embrace and fondle her with a new love, a new admiration – he said the words, just so, explicitly – which, she declared, turning her behind to him huffily, was entirely beyond her modest intelligence. She whirled, and sat up and shouted:

'Are you trying to say that you prefer me as a liar?'

'Husssh! My wild little girleen! Sarah will hear you.'

'I don't give a damn if she does hear me. What does she know about it? She wasn't there. It was she started all this, and you kept at her and at her to make me seem more of a liar.'

'Nonsense, darling. It's just that you have this wonderful Irish gift for fantasy.'

'It's not fantasy. It's true, true, true. Every word of it is true. There may be some detail here or there, some trivial, irrelevant thing, some small thing slipped up, but it's all true. And I am not going to have you and old Sarah Sucklepuss down there stealing my life from me with her bloody old . . .'

And, to his pitying astonishment, she burst into a long, low wail of weeping, sobbing into the pillow like, he thought, as he laid his palm on her wet cheek, a child whose dog has been rolled over by a bus before her eyes.

'You don't understand, Dicky,' she wailed into his armpit. 'It's torture to hear her digging up my life and turning it all into lies that never happened the way she says they happened.'

'But you must have told her they happened that way?'

'I told her the bones. And all she has of anything now is the bones. I can't remember the bones. All I have is the feeling I had at the time. Or else I can't remember at all.'

'Tell her so. Say you forget.'

'It would be like taking her life away from her. All the poor old Sucklepuss has is my bones.'

She wept herself asleep on his shoulder. It is the measure of his distress at what he had done to her, of his natural shrewdness, and of his sensitiveness hidden behind his cocktail-bar laugh that as he lay there, listening to the dim, distant, ceaseless baa-ing, he decided never again to visit Ardagh.

But this was years ago, and since then Mary's life has stopped being the flowing, straightforward river it once was. Not that life ever is like a river that starts from many tributaries and flows at the end straight to the sea; it is more like the line of life on my palm that starts firmly and frays over the edge in a cataract of little streams of which it is impossible to say where each began. Richard has small interest now in her youth. He is rarely amused by her exaggerations: the wind that blew the legs off her, or the bus that went down Fifth Avenue at a hundred miles per hour. Her lovely, lighthearted, featherheaded ways are now her usual scattiness. She finds it more and more difficult to follow Sarah's letters about the latest doings of Ardagh. And the only way Sarah can form any clear pictures of Mary's life in New York is by those intimate gossips, prolonged into the silence of the night, during Mary's precious half-yearly visits to the little house near the end of the Main Street of Ardagh. Yet, it was just when, for this very reason, one might have expected the visits to become either more frequent or longer that they suddenly became so curt that everybody but Sarah foresaw their end.

It all started out of a ridiculous little incident that occurred during Mary's March visit last year. Over the years she had been trying in vain to free herself from Sarah's memory by catching her out in an error of fact. On this wet, March night she suddenly became aware that Sarah was talking of a German air raid on a part of the Irish coast where some old friends of Richard's, working in the American diplomatic service during the war, had had a summer house. Knowing well that no German bombs had dropped on this part of the coast, she felt an overwhelming sense of relief. She did not contradict the Recording

Angel. She did not crow over her. She stayed as quiet as a cat watching a mouse. The whole glorious value of the error was that Sarah must never become aware of it. The night passed with the error uncorrected. At about two o'clock in the morning. Mary woke up as if to the sound of a shot, remembering clearly that a floating sea-mine had exploded on that part of the coast and damaged a summer house. She left Ardagh the next day, only three days after she had arrived, to Sarah's dumb dismay, on the feeble excuse of being worried about Richard's health. 'Oh, Sarah, I live in terror that he'll have to give up the job altogether, he's driven *so* hard!'

Six months later, in September, Mary came again, and left after two days.

They were having afternoon tea on the second day of this visit – it was a Sunday afternoon – in the bay of the front room, looking out on the empty autumn street, with Sarah happily squeezing the last drops out of a long, lightly amusing recollection of the famous night seventeen years before when Mary, still at school, organized a secret Midsummer Eve party to hail the sun rising over the Galtee Mountains. She had rowed her party, five in all, across the river in the dark and lit a pagan midsummer-fire in, of all places, the playing fields adjoining the Mercy Convent. The nuns, rising to sing their Matins, had heard the singing and seen the fire, and raised a terrible row about it, which set the whole town talking for weeks after. Sarah happily followed the history of everybody even distantly connected with the affair down to the hour of that afternoon tea. Her comments were largely a string of *Requiescats*, a ritual habit which always secretly tickled Mary: it was as if the Recording Angel had a secondary job as Lady High Executioner. ('Anna Grey? Died nine years back, Mary. Tommy Morgan? Failing. Failing before his people's eyes. Joe Fenelon took to the bottle, poor boy. Molly Cardew? Ah, God rest her . . .')

Without a pause Sarah suddenly leaned forward and said:

'Mary, tell me! How is Nathan Cash these days?'

'Nathan who?' Mary had said, parrying wildly at the unexpected transition. This sort of thing was always happening – Sarah suddenly producing some name or event about which she was supposed to know nothing.

'Cash!' Sarah said loudly, rather like people who raise their voices when talking to foreigners in order to be better understood. 'Your friend Nathan Cash. The man who was a director of the Bell Telephone

Company in Newark, New Jersey. He married that Jane Barter whose uncle was a partner in Chuck Full O'Nuts before he divorced her last year after playing around, I think I gathered from you, with some other woman, you-never-said-who. And, after all, he didn't marry her either.'

'Didn't he?' Mary said dully, choked with rage against herself for having as much as mentioned Nathan to Sarah.

'When you came last March you told me he was after marrying Carrie Brindle, a rich Jewish girl from Buffalo. Surely you remember?'

Mary could only give a miserable little laugh.

'You told me about it last March! When you came off the *Liberté*. You told me,' Sarah smiled lovingly and admiringly, 'how he gave yourself orchids for your birthday in January.'

'Why, and so he did!' Mary laughed gaily, her anger with herself mounting and spilling. Last March, coming off that damned six-days boat of loneliness, she had had to talk to somebody about him.

'He is a very handsome man,' Sarah smiled gently. Mary stared at her. 'You showed me his photograph.'

'Did I really?' Mary gurgled, and spread her ringed fingers indifferently. 'Richard and I meet so many people.'

Sarah sighed.

'It must be grand to be getting orchids. That was the only time in my life I saw orchids. She laughed at her own ignorance. 'I thought they were passion flowers. I forgot to ask you,' with a happy smile, 'was it Mr Cash gave them to you before you sailed?'

Mary looked swiftly at her, but it was plain that she was not probing. Sarah's questions were always innocent, pointless, without guile. She looked out, frowningly, at the granite brown of the old North Gate, under whose arch the almost-silent Main Street of Ardagh flows into the completely silent countryside. She heard the soft *cric-croc* of a cart entering slowly under the arch from the farther side. The little cart slowly emerged from under the arch, salmonpink, bearing its pyramid of black peat, drawn by a tiny, grey donkey. It *cric-crocked* slowly past her vision. She found herself murmuring as softly and slowly, feeling as she did so that this was exactly how she had been wheedled last March into talking about Nathan:

'I bought those orchids last March. I just had to have them.'

'Why, Mary?' – gently.

'I was feeling very down.'

'What happened to you?' – sympathetically.

'I'd had a terrible quarrel with a friend.'

'Who, Mary?' – tenderly.

'A friend. Nobody you know. A woman. A woman called Gold. Nancy Gold. There was nobody to see me off on the boat. Richard had gone by plane direct to Berne. The cabin looked empty. No flowers. No bottle of champagne. No basket of fruit. When I went down to lunch I stood at the turn of the staircase and saw all those men and women chattering around all those white tables and all the women wearing corsages. I turned back and went up to the florist and I bought me two orchids.'

Neither of them spoke for a while.

'Well, well,' Sarah concluded. 'And so he married the Jewish woman in the heel of the hunt. Is he happy with her, would you say?'

'How should I know? We never meet. I'm not sure that I like him very much really.'

Sarah smiled in loyal admiration.

'He liked you once, though. Enough anyway to give you orchids.'

'That was just one night going to the opera. I thought at the time it was a little plush of him. Still, a woman likes those little attentions.'

'You always liked nice things. You always like those little attentions. I can see why you bought them for yourself on the boat.'

'It was just that I was down in the mouth.'

'And then there was Richard on your mind, too.'

'Richard?' Mary stared at her as if she was a witch or a fortune-teller.

'I mean you were worried about him.'

'Was I?'

'He was ill. You left here after three days to be with him. I knew the minute you came in the door, Mary, off that old boat, that you weren't your old self.'

Mary gave her a desperate look. She got up.

'I think I'll go for a stroll. I have a bit of a headache.'

She went out, under the arch, so unmistakably a foreigner in her high-collared mink coat, her furry hat and her spiked heels that the few townsfolk who were in the Sunday street stared at her, but sideways so as not to be seen staring. She saw none of them, nothing, none of the familiar names over the shuttered shops, unchanged for as long as she could remember – Fenelon the grocer, Ryan the draper, Shorthall's

Garage, Morgan and Corneille, Furnishers, Upholsterers and Under-takers, Saint Anne's Nursing Home and old Dr Freeman's brass plate polished into holes at the corners. The street petered out where a bright yellow signpost directed her across the bridge to the dark yellow furze on the rising foothills.

She leaned over the limestone parapet, lit a cigarette, and glared along the barely flowing river with its shallow autumn pools and its dry beaches. She pounded the parapet with her gloved fist and said, aloud: 'It's intolerable!' Her cigarette ash floated down into the river. On one side of the river were the long gardens at the back of the Main Street's houses, coming right down to the riverbank; and, farther on, plumb with the river, the backs of old donkey-grey warehouses, decaying now, eyeless, little used since the river silted up and ceased to be navigable. The Franciscan belfry was reflected in an islanded pool among the gravel at the bend of the river, and in the pool a sweep of yellow from the far hills that rose to the farther mountains over whose rounded backs the sailing clouds had long ago seemed so often to call her to come away, to come away. Today the clouds were one solid, frozen mass, tomblike, so that if they moved they moved massively, and she could not tell if they moved at all.

She had rowed across the river down there, that Midsummer Eve, with Annie Grey, and Tommy Morgan, and Joe Fenelon and Molly Cardew. She had borrowed her daddy's gramophone and twelve of his gayest Italian records, and halfway across, the records, which she had placed on top of the gramophone, began to slide one by one into the water with gentle plops. Midsummer heat, and a great sky of stars and the whole of Ardagh sound asleep. While waiting for the sun to rise they swam in one of the pools, and then, at the first ghost of light, not light, a hint of morning, they lit the fire and played a muffled 'O Sole Mio' and a wind blew the wood ash into the cups of wine that Joe Fenelon had stolen from his father's shop. She had not thought of that grey dust in the wine for seventeen years. It was, she thought savagely, the sort of thing that Sarah's memories never remembered, along with the gaiety of Corney Canty, and the way redheaded Molly Cardew used to tickle the back of Tommy Morgan's neck so that he would hunch up his shoulders and say, affectionately-irritably, 'Go away, you green frog you!' and poor weak-minded Joe Fenelon's lovely tenor voice singing 'I'll Take Ye Home Again, Kathleen' at every party. The ash in the wine was just another piece of her real life immured, with the bones of everything she had ever done or said, in the vaults of Sarah's infallible memoirs. Would Nathan Cash one day join these dead bones? Had he already gone there, with all she had been through because of him? Would all her life, unless she really went away and left her past behind her?

She blew out a long breath of smoke and threw her cigarette into the river. She would call in to Shorthall's Garage on the way home. The car would come for her at nine in the morning. By evening she would be floating down over the pinewoods on the little hills about the airstrip at Zurich. Blonde hostesses. Pure-white washrooms. ('Just like Newark,' Richard had once laughed.) And her ritual first cup of *café au lait* at the tall counter, while Richard waited with Donna, and Biddy and Patrick. But she did not stir until a soft rain began to fall, a dew, a mist, and she was aware that it was dusk. The streets were empty, the slates shone purple. The turf smoke medicinal in the air. She stopped by the garage, passed on, stopped again, hesitated again, half turned back and then, with a groan, went on to the house. She went upstairs to her room and lay there, with the last pallor of the day in the dark mirror of the wardrobe, until dinnertime.

For their coffee they sat in the bay window. They gossiped amiably, Mary half listening, her head half turned to the footfalls passing down the street to evening Benediction at the Franciscan priory. Sarah said:

'By the way, Mary, wasn't it very sad about your poor friend, Mrs Henry Beirne!'

Mary turned her head a little farther towards the window as if she were trying to hear something out there, but really to hide the look of blank fear that she could feel coming into her eyes. She knew no Mrs Henry Beirne. Her frightened efforts to recall the woman produced nothing clearer than the vague cloud that a drop of absinthe forms in a glass of water, a fume like smoke, a wavering embryo without a face. The last ghostly footstep faded. She whispered, groping for information:

'Yes. It was very sad. How did you know about it?'

'The Dublin papers had it on account of the other woman being related to the Bishop of Kilkenny. I don't think she could be more than thirty-two. Would you say so?'

'Surely more?' – groping still. Could it be a divorce? Or an accident?

Why couldn't Sarah say what happened? Was the woman dead? The wraith in the water began to curl into another as yet undecipherable shape. She said gently: 'Was her age given in the papers?'

'Not at all, but, sure, 'tis easy to work it out. We know she was the Class of Forty-one. Give her twenty or twenty-one at the Commencement, and wasn't it then she first met Henry Beirne? He proposed to her that very evening on the Common. You danced with him at the Ritz that night. You had the gold dress with the cream insets. How many children was it you said they had?'

As the white shape in the water took on a remembered face, Mary barely stopped herself from saying, 'My God, it must be nine years since I saw that bitch Lucy Burbank.' She said, dully:

'Children? Four' – and immediately regretted it, realizing that to say anything precise to Sarah about anything was only laying the ground for more questions next year, or in three or five years' time, when she would have completely forgotten what she had earlier said. They talked a little more about Lucy Burbank-Beirne. Mary never did find out what exactly happened to the woman that was so very sad.

'It's time we lit the lamp,' Sarah said.

It was dark. The rain had stopped and restarted. The footsteps had all returned the way they had come. In another hour the only sound in the long, winding street would be the drip of rain. Not a ground-floor window would be lit. There would not even be a Civic Guard out on a wet night like this. She gathered up the coffee cups and took them out to the kitchen on the old silver-plated salver, with the copper showing through, that her father had won at a golf tournament forty years ago. She returned and lifted off the pink globe of the oil lamp, her back to Sarah, and then lifted off the glass chimney, and put a match to the two charred wicks and watched the flame creep across their ridged edges. She replaced the glass chimney. Still with her back to Sarah, she said:

'I have bad news to break to you, Sarah.'

'Oh, Mary, don't frighten me.'

'I've been trying to get myself to tell you since I came.'

'What is it, love?'

Carefully she replaced the pink globe, aware of its warm light under her chin.

'Richard has given up his job. I came alone this time. I came only to tell you. I must go away tomorrow morning.'

She slowly raised the first wick, and then the second wick, and felt the room behind her fill with light. She heard a noise like a drip of rain, or melting snow, or oozing blood.

'Oh, Mary, don't go away from me!'

She turned. For the first time, Sarah was pleading with her, her little brown face smaller than ever under the great cloud of hair, her two brown spaniel's eyes brimming with tears.

'I must go!' Mary cried, her two fists trembling by her side. 'I must go!'

'I'll never see you again!'

Mary sank on her knees and looped her arms lovingly about her waist.

'Of course you will, you silly-billy,' she laughed. 'You'll see me lots of times.'

They gazed at one another fondly for a long while. Then Mary rose and went to the dark window and drew the curtains together with a swish. Arranging the folds of the curtains, she said, reassuringly, like a mother to a child:

'You'll see me lots of times. Lots and lots of times.'

Behind her, Sarah said resignedly:

'Will I, Mary?'

# The Sugawn Chair

Every autumn I am reminded of an abandoned sugawn chair that languished for years, without a seat, in the attic of my old home. It is associated in my mind with an enormous sack which the carter used to dump with a thud on the kitchen floor around every October. I was a small kid then, and it was as high as myself. This sack had come 'up from the country', a sort of diplomatic messenger from the fields to the city. It smelled of dust and hay and apples, for the top half of it always bulged with potatoes, and, under a layer of hay, the bottom half bulged with apples. Its arrival always gave my mother great joy and a little sorrow, because it came from the farm where she had been born. Immediately she saw it she glowed with pride in having a 'back', as she called it – meaning something behind her more solid and permanent than city streets, though she was also saddened by the memories that choked her with this smell of hay and potatoes from the home farm, and apples from the little orchard near the farmhouse. My father, who had also been born on a farm, also took great pleasure in these country fruits, and as the two of them stood over the sack, in the kitchen, in the middle of the humming city, everything that their youth had meant to them used to make them smile and laugh and use words that they had never used during the rest of the year, and which I thought magical: words like *late sowing*, *clover crop*, *inch field*, *marl bottom*, *headlands*, *tubers*, and the names of potatoes, British Queens or Arran Banners, that sounded to me like the names of regiments. For those moments my father and mother became a young, courting couple again. As they stood over that sack, as you might say warming their hands to it, they were intensely happy, close to each other, in love again. To me they were two very old people. Counting back now, I reckon that they were about forty-two or forty-three.

One autumn evening after the sack arrived, my father went up to the attic and brought down the old sugawn chair. I suppose he had had it sent up from his home farm. It was the only thing of its kind in our house, which they had filled – in the usual peasants' idea of what constitutes elegance – with plush chairs, gold-framed pictures of Stags at Bay, and exotic tropical birds, pelmets on the mantelpieces, Delft shepherdesses, Chinese mandarins with nodding heads, brass bedsteads with mighty knobs and mother-of-pearl escutcheons set with bits of mirror, vast mahogany chiffoniers, and so on. But the plush-bottomed chairs, with their turned legs and their stiff backs, were for show, not for comfort, whereas in the old country sugawn chair my da could tilt and squeak and rock to his behind's content.

It had been in the place for years, rockety, bockety chipped and well-polished, and known simply as 'your father's chair', until the night when, as he was reading the *Evening Echo* with his legs up on the kitchen range, there was a sudden rending noise, and down he went through the seat of it. There he was then, bending over, with the chair stuck on to him, and my mother and myself in the splits of laughter, pulling it from him while he cursed like a trooper. This was the wreck that he now suddenly brought down from the dusty attic.

The next day, he brought in a great sack of straw from the Cornmarket, a half-gallon of porter and two old buddies from the street – an ex-soldier known to the kids around as 'Tear-'em-and-ate-'em' and a little dwarf of a man who guarded the stage door at the Opera House when he was not being the sacristan at the chapel. I was enchanted when I heard what they were going to do. They were going to make ropes of straw – a miracle I had never heard of – and reseat the chair. Bursting with pride in my da, I ran out and brought in my best pal, and the two of us sat as quiet as cats on the kitchen table, watching the three men filling the place with dust, straw, and loud arguments as they began to twist the ropes for the bottom of the chair.

More strange words began to float in the air with the dust: *scallops, flat tops, bulrushes, cipeens, fields in great heart* ... And when the three sat down for a swig of porter, and looked at the old polished skeleton in the middle of the floor, they began to rub the insides of their thighs and say how there was no life at all like the country life, and my mother poured out more porter for them, and laughed happily when my da began to talk about horses, and harrows, and a day after the plough, and how, for *that* much, he'd throw up this blooming city life altogether and settle down on a bit of a farm for the heel of his days.

This was a game of which he, she and I never got tired, a fairy tale that was so alluring it did not matter a damn that they had not enough money to buy a window box, let alone a farm of land.

'Do you remember that little place,' she would say, 'that was going last year down at Nantenan?'

When she said that, I could see the little reedy fields of Limerick that I knew from holidays with my uncle, and the crumbling stone walls of old demesnes with the moss and saffron lichen on them, and the willow sighing softly by the Deel, and I could smell the wet turf rising in the damp air, and, above all, the tall wildflowers of the mallow, at first cabbage-leaved, then pink and coarse, then gossamery, then breaking into cakes that I used to eat – a rank weed that is the mark of ruin in so many Irish villages, and whose profusion and colour is for me the sublime emblem of Limerick's loneliness, loveliness and decay.

'Ah!' my da would roar. 'You and your blooming ould Limerick! That bog of a place! Oh, but, God blast it, why didn't I grab that little farm I was looking at two years ago there below Emo!'

'Oho, ho, ho!' she would scoff. 'The Queen's! The Lousy Queen's! God, I'd live like a tiger and die like a Turk for Limerick. For one patch of good old Limerick. Oh, Limerick, my love, and it isn't alike! Where would you get spuds and apples the like of them in the length and breadth of the Queen's County?'

And she grabbed a fist of hay from the bag and buried her face in it, and the tears began to stream down her face, and me and my pal screaming with laughter at her, and the sacristan lauding Tipperary, and the voices rose as Tear-'em-and-ate-'em brought up the River Barrow and the fields of Carlow, until my da jumped up with:

'Come on, lads, the day is dyin' and acres wide before us!'

For all that, the straw rope was slow in emerging. Their arguments about it got louder and their voices sharper. At first all their worry had been whether the kitchen was long enough for the rope; but so far, only a few, brief worms of straw lay on the red tiles. The sacristan said: 'That bloody straw is too moist.' When he was a boy in Tipp he never seen straw the like o' that. Tear-'em-and-ate-'em said that straw was old straw. When he was a lad in Carlow they never used old straw. Never! Under no possible circumstances! My dad said: 'What's wrong with that straw is it's too bloomin' short!' And they began to kick the bits with their toes, and grimace at the heap on the floor, and pick up bits and fray them apart and throw them aside until the whole floor was like a stable. At last they put on their coats, and gave the straw a final few kicks, and my pal jumped down and said he was going back to his handball and, in my heart, I knew that they were three impostors.

The kitchen was tidy that evening when I came back with the *Evening Echo*. My da was standing by the sack of potatoes. He had a spud in his fist, rubbing off the dust of its clay with his thumb. When he saw me he tossed it back in the sack, took the paper, took one of the plush-bottom chairs and sat on it with a little grimace. I did not say anything, but young as I was, I could see that he was not reading what he was looking at. God knows what he was seeing at that moment.

For years the anatomy of the chair stood in one of the empty attics. It was there for many years after my father died. When my mother died and I had to sell out the few bits of junk that still remained from their lives, the dealer would not bother to take the useless frame, so that when, for the last time, I walked about the echoing house, I found it standing alone in the middle of the bare attic. As I looked at it I smelled apples, and the musk of Limerick's dust, and the turf-tang from its cottages, and the mallows among the limestone ruins, and I saw my mother and my father again as they were that morning – standing over the autumn sack, their arms about one another, laughing foolishly, and madly in love again.

# A Shadow, Silent as a Cloud

In the empty dining room, lit by a single electric bulb hanging from the rosette in the ceiling, the black-marble clock chimed slowly seven times and a sputter of rain tapped at the windows. The three tables, long, white and narrow, arranged like the letter U, looked very white under that single bulb. At one end of the top table there was a waitress, moving slowly from chair to chair, looking at the cards bearing the names of the guests she would have to serve. She was about fifty, but still handsome and well-shaped though a bit on the dumpy side. She murmured the names in different voices to suit her notion of what they might look like. She said *Miss Olive Harold* in a thin-lipped and prim voice. It was a Protestant sort of name, a hard-faced name. She made *Mr Condon Larkin* into a soft, round-faced man. She said *Miss Stella Shannon* twice, it was such a nice name, young, and lovely, and a bit lost. *Mr Kevin Lowry* could be a gloomy sort of fellow, or he could be a jolly, laughing fellow. *Monsignor O'Connell* ... A bit of wood ash fell from the fire, which was quietly oozing wet sap. She made a crooked mouth at the initials of *Professor J. T. G. Quigley's* name. The next card was at the centre of the table, the chairman's place. *Jeremiah J. Collis.*

She looked over at the fire and saw a gate lodge with a thick laurel copse around it, almost a quarter-acre of close-planted laurels, trimmed level at about four feet from the ground, a miniature forest into which she used to crawl on the crinkling brown leaves. There was a bay tree. She looked up across the wide, spreading pasture to the white door pillars of the Big House. Behind it there were the rolling mountains. On quiet days you could hear the tramcars at Rathfarnham village jolting over the junction points. Her lips, without speaking it, shaped the single word, *Templeogue*. She did not notice that the piece of fallen wood was giving out a pungent smell, like laurel burning. She was still there, with one hand on the chair back, smiling at the fire, when the headwaiter came in and switched on all the lights, and then all the other waiters and hired waitresses like herself came in after him in a chattering gaggle. The headwaiter directed them to their stations, and there they stood, as straight as statues, until the first group of guests came hesitantly to the big doorway and began to cluster around the seating plan on the easel beside it.

She recognized him immediately he came in. He was after getting terribly loguey; his hair was grey at the sides; his chin bulged over his white tie; but he was a fine figure of a man still. He passed to his place, talking and laughing with a soft, pretty young woman with coils of fair hair on top of her head. She had a pale face, red lips and a wrinkled forehead. He called her Stella and it was as plain as a pikestaff that he was gone about her. When he sat down she saw the thin patch on top of his head, but when he said over his shoulder, 'The wine list, please,' she thought his voice was just the same voice, only grown older. When she got the wine list and put it into his backward-stretching hand, the professor beside him was saying, 'All right, Jerry, but I warn you that if you don't phrase it very carefully they will misunderstand your motives.' At that he laughed, and his laugh was a boy's laugh.

From that on she was much too busy to look at him again, until he got up to give the toast of 'Ireland', and said, 'You may smoke, gentlemen'. After a while he laid down his cigar and tapped his coffee cup with his spoon, and stood up to give his speech. She moved over by the left-hand table to take a good stock of him. His waistcoat had burst its bottom button, his jowls were flushed from the wine and the heat, but still and all he really was a fine figure of a man.

During the first few minutes she did not take in one word he said, she felt so nervous for him, but she soon became aware that he was entirely at his ease and she started to listen with interest.

'And so, I hope you can now see, ladies and gentlemen, why I have called my address by the slightly sentimental title "Lest We Forget". Because it does seem to me that we architects forget far too much and far too easily in our eagerness to invent, to innovate, to be modern and progressive. Instead, my feeling is that we should encourage our memories to interrupt us in our haste, to pursue us as we run away from them, to surprise and halt us by the richness of the message that the past can lay in our hands, warning us to go easy when we are going too fast and too far. After all, when you come to think of it, what else is memory but the recognition of experience? And' – he held out his hands appealingly and smiled around the tables – 'let's be honest, what else, all too often, is this famous experience of ours – about which we are always boasting to our juniors – what else is it but the lamentable record of our carefully concealed mistakes?'

For that he got a little laughter and ironic applause.

'Now, I don't pretend to any special wisdom, and I am not yet quite as old as the Methuselah of George Bernard Shaw, or,' with a deferential little bow and a smile towards the Monsignor, 'should I have said the Methuselah of that somewhat more famous author, Genesis?'

They all craned to look at the Monsignor. Seeing him smile indulgently, they crackled into a light laughter. At the next sentence she saw, with amusement, the wry way he touched his thin poll.

'Yet even I sometimes become aware of mortal dissolution and feel the falling of the leaves.'

The words and the gesture evoked more laughter. As if he knew that he had their full attention now he leaned forward on his ten finger tips and let his voice become warm and serious.

'Perhaps that is why I feel so certain that I know what we are all afraid of? We are afraid of being thought old-fashioned. And yet can there be any single one of us, whether young or old, who will dare to deny that our profession is as much concerned with the passing away of old things as with their replacement by new things? That we have something to learn from the very things that we are destroying? For is it not true that to create is in some sense to change, and to change is in some sense to destroy? All creative work is a form of destruction.'

He leaned up and held a longer pause of silence than he had dared before, and, for a while after, he spoke quite conversationally, almost carelessly:

'It's very hard, whenever I drive out of Dublin, not to feel a bit sorry when I look around me at the ranks of new and shining houses stretching out and out all around the old battered centre I've left behind me. I naturally feel a sense of professional pride in these new homes, but I feel sad because those new settlements – it is the only word for them – have no tradition, no feel of the past, no memories, and they have been built on fields that, for generations upon generations, were full of associations and memories. In all these building schemes of ours let us never forget that we are bartering something that is as eloquent as it is old for something that, however good and necessary, is as mute and dumb as it is unappeasably strange and new.'

He paused briefly, and in that moment she heard the young man at her elbow whispering across the table to another young man: 'Clever bastard! Here comes the Templeogue job.' Alerted and annoyed, she began to listen more carefully. He was still speaking quite easily, without any flourish of any kind, voice or hands:

'It would be insulting to this Institute of ours to suggest for a moment that anybody here thinks that architecture is just so much mute stone. Every city is the richer for having absorbed something of the vibrations of the living and the dead. It is not merely that we like to know that somebody famous spoke from this loggia or died on those steps; that in our own capital such noble spirits as Edmund Burke, or Oliver Goldsmith, or Tom Moore, or Charles Stewart Parnell, or Patrick Pearse walked these streets or died within the sounds of their traffic – it makes architecture more living that countless humble citizens have hollowed the steps of a church or sat in the benches of some old school. Must we always barter away that livingness of the dead for the weaker pulsations and meaner associations of the passing day?'

With that one passionate question he picked up and tossed away his card of jottings. Then he smiled and was casual again:

'You know, you could evoke a whole century with one glance at Sheridan the playwright's house in Dorset Street. But I challenge even the most pugnacious gentleman among ye to say that he feels his dander rise today as he changes gear among the red-roofed bungalows of modern Donnybrook.'

He let the ripple of chuckles die away. As he went on she thought he threw a glance at Miss Shannon.

'Or could even the youngest and most romantic lady present confess that she ever thinks of poor Pamela, Lord Edward's unhappy widow, as she whirls in the number eight bus past the Frascati of modern Blackrock? It is the same everywhere. It is right and proper to build new homes. Do we have to do it by knocking down the bridges of history?'

At this, the young man near her who had whispered across the table leaned back in his chair and sighed audibly at the ceiling.

'Yet even in my boyhood places like Rathfarnham were still the haunts of wandering tinkers, wild birds and strolling lovers. The rural charm of Templeogue still had that air of seclusion which once drew Charles Lever and his young bride to live and love there among the fields and hedgerows, within view of the rolling drums of the Dublin mountains topped by the Hell Fire Club and the cairns of the Three

Rock. Must this too, this latest place to be threatened by what we grandiosely call Urban Development, also be utterly destroyed? Must we lose entirely the inheritance of our Irish past?'

The earnestness of this sentence won him a clatter of applause. Even she joined in, and all the louder because the contemptuous young man in front of her was now groaning in audible pain into his two fists. Jerry was now racing on eloquently, but she no longer heard him. With bright, moist eyes she saw only the old gate lodge, the laurel copse, the motionless swing hanging from the beech, and under it the oily celandines and the yellow aconites. Besides, her eyes had wandered to Miss Shannon and Mr Condon Larkin. Miss Shannon's left hand hung down by the side of her chair, Mr Larkin's right hand hung by the side of his, and the two hands gently fondled one another. She was leaning forward, chin on elbowed palm; he was leaning back; both were looking up at the speaker. Anyone could tell that they were not paying the slightest attention to his words.

By the time she had done her part in clearing the tables the bar was packed out, but she saw him, taller than all the rest, in the middle of the crush, arguing with Miss Shannon, Mr Condon Larkin, Professor Quigley, and two or three of the younger men, including the contemptuous young man, who had, she now saw, a beaky nose, tousled fair hair and a slight tuft of fair beard, two prominent teeth and fierce, small blue eyes. He was very angry, and as she pushed nearer she heard him saying in a voice loud enough to be heard above the general babble:

'It's all a damned lot of sentimentality. And I don't believe you mean a bloody word of it. And as for dragging in Tommy Moore, may God forgive you! Now, Edmund Burke I'll grant ye! Dammit, I'll even give you Parnell! But, God Almighty, not Tommy Moore!'

Jerry was also angry.

'And what,' he demanded from the heights, 'what, pray, is wrong with Tom Moore?'

The professor looked as if he was trying to calm them both. The toothy young man spat back in an insulting voice:

'He was a sentimentalist, and wurrse than a sentimentalist. He was a calculating sentimentalist. That thing on his sleeve . . . What was it but the price ticket of a turn-coat?'

'Now, now,' the professor intervened, 'it was a heart all the same.

A song like 'Oft in the Stilly Night could not have been composed by a man without real feeling.'

'Feeling! To conceal what? Ambition! Like all sentimentalists he . . .'

The professor shot a frightened look around the bar – they were all talking at the tops of their voices – and laid a hand on the young man's shoulder, saying:

'Nevertheless, Mr Collyer, it is a lovely song. Jerry, raise it for us. Give us a bar.'

'I will, then,' Jerry said. She withdrew as he laid his glass on the counter, crying, 'And if I maul it itself it'll still be a fine song. Silence for your president!' he shouted, and although a few of them gave a mock-serious cheer, gradually the whole bar fell silent. He cleared his throat and began to sing with feeling. As she stood by the door, half in the corridor, listening, others came along from the lounge to listen. She thought it was splendid the way he put his heart into it, in his fine, deep bass voice, especially when he came to the low, vibrating notes of:

> The smiles, the tears of boyhood years,
> The words of love then spoken . . .

He was looking all the time at Stella Shannon, who kept looking from under her worried brows at Condon Larkin, whose eyes kept expanding and contracting nervously in an evident effort to keep sober.

When the clapping ended, Jerry took back his glass with a sweep and winked triumphantly at young Collyer. Before they could resume their argument she sent in the Boots to him. She watched the Boots touch his arm and whisper, and Jerry look out at her over the heads of the crowd. He came towards her, turning to wag a smug finger at the young man, crying, 'When I've squared up for the wine I'll be back. I won't let you get away with it as easily as all that, my young boyo!' He was groping in his tails for his wallet as he crushed through the door out to her. She moved a few feet up the corridor away from the bar and the noise.

'The wine?' he said. 'How much?'

'It's not the wine, Jerry.' She smiled when he opened his eyes haughtily at her use of his first name. 'I see you don't remember me?'

'I'm very sorry,' he apologized. 'I gather I ought to remember you. But as a matter of fact I just don't.'

She laughed and felt herself blushing.

'You once asked me to marry you. I was twelve at the time. My name is Lily Collis now but I used to be Lily Braden when you knew me long ago. I married a cousin of your own – Victor Collis. He was Uncle Mel's son. We used all be playing together by Uncle Mel's lodge at Templeogue. Do you forget?'

He saw a red plush divan beside him.

'Won't you sit down?' he said to her gently.

'Ah, no, it wouldn't be right, I should really be in the lounge now, I'm on duty there, and at the dance afterwards. Am I embarrassing you?'

'Good Lord, no, not in the least. But I am going to sit down.'

He sat, and looked up at her and laughed.

'You used to have long fair plaits of hair down your back. I was gone about you. I used to swing you on the old beech tree. Twenty swings for a kiss. Wasn't that the tariff?' She laughed happily. 'So you married Uncle Mel's boy. There were such a lot of Collises. From Glasnevin, the North Circular Road, Howth, Raheny, and a few on the south side at Cabinteely, and old Templeogue. Do you realize, Lily, that it must be nearly thirty years since I last laid eyes on you?'

'It is, and thirty-seven years ago. I was thirteen when we last saw one another and you were sixteen. You're every bit of fifty-three, Jerry.'

He raised mock-pleading palms, laughing again.

'Spare my last remaining grey hairs.'

'I simply had to speak to you when I heard you talking about the old place tonight. It's marvellous the way you remember it so well. The path through the wood, and the pond behind the lodge, and the old swing and all.'

'And the smell of the wood-smoke,' he said.

'And the geese pickin' in the grass.'

'And the old avenue all weeds,' he laughed.

'And the old stables falling down,' she cried.

'Do you remember the day the hunt chased a fox across the avenue?'

'I see you have it all!' she cried.

They were silent, looking at one another. In the bar a woman's voice had begun to sing 'Has Sorrow Thy Young Days Shaded?'

'They're still at it about Tom Moore,' he said.

In a mirror facing into the bar she saw that the singer was Miss Shannon.

'Uncle Mel!' Jerry was saying, staring up at her. 'He ran away to sea when he was a boy, and came back, and married into the gate lodge. He had a four-master in a bottle in the fanlight.'

'You know that he killed himself in the heel of the hunt?'

'Ah, no! For God's sake!'

'He was left alone in the lodge after Victor married me. One winter he got raging pneumonia and he wouldn't give in to it. They picked him up one night off the steps of the Parnell monument and took him across to the Rotunda hospital. He'd tell nobody who he was or where he lived, so they took him up to the Workhouse and he died there. It was only after he was buried, in the paupers' graveyard, that we heard about it. I think it was a sort of wild revenge he took on Victor for marrying me. But the Collises were always like that – wild and obstinate and vengeful.'

He shook his head, half sadly, half proudly.

'God knows, Lily, and that's a true bill. Do you know that I didn't speak to my father for seven years before he died? And all over nothing but politics. I pushed myself through college under my own steam. When he was gone I had to support my mother and my two sisters. I climbed to the top of the tree with my two bare hands. But, by God, I did it. Nothing stopped me and nothing ever will stop me from getting what I want. Oho! We're an obstinate set all right. Tell me, what happened at all to Uncle Ned Collis?'

She threw her head sideways to laugh again, but this time her laugh was a half groan.

'There was a wild divil o' hell for you. Always hitting the bottle. Once when he was on a batter didn't he lose his ship at the North Wall, and what did he do but dive into the Liffey and swim after it to the Poolbeg lighthouse, where he knew it would be halting. He died raving in New Orleans.'

He had once been in New Orleans. He saw the mists and the lights on the Mississippi. His eyes blazed:

'Divils o' hell, every one of them! My mother often told me about a Collis woman who swam from Ireland's Eye to the Bailey lighthouse around by Balscadden, a swim no man ever did before or since.' He got up and took her hand in his two hands. 'Lily, there's nobody like the old stock. There was always great stuff in us.' He felt her ring, looked at it and back at her. 'Family?'

'Three, two boys and a girl. Not that they're boys any longer. The eldest is married. He went off to England last month. He's a doctor. The second is on a ship; he's a radio officer. Annie's at home; she's a radiologist.' She paused, saw him look over her uniform, smiled proudly. 'You know Victor well – he's the headwaiter at the Oyster.'

'Good Lord, I must have seen him every week of my life for the last ten years. Why didn't he talk to me and say who he was?'

'It wouldn't be right. But leave you talk to him the next time you go into the Oyster.'

'I will.'

But he had the premonition that he would never dine at the Oyster again. She went on:

'Now that the children are grown up I take a relief job like this now and again. For a night, for a week. What do I want sitting at home in Ringsend doing nothing? I'm here just for tonight. Tomorrow, now, I'll go around and see the lakes.'

'So you married and lived happy ever afterwards.'

'Since you wouldn't have me,' she laughed coyly. 'But what about yourself?'

He released her hand.

'I'm an old dyed-in-the-wool bachelor, Lily. I was too busy and ambitious for that sort of thing when I was young, and now that I'm an old codger nobody wants me.'

'Nonsense, Jerry,' she said maternally. 'I saw you throwing great sheep's eyes at Miss Shannon. You'll get married one of these days. But I'm keeping you from your friends, and I ought to be on the job. It was grand talking about old times, Jerry. I'm glad one Collis anyway made a success of his life. You gave a great speech. They're all talking about it in the lounge. They say you're sure to be given the job. What is it?'

He made a little grimace.

'Just a big housing scheme. But all I'm interested in is that whoever gets it should do it properly. Old things are precious, Lily. The older I grow the more I feel it.'

'Of course you should get it,' she declared loyally. 'Who better? And I hope you'll make a packet of money out of it.'

They shook hands warmly. He watched her walking away from him down the corridor. A tidy figure. Handsome. Full of courage. And

damned intelligent. In the bar Stella's song was dying sweetly and
sadly.

If thus the cold world now wither
Each feeling that once was dear . . .

He hesitated, saw a French window beside him, opened it and stepped
out into the night.

The darkness was moist but warm. The whole sky one basketful of
stars. Feeling a gravel path under his shoes, he walked slowly along it
until he heard the lake lapping the shore like a cat, and, as he grew
accustomed to the dark, he made out a small wooden wharf jutting into
the waves in the lee of a boathouse. He smelled laurels, and rotting
wrack and reeds. He leaned against the shed, and half saw the wide
lakes stretching all around, with their black islands, and their peaked
mountains cutting off the stars. The south wind flowed gently and
indifferently over it all.

Afterwards he would say, 'She gave me a bit of a shake, I can tell you.'
Yet what it was in their brief encounter that disturbed him he could
never say. All he knew was that he had felt a shadow, silent as a cloud,
that he had not heeded for many years, and a sudden wish to be alone
with it. He stayed by the lake for the length of three cigarettes.

They had lived recklessly, some of them wildly, all of them
devil-may-cares who took life in both hands and squandered it without
calculation. But because they had lived like that they did not need pity.
Old Ned, diving drunk off the side of the quay and swimming after his
ship? He'd have spat on pity! 'Died raving in New Orleans . . . ' They
had refused, rejected, despised something precious, and powerful and
real, but they were not failures. Failures were another kind of drunk
altogether, fellows like Condon Larkin, hanging around waiting for
somebody's pity to pick them out of the gutter. He whipped his second
cigarette out of his case and lit it with an angry click of his lighter.
Failures are ambitious, calculating people, men who feel disaster in the
softest wind. It was not that they were just reckless. Lily was a Collis.
With her eyes that could skiver you, and her hard little body like a
pony, and her hands like plates, and her three children she'd slaved for,
made one a doctor, one a radiologist, sent one to sea, as she sent old
Victor padding off every morning and evening to the Oyster in his black
tie and his tails. He saw their box of a house in Ringsend, red brick,

three windows, a green door with an iron knocker, one of hundreds like it, near the sooty church by the canal basin, never free of the rattle of the trams, car lights flashing across the ceilings, ships' sirens on the Liffey. He laughed admiringly. Just the sort of woman who would have swum from Ireland's Eye to the Bailey lighthouse and back again. With a gasp of anger he had flicked his cigarette in an arc into the water. 'She knocked me off my stilts somehow,' he would say afterwards. But he would never admit that she had left him with a sense of smallness and shame.

Lighting his third cigarette, he turned in the direction of the hotel and the faint throb of dance music. Young Collyer would probably say that he was slobbering now about the small homes of the living as before about the big houses of the dead. He went on slowly beside a stony piece of beach and the slopping water until he saw to his left the bright windows beaming light down over the lawn to a white garden seat at the edge of the lake. One window was open. Through it he could see the dancers when they moved past it.

Halted, he was looking irresolutely at the window when he heard his name called from somewhere nearby. He made out a rustic summer house with a conical, thatched roof, at the end of a tiny side path. He walked towards it, peered in, and saw two cigarettes glowing in the dark.

'Who's there?' he asked.

'Us,' said Stella's voice, softly.

He flicked on his cigarette lighter and held it like a torch over his head.

'The Statue of Liberty?' Stella's voice asked.

He made out Condon Larkin sitting beside her. Her shoulders were bare, her face pale, her neck as straight as a swan's, and he thought that she was looking at him quizzically. Just before he put out the flame he saw on the table between them a bottle of brandy. He stopped and entered and sat beside her, and, gradually, by the reflected sheen of the lights and the stars, he saw her better, and that her two hands were clasping a brandy glass as if it were a chalice. He felt a great knot of anger against Larkin bulging in his chest but he managed to say quietly:

'Stella, dear, don't you think it would be more prudent for you to sit indoors? Or at least to wear a wrap?'

Her head swayed feebly on her long neck like a daffodil in a slight wind, and she said in a kind parody of his voice:

'Dear Jerry. Prudent Jerry. Surely you ought to be indoors promoting your cause?'

Larkin leaned across her towards him and began to speak in the overslow, overcareful enunciation of all drunks.

'Mis-ter Pres-i-dent, we were discuss-ing you. I want to con-grat-ulate you, most sincerely. On a very subtle speech. Especially that part of your speech that dealt with Templeogue. I sincere-ly hope they will put you in charge of the entire scheme. I sincerely mean that.'

'Shut up, Larkin,' he said crossly.

'Stella! Our Pres-i-dent tells me to shut up. But I won't shut up. Why should I shut up? It was a very fine speech. And I repeat that.'

'All right, Larkin! What you are trying to say, only you haven't the guts to say it straight out, is that all I care about is getting the Templeogue job. Thank you kindly.'

Stella laid her hand on his, softly.

'Jerry! Condy and I have often talked about this. We believe that what you said about creating and destroying being very close to one another is true. Terribly true.'

He realized from her touch and her tone that they were not mocking him: they really had liked his speech. Larkin leaned over again, crushing Stella against him in a blended waft of jasmine and brandy.

'She's right. It's terribly true! "To create," you said, "is to change. And to change is to de-stroy." And why is it true? It's true because every man who creates is a god-damned, flame-ing, bloody ego-tist. That's why I'll always be a dud. No, Stella!' he snarled querulously, shoving her hand away from him. 'You've rubbed it into me often enough. I'm too diffident. I've no ambition. I'm a dud!'

She sighed at Jerry.

'It's why Condy and I liked your speech so much, Jerry. We feel that everybody should be more diffident. Let things grow naturally, like leaves. You know – the lilies of the field and all that. Condy says why should anybody impose his hand on the handiwork of God?'

His anger burst from him.

'But that isn't what I meant at all. We have to create whether we like it or not. People have to live in houses. We have to build for them, and go on building, even if it's only a road, a bridge, a culvert over a stream. We have to go on into the future. What I'd like to do is to

manoeuvre vast schemes for living people about these old towns and
villages, spread on and on and out and out, like an army of tanks
sweeping in wide arcs about some country they want to conquer. We
have to do it. Even if we don't want to do it life will make us do it,
shoving us on behind. We can't help it!'

Larkin started to say something, and then gave up the ghost, his head
sinking into his arms, his glass rolling over to the ground. Almost at
once his heavy breathing showed that he had fallen asleep. For a
moment Stella's hand hovered towards his head, and then slowly
returned to her glass. She whispered:

'I'm afraid he's a weak argument against you. Actually he is a very
good architect. He just hasn't got your drive.'

He said irritably:

'This gazebo is as damp as a fungus. Let's get out of here for a minute
for a breath of clean air.'

She rose, and teetered a little. When he held her arm to steady her
it was like taking a bird by the wing. Outside she lifted her furrowed
forehead to the sky and murmured, 'The stars of heaven.' She had a
strangely worn face for so young a woman. The pose had tautened her
small breasts. He wanted to touch her bare shoulders.

'Stella! You'll never be able to do anything with him. He's not a good
architect. He's not a good anything. He's just a drunk.'

Still upward-looking, she waved a hand in weak deprecation.

'Please, don't bring all that up again.'

'Stella! Is the real reason why you won't have me that I'm too old?'

She did not so much shake her head as let it roll from side to side,
and then it rolled downward of its own weight so that she was looking
out under her wrinkled forehead to where the light from the hotel
touched the water's edge. He asked passionately:

'Why must you always go around picking people up out of the gutter?
Lame dogs. Weaklings. Fellows who . . .'

She silenced him with a hand on his arm, and a backward look at the
summer hut.

'Poor Condy!' she protested softly.

'And why not poor Jerry? Don't I deserve anything? Haven't I worked
for it? Don't I deserve a wife, and a home, and children?'

'Poor Jerry,' she placated with an appealing smile. 'I'm sure you
deserve a lot of things.'

'But not from you?'

'I wouldn't be any use to you, Jerry. I'd always want to be whatever I am, and you would always be wanting to change me. Oh, I know you'd be kind to me, proud of me, preserve one little corner of me to show your friends, but you'd surround me, encircle me, swallow me up the way you would like to swallow up Templeogue.'

They were silent for a moment, both looking out at the dark lake that slopped endlessly.

'So you really didn't believe a word I said tonight?'

'I believed it. But you did not. You are very ambitious, aren't you, Jerry?'

He did not answer her. He became so excited by the hope that she was asking a question about whose answer she was still in doubt that his fists in his pockets began to tremble, and he was made almost drunk by the scent of her body beside him, and the smells of the lake and the shore and the whispering waves. He did not look at her, but he knew that she was swaying gently by his side, looking up at him.

'All I want is you. You'd be my inspiration in everything I did.'

'What a role!'

'I want nothing in the world but you.'

'Not even Templeogue?'

'If I give up Templeogue will you marry me?'

'Yes! Like a shot!'

He said nothing. She lifted her head to the stars and began to laugh mockingly. She stopped suddenly. From inside the hut the sleepy voice groaned her name. She turned and faced the dark opening. She laid a hand on Jerry's arm.

'He's not a bad architect. He should have a job in the Board of Works, looking after old Georgian houses, old churches, old monuments. He has great taste, great reverence. There is a job vacant in the Board of Works. It would suit him perfectly. Could you say a word for him there, Jerry?'

He looked down at her delicate, worried, tiny face.

'Supposing I took that job myself, would you marry me?'

She shook her head drunkenly.

'Jerry! You might as well try to walk on the lake. We are what we are.'

He took her forcibly by her bare shoulders.

'Stella! Stay with me, come away with me.'

She released herself gently, went into the hut and composedly sat down. He saw her hand stroke the tousled head on the table, and he knew in that instant that in trying to save Larkin she would ruin her own life, and all sorts of ideas jumbled wildly into him, such as that there is no such thing as saving your life or squandering your life because nobody knows what life is until he has lived out so much of it that it is too late then to do anything but go on the way you have gone on, or been driven on, from the beginning. We are free to be, to act, to live, to create, to imagine, call it whatever you like, only inside our own destiny, or else to spit in the face of destiny and be destroyed by it. If a man won't do that all he can do is to bake his bread and throw it on the waters, and hope to God that what he is doing – he gazed up and around him – is the will of the night, the stars, the god of this whole flaming bloody unintelligible universe.

He turned and strode towards the lighted windows. The central window of the middle three was a French window, opening on to steps leading to the lawn. He went up there, and stood in the opening, his hands in his pockets, his shoulders back, watching the couples floating by, smiling benevolently whenever his eye caught somebody he knew. Presently he saw, on a settee in a corner, young Collyer and Kevin Lowry with two young women. He advanced towards them jauntily, swaying his shoulders and his tails, beaming at them.

'Well, now!' he laughed, sitting between the two young women and putting his arms around their shoulders. 'Boys, I see, will be boyos, and it follows that girls will be girlos! Here, what are we drinking? Where are the bloody waiters?'

He raised an arm, clicked his fingers, and Lily Collis came forward smiling. He winked at her.

'Tell the wine waiter to bring me two bottles of fizz, Lily. The best in the house.'

She cast a quick eye at the two young women, smiled at him and went off.

He had already turned eagerly to the young men, talking to them rapidly and forcefully. Between them was a low table with a white marble top. From his waistcoat pocket he produced a gold pencil and with vigorous strokes he slashed lines across it to mark roads, avenues, fields, houses. At first they listened to him quizzically, giving one another long impassive looks, but by degrees his energy and his enthusiasm flooded them into the net of the discussion, so that when the champagne came they ignored it, leaning absorbedly over the table, pointing, arguing, laughing excitedly. The dancers floated by, the music drummed. Once he leaned back and glanced through the French window. The stars glinted. The dark lake lapped the shore.

# A Touch of Autumn in the Air

It was, of all people, Daniel Cashen of Roscommon who first made me realize that the fragments of any experience that remain in a man's memory, like bits and scraps of a ruined temple, are preserved from time not at random but by the inmost desires of his personality.

Cashen was neither sensitive nor intelligent. He was a caricature of the self-made, self-educated, nineteenth-century businessman. Some seventy years ago he had set up a small woollen factory in County Roscommon which, by hard work from early morning to late at night, and by making everybody around him work at the same pace, he developed into a thriving industry which he personally owned. His Swansdown Blankets, for example, were the only kind of blankets my mother ever bought. Though old when I made his acquaintance, he was still a powerful horse of a man, always dressed in well-pressed Irish tweeds, heavy countryman's boots, and a fawn, flat-topped bowler hat set squat above a big, red, square face, heavy handle-bar moustaches and pale blue, staring eyes of which one always saw the complete circle of the iris, challenging, concentrated, slightly mad.

One would not expect such a man to say anything very profound about the workings of the memory, and he did not. All he did was to indulge in a brief burst of reminiscence in a hotel foyer, induced by my casual remark that it was a lovely, sunny day outside but that there was a touch of autumn in the air. The illuminating thing was the bewildered look that came into those pale, staring eyes as he talked. It revealed that he was much more touched and troubled by the Why of memory than by the Fact of memory. He was saying, in effect: Why do I remember that? Why do I not remember the other thing? For the first time in his life something within him had gone out of control.

What he started to talk about was a holiday he spent when just under fifteen, in what was at that time called the Queen's County. It had lasted two months, September and October. 'Lovely, sunny weather, just like today.' What had begun to bother him was not so much that the days had merged and melted together in his memory – after so many years that was only natural – but that here and there, from a few days of no more evident importance than any other days, a few trivial things stuck up above the tides of forgetfulness. And as he mentioned them I could see that he was fumbling, a little fearfully, towards the notion that there might be some meaning in the pattern of those indestructible bits of the jigsaw of his youth, perhaps even some sort of revelation in their obstinacy after so much else had dropped down the crevices of time.

He did not come directly to the major memory that had set his mind working in this way. He mentioned a few lesser memories first, staring out through the revolving glass doors at the sunny street. There was the afternoon when, by idle chance, he leaned over a small stone bridge near his Uncle Bartle's farm and became held for an hour by the mesmerism of the stream flickering through the chickweed. As could happen likewise to a great number of busy men, who normally never think at all about the subjective side of themselves, and are overwhelmed by the mystery of it if once they do advert to it, he attached an almost magical import to the discovery that he had never forgotten the bright pleasure of that casual hour.

'No, John! Although it must be near sixty years ago. And I don't believe I ever will forget it. Why is that?'

Of course, he admitted modestly, he had a phenomenal memory, and to prove it he invited me to ask him the telephone numbers of any half-dozen shops in town. But, yet, there was that red hay barn where he and his cousin, Kitty Bergin, played and tumbled a score of times – it was a blur.

'I can't even remember whether the damn thing was made of timber or corrugated iron!'

Or there was the sunken river, away back on the level leas, a stream rather than a river, where one warm September Sunday after Mass he saw, with distasteful pleasure, the men splashing around naked, roughly ducking a boy who had joined them, laughing at his screams. But, whereas he also still possessed the soft, surrounding fields, the imperceptibly moving clouds, the crunch of a jolting cart far away, the silence so deep that you could have heard an apple falling, he had lost every detail of the walk to and from the river, and every hour before and after it. A less arrogant man might have accepted the simple explanation that the mind wavers in and out of alertness, is bright at one moment, dim at the next. Those mad, round irises glared at the suggestion that his mind could at any time be dim.

He pointed out that he knew the country for miles around, intimately, walking it and cycling it day after day: what clung to him of it all, like burrs, were mere spots – a rusty iron gate falling apart, a crossroads tree with a black patch burnt at its base, an uneventful turn off the main road, a few undistinguished yards of the three miles of wall around the local demesne. He laughed scornfully at my idea that his mind became bright only for those few yards of wall.

'Well, perhaps it became dim then? You were thinking hard about other things up to that point in your walk?'

Here he allowed his real trouble to expose itself. He had not only remembered pointless scraps, but, I found, those scraps had been coming back to him repeatedly during the last few days with a tormenting joy, so that here he was, an old man, fondling nothings as lovingly as if he were fondling a lock of a dead woman's hair. It was plain, at last, that he was thinking of all those fragments of his boyhood as the fish scales of some wonderful fish, never-to-be-seen, sinuous and shining, that had escaped from his net into the ocean.

What had started him off was simple. (I reconstruct it as well as I can, intuiting and enlarging from his own brief, blunt words.) A few mornings before our meeting, fine and sunny also, he had happened to go into a toyshop where they also sold sweets. He was suddenly transfixed by the smell peculiar to these shops – scented soaps, the paint on the tin toys and the sprayed wooden trucks, the smell of the children's gift books, the sweetness of the sweets. At once he was back in that holiday, with his cousin Kitty Bergin, on the leas behind her father's farmhouse (his Uncle Bartle's), one sunny, mistified October morning, driving in a donkey cart down to where his uncle and his cousin Jack were ditching a small meadow that they had retrieved from the rushes and the bog water.

As Kitty and he slowly jolted along the rutted track deeper and deeper into this wide, flat river basin of the Barrow, whose hundreds of streams and dykes feed into what, by a gradual addition, becomes a river some twenty miles away, the two men whom they were approaching looked so minute on the level bog, under the vast sky, that Dan got a queer feeling of his own smallness in observing theirs. As he looked back, the white, thatched farmhouse nestling into the earth had never seemed so homely, cosy and comforting.

Ferns crackled at the hub. When he clutched one its fronds were warm but wet. It was the season when webs are flung with a wild energy across chasms. He wiped his face several times. He saw dew drops in a row in mid-air, invisibly supported between frond and frond. A lean swathe of mist, or was it low cloud, floated beneath far hills. Presently they saw behind the two men a pond with a fringe of reeds. Against an outcrop of delicately decayed limestone was a bent hawthorn in a cloud of ruby berries. Or could it have been a rowan tree? The sky was a pale green. The little shaven meadow was as lemon-bright as fallen ash leaves before the dew dries on their drifts, so that it would have been hard to say whether the liquid lemon of the meadow was evaporating into the sky or the sky melting down into the field.

They were on a happy mission. Mulvaney the postman had brought two letters to the farmhouse from two other sons: Owen, who was a pit manager in the mines at Castlecomer, and Christopher (who, out of respect, was never referred to as Christy), then studying for the priesthood in a Dublin seminary. Aunt Molly had sent them off with the letters, a jug of hot tea and thick rounds of fresh, homemade bread and homemade apple jam smelling of cloves, a great favourite of Uncle Bartle's. They duly reached the two men, relieved the donkey of bridle, bit and winkers so that he could graze in the meadow, spread sacks to sit on, and while Kitty poured the tea into mugs Bartle reverently wiped his clayey hands on the sides of his trousers and took the letters. As he read them aloud in a slow, singsong voice, like a man intoning his prayers, it was clear that those two sons had gone so far outside his own experience of the big world that he stood a little in awe of them both. It was a picture to be remembered for years: the meadow, the old man, the smoke of the distant farmhouse, patriarchal, sheltered, simple.

When he laid down the letter from the priest-to-be he said:

'He's doing well. A steady lad.'

When he had read the letter from the mines he said:

'He's doing fine. If he escapes the danger he will go far.'

While Jack was reading the letters Kitty whispered to Danny, thumbing the moon's faint crescent:

'Look! It says D for Danny.'

'Or,' he murmured to her boldly, 'it could be D for Dear?'

Her warning glare towards her father was an admission.

'I see here,' Jack commented, while his father sucked at the tea, 'that

Christopher is after visiting Fanny Emphie. Her name in religion is Sister Fidelia.'

Dan had seen this girl at the Curragh Races during the first week of his holidays, a neighbour's daughter who, a few weeks later, entered the convent. He had heard them joking one night about how she and Christopher had at one time been 'great' with one another. He remembered a slight, skinny girl with a cocked nose, laughing moist lips and shining white teeth.

'Read me out that bit,' Bartle ordered. 'I didn't note that.'

'"I got special leave from the President to visit Sister Fidelia, last week, at Saint Joachim's. She is well and happy but looked pale. She asked after you all. Saint Joachim's has nice grounds, but the trams pass outside the wall and she said that for the first couple of weeks she could hardly sleep at all."'

The two men went on drinking their tea. It occurred to Dan that they did not care much for Fanny Emphie. He saw her now in her black robes walking along a gravelled path under the high walls of the convent, outside which the trams at night drew their glow in the air overhead. It also occurred to him, for no reason, that Kitty Bergin might one day think of becoming a nun, and he looked at her with a pang of premonitory loss. Why should any of them leave this quiet place?

'Ha!' said old Bartle suddenly, and winked at Danny, and rubbed his dusty hands and drew out his pipe. This meant that they must all get back to work.

Kitty gathered up the utensils, Danny tackled the donkey, the others went back to their ditching and she and Danny drove back to where the fern was plentiful for bedding. Taking two sickles, they began to rasp through the stalks. After a while she straightened up, so did he, and they regarded one another, waist-deep in the fern.

'Do you think,' she asked him pertly, 'would I make a nice nun?'

'You!' he said, startled that the same thought had entered their heads at the same time.

She came across to him, slipped from his pocket the big blue handkerchief in which the bread had been wrapped, cast it in an arc about her fair head, drew it tightly under her chin with her left hand, and then with a deft peck of her right finger and thumb cowled it forward over her forehead and her up-looking blue eyes.

'Sister Fidelia, sir,' she curtsied, provokingly.

He grappled with her as awkwardly as any country boy, paying the sort of homage he expected was expected of him, and she, laughing, wrestled strongly with him. They swayed in one another's arms, aware of each other's bodies, until she cried, 'Here's Daddy,' and when he let her go mocked him from a safe distance for his innocence. But as they cut the fern again her sidelong glances made him happy.

They piled the cut fern into the cart, climbed on top of it, and lay face down on it, feeling the wind so cold that they instinctively pressed closer together. They jolted out to the main road, and as they ambled along they talked, and it seemed to him that it was very serious talk, but he forgot every word of it. When they came near the crossroads with its little sweetshop, they decided to buy a half-penny-worth of their favourite sweets, those flat, odd-shaped sweets – diamonds, hearts, hexagonals – called Conversation Lozenges because each sweet bore on its coarse surface a ring-posy in coloured ink, such as Mizpah, Truth Tries Troth, Do You Care? or All for Love. Some bore girls' names, such as Gladys or Alice. His first sweet said, Yours in Heart. He handed it to her with a smile; she at once popped it into her mouth, laughing at his folly. As they ambled along so, slowly, chatting and chewing, the donkey's hooves whispering through the fallen beech leaves, they heard high above the bare arches of the trees the faint honking of the wild geese called down from the north by the October moon.

It was to those two or three hours of that October morning many years ago that he was whirled back as he stood transfixed by the smells of the sweets-and-toys-shop. Forgetting what he had come there to buy, he asked them if they sold Conversation Lozenges. They had never heard of them. As he turned to go he saw a nun leafing through the children's gift books. He went near her and, pretending to look at a book, peered under her cowl. To his surprise she was a very old nun. On the pavement he glanced up at the sky and was startled to see there the faint crescent moon. He was startled because he remembered that he had seen it earlier in the morning, and had quite forgotten the fact.

He at once distrusted the message of his memory. Perhaps it was not that the smells had reminded him of little Kitty Bergin eating Yours in Heart, or pretending to be a nun, or wrestling with him in the fern? Perhaps what had called him back was the indifference of those two men to the fate of the nun? Or was there some special meaning for him in those arrowing geese? Or in the cosy, sheltered farmhouse? Maybe the important thing that day had been the old man humbly reading the letters? Why had the two men looked so small under the open sky of the bogland? D, she had said, for Danny . . .

As he stared at me there in the hotel foyer, my heart softened towards him. The pain in his eyes was the pain of a man who has begun to lose one of the great pleasures of life in the discovery that we can never truly remember anything at all, that we are for a great part of our lives at the mercy of uncharted currents of the heart. It would have been futile to try to comfort him by saying that those currents may be charted elsewhere, that even when those revolving glass doors in front of us flashed in the October sun the whole movement of the universe since time began was involved in that coincidence of light. Daniel Cashen of Roscommon would get small comfort out of thinking of himself as a little blob of phosphorescence running along the curl of a wave at night.

And then, by chance, I did say something that comforted him, because as he shook hands with me and said he must be off, I said, without thinking:

'I hope the blankets are doing well?'

'Aha!' he cried triumphantly. 'Better than ever.'

And tapped his flat-topped hat more firmly on his head and whirled the doors before him out into the sunny street as imperiously as any man accustomed to ordering everything that comes his way.

Through the slowing doors I watched him halt on the pavement. He looked slowly to the right, and then he looked towards his left, and then, slowly, he looked up around the sky until he found what he was looking for. After a few moments he shivered up his shoulders around his neck, looked at the ground at his feet, put his two hands into his pockets, and moved very slowly away, still down-looking, out of sight.

Poor man, I thought when he was gone; rash, blunt, undevious; yet, in his own crude way, more true to life than his famous French contemporary who recaptured lost time only by dilating, inventing, suppressing, merging such of its realities as he could recall, and inventing whatever he could not. Cashen was playing archaeology with his boyhood, trying to deduce a whole self out of a few dusty shards. It was, of course, far too late. My guess was that of the few scraps that he now held in his hands the clue lay not so much in the offer of love and the images of retirement, the girl's courtship, the white farmhouse snuggling down cosily into the earth under the vast dome of the sky, and the old man left behind by his sons, as in the challenging sight of his own littleness on that aqueous plain whose streams barely trickled to the open sea. He said he hadn't thought of it for sixty years. Perhaps not? But he was thinking of it now, when the adventure was pretty well over. As it was. A week later a friend rang me up and said, 'Did you hear who's died?' I knew at once, but I asked the question.

He left nearly a hundred and fifty thousand pounds – a lot of money in our country – and, since he never married, he divided it all up among his relatives by birth, most of them comparatively poor people and most of them living in what used to be called, in his boyhood, the Queen's County.

# The Younger Generation

When the door closed behind Count Toby the bishop's eyebrows soared. He swivelled back to his desk with a groan, took up his pen, and read the last sentence that he had written an hour ago. Then he shook his head like a dog just come out of a river. The finger with the great amethyst ring began to tap the mahogany. He lifted the edge of his cuff, glanced at his wristlet watch, and said aloud, 'Oh, dear, dear!' When he heard the door opening once more he lifted the eyes of a martyr to the ceiling.

'I'm sorry for interrupting you again, my lord,' palpitated Count Toby. 'I just came back to beg you not to say a word about all this to my wife. And I'm very sorry to have occupied so much of your time. I've talked much too much about my unfortunate affairs. You didn't come to Aughty Castle for *that*. And I'm just sending in Bridie with your egg flip.'

He backed out, bumped the jamb, said, 'Sorry, sorry,' as if he were apologizing to the door. He closed it with a tiny click.

'Ninny!' the bishop grunted, swivelled back, gripped his pen in his fist like a dagger, glared again at what he had written, read it twice, read it three times, exhaled groaningly, and tossed down the pen.

He made yet another effort to concentrate on his pastoral. ' . . . and so guide them,' he intoned, 'to a happy union where their own lives shall repeat this same wonderful cycle of love, marriage and parenthood.'

He leaned back and let his eyes wander to the ocean's vast dishes of sunlight. A yacht, miles out, was becalmed in the dead centre of one of those circles of sun. His eyes sank to the rocks offshore, pale as pearls. On the second terrace the gardener was softly raking the gravel.

'Such a lovely place!'

He took out his pouch and his pipe and began, pensively, to fill it. The raking stopped. The only sound then was a thrush cracking a snail against a stone, and the bishop chuckling softly and sardonically into his pouch.

'Poor Toby!' he said.

His finger deftly coaxed the shreds into the bowl.

'Still, gentleman,' he murmured into his pouch, 'this is going just a little bit too far. I suppose it's fair enough for the laity to treat us as their spiritual doctors. As we are, there's no getting away from it, as we are. But really and truly! And yet, gentlemen, we're told that the first ten years of marriage are the worst? Well, we make many sacrifices, gentlemen, but ... ' He let pouch and pipe sink into his lap and looked out to sea again. 'How long can they be ... It must be twenty years...'

Tut-tutting, he resumed the filling of his pipe.

'You know what it is, gentlemen? There's a good deal of truth in the old country saying that the best of wives needs a dose of ashplant medicine now and again. Externally applied, gentlemen. Well laid on, gentlemen. As my old gardener, Philly Cashman, used to say – God be good to him, many a dewy head o' cabbage he stole from me back in County Cavan – "There's only the wan cure, me lord, for shlow horses and fasht women and that's the shtick!"'

As he lit his pipe he looked through the smoke at his unfinished pastoral. Hurling away the match, he puffed fiercely, seized the pen, and with concentration wrote a new heading: 'Duties of Married People Towards Each Other'. He drove on heavily for about five minutes, but it was like pushing a wheelbarrow through mud. There was a knock at the door. The egg flip?

'Come in!'

He achieved another sentence.

'My lord, am I disturbing you?'

He swivelled, and rose.

'Good morning, Miss Burke! I thought it was the maid with my egg flip.' He held out his hand. He noticed that she did not kiss the ring. 'You weren't down to breakfast? Ah, I see you were out riding.'

She might have changed out of her jodhpurs. He admired the handsome, sullen face, the bold wings to the eyebrows; very like the mother; a divil at a point-to-point. She twirled her crop nervously between her fingers.

'My lord, I want to apologize. I mean for last night. It's dreadful that this sort of thing should happen the very first night you stay with us. And you came for rest and – '

She indicated his pastoral with a glance.

'Say nothing at all about it, child. A thing of nothing. These little upsets occur in the best of households. You were just a little upset last night. A bit out of sorts.'

The dark head tilted like a frightened race horse. The eyes, dilated, caught the blue of the sky.

'I wasn't apologizing for myself. Mummy has been like that for months past. You must excuse her.'

'Your mother is a great credit to your rearing,' he said dryly.

She reddened and cried:

'Daddy is a martyr to her; nobody else would stand her for a week.'

'My child! My child!'

'But it's perfectly true. I know my own mother. This has been going on for years.'

'Miss Anne,' he took her trembling hand, 'sit down there and listen to me'. She took the edge of a chair. 'I've known you since you were that high.' He smiled at her paternally. 'I've known ye all since I was a simple curate in this parish thirty-one years ago. Look now, I'm not going to talk to you like a bishop at all but like an old friend of the family. You're not being quite fair to your mother. She's worried about this marriage of yours.'

'Oh, it's natural that you'd take Mummy's side. I quite understand that. It's natural you wouldn't want me to marry a Protestant but . . .'

'Now, that's where you're wrong. It's not at all natural. On the contrary. It's the most natural thing in the wide world for you to fall in love with this young man, why wouldn't you? When a girl is attracted by the twinkle in a young man's eye, or the cock of his head, or whatever else it is that attracts ye in young men' – he invited her smile; she yielded it perfunctorily – 'it isn't of his religion she does be thinking. And if a girl does fall in love with a young man, what is more natural than that she should want to marry him? What is more proper, in fact? And, then, Miss Anne, what would be more natural than that I, or any other priest, would want to see that young girl married to the man she loves?'

She stared at him, darting from one eye to the other, in search of the snare.

'But, Miss Anne, we can't live by nature alone.'

As he waited for her to appreciate his point, he heard the thrush cracking another snail. In a faint impulse of irritation he remembered the Persian fable about the holy man whose first impulsive desires were all fulfilled, disastrously.

'What I mean is, we sometimes have to resist our natural impulses.'

'But,' she almost sobbed, 'Mummy isn't thinking of anything like that. She wouldn't care if he was a Turk. It's just that she doesn't want me to be married to anybody. She's jealous of me, she always was jealous of me, she hates me, and I hate her, I *do*, I hate her!'

'Oh, dear, dear! You know, Miss Anne . . . The present generation . . . When I was a boy in County Cavan . . . Listen to me! A mother is the best guide any girl could possibly . . . She is wiser in the ways of the world than you are. She's . . .'

She laughed harshly.

'But it isn't true, my lord. Mummy isn't in the least wise. She's got no sense at all. What's the use of pretending? Oh, I do wish, my lord – I'm not being rude or disrespectful – that priests wouldn't always talk to me as if I were a girl of fifteen or a servant in the kitchen. I'm a grown woman. And as for Mummy being better than me, well, the fact of the matter is, you must have seen it for yourself last night, she drinks like a fish. She's tight half the day.'

He leaned back and stroked his cheek heavily. He surveyed her coldly.

'Do you love this man very much?'

'Yes.'

He detected a shadow of a pause, and peered at her.

'My lord, I hope you won't mind my saying this. It often seems to me that there is . . . that the Church in Ireland . . . that it caters only to the poor and ignorant and there's no place in it for educated people.'

'Well, Miss Anne, it may be, it may be. But if there is no room in the Church for educated people, what is going to happen to poor me?'

She collapsed. He could see her knees trembling. He raised his hand.

'Tell me, my child, do you belong to any club anywhere? Any club? A tennis club? Anything?'

She was on guard again.

'I belong to the Automobile Club in Dublin. It's useful when I go up for a dance and want to change my frock.'

'All right. Very well. Now, there are rules in that club, aren't there?'

'Yes. Of course.' Watching him carefully.

'And in any other club there are rules? And if you don't like those rules you have to leave the club – or they'll throw you out on your neck. Isn't that so?'

'Ye-e-es. I suppose so.'

'And you may go from club to club, but no matter where you halt there are still rules? Aren't there? And,' leaning close to her and speaking with all the solemnity in his power, 'if you aren't satisfied to obey the rules of any club all you can do is go wandering around the streets like a lost soul. Isn't that so?'

She saw his point. Her eyes fell.

'Isn't that so?' he insisted, almost bullying her.

'In a way . . .'

'Isn't that the whole thing in a nutshell? You want to dodge the rules. Isn't that the holy all of it?'

'I could go to a hotel,' she said wildly.

He had to laugh at that.

'Even in a hotel there are rules. I live in a palace. A palace, God help us! Do you think I don't have to toe the line? All you want is your own will and your own way, without regard to the commands of the Church. Be honest, now. Admit it like a brave girl. Isn't that the beginning and end of it?'

'But there are rules and rules, there are sensible rules, in England Catholics are allowed to marry Protestants under dispensation, why should an absolute rule be laid down here?'

'Because I say so,' he said severely, and felt his back to the wall. 'It is the rule of this diocese. It is *my* rule.'

He looked hastily at his desk to indicate that there was no more to be said. He knew what she would try next if he gave her half a chance, and his face darkened as a hundred unpleasant ideas poured into his mind – Gallicanism, *cuius regio*, Modernism, Loisy and Tyrrell and old von Hügel, who barely escaped by the skin of his teeth, the Tutiorists, centuries of dispute, the souls who were lost in heresy, the souls that were barely saved . . .

She made one last effort, her lovely features buttoned up with anger and despair and humiliation.

'But, my lord, if I lived in another diocese this silly rule wouldn't apply to me.'

'Silly? Thank you very much, Miss Burke.'

'I'm sorry. I'm being rude. I beg your pardon. Our guest. Peace and quietness. The first night...'

'No apologies, Miss Anne. We're old friends. Come to me, child, if you are in trouble at any time. I'll pray for you. Now, God help me, I must write my pastoral.'

When she shut the door, he sat to his desk, took a new sheet and wrote fast: 'Duties of Children to Parents and Superiors.' He jotted down guide words. 'Obedience. Respect. Discipline. Changing times. Young generation. Church as Wise Guardian. Patience and Understanding.' He wrote easily on the last theme.

' ... warm young blood ... In misunderstanding their own true motives ... Yet this spirit of rebellion is sometimes no more than the headstrong impatience of youth, and the Church will gently and kindly guide them from this wayward path back to those sane and wise precepts which the experience of centuries has tested and not found wanting.'

He read it aloud, crumpled the page and hurled it into the wastepaper basket.

The yacht was still becalmed in the centre of an unruffled circle. The door opened after a faint knock and the maid came in with the egg flip. He relaxed.

'Thanks, Bridie. You *are* Bridie?'

'Yes, Father, I mean my lord.' Curtsying.

'Bridie what?'

'Bridie Lynam, my lord.' Curtsying.

'That's a familiar name. Where do you come from?'

'West of Cootehill, my lord.' Curtsying.

'Ah, no?' In huge, boyish delight. 'So you're a Cavan girl? Well, well, isn't that a coincidence! Cootehill? Ah, glory be to God, Cootehill! Well, to be sure and to be sorry.' He beamed at her. 'Bridie Lynam from Cootehill in the County Cavan. I'm delighted to hear that. Tell me, is it long now since you left Cootehill?'

'Only the two weeks, my lord.'

'Only two weeks! Listen – wallowing back into his chair for a chat. 'Is that ould bakery of Haffigan's still at the end of the Main Street?'

'Indeed it is, my lord.'

He stared and stared at her, or, rather, at the cerise wall of Haffigan's Steam Bakery, and then he burst out into a peal of laughter, while the girl smiled and squirmed shyly to see the bishop laughing over such a simple thing.

'Well, Bridie Lynam, if I got a pound for every time I bought a steaming currant loaf at Haffigan's on my way to school! Dear me.' He took a sip of his egg flip. 'I don't think they put sugar in this, Bridie?'

'Oh, my lord' – red with confusion. 'I'll get it, my lord.'

'Do, do, and come back and we'll have a little gosther about old times. Haffigan's Steam Bakery!'

Smiling broadly, he went back to his desk, and to his first page, and began to punctuate. Then he began to alter words. He was straightway writing in his best vein on the joy of parents in their first child. A knock.

'Come in, come in,' he welcomed and wrote on. He became aware that the countess was speaking to him:

'I'm afraid the egg flip was a bit late, my lord. Anne never told me. She forgets so many things. This room is very close. Let me close the blinds. Where you ever in Venice, my lord?'

'Let them be, please. I like the sun.'

As she kept wandering around, patting a pillow, changing the position of a book, tipping a curtain, peering into the garden, he wondered whether her auburn mop was dyed or false.

'Yes! The sun. The sunflower to the sun.' She looked around her distractedly. 'Anne adores the sun. She lies in it all day long. Strange girl. I do hope everything is all right? I simply cannot get trained servants nowadays. I often long for the old days when one whipped one's serfs.'

Suddenly she swooped on her knees before him, and burst into a loud sobbing wail:

'Oh, my lord, help me! Everybody in this house hates me. Everybody is plotting against me. My daughter hates me. I haven't a friend in the world. What will I do? What will I do?' The bishop looked wildly around him. Her wail became piercing. She clawed at his coat-tails. 'They all think I'm just a stupid, blowzy old woman! Day and night, my lord, they are at me!'

Count Toby opened the door and with a look of shame and agony he said, very gently, 'Mary, dear?' The bishop helped her to her feet. With sudden, monstrous dignity she walked out. The count looked miserably at the bishop and closed the door.

The bishop stared at the door until Bridie Lynam came in with the sugar bowl, pale and flustered.

'Thank you, Bridie,' he whispered. As she was about to go, he decided to add: 'I hope you'll be happy here. Nice place. The count is a grand man. One of the old stock.'

'Yes, my lord.' She added: 'I'm leaving next week, my lord. I'm goin' to England.'

He turned his back on her. The yacht was still there.

'That's a long way away. Have you friends there?'

'Yes, my lord' – softly.

He kept his back to her so that she might not feel shy and asked: 'Is there a boy there?'

Her 'Yes, my lord' was so soft he hardly heard it.

'Irish boy?'

'From Cootehill, my lord.'

He sighed.

'They're all going,' he murmured to himself.

He remained for so long looking out at the scallop of clouds along the horizon that when he turned the room was empty. He sat to his desk again. He moved his papers aside. Drawing another clean sheet towards him, he leaned his head on his hand and began to write a letter.

'My Dearest Darling Mother, I often think how kind the good God has been to me to have given me so good a mother. Since I first knelt at your lap to say my prayers . . . ' He wrote on quietly. 'And as it was you who welcomed me home from school so it was to you that I returned every year from college . . . ' He wrote on, finished the page and signed it, 'Your loving son, Danny.' Then he took the sheet and very carefully, very deliberately, tore it into tiny fragments and let them flutter like snow into the basket.

Then he cupped his face in his hands and whispered, like a prayer, 'Tomorrow I'll say Mass for the respose of your dear soul.' Wearily he resumed his pastoral letter, and now it wrote itself quietly and simply. But as he wrote he felt no joy or pride in it, no more than if this, too, were a letter not to the living but to the dying and the dead. He was not interrupted agai∴. By lunchtime he had finished the first draft.

Only Count Toby came to lunch. They talked of old friends and old times. After a while the bishop said, gently, 'Perhaps, Toby, do you think it might be better, conceivably, if I were to leave this afternoon?'

Toby glanced up at him under his sad spaniel's eyebrows.

'Perhaps so, Danny.'

The bishop nodded and began to talk, at random, about the cemetery of Père Lachaise and the wildfire that runs at night along the cemetery paths. The count stirred his coffee in silence: he was remembering how he had taken Anne there when she was fifteen, and how lovely she had looked as she threw herself into his arms at the sight of a little leaping tongue of blue fire among the immortelles on a grave.

'Anne,' he said after a long time, 'has just told me that she is going to take a flat in Dublin.'

'Ha!' said the bishop. 'So she's trying a new club?'

'How is that?' asked Count Toby.

'Ah, nothing! Nothing.'

# Love's Young Dream

I don't remember my first visits to that part of Ireland, although my father often told me that since I was four years old I used to be sent there every year, sometimes twice a year. He was a ship's captain, my mother had died when I was three, and whenever he was at sea and no nearer relative could have me I would be sent off for safekeeping to the County Kildare.

The first visit I remember at all clearly was when I was ten, to my Uncle Gerry's farm near the town of Newbridge. I remember it because it was during this visit that Noreen Coogan pushed me into the Liffey. (Noreen was the only child of my aunt's servant, Nancy Coogan; that year she must have been about twelve or thirteen.) I can still see myself standing dripping on the bank, crying miserably, and my uncle assuring me that Noreen – 'The bold, bad slut!' – would be kept far away from me for the rest of the holidays; at which I began to wail more loudly than before, and he, guessing the state of my heart, began to laugh so loudly at me that I fairly bawled.

I have no clear image of what Noreen looked like at the time, or, indeed, at any later time. All I have clearly in my memory is a vision of a cloud of corn-fair hair, and two large cornflower eyes, and for some reason or other, I always want to say that she had a complexion like sweet peas. Perhaps I saw her at some time with a big bunch of cream-and-pink sweet peas in her arms, or standing in a garden with a lot of sweet peas in it, and felt that the delicate blend of colours and scents was a perfect setting for her. But all my memories of those early visits are like that – both actual and dim, like the haze of heat that used to soften the fair surface of the far meadows across the river, or the swarms of gnats rising and sinking hazily over the reeds below the bridge. I am sure I saw my uncle's stableman, Marky Fenelon, quite clearly, a little man with a face all composed of marbles, from his blackberry eyes to his crumpled chin or his tightly wound ears; but when I heard that he was a Palatine I never asked what it meant and did not care. I was very clearly aware of Nancy Coogan, big, bustling, bosomy, bare-armed and with a laugh like a thunderclap, but when I gathered somehow that she and Marky were courting and would marry some day all that this *some day* meant to me was Never. Is all childhood made up of facts of nature that are accepted beyond questioning? Perhaps mine was prolonged. When I was thirteen I was so vague as to what marrying meant that I much amused Nancy by asking her why some ladies are called Miss and some Mrs. She laughed and said the misses are the ones that miss, which I thought very clever indeed.

One reason why Noreen and my clearer memories of Newbridge go together is that she focused my holidays for me. She was their one clear centre from which everything went outward and to which everything returned. For after I was ten she became as certain and fixed a part of those visits as my first sight of the elongated Main Street of Newbridge, with the walls of the cavalry barracks all along one side of it and the sutlers' shops all along the other; or the peaceful sound of the gun wagons jingling along the dusty roads – they suddenly sounded less peaceful the year the Great War broke out; or the happy moment of arrival at the farm when I would run to meet Marky Fenelon in the wide, cobbled yard and at once hand him his ritual present of a pound of sailor's twist, bought for him by my father; or – one of the happiest moments of all – when I would run into the flagged kitchen to Nancy with her ritual present, which was always a lacy blouse bought in some port like Gibraltar, or Naples or Genoa. At the sight of me she would let out a welcoming roar of laughter, squash me up against her great, soft, bulging bosom, give me a smacking kiss and lift me, laughing and shrieking, high in the air until my head nearly touched the ceiling.

It was the year in which I asked my famous question about the difference between misses and missuses that I also felt the first faintest, least stir of questioning interest in Nancy's and Marky's marathon courtship. It was really no more than an idle question and I had only a small interest in the answer. That day she was making soda bread on the kitchen table and I was sitting up on the end of the table watching her knead and pound the dough.

'Nancy!' I said pertly. 'What's up with you at all that you're not marrying Marky? When are you going to marry him? Marry him tomorrow, Nancy! Go on, Nancy! Will you marry him tomorrow?'

She let out one of her wild laughs and began to scrape the dough from her fingers and fling the scrapings down on the kneading board, saying gaily with each flap of her hands:

'This year! Next year! Sometime! Never!'

'Is it the way, Nancy, that you're not in love with Marky?'

This time her laughter was a quarry blast.

'God love you, you poor child, that has nothing at all to do with it. It's just that he doesn't like having Noreen living with us. Now, go off and play with the cat,' she added crossly, and began to carve a deep cross into the flattened loaf. At once I wanted to stab her cake myself and began begging her for the knife. Anyway, this talk about Noreen and Marky merely meant what I had always known, that they would all be always there waiting for me at the start of every holiday.

One reason why I know I was thirteen that year was that the next time I went to stay with Uncle Gerry I was fifteen, and this I know because I very soon found out that those two extra years made a great difference to all of us. What made the difference was that in my fourteenth year I spent a long summer spell with my three Feehan cousins, some seven or eight miles away from the Newbridge farm over on the plain of the Curragh. There I had another uncle, Ken Feehan, who had some sort of job in connection with the racecourse.

The Curragh is famous for two things, its racecourse on one side of the plain and on the other the extended military settlement, which seems to outline the farthest edge of green with the long faint stroke of a red pencil. This settlement is still known as the Camp, long after its original tent canvas has been transformed into barrack squares in red brick, wooden huts, tin chapels and tin shops. Sheltering belts of stunted firs have now been planted along its entire length to protect it from the bitter winds blowing down from the mountains, whose slow drum roll closes the view to the southeast. From the door of my Uncle Ken's house, a long, whitewashed cottage or bungalow near the grandstand, we looked southeast at the far-off red pencil-line across a rolling expanse of short grass, empty except for a few cropping sheep, scattered tufts of furze and an occasional car slowly beetling along the road that crosses the Curragh from Newbridge to the south.

It was an empty place for three girls to live in. It is also to the point that the plain is of great age. The couple of roads that cross it are the old woolpack roads into Danish Dublin. It is known that the distant finger of the round tower of Kildare, to the west, was grey with age in the twelfth century. There was a racecourse here some two thousand years ago. Weapons of the Stone Age have been dug up in various parts of the plain. I like to think of this silent antiquity whenever I think of Philly, the eldest of my three cousins, standing at night at the door of the cottage – it is the way I always remember her now – staring across the plain at the only thing there that really interested her, the remote lights of the military camp. Whether the Camp had always excited her or not I do not know, but when I first met her, after the outbreak of the war, everything about it did – the news of departing or arriving regiments, the crackle of gunfire from the pits, the distant flash of a heliograph on bright days, the faint sound of regimental bands borne to us on the south-easterly wind. Standing there at the cottage door, she would talk endlessly of all the handsome and brave poor boys fighting and falling at that very moment on the plains of Flanders. She inferred the whole war from the flash of a mirror, the short rattle of rifle fire, the faint beating of drums, a wavering bugle call. She was eighteen.

I have no doubts at all about Philly's looks. She was not pretty but she was not plain. I grant that her nose was a bit peaky, her teeth slightly prominent, her figure almost skinny; but she had two lively brown eyes like an Italian girl, and her dark, shining hair was combed slick back from her prominent profile with the effect of a figurehead on a ship's prow. Her lower lip was always moistened by her upper teeth, her hands were nervous, her laughter on a hair trigger, her moods unpredictable and turning as rapidly as a trout in a stream; and she was a magnificent liar. This, I see, is as much an implication of her nature as a description of her appearance, but it is how she struck everybody who met her – an unflattering impression dispelled completely in one second.

That I have no wish to do more than mention her two sisters, Moll and Una, may suggest further the force of her personality. She overshadowed them completely, although both of them were capable and pleasing girls. She bullied Moll all the time and she forced all the housework on her simply by refusing to do her own share of it. Poor Moll, a soft, rotund, pouting girl, was no match for her and never did anything in self-defence except complain feebly, weep a little, then laugh despairingly and with a wag of her bottom go on cheerfully with her double chores. Philly did not need to bully Una, a gentle, fair-flaxen girl of about my own age – she was too young and delicate for bullying, cycled into Newbridge every day to school at the local convent, and studied endlessly when at home. I think she had realized very early that the cottage was a place to get out of as quickly as possible.

I liked the three of them, but I far preferred Philly. She was more fun, and I liked the streak of boyish devilment in her that always made her ready for any escapade. I suppose she suffered me as being better company than none, and I also suppose that the main thing in my favour was that although a child to her eyes I was at least male. This is not merely an unkind remark. Her reputation had preceded my meeting with her. Back in Newbridge the general attitude to her was that she was a foolish virgin. At the mention of her name my Uncle Gerry had just phewed out a long, contemptuously good-humoured breath. My aunt laughed at her. Once she made the witty and shrewd remark: 'That girl has far too many beaus to her string.' Nancy sniffed mockingly, 'That featherhead!'; but she may have jealously compared her to her own adored Noreen. Marky said, 'Aha! A bold lassie!' Noreen was, by turns, respectfully and scornfully silent, but, young as I was, I smelled envy.

As for her own sisters, they admired her and feared her and did not love her. They assured me privately that her list of boys was as long as my arm. ('Boys' was a popular word at that time – the 'boys' at the Front, our 'boys' in Flanders, and so on.) Their list included a rich trainer from the County Meath, a subaltern from the Camp, a jockey, a farmer from behind Kildare, a publican's son in Newbridge, a young lawyer from Dublin, even a stableboy from the stables of one of the wealthy trainers who, then as now, lived in half-timbered houses all around the edge of the plain behind white rails and clipped privet hedges. I gathered that all of these beaus were met on race days, in the enclosure, on the members' stand, in the restaurant, to all of which places, because of her father, she had complete access. There was more than a suggestion that she met her admirers on varying terms, playing whatever role pleased her fancy and suited their class. Certainly, those days when everybody of her own class swarmed on the open plain outside the rails and only the comparatively few paid to go inside them, the daughter of an employee of the Turf Club would have had to present herself very well indeed to be accepted by a lieutenant, a lawyer or a trainer.

I was torn this way and that by her. In loyalty to Newbridge I knew I should think her a figure of fun, and I could see that she was a little bully and a shrew, but she would sweep me off my feet whenever she started to talk about that Camp, whose lights flickered at night across an empty plain. She turned it into a magic doorway to the world. In Newbridge, everything, I have said, had been actual but hazy. When she talked to me about the real world I heard Life begin to paw its stable floor.

'Listen, lad! When you grow up take the King's shilling! Be a soldier! See the world!' And then, with her wide, wild, white-toothed laugh: 'Or, if it has to be, see the next world!'

I shall never have a dim or hazy notion of Philly Feehan as long as I remember the baking day when the four of us stood at the door of the cottage, the racecourse behind us as empty as a ballroom on the morning after a dance, the plain before us as empty as a bed at noon, and watched a small, slow cloud of dust move at marching pace from the Camp towards the railway station at Kildare, and heard the clear rattle of the parting snare drums. She shocked us all by suddenly crying out with passion, her brown eyes fixed on the little creeping dust cloud, her face pale under her shiny, black coif:

'I wish to God Almighty I was a bloody hussar!'

She taught me how to smoke. I drank my first beer with her in a hotel bar across the plain in Kilcullen. She gave me my first lesson in dancing. Looking back at her now, I see why her type of girl was the ideal of the soldiers of the Nineteen-fourteen War. They had been made to think of themselves as 'boys'. Their ideal woman was the young virgin, still with her hair down, the Flapper, a blend of devilment and innocence – their most highly desired antithesis to rain-filled trenches, mud above their puttees, and shells whining and exploding over their heads all day long.

So, you can guess why my next visit to Newbridge was different from any that went before. I was now turned fifteen. Noreen was eighteen. The others were beyond the years. They behaved to me as always, but I was not the same with them. I had become wary. It began the minute I arrived. When my Uncle Gerry drove the old tub-trap into the cobbled yard through the big tarred gates opened by Marky immediately he heard the familiar clop of the pony coming along the road, I handed the ritual pound of twist over the side to Marky, alighted, asked the usual questions, said 'I suppose ye're not married yet?' and then, as if on an afterthought, 'Oh, and how's our little Noreen these days?'

She must have done something to annoy him specially that day because he said grimly and shortly:

'Oh, very well, I believe! A bit rakish, now and again! But very well. In the best of health.'

I was alert at once.

'In what way rakish, Marky?' I laughed innocently.

'Ah!' He shook his head upward. If he had been a horse I would have heard the rattle of the bit and seen the yellow teeth. 'I suppose it might be through having no father to keep her in order.'

I nodded in sage agreement.

'How long is it now, Marky, since he died?'

He was untackling the pony, detaching the traces from the hames, his face against the pony's neck, but though I could not see him I knew from his voice that he was not going to pursue the subject.

'Well!' he growled into the pony's back. 'It was all a long time ago. Nancy's inside expecting you.'

He could hardly have said it plainer. I went indoors to her and produced the usual Italian blouse. She hugged me and kissed me, but I was too grown-up now to be lifted to the ceiling, and I hugged her back hard and thought she had fine eyes and was a damn handsome woman yet. Finally I said it:

'And how's Noreen these days?'

She turned back to the table and gently lifted the white silk blouse and said in a thick, cosy voice:

''Tis lovely. 'Twill suit Noreen down to the ground.'

'But,' I protested, 'it's for you! My father sent it for you.'

'Tshah! What do I want with finery? I'm gone beyond fineries. But,' smiling fondly, and lifting up the blouse again by the points of the shoulders to look it all over, 'Noreen will look a masher in that.'

No age is at once so insensitive and so sensitive as adolescence. It is one reason why young people are so exasperating to adults. I looked at her with curiosity, oblivious of her maternal devotion, and elegantly leaning against the table I ventured:

'Nancy! If you were married the three of ye would be as happy as three kittens in a basket. And Marky would be a father to Noreen.'

She dropped the blouse in a silken heap, gave me a sharp look and flounced to the fireplace.

'Noreen,' she said to the range, banging in the damper, 'doesn't want him as long as she has me! Anyway, since he won't have both of us he can have neither of us. Have you seen your aunt yet? She'll be expecting you.'

The flick of her skirt frightened me. I did not know what I had touched, but it felt red-hot. All I knew was that this prolonged courtship of theirs was going, if not gone, on the rocks.

That first day I did not run down the road in search of Noreen as I would have done two years before. I walked down to where Coshea's Boreen comes out on River Road and I came on her there, beyond the laundry, leaning over the wall, showing the hollow backs of her knees, chewing a bit of straw, looking across the river at the meadows and the Dublin road beyond them. I stole up behind her, slipped my arm about her waist and said gaily, 'Hello, Sis!'

She just glanced at me and said:

'Do you mind removing your arm?'

'Oho!' Very loftily. 'Touch me not, eh?'

I was so mad I could have spat in her eye, but I pretended nothing – I would not give her that much satisfaction. Instead, I started chatting away about what I had been doing since I saw her two summers ago. She kept chewing the straw and looking idly across the river. I do not remember what precisely I said that made her begin to pay heed to me except that it was my idea of a gentle probe about Marky and her mother, but it made her give me a slow, mocking smile that said, as plainly and scornfully as if she had spoken the actual words of an American phrase that was beginning to be current at the time: 'Well, and what do you know?' – meaning that I had surprised her, and that I knew nothing, not only about Marky and her mammy but about Everything in General, and that I could bloody-well stop pumping her and go away and find it all out for myself the way she had done. I expected her to say at any moment, 'Hump off, kid!' She conveyed it silently. Women do not talk to small boys.

If I had had any pride I would have walked away from her. But at fifteen years and a couple of months you are so frantic to know all about Everything in General that you have no pride, only lots of cunning. I said, very sadly:

'I suppose, Noreen, you think I'm only a kid?'

'How old are you?' she asked, with just a faint touch of sympathy in her voice.

'Going on to sixteen. But everybody,' I said bitterly, 'talks to me as if I were still ten. Have a fag?'

I flashed out my new mock-silver cigarette case. I observed with satisfaction the way she glanced down the road towards the bridge and the end of the Main Street, and then turned and leaned her back on the wall and glanced idly up Cat Lane before saying, in a bored voice:

'I suppose, really, I might as well.'

I noted also that she smoked the way all girls smoke who are not smokers, continually corking and uncorking her mouth. I kept up the role of downtrodden youth:

''Tis well for you, Noreen. I only wish I was eighteen. You can do what you like. My da would leather hell out of me if he caught me smoking. The way he talks to me about my stamina and my muscles you'd think he wants me to be another Jack Johnson. Would Nancy be cross with you?'

'I'd like to see her!' she boasted.

'I know a girl in Dublin who smokes thirty a day.'

This was too much for her.

'You know nothing about girls!'

'Oho! We grow up fast in Dublin!'

I blew smoke down my nose and turned around and leaned over the river wall and spat in the river. She also turned and blew smoke down her nose and spat in the river. For a moment or two she looked across at the golden meadows. Then:

'I'm engaged to be married.'

I was shocked upright.

'You can't be! Not at eighteen! You're too young!'

'I won't get married for a year or two, of course. But I'll get married when I'm twenty. You don't think I'm going to hang around here tied to my ma's apron strings all my bloomin' life?'

'Where's your engagement ring?'

'It's a secret yet,' she said, with another slow, hot look.

I looked at her for a while, torn between disbelief and a disappointment that had something in it of despair. Then I let my cigarette fall into the river. It was like a fellow throwing down his gun. She said:

'Come on and we'll walk down by the weirs.'

I walked by her side until we came to a hawthorn in full spate, listening to her telling me all about her boy. He was a sergeant on the Curragh. He cycled over from the Camp whenever he was off duty and she went out to meet him halfway. He was not going to remain a sergeant for long; he was 'going for an officer', and when he got his commission they would live in London. I asked her if Nancy knew about all this. It was the only thing I said that upset her.

'If you say one word to her,' she threatened, 'I'll cut the thripes out of you.'

After a bit I risked saying:

'If he saw us together now would he be jealous?'

She was pleased to laugh, condescendingly.

'I'd love to see him jealous. He's simply mad about me.'

And she drowned me with talk of the life she was having now as his 'belle', and the life she would have after she was married, until it was I who became mad with jealousy. Do you doubt it? Even if I *was* only fifteen and three months? Dear Heaven! Does nobody in the world know how old it is to be fifteen and three months? Whenever now I see a group of boys returning, say after holidays, to school, of any age between twelve and eighteen, I look most carefully into their faces in search of eyes that correspond to my unalterable concept of fifteen and three months. I look at myself through those eyes. I see my own frustration in them. For how can anybody who has to come close to them not feel their helplessness? Each of them is imprisoned in childhood and no one can tell him how to escape. Each of them must, blind-eyed, gnaw his way out, secretly and unaided. That they may be the eyes of boys who are mathematically fourteen, seventeen, even (I have met them) nineteen does not matter. All that matters is the fear of being on a brink and not knowing what is beyond it. At certain moments all through our lives we touch a point where ignorance is teetering on the brink of some essential revelation which we fear as much as we need it. These brinks, these barriers, these *No Road* signs recur and recur. They produce our most exhausting and hateful dreams. They tell us every time that we have to be born all over again, grow, change, free ourselves yet once again. Each teetering moment is as terrible as the imaginary point of time in Eastern philosophy when a dying man, who knows that within a few seconds he will be reincarnated, clings to life in terror of his next shape or dies in the desire to know it. The particular tenderness attaching to the age which I call fifteen-and-three-months is that it is the first of many such steps and trials and must affect the nature of all that follow.

Since that July I have been in love half a dozen times, but I have never felt anything since like the tearing torment of those few weeks of summer. How I used to fawn on this creature, whose beauty, I now know, was an illusion! How I used to flatter this girl, whom, I was so soon to realize, I should never have trusted, merely to be allowed to sit beside her and secretly feel the edge of her skirt!

'And does he take you to many dances in the Camp, Noreen? But where do you get the dance dresses? I'd love to see you dressed for a dance! You must look smashing! But where do you get this little card that you write the dances on? Did you say that it is a pink pencil that's attached to it? By a pink thread? You didn't *really* mean, did you, Noreen, that they have *six* wineglasses?'

Her least word could crush me like a moth. But from that summer on she had a power over all of us that was like a tyrant's. One night when Nancy flounced in with the supper and banged down the teapot, and whisked out again with a flick of her tail, my uncle said crossly, 'What's up with that one now?' – implying that things had been 'up with' her before now; my aunt shot a glance at me and said, 'Our ladyship is gone to the pictures without taking Nancy. And Marky is gone off to a whist drive.' I wonder they didn't notice me. Cinema, indeed! I saw the road to the Curragh, dark, secret, scented. Thinking of that sergeant, I must have had eyes like two revolvers. Yet I never realized the extent of Nancy's miseries and suspicions until, one day, she frightened me by saying:

'What are you always mooning about for by yourself? You have no life in you at all this year. Was it you I saw wandering out the road by yourself the other night?'

I knew then that she also had been wandering along the roads at dark, searching for her lamb.

For three whole despairing weeks I did not see Noreen at all. Then, quite suddenly, one Sunday morning I collapsed at Mass. My uncle's doctor diagnosed my illness as acute anaemia, but I am satisfied now that it was a traumatic illness. On August the ninth I was sent home. My father got three months' leave to be near me, and I remained at home under his care for the rest of the summer and most of the autumn. Then, towards the end of October, I began to get a bit brighter in myself when he said that I should go to the Feehans and he would join me there for Christmas with his brother Kenneth, whom he had not seen for some years. I argued to myself that Newbridge would be only a few miles away and that I could more tactfully spy out the land from the slopes of the Curragh. As it happened, things turned out very differently from the way I expected.

I had not reckoned with the weather. To understand this, you should see the place as I did that November. In the winter the Curragh seems older and wider. The foggy air extends its size by concealing its boundaries. The grass is amber, as if from the great age of the plain. For one week that November a sprinkle of snow fell almost every day, so that all the bottoms were white and the crowns of their slopes were melted green. At dusk the whole plain seemed to surge against the glimmering cliffs of the distant Camp and only the lights of a travelling car would then restore the earth to its natural solidity. In the cottage life became as restricted as aboard a ship. Only easygoing Moll was content, her tubby figure always moving busily through the pale glow of the house.

On most days there was little to do but watch the horses at the morning workouts – whenever a horse halted steam enveloped its jockey – or, if the air cleared, walk across to the Camp. It was always Philly who proposed this expedition – no other walk appealed to her – even if we did nothing when we got there except buy some trifle at the stores, such as the latest copy of the *Strand* or the *Red Magazine*, or, if she had the money, she might treat herself to a small bottle of scent. Her favourite, I remember, was some allegedly Oriental perfume called Phul-Nana. We might go into the red-painted tin chapel to say a prayer for the boys. Its candles were as calm as light that had gone to sleep, its tin roof creaking faintly in the wind.

I had always thought the Camp a bleak and empty place. During the winter it was as blank and cold as a plate of sheet iron, and as silent as an abandoned factory building. One wondered where all the soldiers were. It was so silent that it was startling to hear a lorry zooming up the hill towards the tower with its Union Jack hanging soggily from the flagstaff. After the lorry had passed into the Camp there was a ghostliness about the long tracks that it had left behind it on the slight snow. Noreen had talked about 'all the fun' that took place here in the winter. When I asked Philly where all the fun was, she said crossly that it all took place at night. I could only imagine, or over-imagine, its supposed liveliness at those hours when she and I would stand in the porch of the cottage gazing fixedly at its flickering until the cold defeated her curiosity and desire.

After about three weeks I suddenly began to feel one night that something had happened between us, standing there under the porch, watching those distant fireflies, sometimes talking, sometimes hardly speaking at all. At first it had the feeling of some form of complicity or collusion. I even wondered whether it might not be that the years between us had dwindled since I last stayed in the cottage. She had been eighteen then. I had been fourteen, divided from her by childhood. Now that she was twenty and I on the brink of sixteen there was barely a rivulet between us. I noted too that she had recently begun to converse more seriously with me. Perhaps that was merely because she was bored, or perhaps it was because I no longer felt obliged by loyalty to Newbridge to think of her as a comic figure, and so felt a greater sympathy with her. She continued to impress me in other ways. The season induced her to do something else that she had never done during the summer: to practise on the old upright Collard and Collard, with its pale-green, fluted satin shining behind its mahogany fretwork. Its strings sounded very tinkly during that snowy week. During the thaw they jangled. One night I found her reading, pencil in hand, and asked, 'What's the book?' It was Moran's *French Grammar*. She was trying unaided to learn the language. I noted the books she was reading – histories, travel books, famous biographies. She borrowed most of these from a widow, much older than herself, living in Kildare, a colonel's widow, whom she had met by chance at one of the meetings on the Curragh.

After I had heard about the colonel's widow I guessed the truth. With the diabolical shrewdness of my age I saw that she was playing, for me, the part of a woman of a certain age with nothing left for her to do but to encourage a young man who still had the world before him. She once said, 'Ah! If I only had my life to live over again!' But, in the end, this pretending to be so much older than she was worked directly opposite to her intentions. In her sense of the dramatic difference between our ages she let down all her defences, as if she were a very, very old lady thinking, 'Nothing that I can say can possibly matter from one so old to one so tender.' The result was inevitable. When a passionate sigh or a deliberate profanity led her to expose her hand I, quietly, read her hand and excited by what I saw encouraged her without guile. In proportion as she responded to the rising sap of my wonder she lapsed into sincerity and I achieved equality. It was for this unguarded moment that I was lying in wait, as my earlier experience with Noreen had taught me that I must if I wished to be treated as an equal.

I think she first realized how far she had lowered her defences the night when, as we sat alone over the parlour fire – Moll was singing in the kitchen, Uncle Ken in bed with his rheumatics and Una studying in her bedroom – I looked at her after she had told some wildly romantic story of army life in India and said, in a tone of voice with which I hoped her older admirers had made her familiar:

'Philly, you have lovely hair. I'm sorry you put it up since I was here before. I'd love to see you letting it all ripple down your back.'

I knew by the start she gave and the abrupt way she said, 'My hair is all right,' that she had recognized the tone. When I kept looking at her with a curved smile and lowering eyes, I was gratified to see the frightened look in her eyes. It meant that I was able to interest her not as a boy but as a man, so that I was merely amused to see her trying to flounder back quickly to the role of the grown woman talking graciously to the young boy.

I was content with this new situation for about a week: that is to say, I played the role of the sixteen-year-old pupil with a twenty-year-old teacher who knows that he is attracted by her, but who feels that it is as much her duty to keep him in his place as it is her pleasure to hold his admiration. Suddenly, I got tired of it. One night, in a temper at some correction she had made, I shut the book with a bang, glared at her, and said that I preferred to work alone.

'But,' she smiled sweetly, 'I only want to *help* you!'

'I don't want you to *help* me!' I cried haughtily.

'Believe me, my child,' she said sarcastically, 'you need a great deal of help.'

'Not from you!' I retorted.

'Master Know-all!'

'And I'm not a child!'

'You are a schoolboy.'

I screamed at her:

'I'm not. I'm not. I'm not.'

She flew into a rage herself.

'Be quiet! Remember that if you can't behave yourself you can't stay here!'

I swept the books from the table, and raced out of the parlour, and the cottage, into the garden, and so through the wicket gate straight on to the darkness and emptiness of the plain.

The night was frosty. Not only the Camp but the whole hollow plain was an iron dish. But I was not aware of the cold as I walked straight ahead, as hot with anger as a man might be with alcohol – that anger of resentment which makes young people cry at the very injustice of being born. It began to die in me only as the exhaustion induced by constant stumbling in the dark, the splendour of the sky, the magnitude of the plain and the cold night air worked on me to cool my rage and fan my desire.

I lay down under the shelter of a furze clump, between the Camp lights and the cottage lights. Once I thought I heard the coughing of a sheep. Then I realized that I was hearing only the wind rattling through some withered thistles near my feet. The wind, the darkness, the stars, the lights, the size of the plain dwindled me and isolated me. My isolation turned all these human and sky-borne lights into my guides and companions. When my head rolled to the north to the lone cottage, to the south to the windwashed campfires, and looked straight up to the stars of the Charioteer, I remember shouting out in my excitement, without knowing what I meant, 'The lights! The lights!' – as if I wanted some pyrotechnic convulsion in nature to occur, some flashing voice to speak. Only the wind whispered. Only the dried thistles coughed.

It was long after midnight when I re-entered the garden. The cottage was quiet. She would have heard the sweetbriar squeaking over the porch, the soft snoring of her daddy, and after a little while, her bedroom door being opened. She must have thought it was Moll, because she said nothing. I heard her gasp when my hand fell on her bare arm, and I whispered:

'It's me, Philly.'

She sat up, whispering, 'What's wrong?' and I heard her fumbling with the matches.

'Don't light a light!' I begged.

'What is wrong?' she whispered again, and the rest of our talk was carried on in whispering in the dark.

'Philly, I don't want to fight with you.'

'That's all right, we both lost our tempers.'

'I'm very fond of you, Philly.'

'So am I, of you. Good night, now.'

'But I'm not a schoolboy.'

'Yes, yes. Go to your room now. Daddy will be raging if he hears you.'

'Philly! You are a grown woman. And I am *not* a boy.'

'I only said it to tease you.'

'Philly!' I could feel my heart pounding.

'Yes?'

'Kiss me!'

'If you don't go back to bed at once I will call Molly.'

'If you don't kiss me I'll run out of the house and never come back again. Never! Never again!'

(She said that my voice rose: 'You were sort of gasping. You were threatening me. I was sure daddy would hear.')

'If I give you one kiss will you go right back to bed?'

I still feel that first kiss, her parted lips, the gateways of the world opening, the stars over the plain shivering, the wind blowing, and her terror as she said:

'Now go!'

'Another!'

She struck a match, lit her candle, and saw me in my trousers, shirt and bare feet. She started to upbraid me, but I saw that she saw at a glance that she was no longer dealing with a boy. I sat on the side of her bed, filled with wonder and delight at her bare shoulders and her dark, shining hair down about them, and the knowledge that she was not looking at me as a boy nor speaking to me as a boy. She gripped my hand and she assured me that in future I would have to keep to myself or leave the house, that she knew now that she had been stupid and foolish to have treated me as a boy, because any woman should have known better, but that she understood now and she hoped I understood, so would I please realize that I was a man and behave like a man? And as she whispered, like this, so seriously, I stroked her bare forearm, and felt the trembling of it and the weakness entering into it, and so must she because she stretched out her clenched knuckles to the wall.

'I am going to call Molly!'

'Just one last kiss?' I begged, staring at the whiteness of her neck and bosom.

Still holding her knuckles to the wall:

'On your word of honour, you will go then?'

'On my word of honour.'

When we parted, two hours later, she upbraided me with a gentleness that affected me far more than anything else that had happened since our quarrel in the parlour.

I lay awake until I heard the cock crowing. I felt no triumph. My delight was chastened by its own wonder. If she thought that I was in love with her she was deluded. I was too supremely astonished by my adventure to be fully aware of her, and when we met in the morning and I looked at her as if she were a mirror I did not recognize myself. Totally unaware that what appealed to her in me was my utter innocence, taking her to be a woman who had seen strange places, known strange people, heard strange things that I had never seen, known or heard, fearing that she was aware only of my utter inexperience, I behaved unnaturally and self-consciously, hurting her cruelly by what I considered were the proper airs of any man of the world on such occasions. I spoke coolly to her, smiled cynically, once I even winked at her. Whatever I did I knew that I must conceal my ignorance from her; for during those two hours, lying close together, we had been as harmless as doves, as innocent as lambs, simply because I – as I thought then, but as I see now both of us – had not known what else to do.

Besides, I now needed above everything else a retirement into silence, secrecy, self-contemplation, spiritual digestion, a summoning of shocked resources. I put on my cap after breakfast, borrowed one of my uncle's walking sticks, put a cigarette into the side of my mouth, waved a 'Tol-lol' to the three girls, and spent the whole day wandering, blind and lost, about the back roads that lead into the great central bogland of Ireland, an earth-lake of purple heather, where you might tramp all day and see nothing stir except a snipe rising with a whir or, far away, a sloping pillar of blue peat-smoke from a turf-cutter's fire. Its emptiness suited my sense of lostness. I had no wish to arrive anywhere. I wanted to remain undestined. All I wanted was that my other lost self should come back to me. In much the same spirit I so obviously avoided every chance of being alone with her that she must, surely, have begun to ask herself, 'Does he loathe the sight of me?' just as I kept saying to myself, 'Does she despise me now? Did it really happen at all? Did she upbraid me, and push me away and draw me towards her again and again?' At last my awe began to defog. Passing her in the little corridor one afternoon, I gripped her hand and said, 'Tonight?' She nodded, then to my astonishment burst into tears, and slipped from me into her room.

That night the barriers rose between us at once. I was frightened by her silence into silence. I was repelled, even disgusted, by the stuffiness of the room, the smelly candle, the tousled bed, our humiliating stealth. We gripped one another at every creak, lying rigid to listen. I could have cried for rage when I was alone again. Our public behaviour became correspondingly gracious. It was of what I would now call a Byzantine formality, a Mandarin formality. My manner would not have shamed a grand seigneur; hers a princess. There also began between us a series of long, maundering talks about love and marriage which could come to no conclusion, which indeed could hardly have made sense since each of us was trying to instruct the other without exposing the fact that neither of us had anything to reveal.

The fact is only too obvious, we both had within us the same monstrous weapon of destruction. She had imagined too many romantic stories; I had imagined too luxuriantly; both of us had imagined outside ourselves. Fountains and flags and flowers were elsewhere, always elsewhere, under the Himalayas, on the plains of France, an eye-cast across the plain. So, when I asked her about those wonderful winter dances in the Camp and she admitted that she had not yet been to one, the thought had no sequence unfavourable to her because, after all, she *had* met a real lieutenant at the races. Still, her nature's lighthouse was not roving as it used to rove for me at the pier's end. What had attracted me in her had been the flare that said, 'This way to the open sea!' I could not avoid seeing that we had both suddenly become dependent: on this cottage (to which we had once turned our backs to look at the lights across the plain), on my uncle, on my father, on the few shillings that they yielded us for pocket money, on the stuffy little timber-lined room with the chamber pot under the bed, and the varnish blistered from the summer heat and one corner of the ceiling damp. The day she clutched me and said, miserably, 'Do you love me at all?' I realized that she had become dependent on me. My father came next day. I immediately asked him if I might go to the farm at Newbridge for Christmas, and I went there that very evening.

It was like going out of a dim room into full sunshine. I saw everything clearly. They had all been right about Philly; she was a silly featherhead, full of vapourings and nonsense. I no sooner mentioned the Camp to Noreen than she at once made me see it for what it was. Even during the two months while I had been at the cottage looking across at the Camp, she had cycled across there to three dances and she described them to me fully and simply. There was nothing now about pink cards, and pink pencils and six wineglasses; and when I cried, 'But you *told* me!' she only laughed and said she had been making fun of me. That sort of thing might happen in the officers' mess on a special occasion, such as a big dinner dance – she was not certain because she had never been to such an event – but I surely did not think that it was the form at the sergeants' mess? She said that if I wanted badly to take her to a dance there her man would arrange it. And it was clear that she meant this, and that she was now in the habit of going wherever she liked, and in every other way behaving like a grown young woman.

Within an hour I was under her spell again. She seemed to be more beautiful than ever. She was the actuality of all I had imagined Philly to be. But it was not only her beauty that held me now – that mane of sunlight about her head, her full lips the colour of a pale tea rose, her body that was just beginning to take on her mother's plump strength. Her real attraction for me now was her blunt matter-of-factness, her wilfulness, which produced more and more sighs from my aunt, and frowns from my uncle and growls from Marky, and – a thing I could never have expected – a sudden flood of tears from Nancy on the only occasion that she talked about her.

'But why?' I asked my uncle. 'Why?'

The solemnly pitying look he gave me said more than his words:

'Nancy gave up a great deal for that girl. I warned her! But nobody can save a mother from herself.'

I discussed it with Marky:

'People have to grow up!' I protested to him. 'Noreen must be near twenty.'

'I foresaw it,' he growled. 'And I was right.'

None of them understood her. And yet I could sympathise with them. There were times when I almost hated her myself, so greatly did I need her, and so well did she know it, and so ruthlessly did she exact the price of my need, day after day. When she started again to dodge me for days it was solely, I knew well, for the pleasure of making me realize how essential she was to me. I realized it only too well. Within two weeks the pattern of the previous summer began to repeat itself – one day made radiant by her company followed by three without her, so miserably blank by comparison that I could imagine that she had plotted the contrast; appointments made only to be broken, or kept briefly and summarily interrupted. It would not have been so humiliating if she had made it clear to me that I was only a foil or a fill-in for her sergeant; but there were days when she treated me as much more than that, and then, without warning, she would slap me down with those damned three years between us.

The end came after I had spent six whole, empty days cycling around the country desperately searching for her. On the afternoon of that fateful seventh day, just as the first suggestion of twilight was entering the chilly air, I turned down one of those aimless side lanes that lead under the railway towards the level bog. I had come there across the Curragh. After the plain, open as a giant lawn, this hollowed lane, deep under trees slung like hammocks from ditch to ditch, gave me a queer feeling of enclosure, secrecy and remoteness. I had been there once before during the summer, also in search of her, and I had then got exactly the same labyrinthine feeling that I was going underground. That summer day the lane had been a pool of tropical heat, a clot of mingled smells from the overgrown ditches teeming thickly with devil's bread, meadowsweet, loosestrife, cow-eyed daisies, greasy buttercups, purple scabious, great rusty stalks of dock, briars hooped like barbed wire, drooping hawks-beard. This winter evening these flowers and weeds were a damp catacomb of shrunken bones. The fallen leaves were squashy. The arms of the trees were darkly shrunken against the lowering sky. Once a bird scrabbled. Otherwise there was not the least sound. It became almost dark where the lane descended under a stone railway bridge before emerging to end at a wooden gate, grey and worm-eaten, leading out to the bog, now so vague in the half-light that all I saw of it clearly was the occasional eye of a pool catching the last gleams from the watery sky.

She stood with her back to me, leaning over the old gate, gazing out over the bog. She started when she heard my step. My heart was battering, but I managed to say, with a pretence of gaiety:

'Hello, Noreen! Waiting for your beau?'

'And what if I am, nosy?'

'Oho! Nothing at all! Is he letting you down tonight?'

For a second she seemed to bend and slacken, and I relished the sight. She recovered herself, with a wicked grin.

'You can be my beau tonight. You're not so awful-looking. You'd pass in a crowd, I suppose.'

I had leaned idly against the gate. I was wearing my school cap. She took it off, threw it on the ground and brushed back my hair with her palm. A brighter gleam flitted through the clouds. A bog pool glinted greenly behind her shoulder. The smells of the dank vegetation grew thicker. My breath came faster.

'You know, kid, if you did your hair properly . . . Have you no sweetie of your own?'

'Yes!' I said. 'Up in Dublin.'

'What's she like?'

I could only think of Philly, red-eyed from weeping. I could not talk about that goose to a girl who was going to marry a sergeant who would soon take his commission as an officer and carry her off to England, a married woman. I shook my head dumbly and gazed into her blue eyes.

'Well,' she said impatiently, 'what does *she* say to you when you walk her out? What do you say to her?' She suddenly dragged my arm behind her waist. 'Here! Suppose I was her, what would I be saying to you now?' I shivered at her touch. 'Go on!' she mocked.

'I don't think you'd say anything. You'd just look at me.'

She looked at me sidewards and upwards from under droopy lids.

'This way?'

'No!' I said furiously. 'More like . . . I dunno how! More like a sheep?'

She detached my arm irritably. Then she laughed at me pitilessly. Peremptorily she put my arm back again around her waist.

'You're a very timid courter. Say something to me. As if I was your girl.'

I whispered, seeing her cloud of flaxen hair against a pale star:

'You're like an angel, Noreen.'

She sighed a happy sigh that was almost a groan. She looked past me up the dark tunnel with heavy eyelids.

''Tis like the pictures,' she said sleepily. 'Go on.'

'I could pray to you, Noreen.'

'Go on,' she murmured, throatily, leaning against me.

'When I see the sun through the window in the priory I think of you, Noreen.'

Her eyes were closed. She muttered, as if barely awake:

'Why does nobody talk to me like that?'

'Doesn't your sergeant?'

She opened her eyes wide, blue-sky-wide, and stared at me enormously:

'What window?'

'The window of Mary Magdalen with the long golden hair.'

She pushed me away and roared laughing at me; perhaps, I now think, at the pair of us; and was there, I have sometimes wondered, a bitterness in her laughing?

'Honest to God you're a scream!' She quietened and looked seriously at me. 'You poor little bastard!' she said. 'I don't know what I'm going to do with you.'

She really did seem to be considering the problem, so that I felt a great warmth of happiness that she should be thinking kindly about me even if she was a grown woman and even if she still thought I was only a boy. Then she stiffened suddenly, and shoved me away. She had lifted her head like a bird that hears a warning screech from its mate.

'Hop it!' she rapped at me. 'Clear out!' – and began to clamber over the gate into the field beyond.

It did not occur to me to disobey. In a daze of shame I went slowly back up the lane to where I had thrown my bicycle against the ditch. Only when I was on the road did I remember my cap, and laying the bicycle aside I went back for it, thinking she had run off into the field beyond the gate. As I came to the bridge I saw them on the other side of the gate, framed by the stone arch, in one another's arms, their mouths locked. Knowledge turned me into a statue. He was not a sergeant. He was not even a private soldier. He was a little buttoned-up lump of a fellow with a coarse cap on his head, peaked upward so that what there was left of salvaged daylight on his little, wizened horse's face made me realize that he could only be a stableman like Marky . Fenelon. As I stood there, petrified, his fist clutched her yellow mop and slowly dragged her head backward. Her mouth fell open like the red gullet of a cat.

I slunk into the ditch. Then I crept away up the lane, jumped on my bicycle and rode off like a madman. I was aware of stars through black branches. Behind me, far away, across the plain, a bugle began to unfold its gay elaborate call. As it came and died away I imaged the illusory lights of the Camp flickering in the wind that had silenced the wavering notes, and I thought of that flickering line not as lights but as lies. Yet I did not feel anger, or disgust, I did not feel deceived, or betrayed, or derided. I felt only a hollow in me full of defeat, now and forever after. It was a secret moment. Nobody knew it. Nobody would ever know it. But as I rode through the Main Street of Newbridge, along one side of which the shops were now lighted, and the girls already parading the pavement, and the soldiers coming out of the barracks across the street, in twos and threes, for a night's pleasure, I kept my head lowered over the handle bars, as if I was afraid that somebody would guess my shame in my knowledge of my defeat.

I had wanted to know what there is to know; to possess life and be its master. The moment I found out that nobody knows, I had exposed myself to myself. I would never do it again. The shame of it was too much to bear. Like everybody else I would pretend for the rest of my life. I would compound; I would invent – poetry, religion, common sense, kindness, good cheer, the sigh, the laugh, the shrug, everything that saves us from having to admit that beauty and goodness exist here only for as long as we create and nourish them by the force of our dreams, that there is nothing outside ourselves apart from our imaginings.

I rode home. I was in nice time for supper. My uncle said:

'That's a fine complexion you have. Been cycling?'

'It was a grand day for it!' I smiled. 'And a grand night of stars.'

He winked at me and began mockingly to hum the barcarole from *Hoffman*.

The next morning as I passed the gate lodge Noreen came out, and with one of her slow, smiling looks, as of a fellow conspirator, she handed me my cap, wet, crumpled and muddy. When I unfolded it I found the silver track of a snail across the lining. I let it fall into the Liffey, where it slowly floated away.

I did not go down there again for a couple of years. By then I was doing medicine at the university. When my Uncle Gerry met me at the station he laughed loudly:

'By Gor, John, I hardly recognized you. They're after making a grand straight fellow out of you. You'd better stop growing up now and start growing out for a change.'

As I watched him lumbering into the old tub-trap I said:

'You're after getting a bit on the heavy side yourself, Uncle Gerry.'

'Anno Domini!' he said, flicking up the pony, who had also got so fat that he had rubbed the paint off the insides of the shafts.

As we trotted along the road I asked after my aunt, and Marky, and Nancy, and the farm, but what I wanted to get on to as quickly as I decently could was whether he had any tips for the July races. It was not until I was unpacking and came on my father's usual presents for Marky and Nancy that I remembered that Noreen had got married a few months back; for there were two Italian blouses this time, one white blouse for Nancy, and one pale-blue marked *For Noreen*, which I took to be a wedding token. I found Nancy in the kitchen, and I could see no great change in her, apart from a few grey streaks of hair, and that she was getting 'right loguey' too. She shouted with delight when she saw me:

'Aha! You're not a child any more! God be with the days when I used to throw you up to the ceiling. But I'm going to kiss you all the same.'

And we kissed with double-hearty smacks and laughs. Then I handed over the two blouses with a mock bow.

'With my papa's compliments, madame!'

'They're gorgeous!' she said, laying the two of them side by side. The arm of the blue fell on the arm of the white. Gently she lifted the blue sleeve and let it sink on its own blouse. 'I'll post it to her. You heard she went off from me in the heel of the hunt? Aye! She fell in with a soldier here in the barracks and followed him to London. It wouldn't surprise me to hear one of these days that his regiment was posted overseas, to India, or Africa or Egypt. Then she'll be gone from me entirely.'

She smiled, but it was a sad smile.

'I'm sorry, Nancy. You'll surely miss her.'

Her smile went. She said vehemently:

'I will not! There was a time when I'd have laid down my life for that girl. I don't care no more about her now than the child unborn.' She smiled sadly again. 'Ye used to be great pals at one time.'

'Yes,' I agreed shortly, and I was glad to turn round and see Marky darkening the doorway.

We greeted one another warmly. I handed him the sailor's twist. As we were flattering one another I wondered if I was expected to make the old joke about his getting married to Nancy, but that year I was in love with a girl at the university and he looked so grey and wizened and she looked so fat that the joke seemed rather stale and even a little unseemly. I got him to talk about the July races, because my uncle had said that he was interested in a horse called Flyaway, and he started to tell me all about it.

Suddenly, as we talked, there was a noise behind us, like a clatter of pigeons rising. It was Nancy rending the blue blouse from the top to bottom, tearing at it savagely again and again, her teeth bared, her eyes out on pins. Marky, undeflected, merely glanced at her and went on talking in his slow steady voice about Flyaway. We heard the bang of the range lid. Staring at him, I got the smell of burning silk. Marky, seeing that I was too dazed to listen, took me by the arm and, still talking about the horse, guided me out into the hot sun of the cobbled yard. I looked back at the kitchen door.

'Never heed her,' he said. 'She's upset. She feels very lonely in herself this long time.'

'Marky! Did Noreen get into trouble or something?'

'No! She just hoisted her sails, and off with her. It was just as well! Seeing her going off there every night with common fellows around the town, and poor Nancy in that kitchen sitting looking at the fire in the range . . .'

'Wasn't it a pity yourself and Nancy didn't make a match of it?'

He looked at me from under his grey eyebrows and said, quietly:

'And give it to say to everyone that I had another man's child under my roof?'

'What matter?' I cried. 'What matter?'

He shook his little bullet head slowly and slowly pronounced judgment:

'It does matter. I heard it said too often that no man nor beast ever loved their young with the fierce love of a woman for her by-child.' He tapped me lightly on the arm with the twist tobacco. 'If I was you I'd put ten shillings on Flyaway,' and he limped away about his affairs.

The natural way back into the house was through the kitchen. Nancy was standing by the range, with the poker in her fist and her greying head to the door. I knew she had heard the lifted latch, but she held her rounded back rigidly against me. I waited. She turned, looked at me and said coldly:

'Well? Do you want something?'

As I looked at her a bugle began to unfold its far-carrying notes from the distant barracks. Then its convoluted call wavered on the changing wind and died away. Did I hear the sparrows chirruping in the walled orchard? Did the ivy at the window rustle? I saw the evening star and the west was already a cold green. Did I smell decaying vegetation? It was the hour when the soldiers would soon be coming out to meet their girls. I made a feeble gesture with my hands, and walked off to another part of the house. I wanted badly to read about Flyaway.

All that happened over forty years ago. I have three children of my own now. One is fourteen, one is nearly sixteen, and the eldest is a few months over eighteen. The middle one is my son. When I happened to look at him the other night across the fire I saw what I felt to be a familiar look in his eyes and all this came back to me. After all, I have now come to the age when memories are meaningful – the age when a man knows that he has lived. The farm has descended to a second cousin, but my family goes down there now and again for a holiday. They tell me that the cottage on the Curragh is completely disappeared, knocked down to make room for a car park. When I talk to them about bugle calls they laugh at me and say: 'Daddy! Buglers, and drummer boys, and gun wagons and semaphores and all that sort of thing belong to the time of the Boer War.' They say you cannot see the lights of the Camp anymore because of the spruce and firs that have been planted there as a shelter belt. But I could always go to the Curragh for the races.

Neither trained horses nor wild horses would drag me down there. The only thing that would tempt me there would be to feel and smell the night over the plain. I daren't do it. I would still see the flickering lights. I would hear the wavering sound of a far-off bugle. And I would know that these things that I could neither see nor hear are the only reality.

# Two of a Kind

Maxer Creedon was not drunk, but he was melancholy-drunk, and he knew it and he was afraid of it.

At first he had loved being there in the jammed streets, with everybody who passed him carrying parcels wrapped in green or gold, tied with big red ribbons and fixed with berried holly sprigs. Whenever he bumped into someone, parcels toppled and they both cried 'Ooops!' or 'Sorree!' and laughed at one another. A star of snow sank nestling into a woman's hair. He smelled pine and balsam. He saw twelve golden angels blaring silently from twelve golden trumpets in Rockefeller Plaza. He pointed out to a cop that when the traffic lights down Park Avenue changed from red to green the row of white Christmas trees away down the line changed colour by reflection. The cop was very grateful to him. The haze of light on the tops of the buildings made a halo over Fifth Avenue. It was all just the way he knew it would be, and he slopping down from Halifax in that damned old tanker. Then, suddenly, he swung his right arm in a wild arc of disgust.

'To hell with 'em! To hell with everybody!'

'Ooops! Hoho, there! Sorree!'

He refused to laugh back.

'Poor Creedon!' he said to himself. 'All alone in New York, on Christmas-bloody-well-Eve, with nobody to talk to, and nowhere to go only back to the bloody old ship. New York all lit up. Everybody all lit up. Except poor old Creedon.'

He began to cry for poor old Creedon. Crying, he reeled through the passing feet. The next thing he knew he was sitting up at the counter of an Eighth Avenue drugstore sucking black coffee, with one eye screwed-up to look out at the changing traffic lights, chuckling happily over a yarn his mother used to tell him long ago about a place called Ballyroche. He had been there only once, nine years ago, for her funeral. Beaming into his coffee cup, or looking out at the changing traffic lights, he went through his favourite yarn about Poor Lily:

'Ah, wisha! Poor Lily! I wonder where is she atall, atall now. Is she dead or alive. It all happened through an Italian who used to be going from one farm to another selling painted statues. Bandello his name was, a handsome black divil o' hell! I never in all my born days saw a more handsome divil. Well, one wet, wild, windy October morning what did she do but creep out of her bed and we all sound asleep and go off with him. Often and often I heard my father say that the last seen of her was standing under the big tree at Ballyroche Cross, sheltering from the rain, at about eight o'clock in the morning. It was Mikey Clancy the postman saw her. "Yerrah, Lily girl," says he, "what are you doing here at this hour of the morning?" "I'm waiting," says she, "for to go into Fareens on the milk cart." And from that day to this not a sight nor a sound of her no more than if the earth had swallowed her. Except for the one letter from a priest in America to say she was happily married in Brooklyn, New York.'

Maxer chuckled again. The yarn always ended up with the count of the years. The last time he heard it the count had reached forty-one. By this year it would have been fifty.

Maxer put down his cup. For the first time in his life it came to him that the yarn was a true story about a real woman. For as long as four traffic-light changes he fumbled with this fact. Then, like a man hearing a fog signal come again and again from an approaching ship, and at last hearing it close at hand, and then seeing an actual if dim shape, wrapped in a cocoon of haze, the great idea revealed itself.

He lumbered down from his stool and went over to the telephones. His lumpish finger began to trace its way down the grey pages among the Brooklyn *Ban's*. His finger stopped. He read the name aloud. *Bandello, Mrs Lily*. He found a dime, tinkled it home, and dialled the number slowly. On the third ring he heard an old woman's voice. Knowing that she would be very old and might be deaf, he said very loudly and with the extra-meticulous enunciation of all drunks:

'My name is Matthew Creedon. Only my friends all call me Maxer. I come from Limerick, Ireland. My mother came from the townland of Ballyroche. Are you by any chance my Auntie Lily?'

Her reply was a bark:

'What do you want?'

'Nothing at all! Only I thought, if you are the lady in question, that we might have a bit of an ould gosther. I'm a sailor. Docked this morning in the Hudson.'

The voice was still hard and cold:

'Did somebody tell you to call me?'

He began to get cross with her.

'Naw! Just by a fluke I happened to look up your name in the directory. I often heard my mother talking about you. I just felt I'd like to talk to somebody. Being Christmas and all to that. And knowing nobody in New York. But if you don't like the idea, it's okay with me. I don't want to butt in on anybody. Good-bye.'

'Wait! You're sure nobody sent you?'

'Inspiration sent me! Father Christmas sent me!' (She could take that any way she bloody-well liked!) 'Look! It seems to me I'm buttin' in. Let's skip it.'

'No. Why don't you come over and see me?'

Suspiciously he said:

'This minute?'

'Right away!'

At the sudden welcome of her voice all his annoyance vanished.

'Sure, Auntie Lily! I'll be right over. But, listen, I sincerely hope you're not thinking I'm buttin' in. Because if you are...'

'It was very nice of you to call me, Matty, very nice indeed. I'll be glad to see you.'

He hung up, grinning. She was just like his mother – the same old Limerick accent. After fifty years. And the same bossy voice. If she was a day she'd be seventy. She'd be tall, and thin, and handsome, and the real lawdy-daw, doing the grand lady, and under it all she'd be as soft as mountain moss. She'd be tidying the house now like a divil. And giving jaw to ould Bandello. If he was still alive.

He got lost on the subway, so that when he came up it was dark. He paused to have another black coffee. Then he paused to buy a bottle of Jamaica rum as a present for her. And then he had to walk five blocks before he found the house where she lived. The automobiles parked under the lights were all snow-covered. She lived in a brownstone house with high steps. Six other families had rooms in it.

The minute he saw her on top of the not brightly lit landing, looking down at him, he saw something he had completely forgotten. She had his mother's height, and slimness, and her wide mouth, but he had forgotten the pale, liquid blue of the eyes and they stopped him dead on the stairs, his hand tight on the banister. At the sight of them he heard the soft wind sighing over the level Limerick plain and his whole body shivered. For miles and miles not a sound but that soughing wind that makes the meadows and the wheat fields flow like water. All over that plain, where a crossroads is an event, where a little, sleepy lake is an excitement. Where their streams are rivers to them. Where their villages are towns. The resting cows look at you out of owls' eyes over the greasy tips of the buttercups. The meadow grass is up to their bellies. Those two pale eyes looking down at him were bits of the pale albino sky stretched tightly over the Shannon plain.

Slowly he climbed up to meet her, but even when they stood side by side she was still able to look down at him, searching his face with her pallid eyes. He knew what she was looking for, and he knew she had found it when she threw her bony arms around his neck and broke into a low, soft wailing just like that Shannon wind.

'Auntie! You're the living image of her!'

On the click of a finger she became bossy and cross with him, hauling him by his two hands into her room:

'You've been drinking! And what delayed you? And I suppose not a scrap of solid food in your stomach since morning?'

He smiled humbly.

'I'm sorry, Auntie. 'Twas just on account of being all alone, you know. And everybody else making whoopee.' He hauled out the peace offering of the rum. 'Let's have a drink!'

She was fussing all over him immediately.

'You gotta eat something first. Drinking like that all day, I'm ashamed of you! Sit down, boy. Take off your jacket. I got coffee, and cookies, and hamburgers, and a pie, I always lay in a stock for Christmas. All of the neighbours visit me. Everybody knows that Lily Bandello keeps an open house for Christmas, nobody is ever going to say Lily Bandello didn't have a welcome for all her friends and relations at Christmastime . . .'

She bustled in and out of the kitchenette, talking back to him without stop.

It was a big, dusky room, himself looking at himself out of a tall, mirrored wardrobe piled on top with cardboard boxes. There was a divan in one corner as high as a bed, and he guessed that there was a washbasin behind the old peacock-screen. A single bulb hung in the centre of the ceiling, in a fluted glass bell with pink frilly edges. The pope over the bed was Leo XIII. The snowflakes kept touching the bare windowpanes like kittens' paws trying to get in. When she began on the questions, he wished he had not come.

'How's Bid?' she called out from the kitchen.

'Bid? My mother? Oh, well, of course, I mean to say . . . My mother? Oh, she's grand, Auntie! Never better. For her age, of course, that is. Fine, fine out! Just like yourself. Only for the touch of the old rheumatism now and again.'

'Go on, tell me about all of them. How's Uncle Matty? And how's Cis? When were you down in Ballyroche last? But, sure, it's all changed now I suppose, with electric light and everything up to date? And I suppose the old pony and trap is gone years ago? It was only last night I was thinking of Mikey Clancy the postman.' She came in, planking down the plates, an iced Christmas cake, the coffeepot: 'Go on! You're telling me nothing.'

She stood over him, waiting, her pale eyes wide, her mouth stretched. He said:

'My Uncle Matty? Oh well, of course, now, he's not as young as he was. But I saw him there last year. He was looking fine. Fine out. I'd be inclined to say he'd be a bit stooped. But in great form. For his age, that is.'

'Sit in. Eat up. Eat up. Don't mind me. He has a big family now, no doubt?'

'A family? Naturally! There's Tom. And there's Kitty, that's my Aunt Kitty, it *is* Kitty, isn't it, yes, my Auntie Kitty. And . . . God, I can't remember the half of them.'

She shoved the hamburgers towards him. She made him pour the coffee and tell her if he liked it. She told him he was a bad reporter.

'Tell me all about the old place!'

He stuffed his mouth to give him time to think.

'They have twenty-one cows. Holsteins. The black and white chaps. And a red barn. And a shelter belt of pines. 'Tis lovely there now to see the wind in the trees, and when the night falls the way the lighthouse starts winking at you, and . . .'

'What lighthouse?' She glared at him. She drew back from him. 'Are ye daft? What are you dreaming about? Is it a lighthouse in the middle of the County Limerick?'

'There is a lighthouse! I saw it in the harbour!'

But he suddenly remembered that where he had seen it was in a toyshop on Eighth Avenue, with a farm beyond it and a red barn and small cows, and a train going round and round it all.

'Harbour, Matty? Are ye out of your senses?'

'I saw it with my own two eyes.'

Her eyes were like marbles. Suddenly she leaned over like a willow – just the way his mother used to lean over – and laughed and laughed.

'I know what you're talking about now. The lighthouse on the Shannon! Lord save us, how many times did I see it at night from the hill of Ballingarry! But there's no harbour, Matty.'

'There's the harbour at Foynes!'

'Oh, for God's sake!' she cried. 'That's miles and miles and miles away. 'Tis and twenty miles away! And where could you see any train, day or night, from anywhere at all near Ballyroche?'

They argued it hither and over until she suddenly found that the coffee was gone cold and rushed away with the pot to the kitchen. Even there she kept up the argument, calling out that certainly, you could see Moneygay Castle, and the turn of the River Deel on a fine day, but no train, and then she went on about the stepping-stones over the river, and came back babbling about Normoyle's bull that chased them across the dry river, one hot summer's day . . .

He said:

'Auntie! Why the hell did you never write home?'

'Not even once?' she said, with a crooked smile like a bold child.

'Not a sight nor a sound of you from the day you left Ballyroche, as my mother used to say, no more than if the earth swallowed you. You're a nice one!'

'Eat up!' she commanded him, with a little laugh and a tap on his wrist.

'Did you always live here, Auntie Lily?'

She sat down and put her face between her palms with her elbows on the table and looked at him.

'Here? Well, no . . . That is to say, no! My husband and me had a house of our very own over in East Fifty-eighth. He did very well for himself. He was quite a rich man when he died. A big jeweller. When he was killed in an airplane crash five years ago he left me very well off. But sure I didn't need a house of my own and I had lots of friends in Brooklyn, so I came to live here.'

'Fine! What more do you want, that is for a lone woman! No family?'

'I have my son. But he's married, to a Pole, they'll be over here first thing tomorrow morning to take me off to spend Christmas with them. They have an apartment on Riverside Drive. He is the manager of a big department store, Macy's on Flatbush Avenue. But tell me about Bid's children. You must have lots of brothers and sisters. Where are you going from here? Back to Ireland? To Limerick? To Ballyroche?'

He laughed.

'Where else would I go? Our next trip we hit the port of London. I'll be back like an arrow to Ballyroche. They'll be delighted to hear I met you. They'll be asking me all sorts of questions about you. Tell me more about your son, Auntie. Has he a family?'

'My son? Well, my son's name is Thomas. His wife's name is Catherine. She is very beautiful. She has means of her own. They are very happy. He is very well off. He's in charge of a big store, Sears Roebuck on Bedford Avenue. Oh, a fine boy. Fine out! As you say. Fine out. He has three children. There's Cissy, and Matty. And . . .'

Her voice faltered. When she closed her eyes he saw how old she was. She rose and from the bottom drawer of a chest of drawers she pulled out a photograph album. She laid it in front of him and sat back opposite him.

'That is my boy.'

When he said he was like her she said he was very like his father. Maxer said that he often heard that her husband was a most handsome man.

'Have you a picture of him?'

She drew the picture of her son towards her and looked down at it.

'Tell me more about Ballyroche,' she cried.

As he started into a long description of a harvest home he saw her eyes close again, and her breath came more heavily and he felt that she was not hearing a word he said. Then, suddenly, her palm slapped down on the picture of the young man, and he knew that she was not heeding him any more than if he wasn't there. Her fingers closed on the pasteboard. She shied it wildly across the room, where it struck the glass of the window flat on, hesitated and slid to the ground. Maxer saw snowflakes melting as often as they touched the pane. When he looked back at her she was leaning across the table, one white lock down over one eye, her yellow teeth bared.

'You spy!' she spat at him. 'You came from *them*! To spy on me!'

'I came from friendliness.'

'Or was it for a ha'porth of look-about? Well, you can go back to Ballyroche and tell 'em whatever you like. Tell 'em I'm starving if that'll please 'em, the mean, miserable, lousy set that never gave a damn about me from the day I left 'em. For forty years my own sister, your mother, never wrote one line to say...'

'You know damn well she'd have done anything for you if she only knew where you were. Her heart was stuck in you. The two of you were inside one another's pockets. My God, she was forever talking and talking about you. Morning noon and night...'

She shouted at him across the table.

'I wrote six letters...'

'She never got them.'

'I registered two of them.'

'Nobody ever got a line from you, or about you, only for the one letter from the priest that married you to say you were well and happy.'

'What he wrote was that I was down and out. I saw the letter. I let him send it. That Wop left me flat in this city with my baby. I wrote to everybody – my mother, my father, to Bid after she was your mother and had a home of her own. I had to work every day of my life. I worked today. I'll work tomorrow. If you want to know what I do I clean out offices. I worked to bring up my son, and what did he do? Walked out on me with that Polack of his and that was the last I saw of him, or her, or any human being belonging to me until I saw you. Tell them every word of it. They'll love it!'

Maxer got up and went over slowly to the bed for his jacket. As he buttoned it he looked at her glaring at him across the table. Then he looked away from her at the snowflakes feeling the windowpane and dying there. He said, quietly:

'They're all dead. As for Limerick – I haven't been back to Ireland for eight years. When my mum died my father got married again. I ran away to sea when I was sixteen.'

He took his cap. When he was at the door he heard a chair fall and then she was at his side, holding his arm, whispering gently to him:

'Don't go away, Matty.' Her pallid eyes were flooded. 'For God's sake, don't leave me alone with *them* on Christmas Eve!'

Maxer stared at her. Her lips were wavering as if a wind were blowing over them. She had the face of a frightened girl. He threw his cap on the bed and went over and sat down beside it. While he sat there like a big baboon, with his hands between his knees, looking at the snowflakes, she raced into the kitchen to put on the kettle for rum punch. It was a long while before she brought in the two big glasses of punch, with orange sliced in them, and brown sugar like drowned sand at the base of them. When she held them out to him he looked first at them, and then at her, so timid, so pleading, and he began to laugh and laugh – a laugh that he choked by covering his eyes with his hands.

'Damn ye!' he groaned into his hands. 'I was better off drunk.'

She sat beside him on the bed. He looked up. He took one of the glasses and touched hers with it.

'Here's to poor Lily!' he smiled.

She fondled his free hand.

'Lovie, tell me this one thing and tell me true. Did she really and truly talk about me? Or was that all lies too?'

'She'd be crying rain down when she'd be talking about you. She was always and ever talking about you. She was mad about you.'

She sighed a long sigh.

'For years I couldn't understand it. But when my boy left me for that Polack I understood it. I guess Bid had a tough time bringing you all up. And there's no one more hard in all the world than a mother when she's thinking of her own. I'm glad she talked about me. It's better than nothing.'

They sat there on the bed talking and talking. She made more punch, and then more, and in the end they finished the bottle between them, talking about everybody either of them had known in or within miles of the County Limerick. They fixed to spend Christmas Day together, and have Christmas dinner downtown, and maybe go to a picture and then come back and talk some more.

Every time Maxer comes to New York he rings her number. He can hardly breathe until he hears her voice saying, 'Hello, Matty.' They go on the town then and have dinner, always at some place with an Irish name, or a green neon shamrock above the door, and then they go to a movie or a show, and then come back to her room to have a drink and a talk about his last voyage, or the picture post cards he sent her, his latest bits and scraps of news about the Shannon shore. They always get first-class service in restaurants, although Maxer never noticed it until the night a waiter said, 'And what's mom having?' at which she gave him a slow wink out of her pale Limerick eyes and a slow, lover's smile.

# Angels and Ministers of Grace

'You can dress now, Mr Neason,' the doctor said. He went back slowly to his desk and began to write.

Jacky, still holding his shirt in his palms, looked hard at him and he didn't like the look of him at all.

'Well, Doc?' he got out in a kind of choke between the rise and fall of his Adam's apple. 'What's the verdict?'

'The verdict is that your heart is a bit dicky, and your blood pressure is high, but otherwise you're all right.'

'A bit dicky?' said Jacky, suddenly crumpling up the shirt in his fists. Still clutching the shirt he sat down. His heart was fluttering like a slack sail. 'What do you mean, dicky?'

'Well, without going into technical details, the fact is you've been overdoing it and your old ticker has got a bit tired, that's all. If you go to bed and rest up for a couple of months and take things easy from this on you'll probably live to be a hundred. If you don't it could become very serious.'

Jacky forgot his fright.

'Rest? In bed? Sure, flat racing begins next weekend!'

'Mr Neason, you are not going to see a racecourse for another two months. If you do you must get another doctor.'

'But, sure, Holy God, I was never in bed for more than four hours any night o' me life! What'll I be doing in bed for two months?'

'You can listen to the radio. And you can read. And, well, you can be listening to the radio. And you can read.'

'Read what?'

'Anything not too exciting. Someone once told me that whenever H. G. Wells went on a long journey he used to take a volume of the *Encyclopedia Britannica* with him. I'll come and visit you now and again.'

'Can't I come and see you?' Jacky asked feebly.

'It'll be safer the other way,' said the doctor, and it was then that Jacky knew he was really bad.

'Can I take e'er a drink?' he asked, now sagging on the ropes.

'A little glass of malt, or a bottle of stout, whenever you feel like it will do you no harm in the world. But keep off women. It takes the blood away from the head.'

'I never had much to do with them,' said Jacky sourly, putting his head into his shirt.

He went home, took a stiff whiskey, told his wife the news and got into bed. When she saw him in bed she began to cry, and she went on crying so long that he had to tell her he wasn't dead yet. At that she buttoned her lips to keep from crying more than ever. She managed to ask him was there anything special he wanted.

'Is there such a thing in the house as an encyclopedia?' he asked.

'Such a thing as a what?'

'An encyclopedia. The doctor said I must read.'

She looked sadly at him and the tears came again.

'Poor Jacky,' she sobbed, 'I never thought I'd see you reduced to this,' and she went away to look.

It did not take her long – there were not twenty books in the house; bookmakers don't collect that sort of book – so she went around next door to Noreen Mulvey, the schoolmaster's wife. She was soon back with a big black book with red edges called *A Catholic Dictionary*.

'Where the hell did I buy that?' Jacky asked.

'You didn't. I got it from Noreen Mulvey. She said 'tis as good as an encyclopedia.'

Jacky looked gloomily through the funereal volume. He found a green rubber stamp inside the cover. *Saint Jacob's College, Putney Green, Middlesex, London*. There were a lot of queer words in black type, of which the first was *Abbacomites*.

''Twill last me out,' he said mumpishly and settled himself to read.

The first article informed him that abbacomites were noble abbots, or count abbots, to whom the courts of the time gave abbacies for pecuniary profit. He was further informed that these abbots included not only the sons of nobles but their daughters, and even their wives.

'Nice blackguarding!' Jacky muttered and settled himself more comfortably to read the next article, which was headed *Abbess*. He read the brief paragraph with interest, especially the part that informed him that in the Brigittine Order and in the Order of Fontevrault, where there were monasteries for both nuns and monks side by side, 'the monks were bound to obey the abbess of the related monastery.'

'My ladies!' he growled sardonically and went on to *Abbots*.

He began to wilt a little here – the article was long and technical – though he rallied at the paragraph describing the bright young abbés, 'fluttering around the Court of Versailles,' who never so much as saw the abbeys from which they drew their incomes. He weakened again at *Abbreviations* and he nearly gave up at *Abjuration of Heresy*, but he was arrested by the *Abrahamites* because it struck him that these fellows were not far wrong when they declared that 'the good God had created men's souls, but the wicked power, or demiurge, had created their bodies'. However, at the end of this article there was a reference to a later entry on Manicheanism, of which Jacky read enough to decide that they were a lot of bloody foolahs and that the writer on Abrahamitism had been right to give them hell.

*Abraxas* bored him. *Absolution* was full of *a*'s, and *b*'s and *c*'s. As for the *Acaeometi* or Sleepless Monks, it was plain that they were another set of born eedjuts. It was then, as he began to ruffle the pages impatiently, that his eye fell on *Adam*. He read this article not only once but three times. When his wife came in with an eggnog she found him leaning back and staring pensively out of the window.

'Come here to me, Eileen,' he said, taking the eggnog with an absent hand. 'Did it ever occur to you that Adam and Eve made nothing at all of going around in their pelts?'

'Everyone knows that,' she said, tucking in the bedclothes.

'What I mean is did it ever occur to you that they didn't mind one bit?'

'I suppose the poor things were innocent until the devil tempted them.'

He cocked his head cutely at her.

'I'll go so far with you,' he agreed. 'But did it ever occur to you to ask how did the devil manage it if they were all that innocent?'

'Why wouldn't he?' she scoffed. 'Isn't it the innocent ones that always fall?'

'Fair enough,' he agreed again, and then in the smug voice of a chess player saying 'Checkmate,' he said: 'But what you're forgettin' is that this was in the Garden of Eden where sin didn't exist.'

'The devil invented it,' she said hurriedly.

'Heresy!' he pronounced and tapped the book. 'I'm after reading it here under *Abrahamites.*'

'Will you have chops for your supper?' she asked.

He nodded without interest.

'It only stands to reason,' he pointed out. 'You can't tempt a man who is so innocent he doesn't mind seeing a woman going around in her pelt.'

'But what about the apple?' she cried.

'Aha! But what *was* the apple?'

''Twas just an apple. Anyway it was something they weren't allowed to have,' she declared with all the vehemence of a woman who knows that she does not understand what she is saying and must therefore say it as emphatically as she can. But Jacky was, by now, beyond arguing along these lines. He said loftily that the Council of Trent left the matter entirely open. She whisked her head in the air, and at the door she turned to remark with proper feminine unfairness, and irrelevance, that it would be better for him to be saying his prayers.

By suppertime he had moved farther on. Conquering all the territory that he touched, he learned much that he had not previously even thought it possible to know about the subject of *Adultery*. It was an article with cross-references to *Marriage* and *Affinity*. When Eileen came back with the supper tray, bearing two fine chops and a glass of Guinness with a one-inch froth on it, she again found him looking thoughtfully out of the window. As she laid the tray on his unheeding lap he said:

'Did you know that a man can't marry his own mother-in law?'

'Your mother-in-law,' she informed him coldly, 'is in her grave this seven years. And when she was alive you hadn't as much as a good word to throw her no more than to the cat.'

'I am not,' he told her with a nice and infuriating blend of courtesy and condescension, 'discussing your mother. It is a question of canon law.'

Her breath went up her nose like the whistle of a train.

'Eat your chops while they're hot,' she said, and went out with prim lips.

Milo Mulvey called in about ten o'clock to offer his condolences to the patient. Eileen told him to save his sympathy because her hero (her own term) was full of buck and guff. She led him upstairs and while he sat on a canebottomed chair by the bed she leaned over the end of it. Milo adopted the false-jolly manner of all visitors to sickrooms.

'Well, Jacky my ould tar,' he cried jovially, 'so this is what slow horses and fast women did to you?' – with a wink at Eileen to take the harm out of it.

'Milo!' Jacky addressed him seriously. 'Do you really believe that a thousand angels can stand on the point of a needle?'

Milo looked at him, and then he looked a question at Eileen.

'He's that way all day,' she said. ''Tis all on account of that book you gave him.'

'Is that mine?' Milo asked, leaning over to glance at the sombre volume. 'Where did you get it?'

'I borrowed it from Noreen today. Worse luck. The professor here said he wanted to read something.'

'You poor man,' Milo said, 'I'll bring you around half a dozen detective stories.'

'Thanks,' said Jacky, 'but I don't want them. This is the most interesting book I ever read in my life. Barring that book of famous crimes you lent me last year when I had the flu. But do you – and this is a serious question now mind you – do you really and truly believe that a thousand angels can stand on the point of a needle?'

'You're very interested in religion all of a sudden,' Milo said suspiciously.

'For a man,' Eileen agreed dryly, 'who wasn't to church, chapel or meeting for the last five years.'

Jacky leaned out of bed and tapped Milo's knee.

'Milo! Will you tell me how the hell's blazes could even one angel stand on the point of a needle, let alone a thousand of 'em?'

'Answer the professor,' Eileen said wearily to Milo.

'Well,' Milo began, a bit embarrassed and not sure he was not being chaffed by the two of them, 'if you are serious about this the answer is, of course, that angels are pure spirits. I mean they can pass through walls and floors and ceilings. I mean they have neither length, nor breadth, nor depth. I mean they are pure intelligences.'

'What you mean,' Eileen said flatly, 'is that angels have no legs.'

'Well,' Milo conceded unwillingly, 'that is more or less what it comes to.'

'The professor,' she said in a long sigh, 'is now about to ask you how they can stand if they have no legs.'

Milo laughed easily. He turned to Jacky. He was a man who loved explaining things, which was why he was a teacher.

'That's very simple, Jacky. Let me explain it to you. You see, when you say "stand" you don't really mean "stand". You mustn't take these things literally. You know very well, for instance, that when you say "going up to heaven" or "going down to hell," you don't mean "up" and "down" the way we mean upstairs and downstairs. It's the same with everything else. I mean you don't think God has whiskers, do you? You follow me?'

He found himself faltering. Jacky was looking at him rather coldly, something like the way a boss-gangster might look at one of his gang who is explaining volubly how he happened to be seen coming out of the headquarters of the police precinct the previous night at half past eleven arm in arm with the district prosecutor. Milo turned to Eileen:

'*You* understand me, Eileen, don't you? I mean it's impossible for us to as much as talk of things of this kind without forming misleading pictures of them. But, of course,' with a fluent wave of his hand, 'that doesn't mean that our pictures bear any relation to actuality. I mean we don't think that angels have actual wings and all to that, do we?'

He laughed cajolingly, anticipating her answering smile of approval.

She did not smile. She looked sadly at him. Then she looked at Jacky.

'Go on, professor!'

'All the same, Milo,' Jacky said, 'I believe it is a fact that the angels can commit sin?'

'Well, they certainly did once,' Milo agreed, but his eyes were beginning to get shifty. 'The fallen angels and all that. Milton,' he added absently. '*Paradise Lost.*'

'And what,' Jacky asked with a polite interest, 'do you suppose they did it with? Having no legs and so on?'

'With their minds!' said Milo wildly.

'I see,' said Jacky. 'With their minds.'

There was a long pause. Eileen came to the rescue with 'Would you like a bottle of stout, Milo?', very much like a boxer's second at the end of the tenth round saying to a man whose only wish on God's earth is that he had never come into the ring, 'Would ye care for a small brandy?'

Milo said that he would, yes, thanks, he would, thanks very much, take a, in fact, yes a bottle of stout if she had one handy. As she leaned up and went for the stout she heard Milo acceding to her hero that a lot of these things are difficult to our mortal understanding, and Jacky magnanimously agreeing that he could see that, and:

'Take the Garden of Eden, now, for example!'

When she came back with the tray she found the two heads together, going word for word through a page of the black book. She observed that Milo looked much less jovial than when he sailed into the room a quarter of an hour before.

Milo did not call in again until several nights later. He had not been in the bedroom for ten minutes, chatting about this and that, when the doorbell rang. Eileen went down and came back accompanied by Father Milvey. She showed his Reverence in, and when he and Milo greeted one another with as much astonishment as if they had not met for six months, she looked over at Jacky, caught his eye and gave him a moth-wink out of a porcelain face. (The parish joke about the firm of Mulvey and Milvey had moss on it.) Father Milvey was a tidy little man, always as neat as a cuff straight from the laundry; and he might have been thought of as a tidy, cheerful little man if he had not had a slight squint which gave him a somewhat distant look. He greeted the patient with the usual sickroom cordiality. Eileen went downstairs for the bottle of whiskey, and after she had come back and helped them all round, and helped herself, she took up her usual position leaning over the end of the bed, waiting for his Reverence to mention the Garden of Eden. He did it very simply.

'Yerrah, what's the big book, Jacky? Oh? I hope it's not one of those American things, all written in words of one syllable and as full of pictures as if the Vatican was in Hollywood. Well, the Lord knows 'tis high time you took a bit of interest in something else besides horses.'

Jacky fended him off just as simply. He pushed the book aside with a casual:

'Ach, it passes the time, Father.'

There was a short silence. Then Milo made the approach direct.

'He had a bit of difficulty there the other night, Father, with the Garden of Eden. As a matter of fact it stumped myself.'

'Oho, is that so?' said the little priest with a cheerful laugh. 'Nothing like beginning at the beginning, is there? And what was that now?' he asked Jacky, and Eileen saw his hand moving slowly to his pocket, and protruding therefrom the corner of a pale-green pamphlet. She foresaw the look of surprise, could already hear the words, 'extraordinary coincidence . . .'

'Ah, nothing much,' said Jacky.

'What was it, though?'

'Hell!' said Jacky.

Father Milvey's eyes strayed towards Milo's. The look plainly meant: 'I thought you said angels?' His hand came back to his glass. He smiled at Jacky.

'No better subject for a man in your position, Jacky. Did you ever hear the one about the old lad who was dying, and the priest said, "Now, Michael, you renounce the devil, don't you?" Do you know what the old chap said? "Ah, wisha, Father," says he, in a very troubled sort of voice, "I don't think this is any time for me to be antagonizing *anybody*!"' He let the laughter pass, and then he said easily: 'Well, what about hell?'

'Fire!' said Jacky. 'I don't believe a word of it.'

His Reverence's face darkened. Help for the humble was one thing, the proud were another matter altogether. He adopted a sarcastic tone.

'I think,' he said, 'the old man I was just telling you about was a little more prudent in his approach to the question of hell-fire.'

Jacky took umbrage at his tone.

'There's no such a thing as hell-fire,' he said roundly.

'Oh, well, of course, Mr Neason, if you want to go against the general consensus of theological opinion! What do you choose, in your wisdom, to make, for example, of those words: "Depart from me ye accursed into everlasting fire prepared for the devil and his angels?"'

'Angels?' asked Jacky, lifting his eyebrows.

Milo intervened hastily:

'I think, Father, what was troubling Jacky there was the question of angels being pure spirits.'

'What of it?'

Jacky, a man of infinite delicacy, lowered his eyes to his glass.

'I must say I fail to see your difficulty,' his Reverence pursued, and put out his palm when Milo restlessly started to intervene again. 'No, Milo! I *like* to hear these lay theologians talking.'

'Ach, 'tis nothing at all, Father,' Jacky said shyly. 'I'm sure 'tis a very simple thing if I only understood it. Only. Well. Pure spirits, you see? And real fire? I mean, could they, so to speak, feel it?'

'Tshah!' cried Father Milvey. 'Suarez . . . ' He halted. It was a long time since he had read his Suarez. 'Origen,' he began. He stopped again. It was even longer since he had read his Origen. He wavered for a moment or two, and then he became a nice little man again. He expanded into a benevolent smile. 'Wisha, tell me, Jacky, why does all this interest you anyway?'

'It just passes the time, Father.'

Father Milvey laughed.

'You know, you remind me of a man – this is a good one, I only heard it the other day . . .'

Eileen leaned up. She knew that the rest of the visit would pass off swimmingly.

It was four days before Milo called in again. Jacky thought he looked a bit dark under the eyes, but he decided not to remark on it. Anyway Milo did not give him time; he threw his hat on the bed, sat on the chair, leaned forward with his two hands on his knees, and stared at Jacky with a fierce intensity. Normally, Milo was a rotund, assured sort of man; his tiny mouth, like a child whistling, pursed complacently; a man as resolutely tidy-minded as the row of three pens in his breast pocket, each with a little coloured dot to indicate the colour of the ink. He did not look like that at all tonight. Jacky looked at his furrowed brow and the deep, forked lines from his nose to his button-mouth, and wondered could he be on a batter.

'Jacky!' he said harshly. 'All this about hell!'

'Yerrah,' Jacky waved airily, 'that's only chicken feed. You explained all that to me. 'Tis all figurative.' To change the subject, he leaned over and tapped Milo's taut knee. 'But, come here to me, Milo, did it ever occur to you that the antipopes . . .'

Milo choked. He sat back.

'Look!' he almost sobbed. 'First it was angels. Then it was fallen angels. Then it was hell. Now it's antipopes. Will ye, for God's sake, keep to one thing. I'm bothered to blazes about this question of hell.'

'Don't give it a thought,' Jacky soothed him. 'You mustn't take these things too literally. I mean fire and flame and all that!'

'But Father Milvey says, and he's been reading it up, that you must take it literally. My God, 'tis the cornerstone of Christianity. All the eschatological conceptions of the postexilic writings...'

'You're thinking too much about these things,' Jacky said crossly.

'Thinking?' Milo gasped and his round eyes flamed bloodshot. 'I've done nothing for four days and four nights but think about it! My head is addled with thinking!'

'I'll tell you my idea about all that,' Jacky confided. 'I believe there's a hell there all right but there's no one in it.'

'That's what Father Conroy says!'

'Who's he?'

Milo's voice became sullen. He explained unwillingly:

'He's the Jesuit that Father Milvey's consulting about it. But Father Saturninus says...'

'I never heard of him. Where'd you dig *him* up?'

'He's the Capuchin who's conducting the mission this week in Saint Gabriel's. The three of them are at it every night inside in the presbytery. You know very well that the sermon on hell is the lynchpin of every mission. Fire coming out of the noses of the damned, fire out of their ears, fire out of their eyeballs, their hands up for one half-cup of cold water – you know the line! Mind you, not that I approve of it! But it always gets the hard chaws, it gets the fellows that nobody else and nothing else can get. Well, Father Saturninus says all this talk and discussion has him off his stroke. Think of it! Every night people waiting for the sermon on hell and Saturninus climbing up in the pulpit knowing they're waiting for it, and knowing he won't be able to do it. Of course, he could easily talk about hell as a lonely, miserable, desolate place where everybody was always groaning and moaning for the sight of heaven and having no hope of ever seeing it, but you know as well as I do that a hell without fire, and lots and lots of it, isn't worth a tinker's curse to anybody.'

'Well,' said Jacky impatiently, 'I don't see how I can help you. If you want to believe in fire and brimstone...'

Milo grasped his wrist. His voice became a whisper.

'Jacky,' he whispered. 'I don't believe one single bloody word of it.'

'Then what are you worrying about?'

'I'm worrying because I *can't* believe in it! I was happy as long as I *did* believe in it! I *want* to believe in it!'

Jacky threw his hands up in total disgust.

'But, don't you see, Jacky, if you don't believe in hell you don't believe in divils, and if you don't believe in divils you don't believe in the Garden of Eden.' His voice sank to a frightened whisper again. He seized Jacky by the arm. Jacky drew back his chin into his chest, and crushed back into the pillows to get away from the two wild bullet eyes coming closer and closer to him. 'Jacky!' whispered Milo. 'What *was* the apple?'

'A figure of speech!'

Milo dashed his arm away, jumped to his feet, gripped his head in his hands and uttered a hollow and unlikely 'Ha! Ha! Ha!' in three descending notes like a stage villain. His voice became quite normal and casual.

'Can *you eat* a figure of speech?' he asked very politely.

'There was no eatin'. That was another figure of speech, like the angels that have no legs.'

'You mean, I presume,' Milo asked, with a gentle and courteous smile, and a delicate shrug of his Rugby-player's shoulders, 'that Adam had no mouth?'

'Adam was a figure of speech,' Jacky said stolidly.

'I'm going mad!' Milo screamed, so loud that Jacky had one leg out of bed to call Eileen before Milo subsided as quickly and utterly as he had soared. He smiled wanly. 'Sorry, old boy,' he said in the stiff-upper-lip voice of an old Bedalian on the Amazon who has rudely trod on the tail of an anaconda. 'A bit on edge these days. Bad show. I only wish I could see the end of it. The worst of it is Father Milvey says it's all my fault keeping such books in the house. And lending them to you. I wish to God I never gave you that book! I wish to God I never laid eyes on it!'

Jacky fished it out of the eiderdown and handed it to him.

'Take it,' he said. 'I'm sick of it. 'Tis all full of "This one says" and "That one says." Have you er'er an ould detective story?'

'But, Jacky! About *hell?*'

'Forget it!' said Jacky. 'Eileen!' he roared. 'Bring up the bottle of whiskey.'

'No thanks,' said Milo, getting up gloomily and putting the obscure volume under his arm. 'Father Milvey is coming around to my place tonight and I'll have to have a jar with him.' He looked down miserably at Jacky. 'You're looking fine!'

'Why wouldn't I, and I living like a lord?'

''Tis well for you,' Milo grumbled sourly, and went out slowly.

After a while Eileen came upstairs to him bearing the whiskey bottle, two glasses and a big red book.

'What's that book?' he asked suspiciously.

'Milo gave it to me for you. 'Tis *The Arabian Nights*. He said not to let Father Milvey see it. Some of the pictures in it will raise your blood pressure.'

Jacky grunted. He was watching her pouring out the liquor.

'Come here to me, Eileen,' he said, his eye fixed thoughtfully on the glass. 'Did it ever, by any chance, occur to you that . . .'

'What is it now?' she asked threateningly, withholding the glass from him.

'I was only going to say,' he went on humbly, 'did it ever occur to you that the bottom of a whiskey bottle is much too near the top?'

She gave him one of those coldly affectionate looks of which only wives are capable, added a half-inch to his glass, and handed it over to him.

'You ould savage,' she said fondly, and began to tuck him in for the night. To show her approval of him she left the bottle by his side.

Left to himself he opened the big red book. He savoured it. He began to relish it. He was soon enjoying it. He snuggled into his pillow and, with one hand for the page and one for his glass, he entered the Thousand and One Nights. Thanks be to God, here at least there were lots and lots of legs. Towards midnight he gently let the blind roll up to see what sort of a night it was. His eye fell on the light streaming out from Milo Mulvey's sitting room across the grass of his back garden: the theological session in full swing. He raised his eyes to the night sky. It was a fine, sweet, open-faced night in May. A star among the many stars beamed at him. There are more things in heaven . . . With renewed relish he returned to the Grand Vizier's daughter. His glass was full.

# One Night in Turin

1

One robin-singing, cloud-racing, wet-grassed Monday morning last April, Walter Hunter came down to breakfast as usual at half past eight – nice time to let him drive at his ease to his office in Cork city for ten, a gentlemanly hour – picked up his neatly folded *Irish Times* from the hall table and roared into the rear of the house, 'Devilled kidneys forward, Mrs Canty.' He glanced at the headlines as he passed out on to his lawn. The glass door flashed sunlight, greenery, and cloudland about his head. He surveyed with pleasure the host of daffodils on his dew-wet fields stretching down to the low tide, the cloud-castles over the harbour, but on crackling the paper wide open forgot all about them, breakfast, his office and work. The first entry in the *Social and Personal* column read: 'The Countess Maria Rinaldi has arrived in Dublin and is staying for a few days at the Russell Hotel.' He lifted his head, looked here, there and everywhere among the racing clouds as if he had suddenly heard the twittering of a flock of duck, turned and walked quickly back into his study to telephone her. Just as his fist closed on the receiver he paused, like a stopped film. For one minute he was immobile. In that minute he remembered the seven occasions – especially the first and last – on which he had seen her since she left Ireland, sixteen years ago.

The first occasion was now part of his blood stream. It had occurred in 'Forty-six. He had gone with Betsy Cotman to Cervinia, ostensibly for the skiing. It was his first trip abroad since the war, that event whose prolongation so insensibly aged us all. Two years before it began he had gone back to study at the King's Inns, belatedly finishing his law studies, feeling himself still a student among students. By 'Forty-six he was coming down the straight to forty; still handsome, with a few interesting flecks of grey on his temples, in perfect physical trim, having already put half of a good life behind him – he knew it all, he would tell you, with a gay wave of his long fingers – and with the clearest intention of holding on to his good fortune as long as possible.

Cervinia, however, had not been entirely a success. Betsy had stayed with him for only three days – she then had to hurry on to St Moritz to establish herself there before her husband came out – but he had seen her go with relief. In those three days and nights he had discovered that she had no interest in anything that she could not manhandle as a form of healthy sport. Her whole life seemed like a long and rich dinner where every course was a repetition of the pleasure of the last course under a different name. Whether she was skiing, tobogganing, mountain climbing, figure skating, or making love, she never altered her tone one jot, never abated her voice by as much as a quarter tone. She had leaped like a chamois from the snow to the bed, from the bed to the snow, oblivious of the chasms that yawned between her inexhaustible store of hearty Anglo-Saxon good cheer and his Irish sensibilities. He waved her good-bye between a sigh of satisfaction and a breath of nausea, and returned deep-breathing to the pure white mountains. He got in four days of middling-to-good skiing, and then the threatened wet snow fell. He came down into Torino to eke out there the last forty-eight hours of his brief holiday. (His father had died during the war, he was in charge of the family business of Hunter and Hunter, so that all his escapes now had to be intense and brief.)

He was delighted to be alone in snow-covered Turin. Never having stayed before in any Lombard or Swiss city in bad weather, he discovered for the first time the merits of those northern arcades which both allow and tempt one to pass sociably and in comfort from café to café. He was excited by the contrast between these crowded cafés and the sense of isolation that he got from the warnings of the white heaps of bomb rubble, the silent white ruins of crumbled houses, the brown desolation of the swollen Po, the great white, empty squares bluishly lit at night by lean streaks of light from lower-floor windows. As he wandered about, he recalled the many trestle bridges over which his train from Paris had so cautiously crawled. He felt like a pioneer postwar explorer. How wonderful, he thought, it could be to be completely cut off here for a couple of months. He would pass his days in one café after another, hot and steamy, smelling of coffee and *nazionales*. He would make the acquaintance of a few intelligent and interesting men in whose company he would forget all about his stupid and slightly humiliating adventure with that fool of a woman.

His first night was not a success. He spent it in a big, chattering café in the Piazza Carlo Felice. There was no trouble at all about making acquaintances – tourists were still few enough to be interesting novelties in 'Forty-six. But he got buttonholed by one old, bearded character who talked with the same inexhaustible and unprofitable energy about war and politics in Italy as Betsy had about hunting and fishing in England and Ireland. Also, that night he had an unpleasant dream. He dreamed of being squashed (right across his smooth, soft belly) by some great collapsing weight – like an ant one crushed underfoot. He awoke and lit the light to drive away the image. Would he feel terrible agony? Or would it be immediate death? Would he, dead or alive or unconscious, wriggle galvanically like a fly in a candle-flame for a second? He thought of brutal writers and painters who have painted such cruel things. Faulkner? Describing a man burned in a plane crash. Hemingway, describing a man thumbing out another man's eye and then biting off the dangling eyeball. Algren. Why do they do it? Exorcising, or indulging their egos?

There was not a sound from the street. The snow silenced every outer noise. We drag our ego with us through life, chained to it, in its power, not it in ours. We are free of it, or seem to be free of it, only in rare hours – relaxed by the achievement of climbing a mountain peak, elevated by the speed of a dangerous ski run, in the quiet hour after love, calmed by the wonder of some splendid view, asleep, when slightly drunk, listening to music. Where had he heard or read of a man of the most strict behaviour who came within an inch of being killed by a falling beam, who said to himself, 'I was as good as killed! Well, then, my past is finished,' and proceeded to spend the rest of his life in the pursuit of pleasure? He thought, for no apparent reason, of Betsy Cotman – and groaned with displeasure. When he awoke, his light was still lighted. The grimness of his dream remained with him for several hours – an unpleasant wash of grey colour across the sunny morning.

He spent the forenoon shopping: a trifle for his cook, she was worth the attention; a trifle for his secretary, poor thing; an expensive pair of gold earrings for Betsy, these affairs had to be finished off in style. The afternoon and evening he spent in three different cafés, where, again, the talk was easy, amiable, and unimportant. He dined well, went to an American film, and on the way home was accosted at a dark corner by a young man who tried to sell him a fake Parker 51 fountain pen. Walter took the pen in his hand, it came apart immediately and the young man burst into tears. Walter took him to a bar for a drink and the young man revealed his misery. He had spent his only five hundred lire on ten of these fake pens, expecting to resell them for two thousand five hundred. He laid them on the marble table – they were all defective. He had been cruelly defrauded. Walter watched him take one apart and fiddle with it, passionately, despairingly. When the top half of the casing would not screw into the bottom half, he burst into tears once more. Walter gave him a thousand lire and they parted like old friends. But as Walter went out he looked back. The young man was again tearing at the pen. He never forgot that image of the young man's despairing efforts to undo his disaster. He often told his friends about it. 'It brought', he would say, 'the whole war, the whole of Turin, down to the point of a pen'.

His second, and last, day passed just as pleasantly. He went to see the alleged Veil of Veronica in the cathedral. He was not impressed. At lunch he met a man with one arm, an unrepentant Fascist who knew, as a certain fact, that Mussolini had never been shot – it was his double who had been shot – was hiding in Switzerland and would return again to lead a resurgent Italy. He listened to some more vague talk in two more cafés, content to sit on there, slowly filling up his cooling-tank with the ice water of their new-found patriotic ideals and his own moral resolutions. By the time he had again dined and wined himself well he was in an entirely pleasant state of mental and emotional euphoria. It was at this moment that his great adventure began.

His eye fell on a poster – they were playing *La Sonnambula* that night at the opera. He hastened around to the theatre, managed to procure a ticket, took his seat just as the lights dimmed, and within minutes he was leaning forward, rigid with excitement. Molly O'Sullivan had walked on to the stage as the miller's daughter, Amina. At once there grew in him the strangest and sweetest sense of secret complicity with her life – the only man in the whole theatre who had known her as a girl, indeed almost as a child, in Ireland. This feeling was so sweet and strong that he immediately resolved never to tell anybody at home in Ireland that he had been in the theatre that night. He resolved not even to send his card around to her. If he did, he would have to meet her in the company of other admirers behind the scenes, where she would simply become public property – the wonderful new soprano who had been discovered in a wayside *taverna* in the wilds of Ireland. She would no longer be the charming young girl on whom he first laid eyes behind the counter of old Katy O'Sullivan's pub in Coomagara – a pub well known to all late travellers between Cork and Kinsale for being open at all hours, for bad whiskey, poor measure, and the blond charms of the daughter of the house – good-looking in a saucy way, he had thought her the first time he saw her, as vain as a peacock, an outrageous flirt, almost too obviously nobody's fool, but, just as obviously, as innocent and (he had quoted Yeats to himself on their first encounter) 'as ignorant as the dawn'. In her crowded dressing room she would neither be that enchanting apparition emerging, in pure white, under pale, cold, greeny moonlight to mourn her lost love, nor the young girl he used to secretly admire in Dublin during the couple of years after her discovery, whom he used to ambush casually in dusty teashops, in the distempered corridors of the Academy of Music, or walking with her fellow students across Saint Stephen's Green, past the old bandstand, the great beds of geraniums, and the statue of George the Third facing the humped bridge over the ponds. He left the theatre as furtively as a kidnapper. He would write to her when he got home. He would come out again in the summer and confess everything to her.

When he got back home to Hunterscourt he bought recordings of the opera, and, that winter, whenever he put them on for his friends he felt again the secret bond that he had formed with her in Turin, so that if one of his guests asked some such simple question as, 'Is this by Verdi?' or, 'Wally, is this the opera with the song that Joyce's ould father used to love?' he would not correct them, he would not hear them, he would say, in the detached voice of the president of the Cork Grand Opera Society, 'There's a rather nice little aria coming up now.' Then, hearing once more the '*Ah, non credea mirarti*' or the '*Ah, non giunge,*' he would lean back in his armchair by the fire to see her again, gleaming like a snow maiden under a canopy of light and music; or see himself, after the performance, half stunned by delight and wonder, sipping brandy after brandy in a mirrored café by the railway station, with his packed bags and his oiled skis on the floor beside him, waiting, long after the crowd had thinned away, for the Rome-Paris Express to pass at two in the morning, drunkenly watching the wet snowflakes melting on the panes, sinking heavily into the palms outside, floating in a white fuzz around the cloudy electric lights, and now and again a soft thunder rolling dully down from the mountains along the tawny valley of the swollen Po. He had no clear recollection of the journey home.

He remembered only her gleaming image, the music, the falling snow, the heavy, silent streets.

One thing about her soon began to disturb him. At first her image came obediently when he called her. Presently he ceased to control her. Now it was she who ambushed him. Her image became so merged with his own being that any least disturbance in any corner of his senses could awaken her from her coiled sleep, until he came to realize that he had had his greatest illusion of power over his thoughts of her when he was most subject to them. He did not write to her. He did not go to Italy that summer. It was as if he feared to meet her. After that it even seemed to him that she spied on him. Whenever the thought of her visited him among his legal cronies, or among his Bohemian-theatrical friends up in Dublin, he became terrified that some day he would talk to them of her, and he went among them no more. More than that – his affairs with women became infrequent, casual and coarse. 'The worse the better,' he said to himself – though not excusing himself, for it was his self-boast that he never deceived himself about anything.

Being a lawyer accustomed to examining other people's motives, he naturally spent many hours trying to understand why he kept on postponing an avowal of his passion for her. After long consideration, he decided that she was like certain lights that can be discerned only by not looking straight at them – a dim star, a remote airport beacon in a fog, a lamp in a distant cottage window. She represented something in himself that he could only approach obliquely and slowly. 'After all, you don't change your politics or your religion all of a sudden,' he caught himself saying aloud to himself one night. Besides, he knew that nobody really lives entirely by what he professes. She was his illogical goddess. He remembered a Catholic friend of his who was always good-humouredly teasing him for being a Protestant – 'next door to an atheist' – meaning a man for whom nothing existed beyond the earth, the body and the understanding. Yet this pious man, he found out, always carried a four-leafed clover in his cigarette case as a luck charm. 'Against what, in your good God's name?' Walter had asked him with a grin. 'Destiny!' said his friend, with a fierce glare.

He did not blame his friend for teasing him. It must have seemed to many that he had indeed lived all his life by the law of passionate pleasure. He had loved sport – hunting, shooting, fishing. Hunters-court, his father's and his grandfather's home before him, was ideal for any man who enjoyed the open-air life: an old Georgian house (originally the dower house of Lord Boyne's estate across the fields) situated twelve and a quarter miles out of town on a hundred and fifty acres of mixed land ranging from rich alluvial soil down to the kind of reedy-quaggy fields that you find so often along the lower Lee. On any fine morning, before driving into his office in his Mercedes-Benz, he could hack about for an hour on his little demesne, or wander with his gun, or if it is high tide sail down the creek into Cork Harbour to cast a line, or swim in his pelt, completely unobserved, or merely lie on his back gazing up at the harbour sky, vast, always cloud-packed, faintly mobile. The house had half a dozen modern loose-boxes. He had plenty of friends glad to come down for a few days' sailing or for rough-shooting on another hundred acres that he had rented and preserved around the hills of Fermoy. As for other pleasures, where could a man be better situated than within a bare twenty minutes of a modern airport with planes for Dublin, and from that onward to any city on the Continent that he cares to choose? He had several times taken off from Cork after a leisurely lunch on Friday, enjoyed two crowded days in Paris, and on Monday morning walked into Hunter and Hunter's on the South Mall, and hung up his bowler hat and his umbrella with as staid and contented a 'Good morning, Miss O' and a 'Morning, Mr Dooley' as if he had spent the weekend reading *Sense and Sensibility*. What his good friends did not realize, of course, was that it palls. After forty, it begins to pall. He had not realized it himself until that night in Turin. Those hesitations ever since, all those oblique and sidelong efforts to see the dim star, the cottage window, the airport beacon in the fog, were – he now knew – his efforts to understand what it was that he had desired and not found in the hunt, the shoot, on the wind-pocked sea, all these casual women.

Having settled on one explanation for his prolonged hesitations and his frightened secrecy about her, he at once decided on two more – that the real reasons he was being cautious were (a) that he was so much older than she and (b) that he really did not know anything about her as a woman. (His great motto about women had always been a minatory, 'They change, you know, they change!') Accordingly, he kept on making and remaking decisions about her, until he suddenly realized that he had, as it were overnight, become two years older, and so had she, which made both his reasons still more cogent. He thereupon wrote several letters to her – and did not send them. He booked train and plane reservations to go out and meet her, and did not go. One morning his paper announced that she had married Count Giorgio Rinaldi, a landowner with some undefined industrial interests near Bergamo. He wrote to her at once, to congratulate her, assuring her that this was what she both deserved and needed. His second and third encounters with her occurred soon after.

These were the years when his holidays happened to take him to the Dolomites: he visited her and Giorgio in their home outside Bergamo. He made these visits nervously, and after much hesitation. They established only that she had ceased to be an opera singer, that she was living in the grand manner, and that she was a beautiful woman of skill and taste, with a high, marble-white forehead, delicately veined, big grey eyes, globular as a Pekinese's, a poreless skin, exquisitely carved lips and a great pile of braided, blonde hair – a rich, mature beauty, with an Italian-style figure. Anybody who had not known her as Molly O'Sullivan of Coomagara could easily have thought she had always been a *contessa*. She was, he reckoned, thirty or thirty-one. He was nearly forty-three.

The next winter he met them twice in Milan; once for dinner before the opera at Crispi's; the second time, after the opera, when the three of them walked, chatting happily arm in arm, across the foggy piazza and through the arcade for late supper at Savini's. It was a gay night, as gay and warm in feeling as the little red table lamps and the chatter of the crowded arcade. She was completely real to him that night, both as Molly O'Sullivan and as the Contessa Rinaldi.

The next summer, when he happened to be motoring along the lakes from Berne to Venice, he called on them one afternoon where they were in *villeggiatura* in a small cottage above Lecco. High up there it was cool. They drank cold white wine. The lake below was a dark blue. They could see the snowy Alps. He noted, with satisfaction, that the marriage was a childless one.

It was on their last, entirely unplanned, meeting, seven months ago, in Rome, that his swift thoughts converged as he stood immobile over the black telephone. That night, he very nearly told her his secret about the snowy night in Turin. Unfortunately, neither the place nor the occasion encouraged the exchange of memories, least of all that kind of memory. She had come to Rome because Giorgio had come there to consult a specialist. He had met her so unexpectedly, with such a shock of delight, that for a moment he could not talk to her, at a diplomatic cocktail party in the Palazzo Farnese. Since she could not dine with

him – she had to go back to the nursing home to dine with Giorgio –
he persuaded her to meet him afterwards at Doney's for a nightcap.

She came, late, so that his nerves were all on edge before she entered,
dressed as she had been at the Embassy, in a costume of raw silk the
colour of alder-flowers, not much lighter in hue than her hair, and even
her wide floppy hat of openwork straw was covered in cream lace, its
white brim fringed about her sun-tanned face. She looked so lovely,
though so troubled, that he regretted he had not selected a more
secluded place than a Via Veneto café. He was relieved that he had at
least chosen to meet her indoors at Doney's, where it is usually quiet
enough in warm weather, when the crowds prefer to sit outside, three
deep on the pavement under the coloured canopies. By ill luck, just as
they sat to a table in a quiet corner indoors, a sudden September
cloudburst fell on the city, and at once the hundreds of gossippers on
the pavement came rushing indoors, laughing noisily at the unexpected disaster, carrying their drinks, obtruding everywhere in the
*salon*, with waiters racing in and out, holding chairs aloft as if they
were going to brain everybody. Even so, as he listened to her telling him
Giorgio's symptoms – she feared the usual malignancy – he was sure he
could detect certain resonances, conveyed by the tone of her voice
rather than by the words, certain undertones not connected with her
fears for his bodily health, taut, nervous, accentuated perhaps by the
rattling rain, the low peals of summer thunder, the gabbling crowd.

He stared at her, crouching, shaking his head in sad condolence,
smiling with affectionate pity across the brown table, his bat's ears
sharpened by his amorous feeling for her. He became aware that her
beauty, tonight, was not only rich but sad, and, on an instant, he was
transfixed by the true meaning of her melancholy and moritural
loveliness. It came to him when the brilliant lights of the chandeliers
suddenly dimmed as if they had all been lowered into the sea, a loud
peal of thunder reverberated over the rain-torn city, and the *salon* sent
up a laughing, cheering scream of mock fright. In that second he saw
her exactly as he had seen her seven years before in the pallid
moonlight of *The Sleepwalker*, her eyelids drooping not for Rinaldi but
for herself. He cunningly threw out a casual remark about the
happiness of Bergamo and coupled it with that gay night in Milan when
they all three had hurried arm in arm across the foggy piazza to the
warmth of Savini's and the cheery vulgarity of French champagne with
the ritual *risotto al salto*. She replied to his remark – he had trembled

while he waited for her reply – with an all but imperceptible lifting of one shoulder. In that instant he knew that they had ceased to love.

He had been about to win all her trust when the dimmed lights rose again into a full white blaze and the crowd cheered and applauded as if they were at the end of an opera. He had turned and glared at the laughing gabblers as if to shout, 'Silence in the court!' When he turned back he found that she was looking intensely at a young couple beside them, bantering one another loudly and happily, hands clasped across the table. Walter gazed, just as enviously, at her exquisitely curved mouth. As if she felt his look she turned swiftly to him, said brightly in a comic, stage-Irish brogue, 'Well, is there e'er a dhrop left in our ould bottle o' fizz?' – and the sole propitious moment of the night was gone.

The storm passed over. The night was warm and bland again. The *salon* emptied. They talked for a while about what they called their past lives. Since they had not talked alone for many years, this was his first real opportunity to observe how her mind had developed in the meantime. As they talked she became so heated about a couple of remembered (or imagined) insults from her early critics that he began at first to fear that she was a blend – not unfamiliar and very displeasing to him – of the wilful and the unworldly. She conveyed a sense of something wanton, something wild, forcibly bearing off a nature entirely simple and innocent like a strong tide carrying a child's boat out to sea. It fitted in with his first impression of her long ago, in that pub at Coomagara, as a proud, flirtatious girl, 'ignorant as the dawn'; as it fitted also with his vision of her at the opera, a sleepwalking snow maiden wrapped in a canopy of cold light and passionate music. Not that he would have minded her being wilful or unworldly; but he was always disturbed by the wilful who are also unworldly. He had met them only too often in his business – the Irish are a litigious people – unpersuadable, passionate men and women coming into his office, saying fiercely, 'I want justice!' or 'I'll fight to my last penny for my rights!' As he saw things, the unworldly man (unless he had abandoned the wilful life struggle altogether, like the priest or the professor) was no man. He was unsexed, weak and womanish. Likewise, the unworldly woman (unless she had left the world to become a nun) was no woman. She was a childlike, retarded, silly creature of no interest to any grown man. In fact to him the words man, woman, wilful and unworldly were mutually destructive. He could not even enjoy novels about unworldly women living in the active world, not even satires about them, such as Jane Austen wrote; they were not grown up, they were not nubile, they were not playing their proper role in life.

They strolled arm in arm to the Piazza Barberini. By this time he was more eager than ever to be certain whether she had or had not been unhappy with Rinaldi; a thousand times more eager to find out why she had been unhappy – if she had been; ten thousand times still more eager to know if she had been worldly enough to have taken a lover. The lights shivered over the fountaining spume of Triton. A *carrozza* and two taxis stood waiting. He simply had to dare ask the question uppermost in his mind:

'Molly, we've known one another for so long you won't be angry at my asking you something. You have been unhappy with Rinaldi, haven't you?'

She did not answer. She shook her head so slowly that she might have meant anything by it, such as, 'Who is not unhappy?' or 'How impossible it is to talk of such things now!' It might have been meant as a rebuff. It was a poor evasion, since by not denying it she had virtually admitted it. Nevertheless, a slight doubt remained. He tried another approach:

'Is it very lively in Bergamo?'

'It is intensely boring. The place is so small. So conservative. So clannish. You can imagine it. You live in a small city yourself, or is it a large town? We both know what Cork city is like. Rainy, too, like Bergamo. If Milan were not so near Bergamo, it would be unbearable. They all go to Milan for their pleasures as people from Cork go to Dublin, or to London. Or,' she smiled, looking crookedly at him, 'to Rome. At first this used to upset me. It seemed so cowardly. Why on earth, I used to ask myself, don't people lead whatever life they want to lead? Rinaldi explained to me that it is universal practice not to. Half the tourists, he pointed out to me, are provincials on the loose. We have some American business acquaintances. One of them is a very intelligent and amusing man from the Middle West. He once said to us that all over the United States, even in the most puritanical parts, certain cities are specially protected or preserved for this purpose. He once described to us what night life is like in Kansas City. I was fascinated and appalled.'

He pressed her arm.

'In so boring a city you must be pestered by would-be lovers?'

'Bergamo is full of feelings of honour.'

Her answers enchanted him: intelligent, evasive, delicately ambiguous, a true woman of the world out of another age.

Her taxi drew up. He lifted her hand to his moustache.

'I'll see you in the spring!' he cried. 'If not sooner.'

Since then he had written to her several times. She had told him in her Christmas letter that Rinaldi had died. He had written his condolences. In March he had asked if he might visit her in April.

Two birds, black as the telephone, darted past his window in a flurry of wings and love song. He slowly lifted the receiver, saying to himself, 'If she will lunch with me today, I will tell her about that night in Turin. If the fact that I have kept that secret all these years doesn't convince her . . . ' He finished it aloud: 'I'll be back here tonight.'

2

All the way up to Dublin he made and remade plans. He would blurt out nothing. There were still one or two things about her that he must probe. Had she really been unhappy with Rinaldi? Had he been unhappy with her? If so, whose fault was it? That possible lover? Would she want to marry again? He counted her years in Italy. Bergamo. Milan. Rome. Venice. What would she now think of Cork city, of Hunterscourt! It could be as fine a setting for her, by God, as Castle Boyne next door to him. At once he abandoned the idea – nobody must know until everything was certain. If he failed, they would call him an old fool, an old goat, an old ram.

He passed thirty or forty miles seeing her in his home. She would sing every year, at their opera. Sometimes it lasted a full week. She could be the queen of the whole county. Of the whole country! They would travel, following the opera to Covent Garden, Paris, Salzburg, the Scala, the San Carlo, Rome, the Fenice. Then, just as he was imagining them walking arm in arm from the Hotel Danieli across the Piazza San Marco into the lanes leading to the Fenice, there jumped into his head a remark made to him by a kind friend in Cork only two weeks before in the Yacht Club – it was actually young Boyne, Lord Boyne's eldest brat – 'You know what it is, Wally? You must be by now the oldest established bachelor in the whole of the County Cork! And, by God, you're *still* eligible.' At the sting of that *still*, he almost doubled his speed. Then he slackened it. He was soothed by the recollection of the image he had formed of her at that midnight farewell by the fountain of Triton: a woman of the world out of another age.

Across the table she looked as beautiful and elegant as ever – those lamplike eyes, the corn-fair hair, poreless skin, tinted eyelids, pallid lipstick, paler nails, Via Monte Napoleone frock (she admitted it), tinkling wrist. But where he had expected a *contessa*, he found a young student She behaved exactly as she had the first time he had seen her in Dublin in her student days, crossing the Green from the Academy with two other girls, laughing aloud, white-mouthed, red-lipped, tongue-showing like a cat. When he mentioned it now, she laughed in the same way, and her strong arm across the lunch table grasped his hand like a boy.

'Isn't it wonderful?' she cried, so loudly that people nearby turned to frown, and remained looking, transfixed by her beauty.

'What,' he asked hopefully, 'is wonderful?'

'My being here, of course! Back where my life began. I've done so much, I've travelled, I've made so many friends, I've been flattered and fêted wherever I've gone, and nothing, nothing, nothing has been so marvellous as this coming back, not just to Ireland only, not just only to Dublin – though it's so beauuuuutiful! – but to this very hotel, on this same old Green, that I used to cross every day on my way to the Academy. Do you remember when we were young, Walter? We used to think this hotel was only for the big nobs? Now I have a suite in it. My bathroom is in pale green, even down to the bidet. My bath is sunk in the floor like a Roman bath. Me! Molly O'Sullivan!' She laughed at her folly. 'What are you doing in Dublin, Walter?'

'I'm on a secret mission.'

'Big business?' – with big eyes.

The waiter, bringing the champagne bottle to show, gave him time to command himself.

'If you must know, I'm here because of a woman.'

She again seized his hand in her boyish grip.

'Who is she? Do I know her? Tell me at once. What fun! Are you thinking of marrying? It's not too late.'

'I'm not young,' he confessed wryly. 'I'm forty-six.'

'If the heart is young! How long has this been going on?'

'For quite a number of years.'

She drew back.

'Then it can't be secret? You said, "a *secret* mission".'

Caught by her great eyes, he felt his chest tighten. He was on the point of confessing everything to her when the bottle popped. While the waiter poured for him to taste he formulated a new plan. When the waiter had poured for both of them, and gone, he said:

'Molly! I'll go to confession to you. The reason I rang you was because I want your help. I'm going to spend three days on my secret mission. Within these three days I'm going to decide. Advise me. It's true you are much younger than I am. But you have been married and I have not. Am I being foolish? Marriage is no joke at forty-six.'

He observed her intently. Her eyes sank slowly to her plate. With her fork she began slowly to divide the orange salmon. Was she guessing? Then she lifted her glass, and her eyes were full of kindness.

'Success!' she smiled. 'Tell me about your ladylove.'

'She is about your age. Your colouring, too. She was married. Her husband died. I'd have married her long ago if I hadn't let her slip through my fingers when I was young. Besides, she was engaged, and I didn't want to upset her.'

He believed he had always been drawn to her, but that she had been always dedicated. He was merely interpreting her vocation as a form of engagement. If he were to explain his meaning to her in this way she would understand immediately. He went on telling her of his long devotion and his long restraint.

'And so,' he finished, 'when she became free again I found all my old feelings lighting up as warm as ever after all these years.'

'I would never,' she said warmly, 'have thought it of you, Walter. I had always thought of you as more interested in your career than in anything or anybody else. Tell me more about her.'

His ladylove – so she had called her – lived in Ireland until she was about twenty-one. She had taken a degree in arts at Dublin University. Then she had gone abroad. To Spain. As a governess. After a year of this an uncle died and left her a small legacy. She immediately went to London. To a school of acting. During the war she fell in with one of the Free French. A young aristocrat. Interested in play production. For four years she did all sorts of acting, including provincial repertory. She twice got small parts in the West End, but she never really succeeded on the London stage, probably because, immediately the war ended, she married her Frenchman. They went to live abroad. In Bordeaux.

She was staring out at the Green. He added that there had been no children. She went on looking out at the Green, slowly turning her champagne glass. He said he had an idea that the marriage had not been entirely happy.

'I,' she said, without turning her head, and stopped.

He leaned forward.

'I,' she said, 'you might say, could have made Rome. Even,' a little less assuredly, 'Naples?' Still less assuredly, 'Even Milan? Instead, I married. I am back,' and she stopped again. She finished, speaking with sudden bitterness, 'where I began. She sounds very interesting.' she said without interest. 'I suppose it was because of her you didn't take any interest in me when I was at the Academy. What is her name?'

'I will tell you her name on Wednesday night, my last night, if you will dine with me.'

She smiled warmly, laying her hand on the back of his hand.

'Very well. But if you have not succeeded in your great adventure it won't be a very happy occasion? And if you have succeeded it won't be with *me* you'll be wanting to dine?'

He laid his free palm on the back of her hand. She castled her free palm on the back of his.

'That,' he said, 'is all you know! I'll be so happy if I succeed that there's nobody on earth I'll want to tell everything to sooner than you – where we will live, and what we will be doing for the rest of our lives.'

She gave him a curious look.

'Tell me where you live. I ought to know your house from the old days. Isn't it called Hunterscourt? Where exactly is it?'

He told her all about his house. She asked him so many questions about the life he led, about the people around him, about his neighbours and friends that he wondered if she had already guessed what he was after. Her questions were a bewildering blend of ignorance and shrewdness, as when she asked, with a knowing air, if all fillies ran faster than colts, or, 'Is it a fact that the Shannon is the widest river in the whole world?' But then, when he would be feeling completely dismayed by her folly, he would find himself being asked some coldly sensible question about current land values in Cork County. Was she a grown woman only by fits and starts? They talked for so long that he suddenly noticed that they were the only two people in the restaurant. He immediately became terrified – he had established nothing, found out nothing, asked nothing to the point of his quest, and here she was collecting her gloves. He said wildly:

'But you should see Cork again yourself. It is really a little Bergamo. With the hills, too! But not the antiquities. Or the sun. We haven't the same food. Or the wine. Why don't you pay us a visit? I have a whole big house eating its head off.'

'As a matter of fact I was half thinking of visiting some friends there.'

He felt a twinge of dismay. He knew nobody in County Cork who could have met her since she became famous.

'Who are these friends?' he asked crossly.

'Old Lord Boyne.'

He felt the bite of jealousy. He had gone across his fields to Castle Boyne twice to dine and had had the Boynes back twice to dinner at Hunterscourt: they had talked of Italy, but never mentioned the Rinaldis. Old Boyne's crumbling demesne wall shut out the world.

'I did not know,' he said coldly, 'that you knew the Boynes.'

'We met them last year. We were all staying at the Villa d'Este. In May.'

'In May.'

How childish! In May, before the tourists came. Then you retired to the mountains, then you might look at the sea, turn up later in Venice, go to Egypt if you had the money, then try the skiing, then return to Milan for the gossip and the season. It was a little common of her, really. He drew the lunch to an abrupt close.

As she walked ahead of him past the cocktail lounge she glanced in and casually waved to somebody in there. As he passed he also looked into its artificial dusk. It was young Boyne, his long legs hooped up at the counter. They raised friendly hands in mutual salute. He got the unpleasant feeling of being spied on. In the foyer she thanked him for the wonderful lunch and half turned to the stairs. In sudden despair he held her hand.

'How long are you staying here?'

'Three days.'

'Let's dine tonight!' he begged. 'You haven't given me any advice at all!'

'*Magari!*'

She had a dinner date. Lunch tomorrow? She was going out of town for lunch tomorrow. He had to be content with dinner tomorrow night – his second day otherwise wasted.

'I know so little about you,' he said plaintively, still holding her hand, looking at her. 'Have you relatives out of town? I mean, that you are lunching with tomorrow?'

'We are lunching at Killeen Castle.'

'We?' he smiled, apprehensively.

'I'm going with young George Boyne, he wants to buy a filly from the Sassoon stables.' She shook his hand. '*A domani!*' she beamed at him. 'And, *caro*, best of luck in your secret mission. *Ciaou!*'

Two steps up, she laid her hand on the newel post, turned gracefully and to his amazement winked at him. As if his secret love were some sort of jolly joke! He followed her with lifting eyes and chin. He frowned at the faint ridge of corset across her taut Italianate bottom. The calves of a peasant. He called to her just as she was about to disappear at the turn of the stairs:

'Molly! I'm being around town. Is there any little thing I can do for you?'

She glowed. Yes, there was a small thing. To collect a package from the cleaners, who, she laughed, do express cleaning but not express delivery.

'It will be a pleasure.'

He turned away, bewildered. Definitely not quite a woman, much more than a girl, yet with all the mature beauty of a desirable woman. He wondered how Rinaldi had handled her. Not easily, he guessed, remembering having read somewhere (he had wondered how the fellow knew it) that no women in the world are more passionate than the Irish and less erotic. The thought explained her. He smiled happily and slyly as he moved towards the desk where the hotel register still lay open after the last arrival. She was still unspoiled. And undespoiled. His smile vanished as his eye fell on George Boyne's signature. He stood in the doorway, glaring moodily at the sunlit Green. He turned back and, from the desk, rang her cleaners.

'Yes!' a girlish voice cried, gleefully and proudly. 'Countess Rinaldi's dresses are all ready.'

Dresses? Yes. Two frocks, one costume and an overcoat. He became scarlet at the idea of her expecting him to carry all that load of stuff through the city's streets. He gave the doorman half crown, bade him have the parcel collected, and went across the street into the Green, whirling his stick with annoyance. Really, he thought, the woman is completely juvenile.

Very different, *very* different, to what she had led him to expect.

3

She stood by the window, the lace curtain in her hand, and watched him cross the street and enter the Green, gaily twirling his walking stick. Dear Walter, always fancying himself the lady-killer. I sometimes wonder is he a homosexual, with all that pomade, and the wavy hair, and the smell of *eau verte*, and the tight waist, and the flower in the buttonhole and the dandy's walking stick.

It's wonderful to be back. A lunch like that now with an Italian and he'd be playing footy with you all the time, pressing your knee, paying you sugary compliments. All poor old Walter wants to do is to talk about himself and amuse you. Just the same, even one little compliment would be appreciated. Such as, I heard about your singing, or, I hope you're going to sing for us in Ireland. I said, So that's why you didn't take any interest in me when I was at the Academy, and he just opened his mouth like a fish. But that is the one great drawback in Ireland – they never ask you about yourself. So you're back? they say. That is achievement enough for them.

She drew a deep, slow breath as if she were about to break into song.

And God knows they are right to have a good opinion of themselves, the kindest people on earth. Look at him there now trotting off so nicely to collect my things for me.

He can't be serious about that woman. Or did he make her up? There never was any such a girl in Dublin in my time or I'd have heard of her. It's another one of his jokes, like Cork being a little Bergamo, with the hills, but without the sun, or the monuments, or the food, or the drink. I must tell that one to George. He'd have made it sound perfect if he'd said, And without the mothers, and the grandmothers, and the aunts, and the great-aunts, and the great-grandmothers. But he couldn't be serious, he'd be crazy, he's bald at the top, fifty if he's a day, and when we were at the Academy we thought he was ages. I well remember that first morning I saw him on the Green, with Lil Boylan and Judy Helen. Judy nudged me and said, Here's the college Don Juan, so I put on a great laugh, pretending not to see him at all, doing the innocent young girl up from the country. His eyes nearly fell out of his head. God help me, I didn't need to do much pretending. Sweet seventeen, and now I'm twice as old and with not much more sense. If it's crazy for him, what about me?

He went out of sight among the trees. She let the curtain fall. She looked at herself in the full-length mirror between the windows. She lifted her chin, pulled in her waist and jerked up the corners of her lips.

Thirty-four, and still thinking of *l'amore*? The last word of the famous first act. I never sang Mimi. I haven't the range. It would be another story if I was an actress like his friend. They can go on forever, like men, but not a singer, or not at my age.

She slowly ran her palm up under her chin to see the crepe gather.

That Fratella woman who cracked in the top C in Foggia! The way they whistled at her! Imagine having to take to the road again. Bari. Taranto. Reggio. Catania. What a night! *Carmen*. The rain and the wind howling in from the sea, and an old chipped enamel bucket plonking like a double bass in the corner of the dressing room at every drop from the ceiling. I got six encores.

She smoothed down her hips, turned to laugh sideways at herself, jacket open, hands on hips, wrenched-back shoulders, tilted chin. *L'amour est l'enfant de Bohème qui n'a jamais, jamais connu de loi. Si tu ne m'aime pas je t'aime, prends garde à toi.*

I suppose I ought to be out in that lovely green sun.

What is keeping him down there? I don't even know for certain how old he is. He says twenty-five but all young men add it on, or grow beards like Aldiberti – but he says it sells his *tessuti* better. All I get out of him is compliments, flattery galore, the old Irish plamaus, but always dodging off like a trout just when I think, He's going to ask me now. Like a little fox. Sly. A darling, dear, furry little fox, with a long brush. Giorgio! He's only a boy. If he was an Italian I'd know he was only after the one thing. Dear God, if he is, what must he think of me?

She jangled her wrist loudly. She went to the window. Two girls, carrying books, passed along the rails. She shook her head over them littley-bittley. She chuckled fondly as they passed away gossiping.

Was I innocent when I went to Italy? I was a total fool. And *still* am! Like saying, I'm back where I began. Letting myself down opposite him.

And even then he didn't pay me a compliment. Does that damn bar never close? *Sono la Contessa Maria Maddalena Rinaldi.* And what is it to the Contessa Rinaldi to be the Countess of Boyne? And anyway old Boyne will live to be a hundred. A little Bergamo? I want a big Bergamo, Rome, Paris, London, New York. God in heaven, do I want the same thing all over again? I was mad to have come. It was God sent him, there's no fool like an old fool, I must be mad, I'll finish off the whole thing, I'll have nothing more to do with him, when that telephone rings I'll just say, very, very quietly, a bit sad, to make it real, there's no need to hurt him, I'll say, Giorgio, a terrible thing has happened, I have just received a telegram from Coomagara where my grandfather lies seriously ill.

The telephone buzzed.

I'm independent of him. I could always live in Dublin. They'd jump at me for the Dublin Grand Opera. I could sing for the Rathmines and Rathgar. I could sing on the radio.

The telephone buzzed.

It couldn't be Aldiberti. He doesn't know where I'm staying. But if I say Coomagara he'll say, I'll drive you down. I.

The telephone buzzed.

She put her handkerchief to her mouth and ran to the window, and then ran back to the telephone, and snatched it up.

'Giorgio! What on earth are you doing down there? No, *caro*, you will *not* come up here. Yes, yes, and I might too if it were Milano again. But this isn't Milano. I will meet you in the foyer. Oh! I have had such an amusing lunch. I must tell you all about it. Such an amusing lunch! Such fun!'

4

Halfway across the Green he stopped dead. He felt that triple pain of emptiness, inertia and frustration which man calls loneliness. He crossed over to the Club. The bar was closed, the library was empty, the billiard table lay under a grey shroud. He walked slowly, killing time, twirling his stick, down the quays to Farquharson and Murphy's about a conveyance that, he knew, could as well be settled in a month's time by a post card. He walked back, slowly, across the Liffey, over Capel Street bridge, along the quays, along Grafton Street, into Knowles's, where he ordered two dozen red roses to be sent at once to her room. On the card he wrote: *Carissima, Red Roses for Thee*. He walked slowly on to Prost's, where he had a shampoo and a hot towel. He walked out to the Shelbourne. He had a word with Leo at the door. He had a word with Christy O'Connor at the bar, and a prolonged Tio Pepe. He then decided to have tea in the lounge. He stood at the door and recognized three old regulars. His breath stopped. She was seated in a corner, laughing gaily with young Boyne. He withdrew quickly and went out. Outside, he bought the *Evening Mail*. He saw, with a groan, that the Rathmines and Rathgar were once again, yet once again, doing *The Mikado* at the Gaiety. There was not a damn thing that he wanted to see, not even a film. He looked aimlessly all about him. He walked to the hotel. He undressed. He went to bed.

He awoke at six. He had a bath. He shaved. He changed. He went down to the front door. He selected Davy Byrne's for his *apéritif* and strolled, with pleasant anticipation, across the Green. The public part of the bar was full of what he called up-from-the-countrys, men and women with felt hats and paper parcels. He was about to persist into the rear lounge when he thought, though he was not certain of it, that he saw, through the ornamental wrought-iron gate, young Boyne's poll, and thought, again uncertainly, that the poll turned and a cold eye glimpsed him. He turned to go, and then, because he had to be certain, turned again and entered through the gate into the lounge bar. There was nobody sitting at the table by the gate. On the small black-topped table he saw two glasses, one half filled. She had not told him who she was dining with. He went swiftly through the bar and out through the rear door, and by the side lane back to the street. He saw nobody there whom he knew. He walked across the street to the Bailey. There he found a red beard talking about vintage cars in a loud haw-haw voice to a black R.A.F. moustache a foot wide. He went down to the Buttery. It was crowded, but there were a few two-splits-behind and a few fast fillies, so he sat up at the bar. He had a word with George and a prolonged Tio Pepe. He was afraid to dine at any city restaurant, so he walked back to the hotel. He got out the Mercedes and drove out of town to the Yacht Club. He parked, reserved a table, and went for a stroll along the East Pier.

He always liked the force of that stony white arm curved against the ponderous sea. Dublin smoked faintly to the west, low-lying as an encampment, sharp-edged as a saw, pensive as Sunday. Great pink

clouds lay like overblown roses strewn along the bruise-blue horizon.
Inch by inch the calm evening began to fade into a dusk the colour of
cigarette smoke. Some townspeople, lured by the calm weather, were
walking on the pier, taking the air, inspecting one another. A few early
yachts, anchored to their reflections, pointed their noses eastward – the
town's best weather vanes. For a few moments he paused to watch the
gulls soaring and sinking about the funnel of the mailboat steaming
gently at its pier. At first he passed many strollers, in pairs and fours,
chatting companionably, but they became fewer the farther out he
walked towards the pier's end with its lighthouse lantern blank and
unrevolving.

Gradually he felt the wide sky, the wide bay and the oncoming dusk
begin to envelop and isolate him. Now there were no strollers at all.
The white tower and the glass of the many-windowed lantern rose
coldly above him. When he looked back he saw a few lighted windows
along the front. He barely made out the seagulls circling above the
mailboat, blue blobs, but he did not hear their cries. The tall windows
of his club were greenly lit. Behind the town the Dublin mountains
rolled, empty and opaque, as if he were looking at them through
smoked glass. Suddenly a yellow finger of light touched the dusty water
of the harbour, moved across it, and then the electric string of lamps
along the front and down the pier were lit. He climbed the stone steps
up the side of the sea wall and went out through the embrasure. There
was the night sea, the cold east wind, the sullen wash and slop of
waves, one star.

How wonderful it would be now to have her, here, by his side, about
to dine with him, hostess of a big dinner party in the club, at the head
of the table, admired, glancing lovingly down its length at him. They
would have lots of parties. How wonderful it would be to turn from this
sea and wind and find her coming towards him now through the dusk,
his phantom, seagull-white, smiling with winged lips. They would
walk back along the stony arm, her soft arm in his. They would dine
in the club, alone, make plans for travel, talk about opera, return to
the city, not needing anybody, together, alone. The chilly wind said,
But she isn't. Away out in the darkness the Kish lightship blinked. The
chill wind said, Aren't you a fool to dream like this? What would one
of your clients, what would Farquharson or Murphy think of you? He
replied, self-mocking, This is another department, and remembered
that somebody (and with a start he remembered that it had been old

Lord Boyne) once said to him, We are rational about everything except our passions and our children. The wind said, It is cold. His shiver admitted it. He descended the steps and walked swiftly back along the dark and empty monolith. It was like some big public building closing for the night.

He was glad to see a fire alight in the club. His table was marked *Reserved*, unnecessarily – it was early in the season for diners. There was nobody in the silent dining room with its empty white tables; its portraits of bearded commodores, its enormous Victorian seascapes bloomed like grapes. Once a man's head appeared around the door, said a cheery good night, and vanished. He heard the voice of a young man bantering the waitress in the kitchen, and her repeated laughter. He had often seen her smile, never heard her laugh. Once he thought how, more than once during the day, he had had half a notion to throw up the whole thing and go back to Cork. Not now! He drank off his claret with determination. Tomorrow night he would put her to the test. Finally.

The lighthouse swept at intervals. He prolonged his brandy, carefully shaping the words he would say to her. His blood thickened. The dark thickened. He dared not look at his watch. There were no hands on its face. The mailboat hooted before departure. Only nine? He called for a cigar. He ordered another brandy and took it into the reading room so that the waitress could be finished with him. He sat in the empty reading room, on the long leather-covered settee, facing the harbour and the beam that slowly circled and recircled the compass of the night. Slowly his courage oozed. She was at this moment dining with George Boyne.

He surrendered, went to his Mercedes, and drove into the bright city, and through it, and out of it, for home, driven by the furies of his own folly, contempt for his indecision, worked-up hate, bitter pride, cruel reason. It was after two when he pulled up at the gate to Hunterscourt. The house was dark. Here, together, when dark came, after dinner, they would not hear a sound unless it would be Mrs Canty in the kitchen rattling cutlery, or the fire puttering at their feet; later they might hear cows munching, or a plane facing out over the sea; latest of all, lying together in the darkness, they would hear nothing at all.

He turned and drove hell-for-leather back to Dublin, chasing his shivering headlights, passing sleeping cottages, dark villages, echoing through empty towns. He would insist on seeing her at breakfast.

5

George was laughing at her across the small, red table lamp. Over its upthrown light his handsome young face, pointed like a fox, his wide, mocking mouth, his madcap eyes, gleamed like a teenage Mephistopheles.

'Tell him at breakfast,' he said. 'Why keep the poor old fathead in misery until dinner?'

When he drew back she had to peer around the red lamp to see him. Usually when he was in this crazy mood she wanted to devour him the way a mother wants to devour a baby. Through her tears she was aware how his air of wickedness suited him.

'I can't believe it,' she protested. 'Old Walter!'

'He's not as old as all that,' he said crossly. 'Be realistic. He's not much older than you than you are than me. He is still considered one of the most eligible bachelors in County Cork.'

'But I assure you – he never uttered one word to me about marriage.'

'Molly! For the last time! He told you he was in love with an Irishwoman. Whom he met when he was a student. Who studied abroad. Who went on the stage, married a foreigner, lived abroad, is now a widow, has your colouring, is about your age. And he said he is in Dublin to try his fortune with her. Isn't that enough? Without the two dozen red roses – and the *carissima*? What more do you want? Unless,' his voice hardened as he again leaned over the little lamp-glow and peered at her with suspicion, 'you've been making it up. *Pour encourager les autres?*'

She leaned back, twisting her rings, surveying his under-lighted face.

Earlier they had strolled around the Green, had tea at the Shelbourne, strolled again, just barely dodged him in Davy Byrne's. They dined happily at Jammet's until the wine and the brandy began to go to his head and he had begun groping under the table.

'I don't want that, Giorgio!'

'Liar!'

'Well, not only that!'

'Then what else do you want? A title?'

'I have a title.'

'Haw-haw! Wop title!'

She made him apologize; he fell into a dark mood, and would not talk. Embarrassed by the waiters' glances – she suspected that they were not unacquainted with his moods – she had quietly proposed that they bring the evening to an end, whereupon he suddenly became plaintive and begged her not to break off on this note. So they drove, in his car, out of the city up into the hills to the turn of the road at Killakee from which all Dublin lies below, a half-dish of lights encircling the dark bay. Far away a lighthouse slowly circled.

She had been afraid there might be more demands for caresses here. Instead, when she withdrew to her end of the seat, leaning against the window, looking down at the lighted plain, he withdrew to his corner. He did not even once touch her hand. They were silent for a long time. Then he said, reverting to an earlier run of talk at the Shelbourne:

'Tell me more about your lunch today. It fascinates me. What exactly, tell me again, did old Hunter say about this woman of his?'

She humoured him, let him lead her through the whole conversation, back and forth, as if she were a witness in the box. When he had exhausted her memory he fell silent. Whenever the wind whispered the lights far below seemed to flicker. In his dark corner he chuckled to himself, his only comment, at that stage, a contemptuous:

'He has no such woman.'

'Poor Walter! He has to pretend.'

'The man is a goose. Dammit, he ought to know the world better by now. He's old enough!'

'You don't need to be so cruel.'

She was the goose. She should not have come. Sullenly from his corner he had said:

'So you have allotted two dinners to him and only one to me?'

If he had said it in simple disappointment she might have presumed affection – not when he said it sulkily, superbly self-concerned, out of the hurt vanity of a young man. She had drawn her coat around her neck, felt all her years, asked him quietly:

'How old are you, Giorgio?'

'I told you.' Crossly. 'Twenty-five. Why?'

'Does one dinner more or less with me mean so very much to you?'

'It could be a test of how much you love me.'

'And how much do you love me, Giorgio? And in what sense, Giorgio, do you love me?'

From his corner, in a very loud voice, as if he had been asked if he liked *risotto*:

'Very much. In every sense. After Milano you should know that.' Then his tone had suddenly changed, softened, deepened: 'I don't know when I met anybody I liked more than you. I'd marry you like a shot if I could.'

'And are you married, Giorgio?' – wanly.

In a furious, sarcastic mutter:

'My mother has other plans for me.'

'So the Contessa Rinaldi is not good enough for the Countess of Boyne!'

At this he had laughed gaily. It was one reason why she liked him so much: his moods could change like the wind scurrying over the surface of a lake. He said:

'I do wish you would understand the way things really happen in this world. It's got nothing to do with your not being good enough. It's simply that you are broke. As a matter of fact my mother has a great admiration for you. From her point of view it's wholly to your credit that you should have been born in that filthy old pub at Coomagara. Why, she holds you up to me as a model of what *can* be done with nothing. She says you are a spirited and clever woman. But you don't know how tough she is. And she's inquisitive as a hen. That time we met you on the Lakes she went snooping all around the hotel trying to find out about you and Rinaldi. It wasn't difficult. One night at dinner, on the terrace – all those little lamps, the full moon on the lake, the little steamer floating by with its dance music – after the three of us had passed your table, bowing, she shook out her napkin, and whispered to my father and me, like the damned old witch she is, "My dears, I've just had the most interesting talk with that tall old lady from Milan. She knows the Rinaldis intimately. They are completely on the rocks, just as poor as we are."'

'Why did she spy on us?'

'Because she saw I was keen on you, of course. Why else?'

'And are you really so poor?' she had asked dully.

'My mother says she's going to turn Castle Boyne into a guesthouse for rich Americans.'

'So that's that?'

'That's that, my dear!'

She had looked across at him, immobile, glaring out over the lighted dashboard at the lights of Dublin.

'Giorgio, are you wondering if I'm wondering whether your story is true or not?'

'It's all too true!'

'Giorgio, tell me. What is your chosen bride like? My colouring? A bit younger? My figure? Lived abroad? Went to – '

'Stop it! She's no age, no figure, no colouring. We have never seen her. My mother says she will be one of the rich Americans.'

She had shivered with pity for him, and said:

'Let's go and dance somewhere. The cold of death is in my bones.'

So they had come down here to this obscure little supper-and-dancing place, somewhere off the windy quays, so dimly lit she could not decipher the travel posters on the walls. They could barely see one another. Now and again other couples would appear out of the dusk on the tiny floor, but there was no telling how few or how many other people were there. They danced to the radiogram. Once she said, 'Do you like this place?' He said, 'No, but what else is there to do?' They ordered *risotto*. He had brandies; to save his pocket she drank beer. She knew he was in his wicked mood when he said, 'These are Italian travel posters. I believe one of them invites us all to come to Bergamo.'

It was after his third brandy that he had leaned over the lamp and cackled:

'Molly, are you really so utterly innocent that you don't know what Walter Hunter is after?'

And then he told her, and she refused to believe him until he beat her down and down. When he saw her in tears he bade her airily not to cry – she could still accept her old beau. Her protestations became feebler and feebler. She surrendered only when he asked her if she had been making it all up, 'to encourage the others'.

She leaned back to survey him, in all three of them, the ridiculous lurches of love.

'I suppose', she said sadly, 'you don't realize that you are trying to bully me, Giorgio. But why should you care? You're as good as betrothed to an American from Minneapolis.'

'I do care!' he cried back at her.

'Yet you want me to marry Walter Hunter?'

'I want you to marry nobody but me.'

She was so astonished by his tone that she snatched the red shade off the lamp. In the naked light his face was transformed. He looked about seventeen, his mouth melting, his eyes misted. Furiously he snatched the shade from her and restored the ruby dusk. There was a prolonged silence, except for the slither of dance shoes and the staccato hiss of a gourd in a Cuban thrum. She collected her bag and gloves:

'I wish I were rich. Innocent child that you are! Let's go. The night is finished.'

'One more dance?'

They did not dance it Cuban-way. They held one another very tight. He made her feel like a mother with a child. Then he called the waiter, fumbled with the bill and his wallet, said brusquely to her, 'I haven't enough, can you lend me a quid?' She did not dare not take the change from him. They walked back arm in arm across the river, around the locked-up Green. Down here in the plain the wind was slight. The stars were out in their legions. In the empty foyer of the hotel he said:

'I suppose I've cooked my goose with you now?'

'There wasn't any goose, Giorgio,' she said fondly, and bent her cheek to be kissed. 'Only a little *poussin*. Sleep well.'

'I'm not going to sleep. It's a fine night for driving. I'll be home in time to see the morning coming up over your little Bergamo. Have a nice breakfast with old Wally.'

She did not sleep until late morning. Her shame kept her awake, and the image of that young face, lean, sensitive, cruel, greedy, madcap, enchanting, lovable, staring through the headlights fleeing before him. She kept turning and twisting in her bed and in her mind away from thoughts of Walter Hunter. It would be a refuge. All her worldly wisdom told her it would be a sensible and interesting and dangerous refuge. So close to George. With his rich American wife? Poor Giorgio!

6

Tired from his long drive, he did not wake until late morning. When he was about to go downstairs he found an envelope angled under his door. It contained a sheet of hotel note-paper bearing a message from her. *Dear Walter, If you are free for lunch do join me in the foyer at noon. I shall be alone. Molly*. He hastened down. She looked up at him with a wan smile.

'This is delightful, Molly! But you said you were lunching with the Killeens?'

'I decided not to go.'

'Our dinner tonight is all right?' he asked.

'We must make it lunch instead, Walter. I cannot dine with you tonight, I am flying to Milan. Let's go into lunch at once, shall we?'

He followed her, aghast. He sat on the edge of his chair, he fiddled with his knife, he stared at her, he told the waiter they did not wish to drink, he called him back.

'Yes, drinks, please,' he panted. 'Molly? Champagne?'

'Please, Walter!' she groaned. 'Not champagne!'

'Two Martinis.'

He glared at her blankly. All his carefully prepared words had flown away like escaped pigeons.

'And tomorrow night, too? Is that dinner gone, too?' He was getting more and more angry. 'Really, this is too bad of you, Molly!'

She could only open her palms and smile sadly. She saw that he was so upset that he was liable to say the first thing that came into his head, and to her dismay, she found that his anger and his misery made him more *simpatico* than she had ever found him before.

'Molly!' he barked. At once he said, 'Sorry!' and laughed, and then coughed, and said, 'I had a wonderful night last night. I dined alone. At the Yacht Club.'

She looked at her hands. Was she expected to ask, Why wonderful? She looked up. He became aware of her pallor. Her eyes were tired, as if she, too, had not slept. It gave her, as on that night of summer rain in Rome, the vanishing beauty of a peach ripened to the full point when it ought to be picked and eaten at once. He said, in a little voice – strange and rather touching to her in a man so broad, big and ruddy:

'You are pale, Molly. It makes you even more beautiful.'

She smiled feebly at the compliment.

'I didn't sleep very well.'

'I did not sleep at all. I drove all the way down to Cork after dinner. And back again.'

She closed her eyes. He too? This, she thought, is one of those things I will laugh at when I am an old woman.

'Rather a long drive,' she said flatly.

'It was after six before I got back. But I didn't mind. I was thinking of the woman I love. From the hill above Saggart I saw the morning sun spreading over Dublin. I was thinking of her, asleep. Her hair strewn on the pillow.'

His pigeons were circling, sinking, coming back to him. His eyes began to glow. Any minute now, she felt, he will come to it. They picked at random from the outsize menu. He lifted his glass.

'You know,' he said, more at his ease now, 'the only times I ever saw you alone you looked pale, lovely, and unhappy.'

'Alone?' she asked, startled.

'Alone, I mean, since we were students. Yesterday. Now. That wet night in Rome. The first time was in Turin.'

'We never met in Turin.'

He leaned forward.

'I did not say met, I said saw. It was in 'Forty-six. Just after the war. I had gone up to Cervinia for the skiing . . .'

He went bit by bit through his story. With apprehension he noted that she paid no attention to the omelette that had been placed before her. She was staring fixedly through the muslin curtains at the Green. By the time he said, 'They were playing *La Sonnambula*,' he saw, with puzzlement, that her eyes were tear-covered. At the end, when he said, 'You walked out on the stage and I nearly died,' she looked straight at him through the water of her tears.

'And you were actually there all the time! Why on earth didn't you come around afterwards?'

They stared at one another; she waiting for his answer, he gaping at her because he no longer knew the answer. His secret image of her had vanished. Rapidly, as if he were racing backwards after it, he tried to re-create the night, talked of the music act by act, of her songs, of her singing, the lighting, the last falling curtain.

'Walter, you know it so well! And you are so right about that night in Turin. It was one of the best performances I ever gave. As I have good reason to know. But why did you never tell me all this?'

He saw himself in that café, waiting for the train at two in the morning.

'I don't know,' he gasped. 'I was so lonely! And I was so happy!'

She threw up her chin and she laughed the strangest laugh, a laugh like a breaking wave, curling and breaking between pride and regret.

'I was happy too. If you only knew! I often wonder was I ever quite so happy since. It was that very night, between the acts, in my dressing room, that Rinaldi came in and first told me he was in love with me.

Do you remember that enormous bouquet I got at the curtain? Great *reine de joie* roses, straight up from Africa, he had telephoned for them that morning to Milan. They came only just in time, the boy ran with them in his arms, from the taxi, right on to the stage. There were snowflakes on them. They must have cost him the earth. But he was always a spendthrift. No wonder we went broke!' She drew in a deep, passionate, hissing, sobbing breath between her clenched teeth, her eyes swimming, her fists crunched together. 'I'm glad we were broke. I'd do it again. It's the only way to live. Not giving a damn.'

'And I,' he said, 'was sitting for hour after hour after the show in a café, drinking, thinking of you, lost in you!'

'Do you know,' she raced on, lost in herself, 'what we did after the show? You should have been there. Rinaldi invited the whole company to a party as his hotel. He whistled up such a party as you've never seen. Dancing, singing, champagne. And when it was all over, and they were all gone, and now that it's all over forever and all gone forever, I can tell you, Rinaldi and I, left alone . . .'

She hid her screwed-up face in her hands. The sensual picture she evoked sent the blood to his eyes. He stared at her, feeling the first pangs of jealousy, loss, creeping lust. He waited until she was blowing her nose, looking at him self-mockingly, fishing for her compact in her bag, glancing about the restaurant to see if anybody had observed her. She said:

'For two years I kept refusing him. Then I decided that I never would be a great singer.' She shrugged. She looked up at him with sudden recollection: 'What did you say you did that night?'

He told her again, with bitter feeling. She shook her head.

'What a *salade* we make of our lives!' she sighed.

'So you were unhappy with Rinaldi.'

'Unhappy? Who said I was unhappy?'

'You have conveyed it to me in a dozen ways. Molly!' he said intensely, leaning over to her. 'Don't try to deceive me. You can't. Don't try to deceive yourself by idealizing him now. You are in the prime of life, your whole life is before you, you can't stop living.' He paused. He asked it quietly, but unmistakably: 'Would you dare look for happiness again?'

She looked at him for a long while. He hid his trembling hands under the table. She lowered her face in her hands and he saw that her hands, too, were trembling. He leaned back and waited for his fate. When she

raised her head and he saw the tears in her eyes again, he knew that
he had evoked the one night of all her life that he could never defeat.
She said, so softly that he had to lean forward to hear her:

'Walter! Nobody ever finds happiness. We make it, the way people
mean when they say, "Let's make love". We create it. For all I know
we imagine it. We make happiness easily when we are young, because
we are full of dreams, and ideals, and visions, and courage. We make
our own world that pushes away the other world – your world, and my
world, old people's worlds. The young despise the world. Didn't you
ever say it when you were young? I'll conquer the world! But you know
what happens to us. That little flame in us that could burn up the world
when we're young – we sell a little bit of it here, and a little bit of it
there, until, in the end, we haven't as much of it left in us as would
light a cigarette. And yet,' she said, frowning through him, 'it is there,
to the end. You feel always you might blow on it, make it big again,
go on to the very end, without giving up, find the thing, discover the
thing, invent the thing, call it anything you like, that you'd always
been wanting. Walter, I am not your thing. You are not my thing. I
have very little courage left in me, Walter. In fact,' she moaned, 'I have
hardly any left in me at all. That's why I'm flying to Milan tonight.
My bags are packed and ready in the hall. Don't come with me.'

She grabbed her gloves and her handbag, shook hands with him
strongly, and quickly left the restaurant.

In the hotel porch, while her suitcases were being loaded on a taxi,
she picked up a coloured post card of Saint Stephen's Green, addressed
it to The Honourable George Boyne, Ringaskiddy, Co. Cork, and
scrawled on it: *I did it well, nobly and virtuously, and you would have
thought me a damn fool. I have all my life to wonder if I was. M.* As
she stepped into the taxi she saw, down along the wine-red line of
Georgian buildings, a gathering of students, girls and boys, outside the
University Club, chattering and laughing gaily. She looked at them
without envy, slammed the door of the taxi, and drove away.

He let the lace curtain fall. He sat on, sipping a brandy. For the first
time in his life he felt the agony that a man suffers in the full awareness
of loss. All his senses are alerted a millionfold. His brain burns like a
forest fire. And he feels as if the essential parts of his body have been
cut out. He saw her hands, her dilated eyes, her convoluted smile. They
were not only her hands, eyes and smile but the beauty and desirability

of everything unattainable in life. From his pocket he drew out her letter of an hour ago and read it. He saw only the force of her wrist, the strength of her body. He saw her as he had never dared to see her before: those firm calves, the breadth of her hips, her narrow waist, her rich breasts, her yellow pile of hair falling down over her bare body. All this he had lost, as a duellist can lose, forever, as a boxer can lose, forever, as a damned soul loses, forever. This, he knew, he had always wanted. He ordered a brandy, and another, and another, until he was left there alone, seeking for her other image in the round, shining snifter, as one seeks in those toy, round globes that when you shake them give the illusion of falling snow, a tiny figure, remote as a fairy tale, white and virginal, smiling out at him. If he could see her like that, the snow falling silently, the arc lamps fogged by it, the soft thunder in his veins, the music weaving in his memory, he would be happy even though he knew that he would never see her otherwise again. Always the proud, rich, sensual image came before him, smiling, full of love, but not for him.

He gave the young waiter who had been patiently attending him a heavy tip, and went out hatless across the Green to the record shop on Dawson Street. An April shower spattered the shopwindow as he sat in the little booth listening to the '*Ah, non credea mirarti,*' looking out at the falling shower, at the passers-by. The song was as pure as a lark in the clear air. It evoked only the image of a naked Venus. He bought it, went across the street to Doran's pub, from Doran's to the gentle dimness of the empty Buttery, from there to Davy's and from there across to the Bailey. All that afternoon and evening and night he ate nothing. There are in Dublin occasions of vice more squalid by far than in cities that have not been cleaned up. When he reeled out of his last pub late that night, he sought out one of these places, and entered his little season of hell.

He woke up about four in the morning, lying in a lane along the garages and stables at the backs of some houses. He felt a cold mist falling on him. There was congealed blood on his forehead. His pockets were emptied of mone . Unheeded, he got back through the empty city to his car outside the hotel, and managed to drive out of the city. He pulled up on the hill above Saggart and got out to wash himself in a stream.

The rain had stopped. There was Dublin's dish of coloured lights below him on the still-dark plain. A cold light touched the underside of the clouds over the Irish Sea. Far away the Bailey lighthouse circled slowly through the pre-morning dusk. He stayed looking over the city and the sea for a long while, watching them slowly become cold and clear, until two sunbeams leaped from below the horizon, a bird threw out a pillar of song, and, as if to its conductor's baton, all the birds at once began to sing like blazes. He closed his eyes and whispered 'Christ!' out of the depths of his delight and misery. Then he went back to the car and drove away into the cold wetness of the morning.

A dream? Ah, well! It wasn't such a bad dream. If only I hadn't tried to make it become real. Still, isn't this the way most of us spend our lives, waiting for some island or another to rise out of the mist, become cold and clear, and ... so ...

## Miracles Don't Happen Twice

I met Giancarlo on the seafront of Bari late one dank night in October. The Adriatic wind was cold. The waves slapped drearily along the Lungomare. Because of the chilly wind and the gusts of rain only a few people were out of doors, although all Bari loves to gravitate every night to the seafront, enjoying the lights of the cinemas, the big hotels, the fish-vendors' flares, and an occasional boat offshore luring the fish to the spear with white, down-thrown lamps. I had paused to look with amusement at a travel poster showing the Tower of London as red as wine under an improbably blue English sky. The lights glistened on the raindrops sliding down it. 'Yes!' I was thinking. 'And I suppose outside Victoria Station the rain is pelting posters of sunny Italy.' A voice at my side said:

'*E freddo stasera, signore.*'

He was a little man, with pansy-dark eyes. He was smiling an engaging smile. He wore a raincoat but no hat and he carried a briefcase. One glance at him and I was in no doubt that he belonged to a large and ancient Italian profession. Then, instead of asking me if I wanted a nice girl, he said comfortingly that the sun would shine again tomorrow, and then, in English:

'You are English, *signore?*'

I said 'Yes,' because I have found in Italy that if I say I come from Ireland either they say, 'Ah, yes! The dykes and the windmills!' or else a haze comes over their eyes and I have to explain that Ireland is an island near England – which I find a little humiliating and they find disappointing. Sometimes, when I really want to please them, I choose to be an American and invent a home in Chicago or Minneapolis.

'I also have been in England,' said the little man eagerly. 'My sister lives in England. Near Bournemouth. Do you know Bournemouth, *signore?* I know it very well. And Poole. And Eastbourne.'

As he chattered on I began to wonder if he were a real professional. Perhaps he was merely an amateur who would presently produce picture post cards, cheap coral brooches or American cigarettes from his little bag, and would mention girls only if all else failed. I fell into talk with him willingly. Bari is not an exciting city; the hours after dinner are the most lonely hours for a traveller; and, anyway, I have a sympathetic feeling for Italian pimps. They are not bad fellows. They are a race outside our world. They do not tempt us. We tempt them. They have no wish to harm us. They will merely assist us to harm ourselves if we so desire.

After a while I said, 'Let's get out of this beastly wind and have a drink somewhere,' and we began to walk past the Old Port towards the Corso, talking about Dorset. But he did not pause at the Corso, for he said kindly: 'It is too expensive here. I know a good place,' and led me onward in o the dark and winding streets of the old town away behind the docks, until, in a particularly dark and narrow alley, we came to a hole in a wall. It was a wineshop, arched, empty, brightly lit. There we sat to a trestled table, over a flask of acrid wine. We were alone.

'And what is your sister working at in England?' I asked.

'Oh! She is not working,' he said proudly. 'She is married to a wealthy paper manufacturer.'

'Really?' I said, deciding that for tonight I would have to be at least a Sheffield steel king.

'But it is true!' he assured me, instantly interpreting my look. 'Veritably true! She went there when she was eleven. Her name then was Federica Peruzzi. Now her name is Mrs Philpot.'

He produced an envelope bearing an English stamp. The dove-grey paper was deckled, embossed with an address in Bournemouth, and signed Federica.

'It happened so,' he explained. 'After the first war I and my sister were only small children. We lived in Altamura, up in the hills. We had nothing to eat. We came down to Bari because we heard the British navy was in the port.' He shrugged and made a face of shame. 'We were begging outside the big hotels on the seafront. What else could we do? All I had to sell was one double-almond. As you know, the double-almond brings luck. And,' he cried, with a vast, baby-faced smile, 'mine brought luck to me. For one night when a sea captain came out of the Grand Hotel I offered him my double-almond. He took it. He looked at me. He looked at my sister. He looked and looked at her. And suddenly he began to weep. "*Signore*," I said, "why are you crying?" He took me aside and he began to ask me questions, but he could not take his eyes from my sister. I was very troubled for her. I was only fourteen, and in Altamura they had said that we should find the big world in the valley a very wicked place.'

Giancarlo wriggled apologetically with his whole body.

'You see, I loved my little sister, and she was only eleven. But the captain soon explained. His name was Captain Edgeworth. He had lost his only child during the war, and he said that Federica was the living image of his Gladys who had died. And as he said this he became sad and wept again. I knew then that he was an honest man.

'The captain gave me fifty lire and told us both to be at the hotel again the next morning at ten o'clock. Oh! What a meal we had that night! It is thirty-four years ago and never since have I eaten a better meal. Never, never, never as long as I live will I forget that meal. All night Federica could not sleep. She kept waking me up and crying out, "Giancarlo! Our fortunes are made! The rich Englishman will take care of us for the rest of our lives." But I said, "Sleep, little one. We shall never see the captain again. Let us be content with our fifty lire."'

Clearly, so far, a true story. Those cries of hope were not invented. They could only have come out of the old Italian belief in magic, miracles, the wheel of fortune, the *Totocalcio* (their football pools), in short, some *deus ex machina* who alone can change the hopeless reality of life.

'But I was wrong, *signore*. The captain was waiting for us the next morning. He said, "Now we go to Altamura". We took the train into the hills. He slept that night in the one bed between me and my father, with Federica asleep at the tail of it. He ate our poor food, roasted herrings and dry bread. He trusted me with all his money. I could have run away with it all, but I did not touch one lire of it. He arranged between my father and a lawyer to adopt Federica, and to change her name to Edgeworth. The next day we returned to Bari and he took Federica with him to England. When he died he left her all his money. She met a Mr Philpot and married him. Now she has two sons. One of them was fighting here in Italy during the war.'

He drew out his wallet and showed me a crumpled family photograph: two youths, a very lean, English-looking papa and a middle-aged woman full of Italian fat.

'And you?' I asked. 'Did the captain do anything for you?'

'Had I not given up my sister whom I loved? Of course, he gave me money. I travelled a little. I have even been to Rome. I became a valet to a rich American lady in Rome. But I was not happy with her. She was not young and she was not beautiful and she was always trying to make love to me. I could have married her and had all her money, but I was young and romantic, and I wanted real love. Once Federica brought me to Bournemouth. I was unhappy there too. I saw that she did not want me any more. I came back to Bari. I fell in love. I got married.'

He removed his raincoat and showed me the tab. It bore the name and address of Burton's in Piccadilly.

'Federica sent me this coat. Sometimes she sends me shirts and shoes. But never any money.'

We had some more wine. He asked me about my life. I described to him my two steel factories near Sheffield. He said he was gratified and honoured to know me. We talked of his life and with a shrug of self-contempt he gave me a glimpse into his briefcase: brooches of orange-pale coral, picture post cards, American cigarettes. I found that he sometimes gets jobs as a waiter. We talked of the *Totocalcio*. I bought a ticket for him from the *padrone*, and selected the teams, and wrote in his name. As I wrote in his name the sound of the wintry wind outside was one with his deep breathing into my ear.

'It will be lucky,' he cried. 'I know it! It will win a prize! Will it not, Giacomo?' – turning to the *padrone*, who merely lifted his shoulders and let them fall again. We had some more wine. It was half past eleven before we rose and went out into the wind and the darkness. As he walked down the lane Giancarlo stopped and turned. I was afraid that he was going, at last, to ask me if I wanted a nice girl, and I dearly hoped he would not. When he did not I hoped that I understood why. We had drunk wine together, we had exchanged confidences, we were friends.

Just then the yellow light from a window fell on a dark-haired little girl of about eleven who had come dashing up to him, clasping him about the knees, saying, 'Momma is looking for you!' He lifted her into his arms, and kissed her passionately. Then he turned slowly towards me, gazed at me in awe, and whispered:

'This is Federica!' And to her, as if he were showing her the statue of a saint in church: 'Little one! This is a rich Englishman who has just arrived in Bari.'

For one entranced moment the two of them gazed at me. By the child's wide eyes I knew that she had often heard poppa's fairy tale. For that one moment, in that dark wind-swept alley, I knew what it feels like to be a god in a machine. Then a gust of rain came blasting down on us. I groped in my hip pocket for a note and crumpled it into Giancarlo's fist, gripped his arm, said the hour was late, said my family was waiting for me at my hotel, cried, '*Arivederci!*'

Half an hour later I was lying in the warmth of my bed in the Grand Hotel delle Nazioni. Outside I could hear the slapping waves and the wind moaning down from Altamura.

# No Country for Old Men

1

One morning last September, all the Dublin papers carried headlines like these:

END OF CARNDUFF TRIAL

ONE YEAR FOR COMPANY DIRECTOR

This is how one daily paper reported the conclusion of the odd affair:

At the Belfast Assizes yesterday, sentences of one year and of six months respectively were passed on Joseph Peter Cassidy (sixty-three), described as a manufacturer and company director, and Frederick Robert Wilson (fifty-seven), described as accountant and secretary. Both men gave their address as Boyne Close, County Louth. Cassidy had been charged with the illegal possession of a revolver and six rounds of ammunition, with being a member of an illegal organization, and with entering Northern Ireland by an unrecognized road on the night of July 15th last. Wilson had been charged with membership in an illegal organization and entering Northern Ireland by an unrecognized road on the same date.

In sentencing the accused, Mr Justice Cantwell said that on the night in question an attack had been made on Carnduff Police Barracks, in the course of which a policeman had been shot dead, and that, after the attack a motor van, the admitted property of Cassidy, had been found only two miles away from Carnduff, its interior heavily stained with blood.

During the trial both defendants insisted that they had no connection whatever with the attack on Carnduff Barracks and that they had entered Northern Ireland on the night in question solely in search of the motor van, which had been removed without permission from the premises of Celtic Corsets Ltd, of Boyne Close,

Drogheda. Cassidy said that he had carried the revolver solely for his own protection.

Mr Cassidy is a well-known Dublin businessman, a widower with one son, managing director of Celtic Corsets Ltd, and of Gaelic Gowns Ltd. Mr Wilson is secretary to the firm of Celtic Corsets Ltd, and is unmarried. Both men took part in the 1916 Rising and served side by side in the First Dublin Brigade during the War of Independence.

Both accused have been removed to Crumlin Road Prison, Belfast, to serve their sentences.

The reports in all the other papers were equally short, not to say meagre. And yet none of us considered that they should have been more informative. The fact is that whenever perfunctory reports like this appear in the Irish papers we all understand at once that the press is laying a finger on its lips either for political reasons or religious reasons or through a sense of personal delicacy. We guess that some decent man is in trouble, or that some unfortunate priest has gone off the rails, or that some public man has been caught, as the Americans say so vulgarly, with his pants down. We approve of this reserve, this proper regard for human feelings, this *gentillesse* (as the French say), because we Irish have a certain hidalgo quality about us. And, anyway, it might be our turn tomorrow. So we draw a seemly cloak of public reticence over the matter, and then – in whatever golf club, or yacht club, or restaurant or pub the characters in question have been accustomed to frequent – we tap the old grapevine to find out what these fellows have been up to. Over the malt we pass our own judgment on them in seemly privacy.

We certainly had to pursue this Carnduff affair beyond public report and private rumour. We all knew quite well that Joe Cassidy is far too cagey to become a member of any illegal organization at his age and with his income. We know him for a sound, law-abiding citizen who has not carried a gun, let alone killed anybody, for at least thirty-five years. We know Freddy Wilson less well, because he left the country nearly thirty years ago, immediately after the Troubles. Nevertheless, those of us who had known him then, or met him since his return to Ireland to work for Joe Cassidy, assured us that if he actually was doing anything illegal in Northern Ireland it was unthinkable that any policeman would catch him doing it.

We found that Joe's only son, Frank, was a member of the Irish Republican Army, and that on that July night it was he who had borrowed the firm's van to take part in a raid across the border. It so happened that when Joe heard about the van he was at a dinner of the Drogheda chapel of the Irish Manufacturers' Social and Patriotic, and his guts being rich of wine, he had become, not unnaturally, incensed against the boy. After all, Frank could just as easily have stolen somebody else's van. Still in his white tie and tails, and full of fire, Joe had jumped into his Jaguar, and with – or so we presumed – Freddy Wilson, he had torn hell-for-leather after the blue van with the pink corset painted on each side of it. Aided by various sympathetic souls along the road, he had picked up the trail and had the good luck to come up with Frank, a bare ten minutes after the raid, across the border, still with the van, trying to get one of his wounded men back to safety. The wounded youth died under their eyes on the side of the road. The rest was easy to imagine.

Joe and Freddy had sent the son racing back across the border in the Jaguar. They then took over the van and the dead boy. We took off our hats to Joe Cassidy and Freddy Wilson and we let it be known to them both that there would be a public dinner at the Dolphin waiting for them when they came out of gaol.

But as the months went by some more details leaked out. For one thing, Freddy had not been with Joe in the Jaguar. Freddy had been in the van with Frank. He had forced Joe's son to take him with him on the raid across the border because he was taking French leave of Celtic Corsets Ltd, with four thousand pounds' worth of bearer bonds belonging to his old comrade-in-arms in his breast pocket. And he might have got away with them if he had not had the bravado to leave a taunting farewell message to Joe behind him.

The rest was true enough. Joe and Freddy had persuaded Frank to take the Jaguar while they stayed with the van. There they were, then, with a dead youth on their hands, at about one o'clock in the morning, only a mile away from a police barracks that had been attacked by bomb and machine-gun fire ten minutes before . . .

2

Joe waited until he heard the Jaguar driving rapidly away. Then he ran back to the fork of the road as fast as his great bulk and the thin pumps he was wearing would allow. As he ran he could hear nothing but the sound of his own panting and the patter of his pumps on the road. He had no torch, so when he came to the fork he snapped on his petrol lighter and by its fitful light he began shuffling through the long grass, bending, peering, groping, and cursing. He could see nothing except the grass until a beam of light from behind his back showed him the staring face of the dead young man at his feet.

'Found him?' Freddy's voice said from behind the beam.

'The bastards!' Joe said. 'We've got to get him into the van and across the border at once. Bring up the van!'

Freddy turned and ran for the van. While he waited for him to return, Joe clambered up on the ditch and saw, a mile away, the kangaroo jumps of the Jaguar's lights making towards the south. He looked left and saw Freddy's lights coming up the road. Then, still farther left, or northward, he saw a third set of lights moving towards the east. The moon was rising and it made the trees against it look very black. Then they were lifting the dead youth, laying him into the back of the van, and Freddy was driving back the way they had come. As he drove Freddy said:

'Did you see the lights of a car away there to the north? It may only be a private car on the main road from Newtown Butler to Clones, but if we are still in the North they may be police or B Specials trying to cut us off. Damnation! I wish I knew to hell where exactly our wandering border is tonight.'

They took a right turn. The headlights likewise turned and moved parallel to them on their left.

'I don't like this at all,' Freddy said. 'See that?' he shouted, and Joe saw what he meant.

It was a letter box inset into a wall, painted in English red. They were still in the North.

When they came to a T-sign they were aware of the other car's lights, now not more than a quarter of a mile to the east. Freddy whirled west, curved under a railway bridge, tore into sixty on the straight, and let out a cry of joy. His headlights had picked up a tattered Southern tricolour hanging from the branch of a tree: they had crossed the border already. He came to a fork, pulled up, turned off his engine, and they both looked back and listened. The lights of the pursuing car were halted about half a mile behind them. They could hear its engine humming in the still summer night.

'This is all very well,' Joe said. 'We're in the South now. But this bloody border loops all over the place. Any road we take, if we take it far enough, might take us back into trouble again. We had better go very carefully, Freddy-boy!'

Freddy let in the gears and sneaked slowly along the road. The lights behind them moved slowly against distant treetops. Freddy pulled up. The lights whirled and vanished.

'I'm afraid to go on. I expect they have a transmitter.'

He got out and climbed the ditch, followed by Joe. He pointed:

'See that? They're going south! I know what's happened. This road must cross a pocket of the South enclosed by two pincers of the North. They're going down the eastern leg of the pocket to cut us off there if we try to cross it.'

'Then,' Joe said, 'let's run across the western leg and get out that way.'

'You can bet your last bullet they have a patrol down that way already.'

'Then we're boxed!' said Joe. 'Have we a map?'

'No! But I see a cottage. I'm going to take a chance on it. We must have a guide.'

'What the hell is the good of a guide if there's no road out of this pocket?'

'We can walk across the fields, can't we? But – and Freddy nodded his head towards the back of the van, questioningly.

Joe looked into the dark maw behind him.

'We'll carry him. I'm not going to let those bastards get him. Once they identify him, all his relations up here will be in the soup.'

They got out and knocked at the door of the long, slateroofed cottage. There was no sound from inside it. They knocked again several times, but they could not hear as much as the sound of breathing from inside. To Joe's surprise, a gun appeared in Freddy's hand. It was that rather old-fashioned type of long-nosed automatic known as a Peter the Painter. Joe knew this type of gun well; he had always carried a Peter the Painter in the old days. As his eye fell on it he remembered in a flash one night when it jammed during a raid in Clanbrassil Street and he would have been a gone man if Freddy had not shot the Black and Tan who was firing at him. Before he could say anything, Freddy had pushed in a pane of glass with the point of his gun and shouted through the hole:

'This is the I.R.A. There's six of us. If you don't come out we'll burn you out. We'll give you one minute.'

After a few seconds they heard a slight noise, and then a man's voice said:

'Come to the door.'

'No tricks!' Freddy shouted. 'We'll shoot!'

They heard a sound of footsteps, and something like a tin basin falling on a stone floor and rotating noisily to rest. A pale glimmer of light appeared to pass the window. A chain rattled and the door opened on the chain, a device Freddy had never in his life seen in any part of the country, even during the Troubles years ago, when he had often been out at all hours of the night in the loneliest mountainy places behind Dublin. His torch showed the face of a pale but unfrightened middle-aged man looking out through the three-inch opening. Impressed by the man's steady look, he said more quietly than he had intended:

'All we want is a guide. We've lost our way and we want to get back on foot across the border.'

'No!' the man said sturdily. 'I'm not going to help you. This may be the South, but a heap of my neighbours are Orangemen. I do a lot of work with folk across the border.' His eye fell on the long-nosed gun. 'Of course,' he went on amiably, 'if you were to as much as point your gun at me...'

Freddy grinned with relief. 'Consider it done,' he said.

'You must do it so that I can honestly swear that you did do it.'

Freddy raised the revolver. For good measure he said cheerfully:

'If you don't help us I'll shoot you where you stand.'

'Wait until I tell the missus and get me boots on. And put out the lights of yon car. We can take no chances.'

Three minutes later the three of them were back in the van. Their guide made no comment on the fact that they were only two and that one of them was in evening clothes. He did observe dryly that they were mighty old to be in the I.R.A. To this Freddy replied:

'We're two brigadier generals. Did you hear the racket our lads made tonight?'

'I heard something like firing in the direction of Carnduff about half an hour ago. And I saw a rocket going up from over thereabouts about twenty minutes back.'

'Twenty minutes! No wonder the patrols are out.'

They drove slowly, in silence and moonlit darkness, until they came to a fork where they turned south and came to a railway bridge. Freddy was silent because he was aware of the presence of danger; the man was silent because he was a Northerner; and Joe was silent because he was thinking about the gun. After driving for what seemed to Freddy like a long mile, the man at his side told him they must now abandon the van and walk the rest. Even when they opened the van doors and lifted out the dead young man he said nothing, only stooping to look into the blankly staring eyes, shaking his head partly from pity and partly to indicate that he did not recognize him. The three of them carried the body south along the track. It was slow walking, and when he halted them and assured them they had not covered a quarter-mile their aging bones could not believe him. He whispered:

'I'm going to leave ye now. If ye followed this road or yon railway line any farther ye'd find yeerselves back inside the border. From this on ye'll have to take to the fields. Go in a straight line with yon red star foreninst ye. After about half a mile or so ye'll pass out through our Gap o' the North. The Gap's not much more than a quarter-mile wide down there, but ye can't miss it if ye remark that it lies between a wide copse of beeches on the west and a low grassy hill on the east. Carry on then and it'll maybe be another half-mile before you come to a wee road. Ye'll be well into the South by then. That road will take ye fair and free anywhere ye like in the Republic.'

They looked ahead of them into the level darkness. The sky was white with stars. In the clear summer sky the moon was now as big and bright as a tin basin. They saw no lights on the plain. They heard no least sound. Freddy whispered:

'Is there any danger that the Specials, if they're out, would cross the Gap to stop us?'

'Every danger! They'd follow a man twenty miles into the Republic if their blood was up. And it'll be up the night. Ye'll have to move slowly and quietly and take no chances. I can do no more for ye. God bless ye! And don't make a sound. D'ye hear that dog?'

They heard a dog barking.

'That dog must be three miles away.'

When they looked around again he had vanished as if he had been a ghost or a leprechaun.

When he had vanished they sat to rest with the dead youth between them on the grass. Joe whispered that that was a fine Irishman and when, if ever, they got safe home he'd send his wife a present of half a dozen Celtic Corsets. They dared not smoke. On a clear night like this the glow of a cigarette would be seen a mile off. The low barking of the distant dog went on baying the moon. Freddy was bending over the nameless youth, looking at him by the light of the moon. The blank eyes stared at the sky. The hair was dark and glossy. The nose was broad with wide nostrils. The open mouth showed fine white teeth smiling at them.

'Do you remember Harry de Lacey?' he whispered back to Joe. 'He was killed in that ambush at Finglas in Nineteen-twenty. This lad is very like him.'

Joe leaned over to look.

'He's not unlike,' he whispered. 'I met Harry's brother Tony only the other day. He has a job in the Dublin Corporation.'

'We don't even know this lad's name,' Freddy whispered. 'We ought to search him. If we're caught or have to run for it we don't want to leave anything on him that would identify him.'

They went through the youth's pockets. He was carrying a heavy Webley forty-five and six spare rounds. Joe thought of Freddy's Peter the Painter and quickly pocketed the Webley and the bullets. Between them they collected a cheap pocketbook, some papers, a pale-blue handkerchief, a full packet of cigarettes, matches, a few coins, a door key, a hair comb, a fountain pen, a gardener's pruning knife, rosary beads and his wristlet watch. Since they dared not light a match to look at the papers or the pocketbook, and the moonlight was not bright enough to read them, they wrapped the lot in the blue handkerchief and buried it carefully under some loose stones directly at the foot of a stanchion wire from one of the telegraph poles along the railway embankment. Then Freddy took a line between a near, lone tree, a copse beyond it, and the red star, and they staggered off, carrying the corpse between them by the armpits and the legs.

It was heavy going, and they advanced very slowly, listening carefully, breathing heavily, resting many times – they were not young and a body is dead weight – and always laying the corpse between them on the dew-wet ground. During the first panting pause Joe tore off his stiff collar and black tie and whispered from where he lay on his back to Freddy, also strewn supine beside him on the grass:

'Where did you get that Peter the Painter?'

'I've had it by me for thirty-five years.'

'If we're challenged will you fire?'

'To the last bullet, damn them!'

'Good man!' Joe whispered.

Freddy was sitting up in angry surprise.

'Did you doubt it? You don't think I'm going to do five years in gaol in Belfast for this?'

Joe hesitated and then said apologetically: 'I wouldn't have asked you in the old days. But we're not as young as we were.'

Freddy lay back. He was silent for a while. Then, softly, he uttered his thoughts, not so much to the ear beside him as to the stars above him:

'I don't blame you. When a man starts to grow away from his youth he gets fond of the world. But you forget that when we grow older still we begin to get sick of it! Dying would be easy now, Joe!'

'Yes?'

'Did you ever read Faust?' Freddy whispered.

'I saw the opera once or twice, at the Gaiety.'

'The opera is no good! They always make Faust an old fellow with white whiskers. That's not true to life. An old bucko like that wouldn't give a damn about being young again. Not after philosophic wisdom came to him. I've read everything about Faust I could lay my hands on. I used to think one time that it was wrong for Goethe to make Faust ruin that girl. I used to think that if Faust was a magician and had all that magical power he should have been able to have any girl without ruining her. As I got older I realized how true it was. It's the whole point of the story. There's no magic strong enough to cheat the world. It was right to make the world, the flesh, and the devil cheat him in the end.'

'There's no such thing as magic!' Joe murmured smugly.

Freddy laughed softly and bitterly.

'I studied that subject very carefully the time I had a tricks and jokes shop in Manchester. I studied white magic and black magic. I studied telepathy, and hypnotism, and spiritualism. I even studied the Black Mass.' He chuckled quietly. 'One time during the war I drew circles on the floor of the shop with chalk, late at night. All the city was under the blackout, and nobody in the streets but the firewardens. Suddenly all the air-raid sirens began to wail. Then the only sound was the bombs and the ack-ack. I raised my voice and I called up the devil. The next second the whole block next to ours went up with a bang. Do *you* believe in the devil?'

'Oh, well!' Joe laughed, evading carefully, as if he did not wish to antagonize anybody. 'But not with horns and a tail, of course!'

'He's there,' Freddy whispered. 'The whole world's a juke box full of his little whiney tunes. You can buy them from him the way you could have bought my tricks and jokes from me. You don't know what I'm talking about! You're too bloody stupid.' He paused and said apologetically: 'I'm trying to explain to you why I tried to steal your bearer bonds tonight.'

'Forget it,' said Joe. 'For the time being,' he added hastily.

'I wasn't able to do it,' Freddy said, 'because you are a better gangster than me.'

He sat straight up and looked down at the youth's face staring at the stars. Joe sat up too. As if still thinking of the devil he whispered:

'I never did any harm to anyone.'

'Apart from existing!'

'I go to confession and Communion every first Friday of the month. I go every year of my life to Lough Derg. That's no joke of a pilgrimage. Three nights fasting and walking on the cold stones. I was often wet to the skin, kneeling in the rain. That ought to help me when my hour comes.'

'I'm a poor sort of Christian,' Freddy said. 'If I ever was one.'

'You ought to do Lough Derg,' Joe advised him fraternally. 'I'm going to do Lough Derg if I get safe out of this bloody kip-o'-the-reel.' He took out the Webley and broke it open. 'Begod,' he whispered, 'he's after firing every bloody round in this!'

He started to eject the spent rounds and reload the chambers.

'That's the ticket,' Freddy murmured, watching him. 'Always back for a win or a place. Put your trust in God but keep your powder dry. Leave us be going. It's near two o'clock. The sun will be up soon after four.'

All over the land there were long, thick swaths of moonlit mist, so that when each took his turn at carrying the dead youth on his back he looked like a giant walking through milk. In this way they moved a bit faster, but Freddy had to halt many times because Joe's knee began to pain him badly, so that he limped and groaned even when he was walking unburthened. His stiff shirt was crumpled like an old sail. His thin streaks of grey hair halved his big rosy turnip of a head. His ruddy face was wet with perspiration. His light shoes were soon soaked with the heavy dew and muddy from a swampy patch on which they chanced in the darkness. During one of their pauses to rest he whispered, looking at the anonymous face looking up beyond him at the studded sky:

'Was it all a waste?'

'He died young,' Freddy said enviously. 'Bliss was it in that dawn . . . People envy us, too. They say we had the dawn, and the whole day after it. Now every day is either a year long or it has only a couple of hours in it.'

And he suddenly thought, in fright, of all the hosts of young men who were killed in the wars of Europe, more of them than the hosts of visible and invisible stars overhead, and he felt that death is always a waste.

'I wasn't thinking of him,' Joe whispered. 'I was thinking of us and all we did in our time.'

'Yah!' Freddy mocked, mocking his own last thought. 'Time is an old man's thought. When you're young you don't need clocks or watches. You measure things by Now. For dogs and boys it's always Now. A Now that lasts forever. Do you remember the long summer days when you were young? Endless! That's because when you're young you're not killing yourself by thinking. You're just doing and living, without an atom of consciousness of the wonder of what you're squandering. "That is no country for old men. The young in one another's arms . . . " Even death is lovely when you're young. But it's a terrible and lonely thing to look at the face of death when you're young. It unfits you for the long humiliation of life. Aye! When a man stops living he starts watching the end of the sandglass dripping to tell him that his egg is cooked. Did you ever examine your conscience, Joe?'

Joe started.

'My conscience? I examine it every month when I go to confession.'

'That's where time and age get a hold of you. They remind you that sooner or later you'll have to set your sail and float out to sea. But you don't know what I'm talking about – you haven't got a conscience.'

'I know right form wrong,' Joe said warmly. 'More than you do! What were you trying to do tonight with my bearer bonds?'

Freddy ignored him. He said coldly:

'We are a childish people. As childish as a boy with his first catapult, or an old stone in a river-bed.'

Joe said, 'Aye!' indifferently and placatingly. He was thinking what a lunatic he had been to bring this lunatic back to Ireland to work for him.

'You know something, Joe? This country was made for young people. Nobody else but them can live in it, or die in it. Look at you and me! We can neither live in it nor die in it. This country is a cheat of a country for old men, that's why all the old men in this country are cheats – cheating the cheat! Look at us tonight. Why don't the bloody British military or the bloody black-coated bobbies or the flaming B Specials come and give us a chance now to fight them and die decent? But – no! They won't. Another bloody cheat! We're not even allowed to die! All we can do is go creeping around eating, and drinking, and blathering and cheating, and making money, and getting old and withered, and beating our breasts like you, you dying sow, up in Lough Derg.' His voice had been rising all the time. Now he suddenly lifted his head like a dog baying the moon and lifted his two fists to the night and screamed at the top of his voice: 'I want to fight! Come out, ye bastards, and fight!'

Joe grabbed him and clasped a hand over his mouth.

'For Christ's sake!' he growled. 'Are ye mad? Do you want them to catch *him*?'

Freddy bowed his head. Then he lifted it and shook it sadly. His calm was as sudden as his storm. He whispered:

'You see? You're caught, even through the dead. I tell you it's only the young who can die well, because they're proud and ignorant and lovely.' He leaned over and brushed away a tender-legged spider from the young man's pallid brow. 'We lost his hat,' he observed. 'Some ould lad will find it and wear it. Like a crown. Do I see the light of a car? Or a window?'

'If you do, you might be seeing the road we're looking for.'

'Come on!'

They struggled on again. Freddy had to do all the carrying now, with the corpse slung backwards loosely over one shoulder in a sort of fireman's lift. He was wet to his knees. He squelched at every step. The corpse's head rolled at every stumble, and its two hanging hands swayed. At the next pause, after Freddy had laid him softly down, Joe said, wiping his face and neck:

'Freddy, would you explain one thing to me? Why was I such a fool as to bring you back here from Manchester?'

Freddy looked ironically at him.

'Because I'm your lost youth. I'm your lost faith. You can never stop remembering the time when you were young and slim, like this poor devil here, when you felt immortal, when you felt grand, when you felt the lord of the world. And you can never understand why you stopped feeling like that. So you wanted to have me around to see how was I handling your problem.'

'Freddy, why was it that when we were young and trying to die for Ireland we all felt immortal?'

'Because time meant nothing to us. I've explained all that to you, you big ballox!'

'We were like angels,' Joe whispered, filled with awe.

'With flaming swords!'

'And now,' said Joe, bitterly, 'I'm selling women's corsets'.

They lay on the grass, the dead boy between them, all three staring up. A star streaked across the sky, exploded and vanished. At long last Joe said, so gently that Freddy barely heard him: 'You called me a gangster a minute ago. Well, I was one, and I'm not ashamed of it.'

Freddy, supine and silent, stared upward at the lofty white ball of the moon. After a while:

'That isn't correct. We *are* gangsters now. But we weren't always. We were killers. In every revolution there have to be killers. But there also have to be men who sanctify the killing. They make it holy, and beautiful, and splendid and glorious. We had a lot of men like that in Ireland once, and as long as we had them life was worth killing. They gave us a faith. Now we're killers still, but there's nobody to kill now so we've gone into business. We use the word in business – "A wonderful killing".'

His eyes focused away from the moon towards the pale blue flowers beside him that were bright even in death. He went on:

'Joe! I'm sick of hearing you talking about all you're trying to do now for Ireland. It won't work. Nothing on God's earth could make corsets holy, or beautiful, or splendid or glorious.'

After a while he became aware that Joe was crying. After another while Joe said:

'If any of the fellows in the Dolphin saw me now they'd think me mad.'

'They're usually mad enough to think you're sane,' Freddy said, and they scrambled up again.

The next time they rested they were sitting back to back by a mossy rock protruding from the stubble of a cut meadow. Joe said sourly:

'A bloody tricks and jokes shop! So that's what you were doing all those years in Manchester? Were you down to that?'

Freddy snorted.

'When I left Ireland in 'Twenty-two I hadn't as much as a penny piece. I was the dis-bloody-well-illusioned revolutionary. Even to think of Ireland made me puke what I never ate. I was so low that first year in Manchester that if I took one step up I'd be in the gutter. I had no skill. I was just a smarty. I met a widow whose husband used to run a tricks and jokes shop; you know the sort of thing – false noses, imitation ink blobs, stink bombs, card tricks, little Celluloid babies that squirt water when you squash 'em, nutcrackers in the shape of a woman's legs, drinking glasses that leak down your shirt front when you use them, cockroaches to drop in a fellow's beer. A cosy little place. With a cosy little room behind the shop. On winter nights, after we put up the shuts, with the soft pink web of Lancashire mist down over the city, we'd sit on each side of the little red eye of the cooking range. Liz would be reading the *Evening Chronicle* – she always preferred it to the *News* for some reason. She'd say, "Freddy wot abaht comin' to see Clark Guyble in *Hearts Aflyme?*" I wouldn't go. I'd be reading a book about Irish history, or thinking, "What is it like tonight in Dublin?" She never knew what I was thinking. She'd say, "Wot are you thinking abaht?" I'd say, "Some new trick". I used to deceive her nearly every night of the year. We lived together for eighteen years. She was killed in the blitz. I found her stark naked in the rubble, sliced in two.'

He half slewed around to Joe. Joe turned to him. He went on:

'While you, you big sow, were here in Ireland, getting fatter and fatter, making corsets with designs from the Lindisfarne Gospels on 'em. I wrote to you for help twice. Did you answer me? Did you, you cur?'

'I was working for Ireland,' Joe protested. 'Building up the country we fought for.'

Freddy took out his Peter the Painter and began to wipe it in his handkerchief. Joe felt in his tails for the Webley.

'That looks very like my old Peter the Painter,' he said.

'It is! I took it with me to Manchester after the Troubles and the Treaty. In memory of the old days when we were all boys together.'

Joe faced him, full of joy.

'Did you really? All those years?'

Freddy slipped off the safety catch of the Peter the Painter. His forefinger padded gently on the trigger. His left hand felt for the bulk of the bearer bonds in his breast pocket. Joe gripped the butt of the Webley. Smiling, they faced one another.

'Freddy!' Joe said quickly. 'After you left Ireland in 'Twenty-two it was the Civil War, when every man had to choose his side, for the Free State or for the Republic, for De Valera or for Mick Collins. I followed Mick.'

'I know it,' Freddy smiled. 'And it was as well for me that I went to England, for if I'd stayed at home I'd have been for Dev. And you'd have plugged me for it!' he added savagely.

Joe gripped his arm. His voice rose.

'I never killed no Irishman!'

'Maybe you didn't,' Freddy agreed, and swayed the gun a little. 'All you had to do was to give the orders. "Is that bastard de Lacey alive yet?" you'd say to one of your pals. And you wouldn't have to say it twice.'

He pointed the gun at Joe as if he merely wanted to emphasize the 'you'.

'Why do you mention that name?' Joe asked in a cold whisper.

'We mentioned it a while ago. But you only mentioned his brother Tony. How well you never mentioned his brother Marky? Marky de Lacey was my best friend, Joe,' he said, and stuck the gun into Joe's side. 'My best friend! And he was found up on the Three Rock Mountain with a hole in his skull. Don't you ever think of him, Joe, when you're up in Lough Derg praying for your rotten carcass? Don't you ever once think of Marky de Lacey?'

Joe's hand made a backward movement, but Freddy stuck his gun barrel deeper into his fat. Joe's voice rose higher still.

'I never laid a wet finger on Marky de Lacey!'

'Oho!' Freddy sighed. 'Wasn't it well for me I went to England!'

Joe's voice rose to a bat's squeak in the warmth of his protestation:

'Not you, Freddy! Not you! Not you!'

Freddy peered at the dark outline of his turnip head and saw the faint starlit shine on the sweat of his temples and he saw the two eyes glowing like a cat's at him. He withdrew the gun.

'Hell roast yeh,' he said exhaustedly. 'If you say so I have to believe you.'

'I do say so, Freddy. I swear it before God Almighty.'

'All right,' Freddy agreed wearily. 'If you swear it before God Almighty. I suppose I really am your last remaining bit of honesty.'

He leaned down and began to brush a stalk of unmown meadowsweet with the long tip of the automatic. He wondered if he should tell Joe why he had really kept it all those years. He decided not to tell, because he did not care any more. He suddenly felt the way a man must feel when he realizes that he has at last become impotent from old age. He clicked on the safety catch. Joe leaned closer to him:

'Freddy, it's what I often wanted to tell you. The real reason why I brought you home was that I wanted to clear up everything with everybody. They say I did things I never did, they put all the blame on me for things other men did, and because I was the boss I had to take the knock, but I never did them. I'd have told you all this years ago only I thought you were another that didn't trust me. It was only when I saw tonight how you kept my old Peter the Painter for old times' sake – and when we're here together helping the young fellows – handing on the torch as you might say – keeping the old flag flyin' – that I knew you'd believe your old pal in the heel of it all.'

Freddy looked at the smooth, young face on the grass. He clicked the safety catch off again. He looked at the great, ugly, sweating head leaning over and down to him, and he smelled the smell of fear. In disgust he clicked the safety catch on again. All his hate was gone.

'Oh, well,' he said, 'if you even only did a tenth of the things they say you did, Lough Derg won't save you. Nor all the fivers you ever gave to old beggarwomen for winter coal. Come on! It'll soon be a new day. Leave us bury him. Leave us bury everything we ever believed in and be shut of them forever.'

They got up once more. Lugging the dead boy between them, they struggled on.

The invisible sun was now glowing beyond the level land to their left. Soon the sky over there became a faint fringe of apricot merging into the mauve night retreating across the sky. They crossed another mist-swathed field and came to a low wall which, they found, edged a little road near the junction of three roads. When they climbed over the low wall and laid their burthen on the dew-wet verge, they both tumbled exhausted on the grass.

'We made it,' Joe said aloud.

'I'm sorry we did,' said Freddy, strewn on his back.

He woke a quarter of an hour later, sat up, and saw a building about five hundred yards up the road, its chimneys standing dark against the bright portion of the sky. In the raw morning light it looked cold and unfriendly. As he got up and walked towards it he suffered a gently pricking pang of realization that he was back in a world so long forgotten that, seen again, it was as unreal as a half-remembered dream. He was looking at a schoolhouse, stone-cut, slated, at least seventy-five years old. He went in through the little iron gate and looked up at the carved plaque on the wall. It was in Irish. They were safely in the South.

Turning around, he saw a cement-faced dwelling house facing the school, all its tawny holland blinds drawn on sleep, its shaggy lawn and draggled flower beds grey with dew. The teacher's house. He looked wider still, oppressed by the intense silence, by the suspension of life, by the half-light; the spread of empty sky and land entered him as an image of Death waiting to enfold his own slight figure alone at its morning edge. He might have been a bather naked by the edge of the sea about to commit himself, to swim out until he could swim no farther. As a youth he would have held out his arms joyously to it, exulting in the adventure. Now, it was not an ocean that invited him; it was just another day. Yet it was also the hour when a man can no longer evade whatever truth he has collected through his life. He felt for his gun again, and as he touched it he felt like a gambler rubbing his last ivory chip between his fingers.

He turned and ran back quickly along the little dusty road to Joe and he kicked him hard on the rump. Joe started awake and groaned with stiffness and pain. Freddy knelt beside him on one knee.

'Joe!' he besought him.

'I'll get rheumatics outa this. I know I will!' Joe said.

'Joe! Leave us go up North for God's sake and let off a couple of rounds at somebody. We don't want to go home now, do we? Joe! You bastard! It's our last chance to do something decent before we die.'

'Die?' said Joe, and let out a gasp of pain as the night scrawled its first revenge on his lumbar regions. 'Begod and I can tell you it would give me the greatest satisfaction to have a crack at those bastards.'

Meaning, Freddy understood miserably, that it would, in other, more suitable, entirely hypothetical and now quite historical times and circumstances, have given him the greatest satisfaction. Freddy clutched his arm.

'Joe!' he sobbed. 'For God's sake, Joe!'

'At night sometime?' Joe temporized. 'That'd be the ticket! Eh?'

'Now!' Freddy wailed. 'You know damn well that once you get back to your office and your desk and your appointments book, and all the photographs of yourself all over the mantelpiece, you'll never do another decent thing to your dying day.'

'It's a pipe dream,' Joe sighed, and felt his hip tenderly. 'Our dancing days are done.'

Freddy rose up slowly and looked down at him. He threw his Peter the Painter into a green-coated pool beside the road. He felt his breast pocket and pulled out the fat, folded envelope containing the bearer bonds. After a second's hesitation he threw the package into Joe's lap. Joe put the package in his breast pocket, took out the Webley, looked at it, glanced mistrustfully at Freddy, and put it back in his pocket. Freddy sniffed sarcastically. Then he jerked his head towards the schoolhouse.

'That's the schoolteacher's house up the road. We'll carry him up there and hide him there under the fuchsia bushes. Your Frankie can come back tonight and bury him. Then we'll walk on until we meet a car. I could do with a whiskey.'

Joe was still sitting on the grey-wet grass, his two hands splayed out on either side of him. As he looked up the road his voice took on a touch of its normal daytime hectoring tone:

'Are you quite sure we're in the South?'

'I'm afraid so,' Freddy said, as impersonally as any secretary to any manager.

Joe, spread-handed, spread-legged, looked up the road, and sank back even more heavily on his behind. He shook his fat head miserably and clutched his sore knee.

'I'm played out.'

'All right. Lie down and rest, you sod! I'll carry it.'

'No,' Joe snarled. 'We carried it together so far. We'll carry it to the end together.'

Once more they struggled up the road, bearing the youth between them, Freddy holding him under the knees, Joe holding him under the armpits; a small man in a grey alpaca coat and a big, burly man in tails, white shirt front, no collar. They laid the youth as far in as they could under the fuchsia hedge of the teacher's garden. Two trushes hopped on the shaggy lawn. The holland blinds did not stir. As Freddy crossed the arms on the chest, a red petal fell on one of the hands and drops of dew sprinkled one cheek. They arranged the branches to hide the body; Joe knelt and recited three Hail Marys, and Freddy, standing, heard himself murmuring the responses as if somebody else were saying them. He was much impressed by the intercession for all sinners at the hour of death. It made him realize that the figure hidden under the flowering shrub was dead. They threw a last glance at the holland blinds and quietly left the garden. Foot-weary, they walked away up the dusty road, heads lowered, a little at a loss at having no burthen to carry, so tired out that they did not advert to the fact that the sunrise was on their right.

Less than half an hour later they were back in the North, facing the guns of a Northern patrol.

Freddy is out now, and back on his job with Celtic Corsets Ltd. After all, as he says to Joe every week when he visits him in Crumlin Road Prison, Belfast, where else can he go? And who else, as Joe replies, would be fool enough to have him? These weekly visits are ostensibly to discuss business, but the part that Joe really loves – though he pretends modestly to wave it away – is when Freddy draws from his portfolio what they call the Manuscript. It is Joe's biography, which Freddy is composing very carefully and very, very slowly. As he reads the latest couple of pages, the prison walls fade, and Death flowers exquisitely again.

# In the Bosom of the Country

Then, suddenly, after all their years of love, ten of them, five a-growing and five a-dying, death came. They were lying side by side in the big, bridal bed under its looped-up canopy of pink silk on whose slope the sunset gently laid the twig-pattern of the elms in her drive. She had tossed aside her fair hair so that it lay in a heavy tangle on her left shoulder, and was pensively watching him brushing up his greying, military moustaches with the knuckle of his forefinger. She started to scratch his shoulder with her nails, gently at first, then a little more wickedly until he turned to look at her. The sunset revealed the dark roots at the parting of her hair and caught a wrinkle at the corner of her eye. Recognizing a familiar mood he smiled nervously at her curl-at-the-corner smile, slightly mocking, shy, minxish, naughty. A prelude to another pretty quarrel? He soon stopped smiling; this time there was substance to her fret.

'Well, my dashing Major? Are you betraying me with one of your great galumphing horsey wenches from the Hunt? Account for yourself. Two months all but a week? And before that how long was it? Keene by name but not so keen by nature? Is this your idea of devotion? Are you getting tired of me?'

'Anna!' he protested.

He wanted to glance at his watch but his left arm still lay under her waist. He glanced at the ruddy sun behind the elm-boles. Half past four? With a sudden blare the telephone rang. 'Botheration!' she snapped, and reached out her long, bare arm for the receiver. He noticed the little purse of skin hanging from her elbow. Poor dear! He really did love her, but, dammit, they weren't either of them as young as they . . . She sat straight up, crying out, 'No! Oh, no!' He heard a few more squawkings from the receiver and her 'I'll be right over!' She hung up and leaped out of bed, scrambling all over the floor for her clothes.

'It's the hospital. Arty's dead. I've lost my poor husband.'

Something there had kept bothering him for days, something out of tune that alerted him, something that did not seem right. It was not the time and the place. Although, dammit, if, instead of the telephone ringing to say that Arty had gone, Arty had opened the door and peeped in he could not have chosen a more awkward moment to impose himself. Nor could it have been guilt – not after all these years. It could not have been anything they said – so little had been said in their haste to dress. It could only be something tiny, like an eye glancing over a bare shoulder or some single word or gesture that was not meant to mean anything but did. Not that he ever got down to thinking it out properly. 'Am I,' he wondered, 'shying off it for fear of finding out?'

A modest man, he knew his worth. She was not the only person who joked about his name. He did it himself. It was inevitable – F.L. Keene. In the army they used to call him old Festina Lente and kept him to the rank of Major. A good old dobbin. Sure and steady. But, at least, he tried to be honest, and he had flashes, dammit. Once, long ago, Anna had asked him how many women he had loved, and he truly replied, 'Only you.' 'You seem very adept?' she had said sceptically, at which he had asked her the same question about herself and she had answered, 'Only you! Oh, of course, I thought I loved Arty when I married him. But I was very young. I soon found out.' Considering him she had said, 'We get on well for a pair of ignoramuses.' He had thought about this for a while and then, to his own surprise, came up with, 'Love is like jungle warfare at night, it keys you up, you feel things you can't see.' (Like now, when that indefinable something passed in the air between them.)

For her part, when he said that about love and the jungle, she had laughed merrily, sensitive enough to respond to his doleful humour, not intelligent enough to define it. It was his great attraction of which he was quite unaware, always to expect the worst – it made him infinitely tender and pitiful towards everybody. 'I am a dull dog,' he used to say to her sometimes and it used to make her throw her arms around him. Her big, stupid, dull, loyal dog would look at her in astonishment and love. She was his opposite, endlessly hoping for the best, and better. Had she been smarter she would have realized that pessimists are usually kind. The gay, bubbling over, have no time for the pitiful. Love lives in sealed bottles of regret.

He went to the funeral, hoping to have a chat with Mabel Tallant, the only person, he hoped, who knew all about the pair of them. There were so many people there that he decided to keep discreetly to the rear of the crowd. He was surprised at the size of the turn-out but supposed that a man cannot be a District Justice without making a pack of friends. Anyway, the Irish have a great gift for death, wakes and funerals. They are really at their best in misfortune. Used to it, I suppose? And sport. Quid pro quo, what? The thing that surprised him most, as he stood watching the mourners file in and out of the church was that while he knew many of them by sight, and perhaps a dozen by name – the vet, the Guards' Inspector, a couple of doctors, shopkeepers from the town, two or three fellows he had hunted with, and those well enough to nod to – he did not know one of them intimately, apart from Mabel Tallant. With her he just managed to get a word: she said she was taking Anna home with her for a couple of days after the relatives left. 'Give her my love,' he whispered hastily. Mabel had smiled sadly and whispered back, 'Everybody can sleep in peace now.'

He drove away, unaccosted by anybody, wondering what the devil she meant, wondering also why the devil it was that ever since he came to live in Ireland he was always wondering what somebody meant about some damn thing or another. He decided yet once more that they had to talk roundabout because they never had anything to say that was worth saying directly. The yews of his drive were dripping as he drove up to his empty house: nothing would do old Mrs Mac but to go to the funeral. The fire was out. Why had he ever come here? But he had been over all that, too. If his uncle had not left him this place he might never have come back from Kenya; and he might have left after the first year if he had not met Anna Mohan. But now? With Africa gone to hell? Package-safaris all over the place. You might as well think of living in Piccadilly Circus.

The week after the funeral, as he was hacking home from the hunt, Mabel rode up beside him. She was red as a turnip from the wind, mud-spattered to her stock, a grey hair drooping from under her hat, and on her right jaw a streak of dried blood.

'Hello, Mabel? Fall? No bones broken, I hope? You know, you are looking younger every day. But, then, we all know you are a marvel!'

'My dear Frank,' she laughed in her jolly, mannish way; she always laughed at everything, 'if you're referring to my great age I assure you I'm not giving up for a long time yet. Even if I am fifty I'm not decrepit. And I don't think you can give me many years, can you? I wasn't tossed, I'm more wet than muddy. I stayed behind with the Master to put back a few poles that we knocked at the Stameen. I've got half the stream in my boots this minute.'

They ambled along for a quarter of a mile with no more than a few tired words about the hunt. They had had three good runs. The Master was digging out the last fox. You have to give the farmers some satisfaction. After another silence he said, 'How is Anna?'

'You ask me?'

'I suppose I should call on her soon. I don't want to be indiscreet, you know,'

'You could be a bit too discreet.'

'I was always discreet about Anna. I owed it to her. Nobody but you ever knew about Anna and me.'

'Knew? Knows? Maybe not, but you've lived long enough in these parts to know that there's damn little goes on here that everybody doesn't suspect.' She hooted gaily, 'Sometimes a lot more than they've any reason to suspect. It fills their lives, I suppose.'

'Anna and I used always say that they might suspect but they couldn't be sure, and that was what really counted.'

'Past history?'

She laughed. He frowned. Not because her laugh suggested some unspoken blame of him but that it echoed certain spoken, and unspoken prophecies about Anna: her unbridled tongue, as of a woman who had been spoiled as a too-pretty girl, her temper, her tears, her enthusiasms, her wanting always to be smarter than she was, her melancholy days that went on and on, her warm days that were too warm to last, like a hot day in summer, her sudden bursts of generosity towards some women and her sudden bursts of jealousy towards other women – always young, pretty women. One by one Mabel had shaken her head over Anna's 'ways', and he had liked her all the more for it because in spite of everything she seemed to love her. Or was it that she, too, felt sorry for her?

It was growing dusk when they got to Bardy Hill. Fumes of fog were lying over the reedy plain. The tired horses slowed to a walk. She tapped his thigh with her crop.

'Frank! You're fooling yourself. I heard a bit of gossip at the meet this morning.'

'What did you hear?'

'Not much. Somebody said, "I wonder is Major Keene going to marry her now."'

He suddenly realized what that 'something' had been. She had said, 'Arty's dead, I've lost my poor husband.' Lost? Or was that the word they said to her on the phone? Dammit, she had lost him ten years ago.

'Mabel! If Arty had died ten years ago, even five, even three, I'd have married her like a shot. We dreamed of it. We lived on the dream of it. Not on the hope, dammit, no! We never said "die". We said, "if anything happened to him". Always talking about how happy we could be together. Just the two of us. Morning, noon and night. Lovers' talk! But, ye know, hope deferred maketh the heart sick. Anna being a Catholic there was no hope of a divorce. And, anyway, she was fond of him. In the end I gave up hope. I'll tell ye something else, Mabel. I was with her the day Arty died. I hadn't been with her for two months before that. And before that I dunno when. That day, I knew it was all over.'

He frowned again when Mabel said nothing. Venus shone, alone, in a green sky above a low spear of clouds. The horses, smelling home, began to trot downhill. They pulled up at Ballymeen Cross – they had each about half a mile to go.

'Do you think she really expects me to marry her?' he asked unhappily.

'I can only give you the woman's point of view. I'd think it damn cheap of you if you didn't make an honest woman of her. It will be pretty lonely for her in that old house at Culadrum. To put it at its lowest a husband is a handy thing to have about a house.' She laughed sourly. 'I should know.'

She jerked the head of her horse, and cantered away. He did the same. Once, and he regretted it, he took out his anger on the animal with his crop. Twice he uttered the word 'Damnation!' A pool of water gleamed coldly on his drive. A blank window held the last of the day. Culadrum would not be much of a home for Anna from now on. He should know.

He ate little, drank too much wine, slept badly, and immediately after breakfast he drove over to Culadrum. He found her in her drawing-room reading *The Irish Times* before the fire, slim-looking in proper black, very becoming, with a tiny white ruff under her chin, and hanging beneath it one of those little pendants called a Lavallière, a small, coloured miniature of Arty as a young man. With her tightbusted dress, and her fair hair done in a coil on the top of her head she had a Victorian look, like a queen in mourning. His heart went out to her. He kissed her and said gallantly, 'Now, my darling, before the whole world you can be all mine!' To his delight she blushed, a thing he had not seen her do for years. They sat in armchairs on either side of the fire.

'Frank! We have waited so long you won't mind waiting another while, will you?'

'As long as you like, Anna.'

'There is a special reason why we must wait a bit. It has to do with local opinion. I want to be married in a Catholic church.'

So, she *had* been thinking about it!

'By all means. I'm not bigoted. In for a penny in for a pound.'

'I want everything to be done regularly. I want to clear up everything. We will live here. In this house our life is before us. All my friends and all Arty's old friends are Catholics. They move in their own circle, just as people do everywhere. I'm not one of the hunting set, as they aren't either, except for one or two maybe. So it is frightfully important that they should all become your friends too. Oh, my darling, it would make all the difference in the world if you were a Catholic!'

He sat back slowly.

'Well, unfortunately, I'm not.'

'Frank! For me? It would make all the difference for me if you became a Catholic. Oh, if you could only become a Catholic, Frank! Won't you? We'd be all together then. And I'd be so happy!'

'But, dammit, Anna, you're not seriously suggesting that they'd look down on you in some way if you married a Protestant?'

'A mixed marriage? They won't have it in this diocese. Anyway we never did it in our family. Even where they do allow it it's a hole and corner affair. It's not the same thing at all. Documents. Guarantees. Back-door stuff. Ugh!'

'It's beyond me.'

She laughed her little curl-at-the-corners Anna-laugh.

'You've lived in Ireland, Frank, for ten years, and I honestly don't believe you still understand the Irish.'

'Is there anything to understand?'

'Besides, there is something else we have to face.'

'Something else? What else, for God's sake?'

'We always said they didn't know. But in our hearts we always knew that they did know. They always do know. Bother them! Oh, they mightn't have known *exactly*, but they must have known that there was *something* between us. Of course, there is one way out of it. If you don't marry me now they will say they were wrong.'

'But I don't want a way out of it. I want you!'

'But, Frank, if we do marry, you see, then they will know for certain that they were right all along. They'd never feel happy about us. They'd always be whispering about our past. We'd see it in their eyes. They might never visit us at all! And you couldn't blame them, could you? But if you became a Catholic, Frank, they'd be so happy about it that they'd forget and forgive everything. Besides, it was always the one thing – I mean if there ever was any teeny, little thing at all – that stood between us now and again. Now when we can be married, if we do marry, at last, at long last – Oh, my darling! – I want us to be one in everything before the world!'

'It never seemed to bother you before?'

'Of course it bothered me. I often cried about it when you left me.'

'Why did you never speak to me about it?'

'I was afraid of losing you,' she said sombrely.

He stood up, went to the window and looked glumly out through the frosty leaf-tracery on the glass. Accustomed to his ways she kept looking at his back under her eyebrows, waiting on his digestion. Presently he did a smart rightabout turn.

'This,' he declared, 'is a bomb-shell. Dammit, it's an absolute bomb-shell. When we couldn't marry you were so afraid to lose me that you never uttered a word about religion, and now, when we can marry, you give me the choice of being a cad if I don't and a Catholic if I do.'

'Darling, if you can't I shan't blame you. And if you can't I am not going to lose you. No matter what it costs me. Unless you want to ditch me, of course?'

'That I shall never do.'

She joined him at the window, and with one coaxing, pussy-cat finger she stroked his moustaches right and left, and kissed his lips.

'Think about it, darling.'

He stared at her, snatched his cap and left abruptly. After driving in circles for an hour he found himself outside Mabel Tallant's house at Bunahown. She was in the stables watching her groom combing her grey hunter. When he told her she laughed so loudly that he saw her gold-tipped molars.

'You're stuck, my boy!'

'But she might just as well ask me to become a Muslim or a Parsee! It isn't fair!'

She laughed gleefully again, then became solemn.

'Frank?'

'Well?'

'Suppose this happened ten years ago when you first fell in love with Anna? Suppose she wasn't married then? Suppose she asked you then to do this for her, would you have done it? Would you have said it wasn't fair?'

He glared at her, shuffled a bit, strode away.

After a week of torture, sitting for hours alone over his fire, or stalking alone about the leafless roads, he drove into town, stiffened himself with a glass of whiskey at The Royal Hotel and asked the waitress where the Catholic presbytery was. She directed him to Pearse Square with an enthusiasm that he found nauseating. The presbytery looked like a home for orphans, tall, Victorian, redbrick, with imitation stone quoins in grey plaster, pointed in black. Every window looked up at the wet February sky over brass-tipped half-screens. He hauled stoutly at the brass bell-handle and stood to attention glaring at the door. He asked the scrubby boy who opened it for the Parish Priest and was shown into a chilly front room. Drawing? Waiting? Committee? Dining? He found himself faced by a lifesize statue of Christ pointedly exhibiting His rosy heart. He turned his back to it. He did not sit down. This was a thing a man met on his two feet.

The door opened, very slowly. The priest who entered was an old man of at least sixty-five or more. He wore a monsignor's russet vest beneath a celluloid Roman collar that brushed the cincture of white hair about his roped neck. His voice was as mild as milk, his manner as courteous as a glass of port. When he told his visitor that he had been a chaplain with the Royal Inniskillings towards the end of the 1914 war, they were both only too happy to sit, smoke and chat about Château Thierry, the Sambre, the Somme, places known to the younger warrior of the two with the reverence proper to ancient history. Then they retired upstairs to the monsignor's sitting-room, the fireside and a whiskey bottle. An old Alsatian bitch lay strewn on the hearthrug between them.

By the time they got down to business the major felt as relaxed in his armchair, prickly with horsehair, as if they had just met in a club. All went well until he uttered the name, Mrs Anna Mohan. The monsignor's eyelids fell.

'Mrs Mohan? Ah, yes! Lives over at Culadrum House. I knew her father and mother very well. I wouldn't say they were exactly zealous Catholics. But they were good people. Hm! Well, well! Anna Carty, that was. A handsome girl when she was a child. I remember now, they sent her to some convent school in Kent. And after that to some place in Switzerland – Lausanne, I believe – to a finishing school. Rather a mistake that. Risky.'

'Risky?'

The word could have connotations.

'Oh, I am not criticizing them. It is simply that I always feel that if a girl is going to live in Ireland it's wiser to bring her up here. She must have been very young when she married Mohan. Why, we buried him only two, three weeks ago. Hm! I see!'

He looked at the major without expression, but it was plain enough that he did see.

'Well, Major? Tell me this. Would I be wrong in surmising that you are doing this chiefly, if not wholly, to please Mrs Mohan?'

'A fair question, padre. Yes, you've got it. That's about the run of it.'

'I mean, you are not being drawn to the Catholic Church entirely for its own sake, are you?'

'I'll be perfectly straight with you, padre, I don't know anything at all about the Catholic Church. I'll go further. I'm not going to become a Catholic, or anything like it, until I know a lot more about the whole thing.'

'Very wise. In other words, you are not asking me to give you a course of instruction. You are just asking me for some preliminary information.'

'Yes! Yes, that's about the run of it.'

'Is there, then, something that particularly interests you, or shall I say that bothers you, about our Church?'

'Why, dammit, everything about the Catholic Church bothers me. Not that I ever thought about it. But I suppose if you ask me a straight question I might say, well, for example, I might say what's all this about the infallibility of the Pope? It's a tall order, ye know, if somebody comes out every day of the week about something and says "That's it! You've got to take it because I'm infallible!" I mean, supposing the Pope came out tomorrow and said Napoleon was a woman, or that a line isn't the shortest distance between two points, or that the Law of Gravitation is all nonsense, you can't deny it, padre, that that'd be a hell of a tall order. You don't mind my being frank about this, I hope?'

The monsignor patted down the glowing tobacco in his pipe with an asbestos finger and said mildly that no, he did not mind at all.

'Not, of course, that what you suggest bears any relation to reality. But I don't mind. I mean, the examples you have chosen are not the very best in the world.' Here he waved his mottled hand. 'Since Mr Einstein, as the old song says, fings ain't wot they used ter be.' He wandered off a bit about Tycho Brahe and the mathematics of planetary attraction until he saw a glaze gathering over his visitor's eyes. 'In fact, His Holiness hardly ever speaks infallibly. The doctrine of Infallibility was pronounced in 1870.' He halted, thinking of such names as Newman and Lord Acton, and went on hastily. 'Since then I don't think the Pope has spoken *ex cathedra* more than ... Is it twice, or three times? And if I may say so, quite enough, too! Though some people might think even that much was excessive. Things change.' He fell into a private thought. 'Change and expand.'

'Only twice or three times? Is this a fact? Dammit, I never knew this! But,' he pounced, 'when he does we have to believe him, eh?'

'Major Keene, I think all this would seem much simpler to us if we were to think of the whole matter as one of obedience rather than of conviction. You are a soldier. You know about obedience. During the war if your colonel told you to advance on Hill 22 with three men and that old Alsatian there and take Objective 46, which you knew quite well was held by a thousand men, what would you do about it?'

'I'd obey at once.'

'Yes. You would obey. Somebody's got to give the orders.'

Keene stared at him out of his two great, blue eyes like a horse facing a jump.

'By George, you're a hundred per cent right, padre! Somebody's got to be boss. Not like all this damned, modern Whiggery we've got now. When everybody wants to be the boss. All those Trade Unions ... But, mind you, you've touched on another question there. Only last Sunday my housekeeper, Mrs MacCarthy, told me that, when she was at Mass, right here in town, one of your curates . . . You won't mind my saying this?'

'Fire away, Major. Fire away.'

'She told me . . . Mind you, she's a bit of an old exaggerator, but I wouldn't say she's a liar, just Irish ye know, she told me that one of your curates said from the pulpit that any girl going around this town in tight jeans was walking straight on the road to hell. Now, that's a bit of a tall order, padre! What do you say to that?'

The monsignor sighed wheezily.

'Yes. Well. We do seem to have wandered a bit from papal infallibility. But, since you raise the question . . . You, again as an old soldier, must know what happens to orders by the time they pass down to the lower ranks. It's a case of the sergeants' mess, my dear Major. The sergeants' mess in every sense of the word, and you know what I'm talking about.'

'By George! Don't I? Ye know, padre, it's a downright pleasure to talk to a man like you who knows the ways of the big world. You make me feel quite homesick for it.'

'So? Obedience! And order. And authority. You revere your Queen. The proud symbol of the power of your Empire. We Catholics revere the Pope. The proud symbol of our Empire. The Roman Empire. You and I, each in his own way, respect authority, desire order and uphold power.'

'Splendid! I can see that. In fact I begin to see a lot of daylight. Ye know, if we had a couple of chats I shouldn't be at all surprised if we found we had a good deal of ground in common. Mind you, I'm not going to be rushed into this. I'm sure that when I start thinking about it I'll come up with a lot of things that bother me. Mixed marriages, for instance. There's another tall order. And, let me see, hasn't there been some difficulty about the Virgin? And then, of course, there's contraception – ran into that a lot in India. I need hardly say my interest in the matter is purely academic.'

'So is mine.'

He rose.

'Why don't you come to dinner next week, Major, when as you say you will have thought some more about it, and we can combine business, if I may so call it, with pleasure. I've got quite a sound port.'

'Aha! I know something about port.'

The monsignor warmed.

'Do you now? Tell me, did you ever take port for breakfast?'

The major guffawed.

'Oh dammit no! No! Not for breakfast, padre!'

The monsignor chuckled.

'Then I am afraid you don't know anything at all about port. Wait until you taste mine. But I'm afraid if you are a connoisseur in wine you had better bring your own. Ah! The great wines of France. 1917. Spoiled my palate. I can't afford vintage wine any longer.'

'I've got a dozen of Forty-nine Beaunes-Villages at home. I'll bring a couple of bottles with me. By God, this is a splendid idea! I beg your pardon, monsignor, here I am cursing like a trooper in the presence of your reverence.'

'Pshaw! I'm inured to it. I remember one morning outside Ypres. Just before we went into battle. Two dragoons fighting, one of them an Orangeman and the other a Catholic, shouting like troopers. They had to be heard – the barrage going right over our heads, hell open to Christians, the captain staring at his wristwatch waiting for the second to go over the top. Do you remember – Ah, no, you're too young! – those old wristwatches with little metal grilles over them? I never heard such language in all my life as that Orangeman was giving out of him. In the end the other fellow, he was a Corkman, shoved his bayonet up within an inch of the other fellow's throat and he shouts, "Look, Sammy! I'm in the state of grace now before the battle, but with the help of God I won't be so handicapped before the day is out, and I tell you if I meet you then I'll shove this blank blank . . ."'

He clasped Keene by the arm for support as he bent over and laughed at the memory of it. Then he straightened and sighed.

'Poor chaps, neither of 'em came back. And I'm sure the good Lord was equally kind to the pair of them. Next Thursday, Major. At nineteen hours. Goodness me, I haven't used that phrase for it must be forty years. We'll be talking of old times together.'

Keene clasped his hand. He left the presbytery, glancing in respectfully at the impassive eyes of the Sacred Heart.

Those Thursday dinners became such a solemn, as well as delightful opening of hearts that within two months the monsignor was straining hard to hold his neophyte from declaring himself a Catholic on the spot. Indeed, one silent April night, during their third month, as he was showing his guest out into the moist emptiness of Pearse Square he said,

'I shall bless the day, Frank, when you become, if you do become, a Catholic, but I confess I shall have one small regret. The end of our little dinners.'

'Nonsense! Why should they end?'

'They will end.'

By the end of April the major was coming up aginst the hard stuff: the one sector of the battlefield to whose ground he returned obstinately, uncomfortably, scarred a little, sometimes approaching it as quietly as if he were on a lone night-raid. They might be talking about books – say, *Adam Bede* or *The Three Musketeers* and he might slip in:

'Padre! Can one never, simply never say that there are times when love conquers all? I mean, is that kind of love always, simply always, a sin?'

'I'm afraid, Frank, it is. Always a sin. I'm afraid there just isn't any way around that one. Nor, I fear, could any clergyman of any persuasion say anything else.' He allowed himself a slim smile. 'You remind me of old Professor Mahaffy of Trinity College in Dublin. He was a great wag, you know. One time he confided, or pretended to confide in a fashionable Dublin Jesuit, a close friend of his, that he felt drawn to the Catholic Church. Very naturally his Jesuit friend was only too eager to pluck the plum. Another glass? "Not a drop is sold till it's seven years old." Well, it appeared that there was just one small obstacle. Just one tiny, little problem. "If you can only allow me," Mahaffy said, and I am sure he said it with a poker-face, "to believe that Christ was not God I will join your Church tomorrow morning." His Jesuit friend is said to have paused for a long time. And at last he said, very regretfully, as I say to you now about adultery, "I'm afraid there isn't any way around that one." There are some things nobody can get around. Not even the Pope. Let alone me.'

Finally, one night, Frank said, plump out:

'Padre! When, and if, you consider me worthy to be received into the Church shall I have to go to Confession?'

'We will, naturally, have to clear up your past. Not that I think it will bother you very much. There are so few sins, and they repeat themselves endlessly. Even boringly. It is only the circumstances that change.'

'I was coming to exactly that. There is a bit of my past that I would like to clear up right away. I want to tell you that I have been in love with Anna Mohan for some ten years. I mean, we have been lovers in the full sense of the word. And I have never felt guilty about it. My fault, no doubt, but there it is. After all, she was only married to him in theory as you might say. He's gone now and words cannot harm him, everybody knows that he was a roaring alcoholic. Don't those circumstances you speak of alter such cases as mine?'

'He was addicted,' the monsignor agreed sadly. 'As for your case, that he was addicted is sad but it is not relevant to the law. Hard cases make bad laws. Nor is it relevant that you did not feel a sense of guilt. A stern moralist might speak to you of an atrophied conscience. I think it is enough for me to remind you that many men, known to history, men like Hitler or Stalin, committed the greatest crimes without feeling any sense of guilt. I can only repeat to you that adultery is a very grave sin. It is even two sins, for it also sins against the law that thou shalt not steal. She was his wife. I do not wish to overstress the point, but it does arise. Furthermore, chastity is not only of the body. In what is commonly called sex the body and the soul are one. You simply have to accept what I say.'

'She did lose something when he died. I have realized that.'

'I think,' the monsignor added, gravely, 'that this is something that it is your duty to clarify.' He paused and then added, pointedly, 'All round.'

'I accept what you say,' his neophyte sighed. 'It is most troubling.'

The monsignor quietly refilled his glass, wondering a little whether his pupil had some extra reason to be troubled.

He had. By now he was also receiving intermittent instruction from Anna, and on those occasions the tender feelings that she aroused in him were at times more than he could control. On one such occasion, looking up at her pink canopy, he said to her, 'Poor Anna! I can see now why you used sometimes to cry. It was a sin.' She smiled her curl-smile and whispered, 'But, sure, it no longer is.'

'Anna! We must not deceive ourselves. We're not married yet, ye know.'

'We are married in the sight of God,' she said and scratched him a little. 'The Church will bless us.'

'The Church must bless us first.'

'Ah, but sure,' she wheedled, 'it's so much nicer before.'

'It will be much, much nicer when you will lawfully be mine before man and God.'

'Darling!' she cried, and scratched wickedly. 'Don't be a bore! Are you a lawyer or a lover?'

'But the monsignor says . . .'

At this she flew into a rage.

'For Heaven's sake, who are you marrying? Me or the monsignor?'

He forbore to reply. He was troubled, and not for the first time, by the thought, 'Is she in more need of instruction than me?' This, however, was something that, in delicacy, he could not broach to her, or, in loyalty, to the monsignor – unless he might, perhaps, act as a go-between?

'Monsignor! I have one last question. To revert once more to my old problem, I do see, now, that I have indeed been guilty of a grave sin. I no longer contest it. It is undeniable. I cannot understand how I ever doubted it. But, supposing I had lain not with a married woman but with an unmarried woman, may I ask, is it in that case permissible for either party to feel just a little bit less guilty?'

'In such a hypothetical case,' his friend said dryly, 'either party would merely have been breaking one commandment at a time.'

'How stupid of me! How is it that everything becomes so simple when you explain it?'

The occasion to relay the consequences of his question was not long in coming. Under the canopy, he gently pointed out to Anna that they would both have to confess all this sooner or later, as one sin on her part, of two on his. She declared at once, and with passion, that she had no intention of doing anything of the sort.

'Do you think,' she cried, drawing blood from him this time, 'that I am going to spoil all our years and years of love by saying now that they were beastly and horrible?' Then seeing in his terrified horse-eyes how deeply she had shocked him, she added, easily, 'One could of course go through the *formality*.'

'Of course!' he agreed, profoundly relieved to find that she really was, after all a Catholic. She went on:

'Why not? One will say that one has transgressed. That's it. Transgressed. To pass over. To step beyond. Beyond the red line. A little.'

'Indeed,' he agreed happily, 'so we will! I'm so relieved! I'm so glad!'

'But, sure, Frank we'll know in our hearts, of course, that we didn't really do anything very bad at all'

'But, my dear Anna, there is the law! *Thou shalt not commit adultery.*'

At this she sat up, seized him by the hair and shook him like a dog.

'Are you calling me an adulteress?'

He sat up, waved his arms despairingly and wailed at her.

'My darling! I sit in judgement on nobody. But,' he said miserably. 'I *have* been an adulterer.'

She stroked his moustaches and kissed him tenderly.

'Not really, darling. That's just an old afterthought you are having now. You were as innocent as a child at the time.'

He sank back and rolled his tousled head sadly on the pillow.

'I'm such a simple sort of chap, Anna, and it's all such a simple thing, and I understand it so simply, and I do wish that you didn't make it all so damned complicated.'

She laughed and laughed.

'I make it complicated? It is I who am simple about it – your new friends who are tying everything up in knots with their laws, and rules, and regulations, and definitions, and sub-definitions that nobody can make head or tail of. I was brought up on all that stuff. I know it. You don't. They are at it all the time. So many ounces you may eat during Lent in France, so many in Spain. You can't eat meat on Fridays but it's no harm to eat frogs, and snakes and snails. I suppose you could even eat tripe! How much interest may one businessman draw on his deal. How much may another draw on another. Do you think anybody can really measure things like that? A baby who dies without being baptized must go to some place called Limbo that nobody ever knew what it is or in what corner of creation to put it. All that stuff has nothing to do with religion. How could it? Do you know that Saint Augustine said that all unbaptized children are condemned to suffer in eternal fire? Is *that* religion?'

'Are you sure Saint Augustine said this?'

'I was educated in Lausanne,' she said proudly. 'It's the home of Saint Augustine. All those stinking Calvinists.' She began to sob into the pillow. 'I wish I'd never asked you to become a Catholic. I wouldn't have if I knew you were going to take it as seriously as all this.'

'Don't cry, my daffodil! In a few months it will all be over and we will never need to talk of these terrible things again.'

She flew at once into a state of total happiness; she clapped her hands gaily.

'Oh, what fun it will be! In a couple of months you will be my loving husband. We'll be welcomed by everybody with open arms, we'll be known as the greatest lovers in all Ireland, the women will envy me and the men will smile at you and clap you on the back. I can't wait for it.'

'God speed the day when I shall at last be received.'

'And I shall be married!'

For six days and six nights he kept away from the monsignor, thinking of all those millions of babies burning in eternal fire, until his whole soul felt beaten all over by devils armed with sticks, and shovels, and red-hot tongs. On the seventh night he invited the monsignor to dinner. Like a good host he kept from his troubles until the port passed. Then, unsteadily, he said, 'Monsignor, I have another question, a small, tiny little problem. Tell me, where is Limbo?'

The old man paused in the act of raising his glass to his lips and looked at him apprehensively. He had dealt with Transubstantiation, Miracles, the Resurrection, Indulgences, Galileo, the Virgin Birth, the Immaculate Conception, Grace, Predestination, the Will, Mixed Marriages, even Adultery. These great mysteries and problems had presented no lasting difficulty either to him or to his dear friend. But Limbo? He knew from long experience how easily the small things, rather than the big ones, can shatter a man's faith.

'Why did you ask me that question?' he said sadly.

'It just occurred to me,' the major said loyally and curled a little at his lack of frankness to his friend.

'I see!'

'Is it true, monsignor, as I have read, that Saint Augustine said that all babies who have not been baptized must burn in eternal fire?'

With a whole movement of his arm the monsignor pushed his glass slowly to one side. His night was in ruins.

'I believe so,' he said, and thrust gallantly on. 'Still, there are other and more benignant views. It all arose, I presume, out of the problem of where to place those unbaptized souls who died before Christ, and those others who died after Him without ever hearing of Him. I believe it was the Council of Florence that decreed it.' He faltered. 'It was a rather confused Council. So confused that I gather that its Acts have perished. It laid down, it was in the fifteenth century, that nobody who is unbaptized may enter heaven. Since then many thinkers have, in their mercy, felt a repugnance to the idea. Many theologians have sought out ways of accepting the doctrine while, as you might say, circumventing, or anyway softening, its melancholy implications. Major! Do you really want me to go into this matter of Limbo? It is not a primal question.'

'It bothers me, monsignor.'

'I see. Well. I do know that one Italian theologian, whose name escapes me at the moment, felt that God might instruct the angels to confer baptism on those children – who might otherwise perish without it. Another theologian felt that the sincere wish of the parent that the child might have been baptized could be a fair equivalent. Saint Thomas felt, humanely, that those children suffer no pain of the body, although they must, indeed, always grieve that they can never see God. Just as a bird, or a mouse, might grieve that it can never be a man, or speak to an emperor or king.'

'How sad!'

'Of course, Major,' the monsignor whispered, 'we have to recognize that we have no purely human right to Heaven. Heaven is a gift God could, without injustice, deny it to us. I suggest it was originally a rabbinical idea.'

The priest looked into the glowing ashes of the fire. The major looked out at the darkness of the night. Through the open window the invisible fields sent in the sweetness of the May-blossom. After a long while the monsignor said, 'There are many mysteries in life that we have to accept in humility without understanding them. Indeed, it is because we do not understand the mystery that we do accept it – and live with it.'

As he drove away the major watched the beams of his car until they touched the last of his yews, and stood there until the smell of his petrol faded in the pure air. He walked up and down his avenue many times. Afterwards he sat before his dying fire until sleep came to him, where he slouched by its ashes.

It was quite early, a bird-singing May morning, gleaming after a light shower of rain, when he faced her fresh and handsome, breakfasting beside her cheerful morning fire. He said firmly, 'Anna, I can never become a Catholic.'

Her cup clattered into its saucer.

'But, Frank, you must! Do you expect me to marry you like a

Protestant in a registry office? Or to live with you for the rest of my life with you in what you now think of as a cesspool of sin?'

'I am proposing nothing. I can think of nothing. It is just that I am too old, or too stupid, to be able to follow you both.'

'You just want to be shut of me.' She raised her tear-filled eyes. 'Or is it that it is I who am too old and too stupid? Why can't you be as I am? After all I am a Catholic!'

'I have sometimes wondered, Anna, what you are.'

Her fury burst about him like shrapnel. She dashed down *The Irish Times*.

'How dare you? Of course I am a Catholic. What's wrong with you is that you want everything to be perfect. As clean, and bare and tidy as a barrack square. That's it! All you are is a bloody English major who wants everybody's buttons to be polished and everybody's cap to be as straight as a plate.'

'But it wasn't I who raised the question of Limbo!'

'To hell with Limbo! If there is a hell! Or a Limbo! What's wrong with you is you're too conceited. You want to cross every I and dot every T. Why do you want to understand everything? Why can't you just accept things the way I do?'

'Do you accept Limbo?'

'I never think about Limbo. I never think about stupid things like that. I think only of God, and the stars, and of Heaven, and of love, and of you.'

'You put me to a great test, Anna. As the monsignor says I must also think of the cross and the nails. Just as he says that in love the soul and the body are one.'

'You're a liar! All this is just a cute device to get out of marrying me. I see through you. I see through your cheap trickery. I see through your dirty Saxon guile. If you were the last man on earth this minute, Frank Keene, I wouldn't marry you now. Please don't come near me ever again!'

She swept out and crashed the door. He retrieved *The Irish Times* from the fire, beat out its flames and went away.

He had no one left to talk to. He had pestered the monsignor beyond endurance. He had never attended the Church of Ireland. Anyway he doubted if they knew very much about Limbo or the Council of Naples. Mabel Tallant would only laugh at him. He had devoted so many years of his life to Anna that he had made no friends. And now she neither loved him nor respected him, and he did not . . . He crushed down the bleak admission.

After three weeks of the blackest misery, he dashed off a letter:

Monseigneur, Mon General, Mon ami,

If I may be allowed to declare my belief in things that I do not understand and to accept in humility things that I do not approve I am ready, at your command, to take Mount Sion, even unaccompanied by your Alsatian bitch. Give me your order. I will obey.

Your obedient servant,
Francis Lancelot Keene,
Major,
LRCPE and LM,
Late RAMC,
Dunkirk, Tunisia, Libya, Egypt, Italy,
Dispatches, medal and clasp, DSO,
1940-1945.
Retired.

The reply came by telegram the next day. At the sight of the single word of command a sudden rage boiled up in him. Who did he think he was? A bloody general? One man? And no dog? Against an army of doubts . . .

He chose July 9th for it, the feast day of two English saints, John Fisher, bishop, and Thomas More, chancellor, both martyrs.

It was raining as he entered the presbytery. In the monsignor's parlour the old Alsatian half looked up at him and sank back into its doze. The two men walked silently across to the church where the monsignor invested himself in his surplice and stole, and the major knelt by the rails of a sidechapel, feeling nothing whatsoever as he repeated the words of recantation and of belief. They then retired to the presbytery where the major knelt by the monsignor's chair for his first confession. During the previous days he had been girding himself for his complete life-story. The monsignor truncated even that piece of the ceremony, saying, 'I imagine I know it all. Women, and drink, and I suppose swearing like a trooper. Unless there is some special sin of your past life that you want to mention?'

Humbly, the major said, 'Sloth,' and got a faint satisfaction from the painful admission.

Then sunshine flooded his heart when the monsignor told him that his penance would be to say, that night, three Ave Marias.

'So little? After so long?'

'God loves you,' the monsignor said, and bade him to say his Act of Contrition.

The major's eyes filled with tears as he heard the murmuring words of absolution mingle with his own. The monsignor then raised him to his feet and warmly shook both his hands.

'My dear friend in Christ. Now you are one of us. Do your best. In the bosom of the Church. And,' briskly removing his vestments, 'let's go back now and have a good dollop of malt.'

Over the glass the major said happily, 'I was afraid I was going to feel nothing at all. Wouldn't that have been awful?'

'My dear Frank, we are strange cattle. Often, even when I say Mass, I don't feel that it is doing me a bit of good. But I know it is, so I do not worry. The heart may be the centre of all things but in the end it's not our feelings that matter but our good works. As you and I know well, more men go weak in battle from feeling too much than from feeling too little.' He chuckled. 'I remember one time we had a Colonel Home-Crean in the Inniskillings who was always carrying on about the martial spirit. He meant well. But the troops called him Old Carry On. It wasn't a bad pun, because whenever he finished one of his speeches he always said, "Carry on, Sergeant."'

The major laughed wryly.

'Pass the buck.'

'I say it still. I say it now, Frank, to you.'

He tore back at sixty miles an hour to Culadrum to meet her, singing all the way at the top of his voice *When the Saints go marching in*. There was a shower, the sun ebbed and flowed, and 'Blow me,' he cheered, 'if they haven't sent me a rainbow!' He hooted his horn along her drive, and there she was running down the steps on to the gravel to embrace him.

''Tis done,' he laughed, and she said, 'You look about seventeen!'

'God loves me!' he said.

'Did you fix up about the marriage?'

'Good Lord! I forgot all about it!'

'You immense dope!' she laughed. 'That was the whole point. Go back tonight and fix it. And do remember – the tenth of August. We've got all the tickets, darling! Promise?'

'You're still sure it's not a bit too soon? I mean that people may think that . . .'

She laughed triumphantly.

'I want them to think! I'll blame it all on my impetuous lover. And, now, you must come and see my new dresses and hats, a whole crateful of them came this morning from Dublin.'

She took him by the hand, and galloped him upstairs to her room's litter of hillocked tissue and coloured cardboard boxes.

'Sit there. And don't dare stir.' She tore off her frock; he sat and beamed at her, in her panties and bra, circling, preening, glaring in the long mirror at herself in pale toques, straw-hats in white, in mauve, in liver-pink, and he was so happy at her childish happiness that for a moment he was terrified that she would next want him to go to bed with her. Thank heaven, she was too excited to think about it. Once as she posed a pale-blue pillbox on the back of her poll, saying, 'Or this one?' he wondered whether she had gone, or when she would go to Confession, and decided that he would not press her about it just now. Perhaps never at all.

They were married before a large congregation in the cathedral. He recognized many whom he had seen six months before at the funeral. He felt a bit self-conscious about his age, and hers, and several times, when it was over, he had to stop himself from interpreting their broad smiles and their hearty congratulations. Still, whether confetti-speck-led in his grey topper and tails outside the church door, or mingling with the crowd in his new pin-stripe at the champagne reception in the Royal Hotel, he felt he had carried it all off like a soldier and a gentleman, talking now with the Inspector about tinkers, now with a very serious young librarian about the publications of the Irish Manuscripts Commission, now with Mulcahy the chemist, about the 'extraordinary' number of women in the town who took barbiturates for 'the narves', or listening in polite astonishment to a curate whom he had never met before weighing the comparative merits of President Salazar and General Franco. Then they were in his car driving off amid huzzas and laughter, down along the Main Street, out into the country for Dublin, for London and Lausanne. They were both tipsy. She was weeping softly. He filled with pity and love.

'You're not upset, darling?'

'It's just my nerves,' she smiled bravely, took a pill from her bag, and was soon chortling once more.

Everything turned out afterwards just as she had foretold. They set up house together in Culadrum. All her old friends, and her late husband's friends, came often and regularly to visit them. They played bridge with them at least twice a week. In the season he hunted three times a week. He took complete charge of her garden. He developed an interest in local archaeology. She was entirely happy, scratched him no longer and wept no more. He enjoyed all the quiet self-satisfaction of a man who, at some cost to himself, has done the right thing and found everything turning out splendidly. As he marched the roads erect, chest out, with his stick and his dog, he was admired, liked and envied by all.

Winter came. The rains and the barometer fell. She began to make excuses about going to Mass on account of the awful weather and her health. At first he found, to his regret, that he was often going to Mass alone. Then he found that he was always going alone. He began to wonder at this, ask questions about it, become testy about it, and at last they argued crossly over it every Sunday morning. There were long silences because of it. Once a whole week passed without a word spoken. He finally realized that she had no interest at all in religion, and had never had. There he felt a great hole opening in his belly, crawling like fear, recurrent as a fever, painful as betrayal, until he could no longer bear his misery alone.

'But, monsignor,' he wailed, 'why did the woman insist on my becoming a Catholic if she doesn't believe in it herself? Why in God's name did she do this to me?'

His friend did not hesitate – he never had hesitated.

'Superstition. Fear perhaps? She has memories of childhood. Of the dark. The thin red line that may not be crossed.'

'But we crossed it over and over again, for years!'

'That was not for ever.'

'Could we not have had a mixed marriage?'

'It could have been managed. Somehow. Somewhere. She wanted the Real Thing. The laying on of hands. The propitiation. The magic touch. I suspect, Frank, that your wife is a very simple woman. We have millions of them in the Church. Full of what I call ignorant innocence.

They don't do much harm to anybody, except themselves. Or if they become vain, or proud, or we press them too hard, then they turn on us like a knife. Don't force her. You have a problem. You took a chance and now you must find some way of living with it, in faith, and courage and trust. Just remember that your wife is a little vain, rather spoiled I imagine, possibly a trifle conceited, too. And, or so I feel, very unsure of herself. Hence her superstition. African missionaries tell me that they are very familiar with it.'

The major stared at him, containing the urge to say, 'Why the hell didn't you tell me all this before?'

'And what is my superstition?' he asked curtly.

'You are different. You worked your passage. Only . . .'

Here he did hesitate.

'Only?'

'Only do not expect miracles. You may, of course, pray for one. I suppose it is what we all pray for really.'

He took to going to early Mass every morning, much to her annoyance because no matter how quietly he stole out of her bed she always woke up, turning over and muttering things like, 'For God's sake isn't Sunday enough for you?' or 'My nerves are shot to bits with you and your blooming piety!' By Christmas he had taken to sleeping alone. By February he was praying for the gift of silence and drinking like a fish. In spite of that he had lost eleven pounds weight by March and was thinking of running away to Malaysia. By April he could no longer keep his food down. And then their war suddenly ended, in an explosion of light. He had gone out one morning into her walled garden to jab, stoically, at the grass and the pearlwort between the cracks of her crazy-pavement. The night had been a blur of wet trees; now a skyload of sun warmed his stooped back. He smelled the cosseted earth, glanced at her ancient espaliers, became aware of a thrush's throat, blackbirds skirling, the chaffinches' in-and-out, the powerful robin, two loving tits that flicked into the gleaming cloud of an old cherry tree propped over his head. As he picked on and on, patiently and humbly, his memory slowly expanded in widening circles out to the covert of Easter Hill, out beyond the furze-yellow slopes of the Stameen river, away out after that great wheeling run of a month ago across the reedy plain, past its fallen dolmen and its ruined abbey, losing the scent, finding it again, five glorious, nonstop, hammering miles of it. As he shifted the kneeler he noticed the first tiny bells of her white rhododendron. Christ was risen. Steaming roads stretched like wet rulers across the bog, past a pub, a garage, a grey National School, under a procession of elms against a foam-bath of clouds. At his toe he saw a blue eggshell.

At that moment a window in the house was lifted. Looking up, he saw her, in her pink morning-dress, leaning on the sill with both hands, staring over the countryside. He had a vision and in a flash it burst on him that everything she saw and he remembered came out of one eggshell. She waved to him, casually. He waved back wildly with his weeder. She retired.

'Monsignor! It was something that could only happen in Lourdes! How right you were! Never force things. Change and expand. Move slowly. Live with your problems. There are no laws for hard cases. Trust and courage solves everything. And, as you say, most of those laws are just so many old-fashioned rabbinical ideas. And the decrees of the Councils all lost! Heaven is a gift. The heart is the centre. Carry on. We can only all do our best. God loves us. Not a single cross word for two weeks! Everything absolutely ticketyboo. Monsignor, you should be a cardinal!'

They had met in the street. The old man had heard him impassively. Leaning forward on his umbrella he lifted his head from his toes for one quick glance, almost it occurred to the major in his excitement, as if he were not a cardinal but an African missionary.

'You say nothing?' he asked anxiously.

'I was just thinking. Frank. An odd thing! When we were in the Connaught Rangers we never said "Ticketyboo". What we used to say was "All kiff!" Hindustani, do you suppose? That's good news.' He shook hands limply, turned to go, turned back, said, 'Carry on, Frank,' and went on his slow way down the street, followed by his friend's wide-eyed stare of puzzlement, annoyance, affection and undiminished admiration. Two days later he attended his funeral. It was a damp day, and it did not do his rheumatism any good.

The next morning was a Sunday. The storm woke him. Through the corner of his blind he saw spilling rain, waving treetops and Noreen the maid, wrapped up in yellow cellophane like a lifeboat captain, wobbling on her bicycle down the avenue to Mass. He felt a twinge in his shoulder. He said, 'Well, I was at Mass yesterday,' lay back and dozed for an hour. He heard the soft boom of the breakfast gong, and

Anna's door open and close. As he went downstairs in his dressing-gown he smelled bacon and coffee. She was sitting by the breakfast table in her morning-gown. The fire blazed cosily. 'Good morning, love,' he said and kissed her forehead.

'Are you going out?' she asked and looked at the overspilling gutters dropping great glass beads of water past the window.

'Arthritis,' he said sheepishly.

'Why, in God's name,' she groaned, 'do we live in this climate?'

'We live where we are fated to live, in the bosom of the country,' and he lifted the chased lid of the breakfast dish.

She frowned. They munched silently. To cheer her he suggested that they might go to Italy in May, to Venice, to Rome, and he began to plan how they could go and what they could see there together. Far away a church bell tolled, on the wet wind, like a bell for the dead. He went on talking very gaily, very rapidly, very loudly. She smiled her curl-smile and said, 'Why not Lausanne?'

'Indeed, indeed! Anywhere! To get away!'

# Dividends

1

As far as Mel Meldrum was concerned *l'affaire Anna*, as he was to call it, began one wet and windy April morning in 1944 when his chief clerk, Mooney, knocked at the door of his sanctum, handed him my letter, marked *Personal* and *By Hand*, and said that the bearer was an old lady in a black bonnet sitting outside in the main office 'shaking her blooming umbrella all over your new Turkish carpet'. I can see Mel glancing at my signature, smiling at his memories of our college days together twenty years before, rapidly taking the point of the letter and ordering Miss Whelan to be shown in to him at once. He rises courteously, begs her to be seated, watches amusedly while she fumbles in her woven shopping-bag, and produces, proudly I have no doubt, a fat, wrinkled envelope containing the £350 in thirty-five white Bank of England notes. He receives it from her with a small bow. It was why I sent her to him; he was always affable, almost unctuous, with old ladies.

My Aunty Anna Maria was my mother's sister. Until she got this small legacy from another sister, who had recently died in a place called Toogong in New South Wales, she had never before possessed such a lump sum. She had existed for thirty-odd years on a modest salary as cook-housekeeper to a highly successful horse-trainer in County Kildare; and then on the small pension he kindly gave her, supplemented occasionally by minute subventions from a nephew here and a niece there whenever we had the decency to remember how she used to stuff us with cakes and lemonade during our summer holidays on the edge of the Curragh where we loved to visit her in the staff quarters of the trainer's house. My father died, in Cork, so she came down there when she was about fifty-five, to live with my mother; and when my mother died she had stayed on, alone, in the city, living in a single room in a battered old fabric of a tenement overlooking one of Cork's many abandoned quaysides – silent except for the poor kids from the lanes around playing and screaming in the street, or the gulls swooping over the bits of floating orange-skin, breadcrusts or potato peelings backing slowly up-river on the high tide. When Mel saw her she was turned seventy. To my shame I had not seen her for twelve years. I had left Cork before she came there, and returned only once, for my mother's funeral. I was now married and living in Dublin.

It had taken me weeks of letter-writing, back and forth, to persuade her to invest her legacy, and I was delighted when she agreed, because I knew that if she did not she would either scatter it in dribs and drabs, or lose it in the street some day, or hide it in some corner of her room and not remember where before the mice had eaten it into confetti.

Mel described in a long, amusing letter how he had accepted the envelope 'with measured ceremony'. He had given her his best advice 'like a pontiff'. He explained to her that the sum was too small for an annuity, and she was too old for growth-shares, so he must advise her to buy 8% Preference shares in Sunbeam-Wolsey. He refused to charge her his usual stockbroker's fee, and, kindest act of all, told her that instead of waiting from one six-month period to the next for her modest dividends (£28 a year) she might, if she so wished, come into the office on the first of every month, and his chief clerk would there pay her the equivalent of her £28 per annum in twelve equal portions. She accepted his offer 'like a queen'. I could henceforth be happy to think of her toddling on the first of every month into Meldrum, Guy and Meldrum, smiling and bobbing under her black, spangled bonnet, and departing, amid the pleased smiles of everybody in the office, with her six shillings and eight pennies, wrapped in two single pound notes, clasped in the heel of her gloved fist.

I sent him my cordial thanks and thought no more about her until exactly one year later when he wrote to me that she had ordered him to sell her shares. It appeared that she had become smitten by a sudden longing to possess a blue, brocaded, saddle-back armchair that she had seen one morning in the window of Cash's in Patrick Steet. It appeared further that for months past 'a certain Mrs Bastable and a certain Mrs Sealy', two cronies as doddering as herself, also in her tenement on Lavitt's Quay, had been telling her that nobody but 'a born foolah' would leave 'all that lovely money' lying idle in Mister Meldrum's fine office on the South Mall.

It was easy enough to hear these two tempters at work on her:

'Sure, Miss Whalen, you could buy all the armchairs in Cork with that much money! And look at your poor ould room with the paint falling off the ceiling like snow! And your poor ould curtains in tatthers on yer winda! Why don't you buy an electric fire that would keep you warm all the winter? And two grand, soft Blarney blankets for your bed? And a pink, quilted eiderdown? And, anyway, sure that measley ould two quid that Meldrum gives you wouldn't buy a dead cat! And supposing yeh die? What'll happen it then? Get a hold of your money, girl, and *spend it*!'

Mel counter-argued and counter-pleaded. I pleaded. I got her parish priest to plead with her. I even offered to buy her the brocaded armchair as a present. It was no use. Mel sold her shares, gave her a cheque for £350, wished her well, and we both washed our hands of her.

I next got a long and slightly testy letter from Mel, written on the first day of the following month of May. It began, 'Your good Aunty Anna has this morning turned up again in my office, bright as a new-born smile, bowing and bobbing as usual, calmly asking my chief clerk Mooney for what she calls, if you please, *her* little divvies...'

In dismay he had come out to her.

'But, Miss Whelan, you've sold your shares! Don't you remember?'

Aunt Maria smiled cunningly at him.

'Ah, yes!' she agreed. 'But I didn't sell my little divvies!'

'But,' Mel laughed, 'your dividends accrued from the capital sum you invested. Once a client sells his shares he withdraws the capital and there can be no more dividends. Surely you understand that?'

At once Aunty Anna's smile vanished. A dark fright started at the bottom of her chin and climbed slowly up to her eyes.

'Mister Meldrum, you know well that I didn't sell me little divvies. I want me little divvies. You always gave me them. They belong to me. Why can't you give them to me now the way you always gave me them at the first of every month? Why are you keeping them back from me now?'

'Miss Whelan, when a client sells his shares they are gone. And when they are gone the dividends naturally cease forthwith. You instructed me to sell. I did so. I gave you back your money in a lump sum. If you now wish to give me back that lump sum I shall be most happy to buy you more shares and your dividends will begin again. Otherwise we have nothing for you.'

Aunty Anna had burst into floods of tears, and she began to wail, with the whole office staring at the pair of them.

'What do I want with shares? I don't want any more ould shares. I gave you back me shares. Keep 'em! I don't want 'em. All I want is me little divvies. And anyway I haven't the money you gave me, I bought an armchair with it, and an electric fire from the ESB, and a costume from Dowden's, and I gave fifty pounds to the Canon to say Masses for my poor soul when I'm dead, and I loaned ten quid to Mrs Bastable on the ground-floor, and ten quid to Mrs Sealy on the third floor back, and what with this and that and the other all I have left is a few quid, and I don't know where I put 'em, I'd lay down me life I put 'em in the brown teapot on the top shelf but when I went looking for them yesterday I couldn't find them high nor low. Mrs Sealy says I must have made tea with them, but I tell you, Mister Meldrum, I wouldn't trust that one as far as I'd throw her. Mister Meldrum, give me me little divvies. They're all I have to live on bar that mangy old pension. I want me divvies here and now, if you please, or I'll go out there in the street and call a policeman!'

Mel led her gently into his inner sanctum, together with his book-keeper, and the two of them spent an hour explaining to her, in every way they could think of, the difference between shares and dividends. They showed her the receipt for the purchase of the shares, for the dividends they had earned over the year, the notation of the re-sale of the shares, and the red line drawn clearly at the end of her account to show that it was now closed for ever. They might as well have been talking to the carpet. Aunty Anna just could not understand that he who does not speculate cannot accumulate. The upshot of it was that she became so upset, and Mel became so angry with her, and then so upset because he had upset her that, to comfort her, he took £2 6s. 8d. out of his pocket, the equivalent of what she had hitherto lawfully drawn every month, told her that this was the end, the very end, and that she must now reconcile herself, firmly and finally, if she would be so very kind, to the plain fact that she was no longer in the market for anything. And so he showed her out, bobbing and smiling, and happy, and (he hoped), convinced. He was most forbearing about it all. Three pages he wrote about it to me. All I could do was to write him a properly apologetic and deeply grateful reply, enclosing my cheque for £2 6s. 8d., which, I noted, in some surprise, he duly cashed.

On the morning of the first of the following month of June he was on the telephone. His voice over the wire sounded rather strangled.

'Your good aunt is back here in my office again. She is sitting directly opposite me. She seems to be in very good health. And in good spirits to boot. In fact she is beaming at me. Nevertheless she is once more demanding dividends on shares which she does not possess. Will you kindly tell me at once what you wish me to do with, for, or to her?'

'Oh, Lord, Mel! This is too bad! I'm very sorry! I'm awfully sorry. Look, Mel, couldn't you just explain firmly to the old lady that...'

At this his voice rose to a squeak of utter exasperation.

'Miss Whelan has been in my private office for the past three-quarters of a bloody hour with my book-keeper, my assistant book-keeper, my chief clerk...'

'Mel! I'll tell you what to do. Just give her the two quid six and eight and I'll send you a cheque for it this minute, and then tell her never, just simply never, to darken your doors again.'

Mel's voice became precise, piercing, priggish and prim in a way that suddenly recalled to me a familiar side of his nature that I had completely forgotten until that moment.

'I have no hope what-so-ever of achieve-ing the entire-ly de-sirable state of affairs that you so blandly de-pict. I am afraid the time has arrived for you to come down to Cork in person and talk in person to your good aunt. Furthermore, I must tell you that your proposal about a cheque is totally contrary to my principles as a man and as a stockbroker. It is contrary to the whole ethics, and the whole philosophy, the whole morality of stockbroking. It is inconsistent, unrealistic, unprofessional and absurd. As I have explained to Miss Whelan, he who saves may invest, he who invests may accumulate, he who does not save may not...'

'Mel, for God's sake come off it! How the hell can she save anything at all on that measley old pension of hers? Who do you think she is? Bernard Baruch? Henry Ford? John D. Rockefeller? Gulbenkian?'

'In that case,' he retorted, 'it is as absurd for her to expect as it would be unrealistic for me to pretend that she is entitled to returns on non-existent capital. In the name of justice, equity and realism, above all in the name of realism, I will not and I cannot pretend to pay any client dividends that simply do not exist ... Excuse me one moment.'

Here I could hear a confused babble of voices as of four or five people engaged in passionate argument, 161 blessed miles away from my study in Dublin.

'Hello!' he roared. 'How soon, for God Almighty's sake, can you come down to Cork and settle this matter with your aunt?'

I saw that there was no way out of it. It was a Friday. I said that I would take the morning train on Saturday.

'I will meet you at the station.'

'Is this an order?' I asked wryly.

His answer was clipped. He recovered himself sufficiently to add 'Please!' and even to mention that I could get some sort of ragtime lunch on the train. When I said I would be there, he calmed down. He expanded. He even became amiable. When he broke into French I remembered how, in his student days, he used to go to France every summer and Easter with his widowed mother.

'Bon! Nous causerons de beaucoup de choses. Et nous donnerons le coup-de-grace à l'affaire Anna, et à ses actions imaginaires' – and hung up.

*Actions?* My dictionary told me that the word means *acts, actions, performances, battles, postures, stocks, shares.* As I put back the volume on its shelf I remembered how good he always used to be at social work among the poor of Cork. I also wondered a little how such a man could see nothing wrong with giving charity outside his office in the name of Saint Vincent de Paul but everything wrong with the idea of bestowing largesse inside it in the name of pity. I also realized that I had not met him for some twenty years.

2

It was a perfect June morning. All the way down from Dublin to Cork the country looked so soft and fresh, so green and young, and I lunched so well that my heart gradually warmed both to Aunty Anna and to Mel, the dual cause of this pleasant excursion back to my homeground. As the fields floated past and the waves of the telegraph wires rolled and sank I started to recall the Mel I used to know. Indeed if anybody at that moment had asked me about him – say, that old priest half dozing on the seat opposite me – I would have launched on a eulogy as long as an elegy.

Stout fellow! Salt of the earth! As fine a chap as you could hope to meet in a day's march. Honest, kind and absolutely reliable. The sort of man who would never, simply never let you down. A worthy inheritor of his father's and his grandfather's business. Handsome, strong, tall, always well dressed – in the old days, we all thought him a bit of a dandy. And so easy! As smooth and easy as that bog-stream outside there. Oh, now and again he could be gruff if you rubbed him the wrong way, and he was sometimes given a bit to playing the big shot. And by that same token he always boasted that he was a first class shot. A real, clean-living, open-air man. What else? Well informed about music. And the opera. Spoke French well – those visits abroad with his mother. A strong civic sense, always proud of his native city. Who was it that told me a few years ago that he is up to his neck nowadays in all sorts of worthy societies in Cork? The Old Folks Association, the Safety First Association, Saint Vincent de Paul, the Archaeological Society, the Society for the Prevention of Cruelty to Animals, the African Mission Brotherhood . . .

I glanced across at my old priest. He was looking at me as if I had been talking aloud to myself. I turned to the fields.

'Well . . . Not exactly sociable, I suppose. Unless a committee meeting in a hotel room can be called a jolly sociable occasion.'

Come to think of it, he always did keep a bit to himself. Not stand-offishly, more of a class thing, being so much richer than the rest of us. Or was he a little shy? And I did hear recently that he has given up shooting and taken to bird-watching – from a weekend cottage he has outside Cork, some place along the valley of the Lee beyond Inniscarra. His private hide-out where he can 'get away from it all'.

The old priest was still looking at me. I turned to watch a racing horse.

'All? I suppose he means the roaring traffic of Cork, which, when I was a student, chiefly meant jarvey-cars, bullocks, dray-horses and bicycles. It is a quiet place. Not really a city at all. And then, of course, we mustn't forget Cork's famous social whirl. Bridge every night, golf every Saturday, and, for the happy few, a spot of sailing in the harbour over the weekend. And tubs of secret drinking in hotel lounges for the happy many, stealing in discreetly by the back door. Or were they the unhappy many? Cork can be a pretty grim place in the winter. As I well know! Lord! don't I know!'

A sunshot shower of rain flecked the windows of the train.

'We may as well face it. Cork is a place where it rains, and rains, and rains, with an implacable and persistent slowness. A frightful place, really, in the winter! Of course, if you have enough piastres you can knock out a good time even in Cork. But you have to have the piastres. And I never did. Mel did. And lots of 'em. Rich? Very. At least by Cork standards. A tight, bloody hole, full to the butt of the lugs with old family businesses that keep a firm grip on their miserly homesteads.'

Was that priest raising his eyebrows at me?

'Naturally, he's a Catholic! A most devoted Catholic. No! A baptized, confirmed and unmarried bachelor. That is odd – because he always had a great eye for the girls. Funny I never thought of it before. In Ireland you don't, somehow. You get so used to the widowed mother in the background, or the uncle who is a bishop, or the two brothers who are priests, or the three sisters who are nuns. The tradition of celibacy. But, by God, he did have that roving eye! Why didn't he marry? And he was quite good-looking. Even if he has slightly prominent teeth, and a rather silly, affected way of shaving that leaves a tuft of hair on each cheekbone.'

I closed my eyes to see him better. I wondered why the hell I was coming down here at all.

'He must be forty-six or forty-seven by now. If his taste in clothes is what it used to be he will be wearing a check sports coat with two splits behind and a check cap slightly yawed over his gamesome eye. The country squire's weekend costume.

'Is there,' I asked the priest, 'a train back out of Cork tonight?'

He smiled crookedly.

'There is. A slow one. You're not staying long with us, I see?'

'I have to get back tonight.'

I felt my face flushing. My wife is not well. My youngest daughter has a fever. I am in a bad shape myself, Mel. In fact I am running a temperature of 102°. My brother is arriving from London on Sunday morning. My best friend is dying. My uncle died yesterday. I simply have to go to his funeral.

'Are you sure, Father, there is a train out of Cork tonight?'

'There is. One of these days they say we are going to have our own airport. With aeroplanes.'

The rain stopped and the sun burst out, but I did not trust it one inch. I recognized familiar fields. Poor-looking fields. The rain. The cold. My poverty-stricken youth in Cork. We passed Blarney. Then we were in the tunnel, and though I knew there is this long tunnel into Cork I had forgotten how long it was, how smelly and how dark.

He was the first person I saw on the platform, in his tweeds and his sporty cap. The wings of his hair were turning white. His teeth were much too white to be his own. He wore spectacles. We greeted one another warmly.

People talk of well-remembered voices. I recognized his slightly hectoring Oxford-cum-Cork accent only when he said, 'Well. So we got Your Highness down to Cork at last?' I laughed, 'Why do Cork people always say "up to Dublin" and "down to Cork"? Here I am, like Orpheus.' He sniffed by way of reply, and we went out of the station yard teasing one another amiably about our advancing years, sat into his white sports Jaguar and shot across the station yard like a bullet.

3

'Well?' I said. 'And how did you finish up yesterday with my dear old Aunty Anna?'

He pretended to be coping with the traffic – at that point a dozen bullocks lurching wild-eyed all over the street before the howls and waving arms of two equally wild-eyed drovers. Then, with a sheepish side glance and a grin that was clearly meant to involve me in his illogicality, he said:

'I gave her the odd two quid again. She will obviously be back in a month. And every month for the rest of her life. Unless we do something drastic about her.'

'I see. Are we going to beard her now?'

'No! I don't work on Saturdays. And I'm not going to break my rule of life for that accursed old hairpin. I'm driving you out to my Sabine farm. We've got the whole weekend. We'll talk about her tonight after dinner. And not one minute before!'

I bridled. After all, I was very fond of my Aunty Anna, even if I had not visited her for the last twelve years, and I objected to being shanghaied like this without as much as a 'If you'd like it', or 'If you can spare the time', or 'By your leave'. Was he at his old game of playing the big shot? The bossy businessman? At close quarters, over a whole weekend, was he going to turn out to be an awful bore? However, he had been very kind to Aunty Anna, and I had got him into this mess, and I was under an obligation to him, so I said, as pleasantly as I could, 'That's very kind of you, Mel. I can see my aunt tomorrow morning, and I'm sure there must be an afternoon train home.'

'If that's what you want,' he said, rather huffily. Then he said, cheerfully, 'If there is a train to Dublin on Sundays I'm sure it takes about ten hours.' Then he said, so smugly that anybody who did not know him could well have taken an immediate dislike to him, 'You're going to like my cottage – it's a real beauty. Nobody in Cork has anything like it!'

I did not talk much during the drive into and out of the city. It reminded me too much of my father and mother, of my lost youth. He blathered on and on about its great future, its economic development, the airport they were sure to have some day, as if he were the Lord Mayor of the damn place. Then we were out of it and in the country again, and presently – it cannot have been more than twenty minutes at his mad speed – he said, 'Behold my Sabine farm!'

At first glance, through the trees, it looked like the sort of cottage that would make any estate-agent start pouring out words like 'rustic', 'picturesque', 'antique', 'venerable', 'traditional', 'old-world' and every other kind of pin-headed euphemism for damp, dirty, crumbling, phoney, half ruined, fourth-hand and thoroughly uncomfortable. When we drew up by its little wooden gate, it turned out to be the sort of dream-cottage you meet in English detective stories, or on the travel posters of British Railways. It stood under its trim roof of thatch on a sunbathed sideroad, in about two acres of orchard, kitchen garden and lawn, facing a small, old church with a not ungraceful spire in brownstone directly above the Lee murmuring far below in a valley scooped aeons ago out of the surrounding hills and covered now with young pine-woods. It was long, low and pink-washed, with diamond panes in its small windows, and its walls were covered by a thick curtain of Albertine roses that would be a mellow blaze within a week or two. The door, painted in William Morris blue, was opened by a brown-eyed young woman whom he introduced as, 'My housekeeper. My invaluable Sheila.' The living-room was long and low-ceilinged, furnished in elegant Adams and Chippendale, carpeted in pale green from wall to wall, with an unnecessary but welcoming wood fire sizzling softly in an old brick fireplace. Later I found that he had put in central heating, electric light and an American-style kitchen. His Sheila brought us Scotch, water and ice-cubes, and we sank into two deep armchairs beside the fire.

'You seem to live pretty well, friend,' I admitted grudgingly.

'I like the simple life,' he breezed. 'But I'm not simple-minded about it, I'm a realist.'

I humphed internally. I recognized the common illusion of most businessmen that writers are all mental defectives, dreamy romancers with about as much commonsense as would fit in one of their small toes. Really, I thought again, all this might well turn out to be a frightful bore.

I became aware that his housekeeper was still standing beside us. Her brown eyes reminded me of two shining chestnuts. If her chin had not been a shadow overshot she would have been a beauty. What struck me most about her was not, however, her face, her trim figure or her straight back, but her air of calm self-possession. He gave her a quick, all-over glance.

'Well, my dear? What are you giving us for dinner tonight?'

'Two roast chickens. Parsley potatoes. New. Your own. And fresh peas from the garden.'

'And for sweet? Apart from yourself?' he asked, with that kind of gawky smile with which elderly men try to curry favour with scowling children, and that celibates overdo for handsome young women.

'Apart from myself,' she replied calmly, 'there will be an apple pie. They are the last apples left in your loft.'

'With cream?'

'Naturally.'

'And the wine?'

She nodded to two bottles standing at a discreet distance from the brickwork of the fireplace. Gevrey Chambertin: 1949.

'Excellent. We will dine at seven-thirty.' He turned away from her. 'Drink up! I saw two kingfishers flashing along the river last week and I want to check whether they are still there. They've just got married,' he added, with a raise-your-eyebrows grin at Sheila, who tossed her head and went off about her business.

'And where did that treasure come from?' I asked, carefully keeping the note of suspicion out of my voice, and noting inwardly that twenty years ago I would have started to pull his leg about her.

'Pure luck. She is a typist in my office. I used to have a dreadful old hairpin, as old and almost as doddery as your mad aunt. Then I suddenly found out that Sheila lives halfway between here and Cork, in a labourer's cottage on the side of the road. When I suggested to her that she might lend a hand and make some extra cash she jumped at it. Every Friday night I drive her home from the office on my way here, collect her on Saturday morning, and Bob's-your-uncle.'

He gathered up his binoculars, notebooks and camera, and we went off after the kingfishers. I enjoyed every minute of it, tramping for about three hours up and down the river bed. He found his kingfishers, a nesting heron, and became madly excited when he picked out through his binoculars, and let me also see, a buff-coloured bird about the size of a thrush but with a long beak, a crest and black and white stripes on its wings, perched on a tall beech tree.

'Can it,' he kept saying in a shouting whisper, 'but it can't be, can it *possibly* be a hoopoe?'

He entered every detail in his field notebook, date, hour, tempera-ture, compass bearings and heaven only knows what else, and he became so boyish about it all that my earlier annoyance with him vanished completely. When, on the way home, I asked him casually how old he was, and he said 'Forty-seven', my earlier suspicions also vanished. He was at least twice her age. By the time we got back to his cottage I felt not only so pleasantly tired but so pleasantly relaxed that I told him I had decided not to return home until the Monday morning.

The wood fire, now that the evening chill had come, was welcoming. I found that there were two baths, and lots of hot water. I wallowed in mine for twenty minutes. When we both emerged his Sheila made us a shaker of martinis, and through them we moved leisurely into a perfect dinner. She had not roasted the chickens, she had broiled them *en papilottes*. She must have spent an hour on the apple pie alone – my wife, who is a first-rate cook, could not have improved on its delicate crust.

'Did you teach her all this cooking, Mel?'

'I confess I have tried to play Professor Higgins to her Pygmalion. But only,' he winked, 'as to her cooking. So far.'

By the time we had finished off the two bottles of Burgundy and retired to our armchairs before the fire we were the old – that is the young – Mel and Sean. She lit two shaded lamps, brought us Italian coffee, a bottle of Hine, two warmed glasses, the cigar-box and our slippers.

'Wonderful woman!' I murmured. 'I hope you never lose her.'

'She is useful,' he agreed shortly, poured the brandy and, like me, stretched out his long legs to the fire.

For a while there was not a sound except the sizzle of the logs and an occasional slight tinkle from the direction of the kitchen. The deep, darkening country closed around us in such utter silence that when I strained my ears to listen I could hear, deep in the valley, the whisper of the river. Did I hear a pheasant coughing? Drowsily I remembered that he had said that we would talk tonight of Aunty Anna. I had no wish to talk about Aunty Anna, and by the sleepy way he was regarding the fire through his brandy glass I hoped he felt the same. Then I heard his voice, and with something sharper than regret I gathered that he had begun to talk about himself.

4

'Sean, I'm very glad you came. For a long time now I've been working out a certain idea, something rather important, and I want to try it out on you, just as a sort of test.'

Just barely holding off the sleep of bliss, I nodded easily.

'Did it ever strike you that every man – which includes every woman – is his own potter? I mean, that sooner or later every man takes up what you might call the clay, or the plasticine, or the mud, call it what you like, of his experience of life, and throws it down on his potter's wheel, and starts the pedal going, and rounds it up into a shape? Into what I call his idea of the shape of his whole life? Are you following me?'

I nodded myself awake.

'Good! Now for the big snag. It is, why do we do this? I can't say we do it to please ourselves, because we can *have* no selves – can we? We can't *see* ourselves – can we? – or *know* ourselves – can we? – and therefore we cannot *be* ourselves – can we? – until we have made this shape, and looked at it, as one would look in a mirror, and said to ourselves, "That's me! That's my vocation. My ambition. My politics. My faith. My whole life." I mean,' he pounded on, with a force of energy that made me even more tired and sleepy than before, 'I cannot say "That's me" until I have made my shape, because there is no *me* until I have made my shape. Therefore I can get no real pleasure of it all until the job is actually done. That's a pretty disturbing thought, what-what?'

I pulled myself awake. What had I walked into? Two nights of this twaddle? There simply had to be an afternoon train tomorrow!

'And when the job is done, Mel?'

He gave me a powerful slap on the thigh.

'Then I begin to live. When I at last know exactly what I am, I at last know exactly what I want to do, because my shape, my image, now tells me what I do want to do.'

I sighed and stretched.

'And then, Mel, some other fellow comes along and he looks at your portrait of the artist as a young dog, and he says, "No! This may be some crazy dream Mel has of himself, or some crazy dream he has of the world as he would like it to be, but it's not our Mel, and it's not our world."'

'Ha-ha, and I might say the same to him, and to his world?'

'You certainly might. But, of course, I hope you're not so daft as to deny that all the time there must be a real objective world outside there? Made up of stockbrokers and tax-collectors, and physicists, and isoprene, and polmerization . . .'

'By the way, rubber is going up.'

' . . . and gravitation, electricity, atomic weight, blood pressure, measles, kids getting sick, old people dying and kingfishers mating, and so on and so on. And a real, objective you, me, and Tom, Dick and Harry inside in each one of us, and no fancies and no fooling.' I laughed. 'Mel, you're a joy! I'm glad to inform you that you haven't changed one iota since the days when we used to come out from old Father Abstractibus's philosophy lectures, long ago in University College, Cork, and lie on the grass of the quadrangle, and talk for hours about the Object and the Subject and "What is Reality?", and "What is the stars?", and never got one inch beyond chasing our own tails. And here you are, still at it! It's a pointless pursuit, and I'm in no mood for it. Mel! If we have to talk about anything at all on top of that wonderful dinner, and that marvellous Gevrey Chambertin, and this perfect brandy, let's talk about a painfully real subject. Let's talk about my Aunty Anna.'

'That,' he said calmly, 'is what I am talking about. About people who live in imaginations, and fantasies, and illusions about themselves. What, so far as I can see, the whole blessed world is doing all the time. Including your dear Auntie Anna Maria Whelan.' He stretched out his foot and touched my ankle with the toe of his slipper. 'Do you know what your dear Auntie Anna did with that three hundred and fifty quid?'

'You told me. She bought an armchair, and an electric fire, and an eiderdown, and curtains, and Masses for her soul, and she gave loans to . . .'

'Rubbish! That's what she said. She bought a fur coat with the three-fifty quid.'

'You're a liar!'

'She is the liar.'

'Then you're joking.'

'It's no joke, my friend. The old divil had the cheek to have it on her back when she came into my office yesterday. When she went out I had a brain-wave. I rang up a friend of mine who works with the Saint Vincent de Paul's in her part of the city and I asked him to drop around and have a look at her place. No armchair, no electric fire, no eiderdown, no new curtains, no nothing. And as for those loans that she invented, as he pointed out to me, the poor don't give anybody loans of ten quid a time. Ten shillings would be more like it. If that! You talk very glibly about the "real, objective world outside there". You don't seem to know so very much about it, after all, do you?'

His air of condescension infuriated me.

'It was probably a cheap, second-hand coat!'

'I checked up on that too. Cork is a small place, and there aren't many shops where you can buy new fur coats for a sum as large as that. I rang up Bob Rohu and I told him the whole yarn. I hit a bull's eye at once. He sold it to her himself. He remembered the transaction very well – as you might expect. A poor old woman like her doesn't come in every day to buy a bang-up fur coat. She paid him two hundred and seventy-five pounds for that fur coat. In notes.' He paused. He concluded with sardonic formality, 'You perceive my trend?'

I was furious, chastened and filled with pity for my Aunty Anna. I saw also that whatever picture Mel had made of himself it would not show him as anybody's fool. I could have choked him. Here was I, who had known Aunty Anna all my life, a man who was supposed to know something about human nature, and here was this fellow who had only met Aunty Anna three or four times in his life, pitilessly exposing her to me as a woman perched out there for thirty years on that big, grassy, empty plain of the Curragh of Kildare, working, since she was twenty, for a wealthy trainer, seeing his rich, horsy clients coming and going in all their finery, and thinking, as she grew older and older, with no man ever asking her to marry him – Why the hell had I never realized that she would think it? – that she would never possess anything even dimly like what they possessed. Until, by pure chance, at the age of seventy-odd, she finds herself drawing dividends like the best of them, trading in the stock-market just like the best of them, being received like a lady by the best stockbroker in Cork – and sees that fur coat in a shop window.

Mel was slowly rolling his brandy around in his brandy glass and watching me slyly.

'Interesting, isn't it?' he said.

'Very,' I said bitterly. After a while of silence I said, 'And this is why she won't get any more of what she thinks are her little divvies? Even if I agreed to pay you for them?'

He answered with anger, almost with passion:

'It is. The woman is fooling herself, and I refuse to encourage her. She is trying to make nonsense of everything I believe in. And I won't let her do it. Would you, as a writer, write something you didn't believe to be true?'

'Don't be silly! I'm pleased and proud any time I think I'm able to tell even one tenth of the truth.'

'Would you, if you were a doctor, tell lies to a patient?'

'Doctors have to do it all the time. To help them to live. To make it easier for them to die.'

'Well, I don't and won't tell lies. Facts are facts in my profession, and I have to live by them.'

'You gamble.'

'I do not.'

'You encourage your clients to gamble.'

'I do not.'

'Then what do you do for a living?'

'I hope.'

We laughed. We calmed down.

'What about charity, Mel?'

'I would have no objection to giving your aunt charity. I like the old thing. She is a nice poor soul. And my friend in the Vincent de Paul assures me that she is a very worthy creature. In fact I'd be quite happy to pay the old hairpin ... ' Here the chill caution of the trained businessman entered his voice, 'I'd be quite happy to go halves with you in paying her the equivalent of her blasted divvies every year. But not as dividends! Strictly as a gift from the pair of us.'

'Mel, that's kind of you! Our whole problem is solved. Let's give her the £28 a year as a present. What are you looking at me like that for?'

'She won't take it.'

'Why won't she take it?'

'Because it's charity. And she doesn't want charity. The poor never want charity. They hate it because it makes them feel their poverty. Any of them that have any pride left in them. And that old lady is stiff with pride. You could take a gift from me, I could take a gift from you, Queen Victoria would have taken all India and hung it on her charm bracelet without as much as a thank you. But not the poor! However, try her. Take the Jaguar tomorrow morning and drive into town and take her out to lunch. I bet you a tenner to a bob she'll refuse.' He rose. 'Ah! Here we are!'

This was for our housekeeper, waiting, ready to be driven home. She was wearing a small fur hat and a neat, belted tweed coat. From under her hat her dark hair crooked around each cheek. Now that she was wearing high-heeled shoes I noticed how long and elegant her legs were.

'That,' said Mel, surveying her, 'is a darling little hat you have.'

'I had it on this morning,' she said quietly. 'But men never notice anything.'

'Where did you get it?'

'I bought it of course. It's wild mink. I've been saving up for it for years. I got it at Rohu's.'

'Good girl!' he said enthusiastically, and looked at me in approval of his pupil, while I wondered if he knew how much even that little dream of wild mink cost her. She might well have been saving up for it for years. 'I'll bring around the car. I won't be long,' he said to me. 'Play yourself some music while we're away. I've got some good records.'

When he had gone out I said to her, 'Won't you sit down while you are waiting?' and she sat sedately on the arm of his vacated chair and crossed her pretty heron's legs.

'Do you like music, Sheila?'

'I used to like only jazz. Recently I've come to prefer classical music. Mr Meldrum has been introducing me to it. Shall I show you how to work the machine? It's new and he is very particular about it. It has two extensions. They give you the impression that you are surrounded by an orchestra. Oh!' lifting the lid and looking in. 'There's a record on it. Yes, here is the jacket – it's *The Siegfried Idyll*. Would you like to play this one. Or would you perhaps prefer something more modern?'

(I thought, 'You may only be a typist in his office but you have the manners of a woman of the world.')

'Yes, I'd like to hear that again. It's years since I heard any Wagner. Do *you* like it?'

'We've played it so often now that I'm just beginning to understand what it's all about.'

'And what is it all about?' I smiled.

She switched on the machine and closed the lid.

'I suppose it's about happiness through love. It takes a little time to warm up. Then it works automatically.'

I glanced at her. Was she a deep one? His horn hooted from the road. For the first time she smiled. She had perfect teeth.

'I must be off. Don't let the fire die down. He sometimes sits up late. There are plenty of logs. And I've fixed the electric blankets at Number Two heat, so they will be nice and cosy before you have finished your last nightcaps. Goodnight.'

When she was gone I walked to the window to look after her and saw that a vast moon had risen over the dark hills surrounding the valley, touching their round breasts as softly as a kiss. He and she stood arm in arm looking at it, he leaning a little over her, pointing up to the moon as if he were showing it to an infant, and saying something that, for once, must have not been off the mark, because she swiftly turned her face up to him and laughed gloriously. Just as he touched her furry cap with his finger the record behind me fell into place and a score of violins began whispering, pulsing and swelling around me as power-fully as the immense moon. In that second I had no more doubts about the pair of them. He released her arm, opened the door of the car for her so that its carriage light fell for a second on her radiant smile. He banged her door, got in on his side and shot away. I returned slowly to my armchair, my brandy and cigar, and stared into the flickering fire.

Gradually the idyll rose in wave after wave to its first crescendo until the bows of the violins were so many lashing whips of passionate sound. The lunatic! Sitting here, of nights, in this silent valley, with her opposite him, listening to music like this Christmas morning music, composed by a lover for his sleeping beloved. If it made me wish to God I was at home in bed with my wife what, in heaven's name, must it do to him? I suddenly remembered something that made me snatch up the jacket of the record. I was right. Wagner wrote that love idyll when he was fifty-seven, having fallen in love with Cosima Liszt when he was in his forties and she in her twenties, and I began to think of other elderly men who had married young women, finding them even in that tight little city a few miles away. Wintering men plucking their budding roses. Old Robert Cottrell, the ship-owner, who married a barmaid out of the Victoria Hotel. Frank Lane, the distiller, who at sixty picked a pretty waitress out of The Golden Tavern. And who was that miller who, after being a widower for twenty-five years, fell in love with one of his mill-girls and had children by her, younger than his grandchildren? It is the sort of thing that can easily happen to men who have lived all their lives by the most rigid conventions, and then suddenly get sick of it all and throw their hats over the moon.

I became more calm as the music slowly died in exhaustion of its own surfeit. He was as open as a book – all that talk of his about men taking the clay of life and making a self-shape of it. Of her I knew nothing except that he had said she lived in a roadside cottage and, as he must know well – and he would be the first to say it – that a rich stockbroker would be a wonderful catch for her. I started to walk restlessly about the house. By error I entered his bedroom. I shut the door quickly, feeling that I was floundering in deep and dangerous tides. The covers of his bed had been neatly turned down at an angle of forty-five degrees and on his pillow there lay a red rosebud. I went to bed and fell into such a sound sleep that I did not hear him return.

When I woke up it was blazing sun outside and the cottage was empty: he had presumably gone to Mass and to collect her. When they came in he was wearing the rosebud in his lapel. After breakfast I took the Jaguar and drove into town to meet my Aunty Anna.

5

The city was full of the sound of church bells but there was hardly a soul out along the quay where she lived. Even the gulls were silent, floating on the river or perched along the quayside walls. I drew up outside her old fabric of a house, its railings crooked, its fanlight cracked, its traditional eight-panelled door clotted with years of paint asking only for a blowlamp and a week's scraping to reveal chiselled mouldings and fine mahogany. I sat for a while in the car thinking of the Aunty Anna I knew and the best way to handle her.

She had always been a soft, slack, complaining creature with, so far as I knew, no keener interests in life than backing horses, telling fortunes on the cups and cards, eating boiled sweets and reading violet-coloured penny novelettes. I should have brought her a box of chocolates. I drove off and managed to find a shop open that sold them. It may have been, it occurred to me, this love of boiled sweets that used to give her so much trouble with her teeth; they used to pain her a great deal and several of them were decayed in the front of her mouth. At that time there was some kind of pulp, paste or malleable wafer that poor country folk used as a dental stopgap to hide these marks of decay on special occasions. Or perhaps it was only white paper chewed-up? She used it constantly and it made her teeth look like putty. The poor woman had also had an operation performed, unskilfully, on her left elbow, which had a moist hollow, like a navel, where the point of the ulna ought to have been; she used to nurse it all the time with her fondling right hand, especially on cold or windy days. Would the poor old thing respond to the idea of going to a good surgeon? Or I could, perhaps, tempt her with some good, stout, comfortable dresses: my wife could easily get those for her. Not that I feared, looking up at the crumbling bricks of her tenement, that I would have any difficulty in persuading her to accept an annual gift, and I thought back to those days on the rolling, green Curragh when she had at least had every comfort, the best of food and healthy, country air, and I realized that she should never have left her base, and that the ideal, but now impossible, thing for her to do would be to go back and live in the country where she belonged.

A few minutes later I was holding her weeping in my arms in her one room where she had cooked slept and sat day after day for so many years, and as I smelled the familiar, indefinable musk of urban poverty, suggestive mainly of sour clothes, bad sewage and fried onions, I was overcome with shame that I had not visited her once during the twelve years since I left Cork to be married. I kissed her, and she kissed me, as maternally as if I were still a small boy. Then I stood back, looked at her and got a shock of memory. She had a face like an old turtle, she was humped like a heron and she was rouged. Long ago, my mother had laughed one day and said she did it with geranium petals rubbed lightly in pale-brown boot polish. I noted, too, that all her decayed teeth were replaced by a good denture, and that her hair was tinted and blued. Like a boy I endured the reproaches that she poured over me, and then, eager to be out of that jumbled, stuffy room, I bustled her to get ready and come out to lunch at the Victoria Hotel.

She put on her fur coat, and a small, ancient straw hat, gay with white daisies. Once she was dressed she became rigid with what Cork calls grandeur, as when she said: 'This is quite a nice little car,' and started talking about all the much grander cars she used to drive in at the Curragh Races. At lunch she held her knife and fork at right-angles to her plate, sipped her wine like a bird, drank her coffee with the little finger crooked, hem-hemmed into her napkin like a nun and small-talked as if she were royalty giving me an audience, all of it gossip and chit-chat about the gentry of the Curragh and their fine ladies and great houses. At the end of the lunch she produced a compact, powdered her nose, examined her face intently all over and delicately applied a pink lipstick. She evaded all my efforts to talk of old times until we moved into the empty lounge where I had a stout brandy. She preferred a gin-and-lime. At last I did lure her out of her glorious past to my proposal that I should give her twenty-eight pounds a year (I carefully left Mel out of it) as a little gesture, 'For old times' sake, *Aunty*?' – trying to make her stop being Her Majesty, and become my Aunty Anna again.

She made short work of me.

'No! Thank you very much. Now that I have my divvies I don't need it.'

From there we went back and forth over the whole thing, over more brandy and gin, for two fruitless hours. Gifts she would ('of course') not accept. Her divvies she would ('of course') not renounce. By the end of it I had gained only one point. She said, coldly but with spirit, that if 'that man' denied her her rights she would never darken his door again.

'I will have nothing more to do with this so-called Mister Meldrum. I am finished with all fraudulent stockbrokers for ever.'

It was four o'clock before I surrendered, furious, rejected, humiliated and exhausted. I drove her around the city, slowly at her queenly request, in my white Jaguar (in which, I told her, I had arrived from Dublin that morning), and ended up at her door amid a crowd of lane kids oohing and aahing at what one of them called Snow White's car. I promised faithfully to visit her again next summer, kissed her goodbye, excused my haste by saying that I had to be back in Dublin before nightfall and drove away amid the huzzas of the tiny mob. As soon as I got around a corner I paused to rub off her lipstick. I felt very proud of her, I despised myself, and I hated Mel and all that he and his kind stood for – by which I do not now know what I meant then, unless it had something to do with the corrupting power of money over us all.

I was in no mood to face his guffaws of triumph. I parked the Jaguar on the empty South Mall and went wandering through the silent, Sunday streets of this city of my youth, seeing little of it. I was too angry, and too absorbed in trying to devise some means of helping her, and at every turn bothered by unhappy thoughts about Mel and myself, and about whatever it was that the years had done to us both. Was he right in saying that I knew nothing about poor people like Aunty Anna? His Sheila was a young, pretty Aunty Anna, poor like her, being drawn now, as she had been, close to the world of wealth. What did he really know about her? The question brought me to the point – I was then leaning over the old South Gate Bridge, looking down into the River Lee, far from sweet-smelling at low tide – thinking again not of him alone but of myself and him, as we were when we were here, at college together, years ago. What did I really ever know about him? My Aunty Anna was dead, replaced by what would have been described in one of her violet-covered novelettes as 'Miss Anna Whelan, A Country Lady in reduced circumstances', with nothing left to her from her better days but her memories and her fur coat; defrauded and impoverished of thousands of pounds – her lost fortune would be at least that much within a matter of weeks – by a slick stockbroker. Had my Mel ever existed?

We are not one person. We pass through several lives of faith, ambition, sometimes love, often friendship. We change, die and live again. In that cosy cottage of his had I been the guest of a ghost? Myself a ghost? If he was a new man his Sheila might know him. I did not. For all I knew, she was creating him. All I knew, as I rose from the parapet and walked back to the car, was that I must return to his cottage, as I must leave it, in the most careful silence.

I got back in time to join him and the local curate in another of Sheila's cool five-to-one martinis. Over the dinner, which was just as good as the one the night before, I left the talk to Mel and his guest, all about archaeology, birds, the proposed airport, Cork's current political gossip. I envied the pair of them. Nobody in a capital city can ever be so intimately and intensely absorbed about local matters as provincials always are about the doings and the characters of their city-states. The curate left early. Mel drove Sheila home immediately after. He returned, within twenty minutes.

I was standing with my hand on the high mantelpiece of the fireplace listening to the *verso* of the *Siegfried Idyll*, the end of the last act of *Die Walküre*. As he came in I raised a silencing hand, excited as I was by the heroic loveliness of this music that lays Brünhilde on the mountainside in Valhalla, at the centre of encircling fires through which a young man, who will be Siegfried, will one day break to deliver her with a kiss. Mel threw himself into his armchair, his hands behind his head, and we both listened until the music ended and the silence and the dark of the country began to hum again in our ears. For a while we said nothing. Then I did what I had promised not to do.

'Well?' I asked, looking down at him.

'Well?' he said, looking up at me.

'Do I congratulate you?'

'On what?'

'On your Brünhilde.'

Lazily he rolled his head on the back of his chair.

'Meaning no? Or that you don't know?'

Again he slowly rolled his head.

'Giving nothing away? Mel, you used not to be so damn cautious. What has happened to you? Come on, Mel, take a chance on life. Begin by giving Aunty Anna her divvies.'

'Aha? So she refused our gift?'

'She refused. Also she will trouble you no more. She is now convinced that you are a fraudulent stockbroker who has robbed her of a fortune. Come on, man! Gamble for once in your cautious life. Stop being a fraudulent broker.'

'Are you suggesting that I should let your aunt blackmail me?'

'I'm suggesting that you forget the idol you have made outside in the woodshed. It's not you. It can't be you. The Mel I knew can't be that fancy portrait of an unbreakable, incorruptible, crusty, self-absorbed old man, stiff-necked with principles and pride and priggishness. It is a false god. Kick it out on the rubbish heap. When you have made yourself a real image of yourself you'll find there is nothing so terribly frightening about giving Aunty Anna her divvies – or marrying Sheila.'

I had said 'frightening' because immediately I started suggesting that he was different to whatever he wanted to be I had seen his eyes under his blond eyelashes contract, a blush appear on his cheekbones under their grey outcrops of hair, his mouth begin to melt. With a flick he threw away the sudden fear.

'I haven't changed. I am what I am, always was and intend always to be. And if I am a prig, as you so kindly call me, I'm content to be a prig. It's better than being a cockeyed dreamer like you and your mad aunt.'

'Then why are you playing with the girl?'

'I am not.'

'In that case you might wipe that lipstick off your cheek.'

'You know nothing about her.' He paused. 'She has a boyfriend. He was waiting for her again at her cottage tonight.'

'I shouldn't be surprised if she had a dozen boy-friends. A girl as pretty as that! You have seen him often?'

'I have. He comes around here on his motor-bicycle whenever she stays a bit later than usual. Just to offer her a lift home. Just by way of no harm. Each time, she goes off with him at once. I followed them one night. I saw them kissing and hugging under a tree. If she can deceive him she could deceive me. If I married her I might be unhappy all my life, I'd be jealous and suspicious of her all my life.'

'You make me sick! *You* might not be happy? Why don't you say she might not be happy? What sort of a thing do you think marriage is? One long honeymoon? Happiness is a bonus. You smuggle it. You work for it. It comes and goes. You have to be in the market to snatch it. Where's your realism? He who does not speculate cannot accumulate. Stop being such a coward! Live, man, live!'

'I prefer to be logical.'

'Then you certainly will not give Aunty Anna her imaginary divvies, and you will have to sack your imaginary Sheila, and then you will be very unhappy indeed.'

'I may be. It will wear off. And, anyway, it's none of your damn business.'

For a couple of moments we looked at one another hatefully. Then I turned and without saying goodnight went to my room. Almost immediately I heard the front door slam. Parting the curtains I saw him stride down the path, out into the moonlit road and around the corner under the deep shadows of the trees towards where we had gone yesterday to watch the kingfishers, the nesting heron and that unlikely, crested, exotic bird. For a second my heart went out to him. Then I shrugged him off in despair. I was awakened – my watch said it was two o'clock – by the sound of the Brünhildeian flames wavering, leaping, pulsing from their mountaintop among the gods. I, in bed, he, by the ashen fire, listened to it together. After it died away I heard his door click.

In the morning I rose to find him already up and in his spotless yellow-and-white kitchen making coffee and toast.

'Morning, Mel!'

'Hello! Sleep well? I'm the cook on Monday mornings. She leaves everything ready, as you see,' nodding to the napery, china and silverware on the table.

She had even left a tiny bouquet of polyanthuses, alyssum and cowslips in a vase.

He was dressed for the city in his black jacket, with black and grey-striped trousers, grey Suède waistctoat, stiff white collar and striped shirt, a small pearl tie-pin in his grey tie. Over the coffee he talked about birds, and for that while, as on the Saturday, he was again his old attractive, youthful, zestful self. He talked of the hoopoe, saying, 'It cannot have been one – they pass us by in the spring.' He talked about night-jars. He sounded knowledgeable about owls. When we were ready to go he saw to it that every curtain was drawn ('The sun fades the mahogany') and every window carefully fastened, took down his bowler hat and umbrella, double-locked the door, felt it twice, looked all over the front of the cottage, and we drove off into another sunbathed morning.

On the way into town we picked up Sheila outside her roadside cottage, and after that we did not speak at all until he dropped her at his office. There I tried to insist on his not seeing me off at the station – he was a busy man, Monday morning and all that, he must have lots to attend to – and he insisted against my insisting, and we almost squabbled again before he gave in so far as to go into his office to ask if there was anything urgent. He brought me in with him, and formally introduced me to his chief accountant and his book-keeper. While he ruffled through his mail, I chatted with them, and noted the Turkish carpet, and all his modern gadgets, and thought that this was the place where Aunty Anna began to change. At the station he insisted on buying me the morning papers, and on waiting by my carriage door until the train should carry me away. I thanked him for our enjoyable weekend, assured him I meant it, praised his cottage, remembered the food and the wine, promised that we would meet again, to which he nodded, and exchanged a few polite, parting words. As the porters started to slam the last doors, and pull up the windows against the rank smells of the tunnel at the platform's end, he said, his pointed face lifted below my window, his eyes sullen above the two little tufts of greying hair on his cheekbones:

'You will be pleased to hear, by the way, that I have decided to give your aunt her dividends, as usual. Naturally, we go halves in that.'

I leaned down and grasped his shoulder.

'And marry Sheila?'

'I know when I'm licked. I'm going to give her the sack this morning. I'll have to get a new housekeeper. I am going to ask your Aunty Anna.'

'But she's seventy! And a lady in reduced circumstances. She will refuse.'

'Not when she sees my cottage,' he said arrogantly. 'I'm only there on weekends. She can imagine she is a real lady for five days in the week. Not bad! And she has been a cook. And she won't tempt my flesh. Hail! And Farewell!'

The train started to puff and chug and he and the platform slid slowly away.

Seconds later I was in the tunnel. My window went opaque. I got the rancid smell of the underworld. 'And Farewell?' Evidently I was not, it was a just judgement on my presumption, to meet him ever again. I had probed, I had interfered, I had uncovered his most secret dream and destroyed it by forcing him to bring it to the test of reality. I had been tiresome in every way. I had counted on finding the Mel I had thought I had always known, felt affronted at finding him rather different, tried to make him more different, and yet at the same time have my old Mel, and was furious when he insisted on remaining whatever he thought he always had been. In such irreducibly plenary moments of total mess, shame and embarrassment the truth can only be trite, though none the less the truth for that. Youth only knows embryos. Life is equivocal. Life is a gamble. Friendship is frail. Love is a risk. All any man can do when fate sends some shining dream his way is to embrace it and fight for it without rest or reason because we do all the important things of life for reasons (It *has* been said!) of which reason knows nothing – until about twenty years after.

For that mile of tunnel I had them all there together with me in that dark carriage, with the cold smell of steam, and an occasional splash of water on the roof from the ventilation shafts to the upper air. Abruptly, the tunnel shot away and I felt like a skin-diver soaring from the sea to the light of day. Green country exploded around me on all sides in universal sunlight. Small, pink cars went ambling below me along dusty side-roads to the creamery. Black-and-white cows munched. Everywhere in the fields men were at their morning work. I opened the window to let in the fresh air. Then, with only occasional glances out at the fields floating away behind me, and at certain images and thoughts that became fainter and fewer with the passing miles, I settled down to my newspapers and the gathering thoughts of my home and my work.

I have never seen him since, although we are both now ageing men, but, perhaps three times, it could be four, as if a little switch went click in my memory he has revisited me – a dubious shadow, with two grey tufts on his cheeks and a long nose like Sherlock Holmes . . . No more. He did write to me once, after – not, I observed, *when* – Aunty Anna died, in his service, aged eighty-one. Piously, he had attended to everything. He enclosed some snapshots that he had found in her bag: herself as a young woman, horses on the Curragh, myself as a young boy. In her will, he mentioned, she had bequeathed her dividends to him.

# The Heat of the Sun

They never said, 'Let's go down to Rodgers', although it was old Rodgers who owned the pub; they said, 'Let's go down to Uncle Alfie.' A good pub is like that, it is the barman who makes it, not the boss. They gave their custom to Rodgers, they gave their confidence to Alfie. He knew them all, some of them ever since they were old enough to drink their first pint in a pub. He knew their fathers, mothers, brothers, sisters, girls, prospects, wages, hopes, fears and what they were always calling their ideas and their ideals and that he called their ould guff. Always their friend, sometimes their philosopher, he was rarely their guide. Your da gave you money (sometimes) and you hardly thanked him for it. Alfie loaned it. You da gave you advice and you resented it. Alfie could give you a rap as sharp as lightning, and you accepted it because he gave it as your equal. Your da never had any news. Alfie knew everything. He was your postman, passing on bits of paper with messages in pencil: 'Deirdre was asking after you, try 803222, Hughesy.' Or, 'For Jay's sake leave a half-note for me, Paddywhack.' He might hand you out a coloured postcard with a foreign stamp, taken from the little sheaf stuck behind the cash register. The sheeting around the register was as wall-papered as a Travel Bureau with coloured postcards from all over the world. Best of all, he was there always: his coat off, his shirtsleeves rolled up, his bowler hat always on his balding red head, a monument in a white apron, with a brogue like an echo in an empty barrel.

You pushed the two glass doors in like a king.

'Hi, Alfie!'

'Jakus, Johnny, is that yourself?' With a slap on the shoulder and your drink slid in front of you unasked. 'Fwhere were you this time? Did yoo have a good voyage?'

'Not bad. Same old thing – Black Sea, the Piraeus, Palermo, Naples, Genoa. Crumby dumps!' Your half pint aloft. 'What's the best port in all creation, Alfie?'

'As if yoo needed to ask me!'

'Here's to it, and God bless it. *Dublin town, O Dublin town / That's where I long to be, / With the friends so dear to me, / Grafton Street where it's all so gay. / And the lights of Scotsman's Bay.* Theme-song of every poor bloody exile of Erin. Up the rebels. Long live the Queen of Sheba. How's Tommy? How's Angela? How's Casey, Joanna, Hughesy, Paddywhack? Does my little black-eyed Deirdre still love me?'

'Paddy was in on Chuesday night. He's working with the Gas Company now.'

'Poor old Paddywhack! Has he the gold wristlet still? And the signet ring? Will the poor bugger never get a decent job?'

'His wife had another child. That's six he has now.'

'Sacred Heart!'

'Hughesy is going strong with Flossie.'

(He noticed that Deirdre was being passed over.)

'Sure that line is four years old. When is the bastard going to make an honest woman of her?'

'Is it a busman? She's aiming higher than that. The trouble with yoo young fellows is ye pick gurls beyond yeer means. Yeer eyes are bigger than yeer balls. Leave them their youth. Wedded, bedded and deaded, the world knows it.'

He was anti-woman. Everybody knew he had a wife somewhere, and three kids, separated five years ago. She was before their time – none of them had ever seen her. Poor old Alfie! In hope and in dreams and in insecurity is life. In home and in safety is . . . He should know, he had it every time he came home. Like tonight:

'Oh, no! Johnny! You're not going out from us on your first night home? We haven't seen you for four months! And your father and me looking forward to a nice bit of a chat. About your future, Johnny. About your plans, Johnny. About your prospects. Sit down there now and be talking to us.'

You sat back. They talked. You mumbled. The end of it was always the same. After another half-hour of twitching you said it again.

'I think I'll drop down to Uncle Alfie for an hour to see the boys. I won't be late, Mum. But leave the key under the mat. Don't wait up for me, I'll creep in like a mouse.'

Hating the way they looked at one another, knowing well that you wouldn't be in before one in the morning – if then – shoes in hand, head cocked for the slightest tweak of a bedspring upstairs, feeling a right bastard or, if with God's help, you were tight enough, feeling nothing but your way. Hell roast 'em! Why couldn't they understand that when you cabled, 'Coming home Thursday stop love stop Johnny,' it meant you wanted to see them okay, and you were bringing presents for them, okay, and it would be nice to have your own old room, okay, but what you were really seeing was the gleam of the bottles, and the wet mahogany, and the slow, floating layers of smoke, shoulders pushing, hands shooting, everybody talking at the top of his voice to be heard and old Alfie grinning at ye all like an ape. God Almighty! When a fellow has only seven lousy days shore leave . . .

It was dry October, the softest twinge of faintest fog, the streets empty, a halo around every light, a right night for a landfall. Tramping downhill, peaked cap slanted, whistling, he foresaw it all. A dollar to a dime on it – Alfie would resume exactly where they left off four months ago:

'Johnny! It is high time yoo thought of settling down.'

'Gimme a chance, Alfie. I'm only twenty-three. I'll settle down some day. Why don't you say that to Loftus or Casey?'

'Loftus will find it hard. With that short leg. Anyway I mean settle down ashore. That wandering life you're leading! It's no life!'

'I'm not ready, Alfie. I want to meet the right girl. I'm mad about Deirdre, but she's always talking about motorcars, and houses in Foxrock, and Sunday morning sherry parties. I'm not sure of her. The right girl is damn hard to find. It's a funny thing, Alfie, all the nice women I meet are married women.'

'An ould shtory. And the ladies tell me all the nice men are married men. I think the truth is that no wan is ready until they know by heart the music that tames the wild bashte – know it and are beginning to forget it. I don't think Deirdre is the right sawrt for you at all, Johnny. She's too expensive for you. She's too ambitious. She's like Flossie – playing with Hughesy, trying to learn the chune on the cheap, as you might say. Johnny! If I were you, I'd choose a woman of experience. What'd suit you, now, down to the ground would be a nice, soft, cosy, widow-woman that knows every chune in the piper's bag.'

'Oh, for God's sake, Alfie! With a wooden leg? And a yellow wig? And a blue bank-book? I'm young, Alfie. What I dream about, in the middle watch, looking up at the stars, is a young, beautiful, exquisite, lovely, fond, right-dimensional Irish girl of eighteen. Like my little Deirdre.

Pure as the driven snow. Loyal and true. Gentle as the dawn. Deirdre, without the motor-car!'

Alfie would draw up from the counter and make a face as if he was sucking alum.

'You could sing it if yoo had the voice for it. "*She was luvely and fair, as the roase of the Summer, But it was not her beauutye aloane tha-at won me . . .*"'

He would snatch it from him tonight:

'"*Oh no! 'Twas the truth in her eyes ever dawning, That made me love Mary, the Rose of Tra-a-leee.*" A hundred per cent right, Alfie. Lead me to her.'

'I wouldn't give you two pinnies for a gurl of eighteen – she couldn't cook an egg for you. And dimensions are all very fine and dandy, but they don't lasht, boy. They don't lasht! Did I ever tell yoo about the fellow that married the opera singer? She was like an angel out of heaven on the stage. In the bed she was no better to him than an ould shweeping brush. He used to wake her up in the middle of the night and say, "Sing, damn yoor sowl!"'

Aboard ship he had told them that one many times. Always the old deck-hands would nod solemnly and say, 'And e's dead right, chum! Feed me and love me, what more can a man ask for?' Well, if he said it tonight he would be ready for him; drawing himself up, with one hand flat on his top, left, brass button:

'Alfie! In this rotten, cheating, stinking, lousy, modern world my generation is going to *fight* for our ideals!'

Four miles out over the shadow sea the light on the Kish bank winked drowsily. Fog? It was so quiet along the promenade that he could hear the small waves below him sucking into the rocks. Wind soft from the south. The only person he passed was a Civic Guard in a cape. He turned right, then left, passed the Coal Harbour, wheeled right again, left, and there were the lights flowing out on the pavement. He pushed the two glass doors in like a king.

'Hi! . . .'

He stopped. The young barman was staring at him with uplifted eyebrows. He looked around. The place was like a morgue. He recognized old Molly Goosegog, her fat legs spread, soaking it up as usual with the one-armed colonel. Three business types, their hats on, hunched over a table, talking low. In the farthest corner two middle-aged women were drinking gins and bitters. Dyed, dried, skewered and skivered, two old boiling hens, cigarettes dangled from their red beaks. He moved slowly to the counter.

'Where's Alfie?' he asked quietly.

'On leave.'

'Alfie never took leave in his life unless he took leave of his senses.'

'Well, he's on leave now. What can I get you, sir?'

*Sir!* Sullenly he said, 'A large whiskey,' although he had been planning a night of draught porter. Alfie would have said, 'Johnny! There is no such thing on earth as a *large* whiskey.' Or he might have said nothing but come back with a half pint of draught and said, 'That'll be better for you.'

Was it because it was Thursday night? Nobody much ever came on Thursday night: less even than came on Friday night. Everyone stony. Behold my beeves and fatlings are all killed, and nobody cometh to eat them. Seven lousy nights and the first a flop? Go forth into the highways and by-ways. From pub to pub? The whiskey appeared before him. The barman stood waiting. He looked up.

'Four and sixpence, sir.'

With Alfie, you let it run for a week, for two, for three, for as long as you liked. Then you asked, 'What's on the slate, Alfie?' and, if you were flush, you paid a half-note over and above for future credit. Man knoweth not the hour nor the night. He paid out four shillings and a sixpenny bit. The barman rang it up and retired down the counter to lean over his *Herald*.

'How long is Alfie going to be on leave?'

The fellow barely glanced up.

'I don't know, I'm only here this past two weeks.'

'Is the boss in?'

'He's gone down to the chapel. The October Devotions.'

Thinking of his latter end. *Dies irae, dies illae.* Back in Newbridge with the Dominicans. All Souls Night. He glanced at the door. Would there be anyone down at The Blue Peter? Or in Mooney's? Maybe in The Purty Kitchen?'

'Any message for me there behind the old cashbox?'

'Name?'

'Kendrick.'

The barman, his back to him, went through the light sheaf. Without turning he said, 'Nothing,' shoved it back and returned to his *Herald*.

Out of sight out of mind. Bugger the whole lousy lot of them! And Deirdre along with them! The glass doors swished open and there were Paddywhack and Loftus. He leaped from his stool.

'Hi, scouts!'

'Johnny!'

Handshakes all round. Paddy was as hungry-looking as a displaced Arab. His shirtsleeves too long. The gold wristlet. The signet ring. Loftus, as always, as lean and yellow as a Dane. Hoppity Loftus with his short leg. He never worked. He was a Prod and had an English accent, and he lived off his mother. All he did was to get her breakfast in the morning and have her supper ready for her at night. She worked in the Sweep.

'Name it, boys! I'm standing!'

Paddy looked thirstily at the glass of whiskey.

'Are you on the hard tack?'

'Naw! Just this bloody place gave me the willies. The usual?' He commanded the barman. 'Two halfpints. Make it three and I'll use this as a chaser. God, it's marvellous to see ye! Come on, come on! Give! Give! Gimme all the dirt. Tell me more, tell me all. Are you still with the Gas Company, Paddy?'

'I'm with a house-agent now. Looney and Cassidy. In Dame Street.' He made a fish-face. 'NBG Paid on commission. Just to tide me over a bad patch.' He laughed cheerfully. 'The wife is preggers again.'

'Paddy! I dunno how you do it.'

'I'm told,' said Loftus lightly, 'that it's a very simple matter, really.'

'How's your mother, Loftus?'

A rude question. Loftus shrugged it away. They took their drinks to one of the round tables. Paddy lifted his glass.

'Johnny! You don't know how lucky you are. A steady job, cash in your pocket, a girl in every port.'

'And as brown,' said Loftus lifting his glass, 'and as round as a football.'

'Me round?' he shouted, ripped open the jacket of his uniform and banged his narrow waist. 'Feel that, go on, feel it! Hard as iron, boy! Eight stone ten. You,' he said condescendingly, rebuttoning, 'must be about ten stone eight.' He paused. Then he had to say it: 'Does Deirdre still love me?'

Loftus's eyes glinted as he proffered the sponge on the spear.

'I saw her two weeks ago in a red Triumph. A medical student from Trinity, I believe. She looked smashing.'

His heart curdled, his throat tightened, he laughed loudly.

'So the little bitch is betraying me, eh?'

He could see her, with her dark hair curled down on one shoulder as if she had a monkey on her head. The red lips. The high bosoms.

'It's just because you're not around much,' Paddy said comfortingly. 'Wait until she hears you're home!'

'How are all those girls of yours?' Loftus smiled. 'In foreign parts.'

Paddy poured sad oil.

'Too bad about poor Alfie?'

'I heard nothing,' he said sourly. 'Nobody writes to me. Where *is* the ould devil!'

'You didn't know! Hospice for the Dying. Cancer. These last three months. It'll be any day now.'

It gagged him. There was a long silence. His first death. The double doors let in Hughesy and Flossie; their oldest and youngest – a blonde mop, black lashes, a good looker, but not a patch on his D. Their welcomes were muted. They sat down stiffly like people who did not mean to stay.

'"Here,"' he chanted mournfully, '"here, the gang's all here."'

'Not all of us,' Paddy said.

'This is a committee meeting, really,' Hughesy said, taking charge of it at once. 'Well?' he asked Paddywhack and Loftus. 'How much can we raise?'

'We're gathering for Mrs Alfie,' Paddywhack explained. 'She hadn't a sou.'

'I managed to borrow five bob,' Flossie said, taking two half-crowns from inside her glove and laying them on the table.

'That,' said Hughesy, putting down half a crown, 'is all I can manage.'

Paddywhack squirmed and said, 'Six kids and another coming, and Thursday night.'

Loftus showed empty palms. 'Unless I could pop something?'

He felt worse than a wanderer – a stranger.

'Mrs Alfie? How in God's name did ye meet *her*?' he asked Hughesy.

'It was Alfie asked us to keep an eye on her and the kids. I saw him again today,' he told the others.

'How is he?' he asked.

Hughesy looked away.

'Alas, poor Yorick,' Loftus said. 'A skull!'

Flossie began to cry.

'But where's the rest of the gang? Joanna, and Tommy, and Angela and Casey.'

He stopped short of Deirdre. Paddywhack shook his head and made faint gestures.

'I nearly didn't come myself. Can you manage anything, Johnny?'

He took out his pocketbook and planked down a pound note.

'Good man!' said Hughesy, and looked up at the barman standing over them, and down at the pound note. He smiled apologetically at Johnny. 'Any more of that nice stuff?'

'Come on, scouts, I'm standing. If it's to be a wake, for Christ's sake let it be a wake. What's yours, Flossie? Still sticking to the dry sherry? Hughesy? The old pint?' He nodded to the barman, who departed silently. 'Let me in on this. Tell me all about Alfie.'

As the drinks warmed them they talked. A man, by God! A true friend if there ever was one. They don't often come like that nowadays. True from his bald head to the soles of his feet. Tried and true. A son of the soil. A bit of old Ireland. Vanishing down the drain. Not one bit of cod about him. His jokes ... We shall not look upon his like again. The pound note melted. Paddywhack said, 'Life is a mystery all right. She looks such a nice woman, and she *is* a nice woman, and full of guts, not one word of complaint, and three kids. What in God's name happened to them?' They told him, asking how she lived, that she used to work as a dressmaker. 'Yes, he did!' Loftus answered him. 'After a fashion, he did. He supported her. After a fashion.' Flossie said she would never come to this pub again. They agreed with Hughesy that Dublin wouldn't be the same without him. She said the fact was he had nothing to do with all those ... They followed her eyes down to Molly Goosegog and the one-armed colonel, and the three business types, and the two boiled hakes with the gins and bitters. Hughesy slapped the table. 'And that's a true bill, Flossie! He was one of us. Old in body but young in heart. You agree, Johnny?' He agreed that Alfie was the only man he ever met who understood them. 'He fought for his ideals.' They talked of understanding, and ideals, and truth, and true love, and how well Alfie understood what it means to be young, and to believe in things, that was it – to believe in things. A second pound was melting, and it was after ten, when Flossie said to Hughesy that she must go home soon.

'Mind your few quid, Johnny,' Hughesy said. 'What's left there will be enough. A dozen bottles of stout, say a dozen and a half. Just to cheer her up. We'll drop around for a minute, Flossie. Just to cheer her up.'

'One for the road,' he insisted, and held them. They leaned back.

It was nearly eleven when they left in a bunch, carrying the three brown-paper bags of stout, out into the dry streets, the nebulous night, under the dim stars and the gathering clouds that were lit by the city's glow. Loftus said it was a fine night for a ramble. Hughesy laughed and said, 'Or for courting.' Two by two, hooting merrily backwards and forwards at one another, they wound up among shaggy, dim-lit squares with names like Albert Gardens, Aldershot Place or Portland Square, all marked on green and white tablets in Irish and English, until they came to a basement door and, stepping down to it, rang and waited in a bunch under a stone arch. In the dark they were suddenly silent, listening. A light went on over the door. She opened it.

Alfie's youth. She was soft and welcoming. All the parts of her face seemed to be running into one another, dissolving like ice-cream in the sun, her mouth melting, her blue-blue eyes swimming. A loose tress of her grey-fair hair flowed over a high forehead. Her voice was as timid as butter. She was not a bad-looking woman, and for a moment a little flame of youth flared up in her when they introduced him to her, and she laughed softly and said, 'So this is Johnny! He said you were the baby of the lot.' She held his hand in her two hands, moist and warm as if she had been washing something, and he remembered a line from a poem they used to read at school, long forgotten, never understood. *Fear no more the heat of the sun...*

'Glad to meet you, Mrs Alfie,' he said and realized for the first time that he did not know Alfie's name.

'We brought a few drinks,' Hughesy explained. 'Just to brighten the night.'

'Come in, boys, come in. Talk low,' she begged. 'Jenny is only just gone to sleep.'

The low room was small and untidy, and smelled of soap. The fire was ashen. She had only two glasses. They sat in a circle and drank out of cups, or from the bottle-necks. Moist cloths hung drooping and wet on a line; the stuffing of the chairs tufted out, he saw a toy horse with three legs, torn green paperbacks, a house-of-cards half collapsed on a tray. Staring at her, he heard nothing of their whispering; both surprised and pleased to hear her laugh so often. He became aware that Hughesy and Flossie were fading out, for the last bus. Around midnight Paddywhack said he must give the wife a hand with the kids, and slid away. She put a few bits of sticks in the grate and tried ineffectually to remake the fire. Then Loftus clumped off home to his mother and there were only the two of them in the room, stooping over one flicker in the ashes, whispering, heads together.

Only once again did she mention Alfie; when she said, 'They're a grand bunch. Ye are all good boys. Decent young men. It was what he always said about ye.'

'Did you see him often?'

'Hardly at all. He might drop in after he shut the pub. To see the children. He told me he was always at ye to settle down. Hughesy, and Flossie, and Casey, and Loftus and you. Do you like Loftus?'

'He's cold. And bitter.'

'Is Deirdre your girl?'

'Yes. But I think she's letting me down. Did you meet her? She's a smasher.'

'She is a beautiful girl. I don't want to interfere in your life, Johnny, but I would be inclined to think that I would nearly say that she might have a hard streak in her.'

'Not like you?' he smiled.

'I'm not faulting her. A woman must think of her own good.'

There he was off, full-cock, about youth, ideals, loyalty, truth, honesty, love, things that only the gang understood, everybody else talking to you about your future, and good jobs, and making money. 'Ireland is the last fortress. The Noah's Ark of the world. No place like it.' And he should know, an exile! She agreed, she agreed. She said, 'The people here are warm and natural still in spite of all.' He was with her, all the way with her. 'We are not materialists. Not the best of us.' At that they were both off, whispering breaking into louder talk, hushing, glancing fearfully at the door of the bedroom.

The last flicker of the fire died away. They drank the last bottle of stout between them, passing it from mouth to mouth. Her voice grew softer, her hand when she held his was padded like a cat's. The night became a fugitive. Faintly a foghorn in the bay moaned through a muffled blanket. He looked out and up through the window and saw a yellow blur of street light, and the mist that clung wetly to a fogged tree. She got up to make tea. He followed her into the messy kitchen to help and talk. They came back and she put a few more futile chips of sticks on the warm ashes. She laughed at the slightest thing – when the toy horse toppled, or when he told her about the dog, kicked, and beaten, and mangy, that he bought in Palermo, and how it swam ashore back to its Moorish slum. Or that night in Odessa in the YMCA when he got into a fight by pretending the C stood for Communist.

When it was two o'clock he said, 'You must send me away.' She said, 'Listen to the dripping outside. Oh, don't go away, Johnny!' He said, 'You must sleep.' She said, 'I don't know what sleep is,' and held him by his wrist, frightened to be left alone. 'Listen to the drip-drop,' she wheedled. 'And look! It's yellow as mustard outside. Sleep here. Sleep in my bed. We're friends, aren't we? Just lie and sleep. You're a good boy. I know you. Go in there and lie down.' She led him into the bedroom with its unmade bed. He barely made out the child asleep on a camp-bed, one arm hooped around its head. She took her nightgown from a chair and went out.

He hung up his jacket, removed his shoes and lay down, gazing out the door at the yellow blur of the street lamp. It was as cold as the grave in the bed. She came back in her rumpled nightdress, her hair about her shoulders, got in under the clothes beside him and put out the light. The yellow street lamp bleared in through the bedroom door.

'It's bloody cold,' he said.

'We'll soon warm up. You should have taken your clothes off and got under the blankets, sure what does it matter?'

They lay in silence for a while, hearing nothing but their breathing and the faint, far fog-horn. He moved closer and began to whisper into her ear about what it means to be homeless, and she whispered to him about the time she came up to Dublin for the first time from County Cavan, for her honeymoon. She never once went back there. He whispered to her, 'You are a heroine.' She said, 'You're a good lad, Johnny.'

After a while more she said, 'We must sleep,' and he lay on his back, his hands clasped behind his head. After a long while he said, 'Deirdre is a bitch,' and she said, 'She is very young.' After another while he whispered, 'Try to sleep,' and she whispered, 'Yes.' After another long time he said, 'You're not sleeping. You are thinking of him. When will you know?' She said, 'It might be any minute. Then I'll sleep. And sleep. And sleep.'

Sleep stole on him. He woke abruptly, at five o'clock. She was no longer in the bed. He saw her in the front room, a man's overcoat on her shoulders, leaning her elbows on the window-sill staring out. In his stockinged feet he went to her and put his arm around her shoulder.

'You can't sleep?'

She did not stir. Her face had melted completely, her two cheeks were wet. He did not know what to say to her. By the cleansed lamplight outside he saw that the fog had lifted. She whispered. 'It's all over.'

'You can't tell!'

'I know it. I'll go out and ring the hospital at six o'clock. But I know it.' Her face screwed up and more tears oozed from her closed eyes. 'You'd better go, Johnny. Your people may be worrying.'

He dressed, shivering, among the empty bottles of stout on the floor, some of them standing to attention, some of them rolled on their sides. He put on his peaked cap with the white top, patted her hooped back, said, 'God help you,' and went out up the steps to the street level. It was black as night. From the pavement he looked down at the shadow of her face behind the misty glass, lifted a hand and walked away.

When he came to the Coal Harbour he halted on the centre of the railway bridge and leaned his hands on the wet parapet. Six miles across the level bay the string of orange lights flickered along the shoreline, and farther west the city's night-glow underlit its mirror of cloud. The harbour water, dark as oil, held the riding-light of a coaltub. He drew in deep breaths of the raw air and blinked his sanded eyes. He said quietly, 'I still love you, you bitch.' Then he lifted his head, put his two palms about his mouth like a megaphone, and howled in a long, wild howl across the bay, 'Do you love me?'

The city lay remote under its dull mirror.

He rubbed the stone and remembered, 'Quiet consummation have; and renowned be thy grave' – and marched homewards, arms swinging, chin up, white cap slanted. The water of the main harbour was inscribed by a slow wheel of light. Far out from the Kish bank a flight of light beamed and died at regular intervals. The whole way home the only sound he heard was a faint, faraway humming like a bee, a dawn-flight out of Dublin across the sea.

As he stole indoors a voice whispered, upstairs, 'Are you all right, darling?'

'Okay, Mum!'

'Daddy's asleep.'

'Okay, Mum.'
'Sleep well, love.'
'Okay, Mum. I'll sleep. And sleep. And sleep.'

# The Human Thing

It is not always cold in the Basses-Alpes – but on that late September evening (was it as long as ten years ago?) when I rang his presbytery bell it was very cold. The only answer to my call was the wind funnelling down that tiny, flagged street of his, narrow as a bedspread and smelly as a bedpan. It was like aerial gunnery aimed over thirty miles of forests and ravines to strike the sea five miles out beyond the warm beaches of Nice where I had toasted myself that morning in the Riviera sun. Was I to have to spend the night alone up here in Argons? And, if so, was there even a half-decent hotel in Argons? It would be dusk within an hour. I rang again and pressed for shelter against his studded door. Suddenly it opened and a woman passed hastily out into the narrow street. All I saw was a snapshot glimpse of a brightly made-up mouth in a dark face, a stocky figure, well dressed, a bit over-blown in the Italian way that you so often see along this border. Afterwards I wondered if she had been wearing a long black veil like a war-widow. The old housekeeper all but closed the door after her, glared at me with two sooty eyes from under a top-knot like the ace of spades, accepted my card and my tiny letter of introduction, closed the door within an inch of its jamb and backed into the house. This meant at least that he was at home, and I straightway forgot everything except what the Abbé de Saint Laurent had told me about him a few days before in his sunbathed little study in Nice.

'Argons?' he had said. 'In that case I know the very man for you. You must call on my good confrère the Abbé Morfé. He will tell you everything you want to know about the traditional life of the Basses-Alpes.'

And straightway sat to his desk and began to write on a small sheet of paper, murmuring over one sunlit shoulder as he wrote:

'He is not French, of course. Although you would never suspect it he has been with us so long – for at least twenty years. He is an Irishman. One of several who volunteered for the French mission after the War, when we were badly in need of priests. As we still are! You may talk to him freely. Not,' he smiled back at me around the corner of his glasses, 'that you will need to. He will do the talking. How do you spell your name? Thank you. A very outspoken man. Sometimes, I think, a little too outspoken. But,' and here he turned right around to me, 'zealous! Beyond my vocabulary. A downright man. And absolutely fearless.' He turned back to his desk to inscribe the tiny envelope. 'The perfect priest for the mountains. Ireland, as you must know, was never Romanized. So you, as an Englishman . . . ' (He did not observe my sigh; I am always being mistaken for an Englishman.) ' . . . will understand readily what I mean when I say that he represents the best, the very best of *l'église des barbares.*'

He folded his small letter into its small envelope, handed it to me courteously, and wafted me upwards and onwards towards nether Gaul.

As if under another wild blast of wind the door was flung open. I saw a powerful-looking countryman. His face was the colour of raw bacon cured by the sun and the wind. In his left hand he held my card, in his right a fat claw-hammer which he flung behind the door with such a clatter that for a second I was taken aback by the violence of the gesture; all the more so because he was shouting back into the house, '*Mais, je vous ai dis que je ne la connais pas!*' He turned back to me, warmly welcoming, cried, 'Come in, Sean! Come in!' and I was straightway back in the County Mayo; though in Ireland only a Protestant clergyman would have looked so indigent. His soutane was old and dusty, his boots were unlaced, he wore an old, fraying straw hat on the back of his balding poll, he was smoking a pipe mended with twine.

'I was making a coop for the hens!' he said.

'I'm interrupting you?'

'The most pleasant interruption in the world!' he laughed, and with one big hand on my shoulder he drew me in and invited me to stay not only for the night but for as long as I pleased: to which I cautiously replied that it could, alas, only be for one night. When we were in his living-room – oh! the joy of that sizzling log fire! – he at once produced a full bottle of Tullamore Dew, which, I noticed, was not only dusty but had never been opened. He sank as slowly as an elephant into his leather-covered armchair and began to talk non-stop about Ireland.

Everything in the room was of the region, and it was all as darkly impersonal as a convent: the hand-wrought firedogs, the heavy furniture that had obviously been made on the spot a long time ago, the greying, pious prints, the brown tiles, the adze-marked beams under a ceiling that had once been white plaster and was now tea-coloured from years of wood smoke and nicotine. As my feet thawed my heart rose – all this was exactly the sort of thing I needed for my article. But for well over an hour he did not give me a chance to ask him any of the questions that had brought me to his door – he asked all the questions, and rarely waited for my answers. I could see only three tokens of our common country: the until-now unopened bottle of whiskey; the corner of *The Sunday Independent*, still in its folder, still bearing its green Irish stamp, edging out from under the papers of the *midi*; and a small cushion embroidered with green and red leprechauns bulging from under his fat elbow. I could imagine it coming to him, with 'Merry Christmas', from some distant Deirdre or Mary.

At long last he let Ireland drop. Touching the Abbé's note (a little frigidly?) he said:

'Well, so you are going to write about us? And what have you discovered so far, pray?'

'More or less what you'd expect.'

'And,' a little guardedly, 'what would I expect?'

'What every traveller in a strange place expects, that the truth about every place is the sum of everybody's contradictions.'

'Such as?'

'Well, for example, everybody I meet east of the Var tells me that the old, traditional life now exists nowhere except west of the Var, and everybody west of the Var tells me that if I want to see the old ways I must come up here into the mountains. What would you say to that?'

He sniffed, and at once struck the chord that dominated everything else that was to follow.

'Do you know phwat it is?' he said in a buttermilk brogue, with a buttermilk smile, 'I'm not sure that I'm fit to tawlk about this ould counthry at all, at all. 'Tis a quare counthry. To tell you the honest truth, Sean, I'm gettin' a bit fed up with the Frinch. I have to live with them you know.'

Meaning that I was just a tourist? The jab and the brogue delighted and alerted me. A false brogue, as every Irishman knows, is a sure sign that the speaker is about to say something so true that he wants to blunt the edge of it by presenting it as a kind of family joke. I said, adopting the same sword-in-the-scabbard technique:

'Shure and all, isn't it a bit late in the day for you to be feeling that way now, Father? After all your thirty-odd years shepherding thim?'

He looked at me unamiably. A point apiece. We were playing that ancient Irish game known as conversational poker, a game which nobody can win and nobody can lose because nobody may utter the open truth but everybody must give and take a few sharp little smacks of it or the game is no good at all.

'Better late than never,' he said sourly. 'As is the way with most of us?'

He began to talk slowly. Was he feeling his way into my mind? Or into his own? He casually refreshed my glass. But as we progressed I thought I noticed a difference in his way of playing the Game: if we were playing the Game. After all he was a priest, and a French priest, and a French priest of the mountains – a man, that is, for whom the stakes in every game are infinite.

'The Basses-Alpes? Mind you, Sean, the Basses-Alpes aren't such a bad country. Not rich, of course. Anyway not rich the way the coast is rich. But it has things the coast never had and never will have. There are people who like to bask on the Riviera, who like to have Nice sunny apartments and Nice sunny congregations. But, sure, the Riviera isn't country at all! What is the Riviera but one blooming esplanade forty miles long? A string of international resorts without a stem of local character? Without any character! Without any values except cold, commercial cash values. But we aren't poor either. The land down there, you've seen it, is all ravined and gorged. Hard, stony uplands. With their olive groves abandoned, and their villages crumbling, or turned into tourist traps, and their farmhouses for sale to foreigners. And all the young people going. Gone! Lured away down to the bright lights along the coast. All of them wanting to be croupiers, or traffic cops in white helmets, or factory workers in white overalls. When I think of places like St Paul! A sink of iniquity I call it. For all I know it may be a place that you like to visit. And for good reasons, comfortable hotels, good food. But fifty years ago that was a decent, little country hill village. What is it today? Packed to the last corner with what, with who? The *haut monde*! Paahrisians! In bikinis and beach pyjamas! Do you know who the organist in that little church is today? A Protestant! And glad to have him. And now don't start talking to me about arty-arty chapels like that one by Matisse up in Vence. A chapel? It's a bathroom designed by a freethinker.'

'Was Matisse a freethinker?'

'You can have him! Listen! There's one thing on earth that I can't stand and that's milk and water Catholics.'

His eyes glinted. If this was, by any chance, a jab at me, maybe we were still playing the Game. He went on:

'Up here it is different. Up here the forests mean – well, you might call it comparative wealth for some and a good living for all. So our people have stayed on. The bright lights are farther away.' His voice slowed. 'Yes, our people have stayed on.'

'And,' I leaned forward eagerly, 'kept the old life ways?'

He knocked his pipe out with slow, careful taps on the head of a firedog. I had the feeling that the Game was over.

'I'll explain to you what I mean by milk and water religion. I know of instances of women in these parts deliberately going off and having affairs – and I mean respectable, married women with families – for no reason but because it is the modern fashion. Women born and reared in these parts, copying, that's all it is, the ways of places they think better than their own. To be as smart as the best. To be in the fashion. I find that utterly contemptible.'

He was so passionate about it that I demurred, though cautiously since he felt so strongly about it.

'Surely,' I proposed gently, 'one must go by cases? I mean a woman might be terribly unhappy. Her husband might be a boor, or a bore, or even a drunk. She might have met with some man whom she wished she had married, some man she loved or thought she loved...'

'That has nothing whatever to do with it! I could understand it if there was a bit of real passion in it. I could make allowances. I could even forgive it. It is my job to forgive. But they do it for the most vulgar of all reasons, just to be up to the minute. To be *à la page*. They do it simply to have something to boast about at the tea-table.'

'And the men?'

'The same! People like that have no religion, no character. They have nothing. That's what I mean by milk and water religion.'

'And for this you blame the gentry?'

'I never mentioned the gentry.'

'You said they want to be as smart as the best. To be in the fashion. Which best? Whose fashion? The nobs'?'

'You never get this sort of thing among the gentry, certainly not among the real noblesse. Oh, of course, you will find sinners among them, as you will everywhere. The flesh is the flesh, high or low. We are all creatures of the flesh. But this thing doesn't come from the flesh. It isn't even honest sensuality. It comes from the corruption of the mind. It comes from meanness of the mind. It's plain, vulgar, bloody tomfoolery. It is indifference. It is spiritual death. It is apostasy.'

He slapped the side of his armchair. An uncomfortable silence fell on us. Was he always as irascible as this?

'Maybe I'm in a pessimistic mood,' he grumbled. 'Gimme your glass. I'm a bad host. Maybe what I need is a week after the grouse in County Mayo.'

'Aye,' I said, more than willing to return to the Game. 'They say there's nothing like a good grouse for a bad theologian.'

'Why is it bad theology, pray?'

'Well, after all, "the greatest of these is charity".'

'Oho! There is always charity.'

(He sounded as if he was a bit sick of charity.)

'This couldn't be a long backwash from the French Revolution? I notice your little street here is called the Rue Carnot.'

'There is also,' he parried back, 'A Rue Saint Roch. That's San Rocco. The good Italian influence. The bond with Rome.'

'Yes!' I said dryly. 'I noticed that Italian influence. In the Place Garibaldi.'

He snarled it:

'That crew!'

We both laughed. (There really is a lot to be said for the urbanity of the Game.) Just then old Ace of Spades came in to say in her sullen voice:

'Dinner is served, Father. And that lady telephoned to say the funeral will be tomorrow at nine o'clock.'

He looked hard at her.

'Anastasia, do you know this Madame Bailly?'

'She has been living in Alberon this five years.'

'Funny that I can't remember her. I'll just ring Father Benoit.' He turned to me. 'He is one of my curates. We have a big parish. We divide it among the three of us.'

I had driven up through Alberon: one of those small places with a couple of sawmills, and with more garages than hotels, which means that everything goes stone-dead after October when the big passes get clogged with snow.

'Let's eat!'

We went into his dining-room. As he flung out his serviette, tucked it under his jaw and began to pour the wine, he said:

'The poor woman's husband was killed this afternoon in an accident. A tree fell right across his back. He owned a hotel, a garage and a sawmill in Alberon. She came about the funeral.' He paused in the act of filling his own glass. 'Bailly?' I know a couple of Baillys around Grasse. And,' he growled, 'nothing much good about any of them'.

'Liberals?' I teased.

'Puh! You mentioned Garibaldi. And Carnot. It would be very interesting study for you to find out at what date these names came in . . . and at what date a lot of other things began to come in.'

We talked at random. Presently he said:

'I don't want you to misunderstand me about the gentry. When all is said and done they are still the best people in France. They're on the way out, of course. They have no political gumption. And no money. And no influence. Your Liberals, as you choose to call them, are pushing them over the last edge of the ravines. What's left of them.' He sipped his wine and frowned. 'Bailly? Somehow or other that name keeps ringing a bell somewhere in what's left of my poor old head.'

'Haven't you the Liber Animarum?' I asked, meaning the thick, black notebook I had been shown once in an Irish presbytery by an old priest who had once been a dear friend of mine. These stubby books have a page to every parishioner: name, business, address, married or single, whether he practises his religion or not, and sometimes, though rarely, a more intimate comment if the priest considers it necessary to probe more deeply. He snorted.

'Ha! Liber Animarium, how are you? 'Tis easy seen that you come from Holy Ireland. Themselves and their card-indexes. What I call IBM Catholicism. It's as much as my two curates and myself can do to get around to visiting our parishioners once every two years. If that! And sometimes none too welcome at that! Have you any idea at all of the size of our parishes? If it wasn't for our housekeepers . . .' He stopped dead. He sighed. 'I must be getting old. I'm losing my grip.'

He rang the little brass bell on the table and waited for her to appear at the door.

'Tell me,' he said. 'Do you really know this Madame Bailly?'

'Everybody in Alberon knows her.'

'Yes, yes, you told me she is from Alberon.'

'I said she lives in Alberon.'

He pushed his chair back and faced her.

'Anastasia! What are you trying to say exactly? Where did she come from?'

'Cannes.'

'And Bailly married her and brought her to Alberon five years ago?'

'M. Bailly's wife and four children are living in Grasse with his mother.'

There was a long silence. He said, 'Bailly sent them away?'

Her sooty eyes stared at him. Her shoulders barely moved. He thanked her and nodded her out. He pushed his dinner away and his face was pale about his tightly clenched lips – the only part of that ruddy face that could grow pale.

'Five years! What sort of a priest am I? What sort of a parish do I run? Under my very nose! And now this person has the insolence to come here and ask me to give him a Christian burial! I'll soon put a stop to that!'

'My God! You can't refuse to bury the man? You can't let him be put into a hole in the ground like an animal?'

'And do you think that after leading this kind of life, giving public scandal for five years, openly and brazenly, that I am going to give him public burial now as a good Catholic? What would my parishioners say? What would they think? Do you think that it's for this I came here thirty-three years ago, to bless scandalmongers like those two apostates?'

'Isn't that a bit extreme? Sinners, yes. Call them that if you like. That, of course. But in mere charity . . .'

'Charity! Everybody always talks to me about charity! What is charity?'

'Love, I suppose. I suppose those two unfortunate people loved one another.'

'And his wife? And his four children? Did he love *them*?'

'But he may, even at the last minute, have hoped for forgiveness. If you had been there when that tree fell on him would you not have given him Extreme Unction? Anointed his eyes, and hands, and mouth, and prayed for his forgiveness?'

Outside, a wild rush of wind rattled leaves against the pane like a million clamouring fingers.

'Well, I was *not* there,' he said heavily. 'He died as he lived, struck down by the hand of God. I'm going to phone Father Benoit.'

Alone in the room I tried to visualize that stocky Italianate woman I had seen hurrying away from his door. I tried to see her and her dead lover in their hotel in Alberon, and I realized that this was one life story that I would never know. All I could imagine was a hundred spade-heads like old Anastasia in that little hill town besieging her with their cruel silence and their bitter eyes. He came back and slumped into his chair.

'He is out.'

I sat opposite him and I thought: 'And here is another life-story that I will never know!' After a few moments he said, quietly:

'Charity, Sean, is a virtue. It is, as you say, love – the love of all things through God, the love of God in all things. As for your love, human love? It is that, too. As Saint Bonaventure said, it is the life that couples the lover to the beloved. *Vita copulans amantem cum amato.* But it is that in the name of God, for God and by God. One act of love in a lifetime is an immensity. But one mortal sin can of itself destroy all love, and all life, as that man destroyed two lives over and over again before the eyes of the world.' He stopped and got up again. 'This thing must be ended publicly! As it was begun publicly. I must go down there at once.'

'Tonight?'

We both looked at the window. The mistral was at its full force. A wild sheaf of leaves whirled horizontally past the window.

'Let me drive you,' I offered, miserably.

'I'd be glad if you did. I'm in no fit state to drive.'

We buttoned ourselves up in our overcoats, pulled on our berets, and crushed into my little Dauphine. He directed me on the long, winding road where the woods on each side waved in one solid mass like a turbulent sea. I was too busy watching the road to talk. All the way he never spoke except to say 'Fork left', or 'Right here'. I felt like a man driving an executioner to the place of execution and I did not know which of the two of us I disliked the more at that moment. When we entered Alberon the streets were empty and dark. Two cafés were lighted, their windows opaque with condensed moisture. He suddenly said, revealing that he had been thinking in that language:

'*C'est dans la Place . Il s'appelle Le Chamois.*'

It was a three-storey house with the usual Alpine roof pitched to a peak and smoothing out at the base to let the great weight of snow slide down and melt on the gutters. On the ground floor there was a café, all dark and buttoned-up. Two windows on the storey above it were lighted. When he got out and was ringing at the door I withdrew to the centre of the little Place to park and wait. It took a couple of rings to produce an answer. When the door opened I saw, against the light inside, the dark outline of the woman who called herself Madame Bailly. He stepped inside at once, the door closed. I was alone with the mistral, the darkness and the empty Place.

The perfect priest for the mountains. Getting a bit fed-up with the Frinch. Nice people and Nice apartments. Absolutely fearless. Downright. A finger on a switch lit up two more windows upstairs. *Vita copulans amantem cum amato.* Would he be laid out in there on his bed of love? Zealous beyond my vocabulary. The mistral blew around and around me in moaning circles. Two men, an older and a younger, came, heads down, into the square from the left. I saw them pause at the closed-up Café le Chamois, look at its dark window, making some gestures that could only mean, 'Ah yes! I heard that . . . ' Then one of them stretched his arm forward and they went on again, heads down, to, I presumed, one of the other cafés, where no doubt as in every house in the town . . . I started the engine and turned on the heat.

After another long wait those two extra windows went dark. Still he did not come out. One mortal act of love in a lifetime is an immensity. One mortal sin can destroy the whole of that love and of that life for ever. Damn it, why doesn't he finish her off quickly? That, at least, would be a small act of Charity! A big truck and trailer laden with long baulks of timber trundled into the square and out at the other end. Then only the wind and the darkness again.

At last a flood of light beamed out on the pavement as the door opened and I saw his great bulky outline. He was shaking hands with the woman in black. As I peered forward I saw that it was not the same woman. He bowed to her and looked around for me. I drove over to meet him. She slowly closed the door, he clambered in, and silently waved me onward.

I could not see his face in the darkness but by the dashboard light I saw his hand, lying loosely on his thigh, shaking like a man with the palsy.

'Well?' I asked.

He spoke so softly I could barely hear him.

'I could not believe such love existed on this earth.'

'Madame Bailly?'

'She came down from Grasse. With her four children. For the funeral.'

'There will be a funeral?'

'Could I refuse his wife?'

'And the other?'

'The two of them are there together. Comforting one another.'

No more was said until we were back in his living-room, in his dark presbytery, in his tiny, smelly street. There, standing by the grey ash of his dying fire, still in his beret and his long overcoat, he turned on me a face twisted by agony and cried:

'Did I do right?'

'You did the human thing, Father.'

'Ah! The human thing?' He shook his head, uncomforted. He laid his hand in a kindly way on my shoulder. 'Sleep well, you!' – as one who would not. 'And I never told you anything at all, at all, about the ould Basses-Alpes!'

I hardly slept at all. All night the wind moaned through his narrow street, down over every forest, village and black ravine. Were those two women awake? I wished I was down where the bright lights of the esplanades glinted in the whispering sea.

# One Man, One Boat, One Girl

1

The first time I met Olly Carson I was sitting on a crate with T. J. Mooney in the Despatch Yard of the factory during the lunch break, each of us holding a bottle of Guinness in each fist. We were celebrating two famous birthdays, my twenty-first and his thirtieth, and T.J. was giving out the score about *Man and Superman*, his favourite anti-female tract. Olly came by, stopped, looked at the two of us out of his comical gooseberry eyes, winked, pulled another bottle of Guinness out of his lunch-bag, sat up beside us without being asked, and started at once on a bawdy story about a barmaid and a champagne cork. From that moment we were a cabal. When he told us that he had only just come over from Sheffield and did not know a soul in Cork I nudged T.J., he looked at me, I raised my eyebrows, and he nodded. Straightway we introduced Olly to the Rules of the River. One man, One boat, One girl.

The next Sunday, by way of initiating him, we sent him off down the Marina while we were getting out the boats from the rowing club. In those days, before cars started ruining the roads, before outboard-motors, and caravans, and cinemas, and Telly, and touring buses, and Teddy Boys and all this bloody modern fal-lal, the Lee used to be full of boats every Saturday and Sunday, and the Marina full of strolling couples from dawn to dark. As T.J. once said there were as many marriages made on the Marina as were ever made in Heaven.
  'Why don't we fix up with the girls beforehand?' Olly asked.
  'That,' T.J. explained, 'is on account of Rules four, five and six. Adventure. No attachments. And no regrets.'
  'Suits me!' says Olly and off he went.

Within fifteen minutes he was back leading two of them by the grin.

He trotted off again and he was back almost as quickly with a real dazzler for himself. After that he became the official Club Decoy. God knows what he had for the girls. He was no beauty. He had a pug nose and hobby-horse nostrils. He was strong and powerful but in a bathing dress he had stubby thighs and legs like a grown-up circus dwarf. He had no least idea how to dress – he always wore brown shoes with a dark suit, and on the river he wore his bowler hat even with his coat off. His pay packet was no fatter than Jim's or mine or anybody else's at the works. If it was not for his two rakehell eyes I do not know what he had for the women. Whatever he had they used to swing out of his arm, gazing adoringly and uncertainly into his two pop-eyes as if he was Rudolph Valentino in person.

'What's the trick, Olly?' I once asked him. 'Do you spray 'em with Secrets of Venus out of your cuff? Or drop cigarette-ash into their lemonade?'

Olly was very serious, very English, no matter what you asked him.

'I ain't got no tricks, Alphonsus,' he said. 'I think maybe the fack o' the matter is I've got a kind heart for the girls. They trust me, see? Or maybe the fack o' the matter is I'm not afraid of 'em, like all you bloomin' Irish.'

'That,' said T.J., prophetically as I now see, 'is where the ferry-boat will leave you some day. You'd be wiser to be afraid of 'em. As Shaw says . . .'

'Oh, F. Shaw!' says Olly.

'I beg your pardon,' says T.J. 'G. B. Shaw.'

In the end T.J. decided that they trusted him but that they thought he was a bit of a mug; but then, as he said, regarding me pityingly:

'You are a bit of a mug, too, Al, so the mystery remains.'

Will somebody tell me what has happened to time? There were a hundred hours in every one of those long Saturdays and Sundays on the river. And is it only in memory that it never rains, and that all girls are gamesome? Inside one month of that first season with us Olly knew every creek on the river, every stream on every creek, every field on every stream where you could tie up and get down to business, as cosy as a squawl of kittens in a basket, full of peace and joy and contentment the livelong day. In the late evening – lightsome until eleven o'clock in June – we would foregather and row home, tail to prow, like a little musical armada, T.J. swinging his old roundy concertina, me with my trumpet and Olly had a voice that made Caruso sound like a tomtit. When we came to the lights of Montenotte we used to wake the echoes in the hills.

I will never forget one late August night, it was our second season together, when we drew up for a rest opposite the old Shandon Rowing Club on the Marina. Before you could sing A to a tuning fork we had the boys and girls creeping out of the shadows of the avenue two by two down to the edge of the quay, sitting on the limestone wall, legs dangling, chiming in harmony all the songs you ever heard out of Grand Opera, Victor Herbert, G. and S., all those nice, sentimental, happy, pre-bloody-jazz-age songs like *By the Light of the Silvery Moon*, or *Farewell My Own*, *Light of My Life*, *Farewell*, or *Home to Our Mountains*, or

> *The moon hath raised her lamp above*
> *To light the way to thee, my love . . .*

The night came down like a curtain over the elm trees. Across the river the engine of the last excursion train from Youghal was blowing sparks up to the stars. The excursionists were waving their handkerchiefs out of the windows like mad, and the lights in the hundreds of houses up on the hill were dancing like fireflies. It was near two in the morning before we got home. We had to hire a sidecar and dump the girls on tip-toe, one by one, fifty yards from their doorsteps and their frothing fathers. We never saw them again. 'No attachments. No regrets.' No wonder you get all those angry young bums nowadays. They never knew how happy the world was between the two wars. Sheer heaven!

2

We had three good summers of it – and then the inevitable *femme fatale*!

It was a Sunday morning, blue sky, wind from the SW, boats almost ready – rugs, grub, cushions, concertina, trumpet – and T.J. was just about to say to Olly, 'Off you go, boy, collect the flesh!' when Janey

Anne Breen hove into view. I knew her slightly through a third cousin of mine, a very pretty girl named Fan Looney; the two of them used to go off together once a week saving sinners with the Ladies' Saint Vincent de Paul. Without thinking, I said:

'Hello, Janey Anne!'

'Good morning, Alphonsus,' says she. 'Off for a little row? Very good. Very healthy.'

I introduced the boys, we chatted for a bit, and before I could warn Olly he did it. It must have been pure reflex action because she had, and still has, a thin hardbeak smile, mousy hair, as dry as a Temperance Club cat and crimped like corrugated iron, two peg legs the same width all the way up stuck into size eight shoes, black and squat-heeled, with big, black bow-knots, and she was wearing, as she always did, and when I saw her the other day she still was wearing it, an electric-blue frock that T.J. said always made him think of methylated spirits. If she had anything at all that you could look at it they were her two goofy eyes, sweety, softy, eyes, twice their natural size behind her thick, rimless spectacles, and two big front teeth lying white and wet on her lower lip as if she was always saying fuf-fuf. Whatever made him do it, Olly slips his arm around her waist and says, in his best Harry Lauder accent, 'Coom on, lass, what about a kiss and a squeeze for poor old Olly, eh?' She gave him a crack across the puss that you could hear echoing across the Marina half an hour after, and off she stalked, nose and specs in the air, her heels digging holes of anger in the ground, and Olly picking up his bowler hat off the grass and gazing after her with his mouth open and T.J. in the splits of laughter.

T.J. always had a very strange way of laughing. He used to bend over as if he was trying to kiss his knees, his hands trailing the ground, for all the world like a cow laughing at a pound of butter. That was the way he was now, and me leaning across his back, patting him like a baby with the hiccups. As soon as he could talk he explained matters to Olly.

'No, Olly! No, boy! Not with black shoes and bow-ties to them. Not with specs. Not with a Child of Mary medal around her neck. Not with no mother, a brother a priest, and a sister a nun.'

'Nun?' he says. 'You mean locked up for life in a bloomin' convent?'

'That's the idea,' I said. 'And if somebody doesn't pick Janey Anne up very soon she'll be locked up too in about a hundred yards of nun's veiling. She's a good girl, Olly. G-O-O-D. One of those girls you read about in ancient books.'

He stared after her, gargling.

'Pure,' says T.J., 'as the driven snow. Now off you go, Olly, like a good boy, and find us a couple of nice bad girls like you always do. Young, and tender and jumping like April lambs.'

He trotted off after her, caught up with her, and took off his hat and began adulating in front of her.

'For God's sake,' says T.J. watching him, 'surely he's not trying to persuade that stick to come on the river with him? She must be turned thirty if she's a day.'

We watched the two of them walking away from us along the path, Olly with his hat in his hand, angled sideways towards her, bowing like a shop-walker, and her ladyship talking down the side of her arm at him as if she was ticking off a bold, bad doggie. They went on, and they went on, along the path, under the trees, around the bend of the Marina, out of sight. We sat down to wait. After half an hour T.J. jumped up and said, angrily, 'Come on. We'll take one boat between us.'

We rowed down the river, not speaking, until we passed the end of the Marina. I was stroke. I said over my shoulder:

'Do you see what I see?'

The two of them were sitting on the last bench of the Marina and they were laughing.

'So be it!' says T.J. 'He can have his attachment. And his regrets.'

'We might have a few regrets, too.'

'You're young, boy, you'll find you get over these things.'

I could not see his face but I did not like his tone. He sounded like a bitter old man.

3

They were married that July, and I had to drag T.J. to the wedding, the usual hole and corner affair in the presbytery, Olly being a Baptist and sticking to it; and after the honeymoon I had to drag him with me to visit them in their little garden flat on the Lower Road, a bare hundred yards from the river. I think T.J. came only because it was a damp night and he had nowhere else to go.

'Anyway,' I said, as I squeaked open the garden gate, 'it's only polite. This looks like a cosy little love-nest.'

'Says the setter to the snipe.'

He was just after buying a pure bred, golden setter pup, named Babs, spayed.

'I bet you tuppence we'll have to leave Babs outside,' he said. 'And I bet you we won't get a drink either.'

She opened the door. Specs, bird's eyes, wet teeth, electric-blue dress. An old black mongrel cocker ran out and in a second the two dogs were at it. She retrieved the mongrel.

'Come to mumsy-wumsy,' she says, almost suckling him. 'Poor little Charlie-Barlie. Bold, bad, foxy dog! Boo!'

'Bitch,' says T.J. coldly.

Olly was behind her, grinning.

'Charlie's a present from an old admirer,' he says, with a lewd wink.

'Oliver!' she upbraided. 'He is not. Charlie-Barlie,' she explained primly, 'was left in my care a year ago by an old friend who had to go to sea.'

Olly pinched her behind.

'Old friend? Ha-ha!' and he winked at us again.

We had to leave Babs outside, tied to the railings.

'Won't you wipe your feet?' she begged. 'I did the lino today.'

We could smell it. Brand new, red roses climbing all over golden lattice-work. She had the Infant of Prague on the wall with an electric bulb glowing in front of it. She had a holy-water font on the wall, too. For spite T.J. dropped his cigarette ash into it. The little parlour was as neat as an altar. They sat on each side of the fire, and T.J. and me sat on a new settee against the opposite wall. Olly produced two bottles of Guinness and poured them for us. She took away the bottles and the corkscrew and we knew that was that.

'Well,' I said, friendly-like, 'and how did the honeymoon go?'

'Guess where we went?' Olly grinned.

'London? Isle of Man? Killarney? Southend? Brighton?' Olly grinned a No to all of them.

'We took a rowboat and set off to explore the river. Lots of nice little cosy corners down there, eh?'

He clicked his tongue and raised shocked eyebrows.

'Oliver!' said Janey Anne, and we knew that he had told her all.

If T.J.'s slow smile was a knife it would have cut his jaw off.

'Nice time?' I asked Olly, and his tone changed.

'So-so!'

'It rained,' she grimaced.

'A little accident,' he gestured.

'Oliver rocked the boat,' she said and glared at him.

'As a matter o' fack, poor little Janey fell into the river. She got a bad cold. She lost her glasses. So we came home.'

Jim made a very sad face and looked very happy. Then he slowly began to go as white as cheese because Olly had started in on the story of the blind salesman who met the deaf whore. This was always a thing about T.J. Any story you liked among men, but a single off-colour word in the presence of women made him go white with anger. I looked at Janey Anne. She was chuckling. Olly finished his yarn, winked at me, and looked expectantly at Janey. Her face at once did a quick curtain and she said severely:

'Oliver!'

He guffawed. His gooseberry eyes rolled in their sockets. He said:

'Did I ever tell you the one about the barmaid and the champagne cork?'

'Yes,' said Jim like a bullet.

That did not stop Olly. Janey Anne gurgled. Olly finished, winked, waited, got his 'Oliver!' and guffawed happily. He then started in, at length and detail, on our river days. T.J. looked four times at his watch. He held his empty glass between his clasped hands as if he was trying to press it to bits. Janey listened, radiant until it was all finished with Olly singing our Barcarolle, *River girls, O river girls, How we love your dancing curls*. Then she snapped down the black curtain and said to T.J.:

'I think you have been a bunch of very bad boys, Mister Mooney. I am really shocked at you. After all you are older than Oliver. Not to mention poor Alphonsus there, and he's only a boy.'

Oliver, lolling in his armchair, beamed at us both. His beaming face said it for him:

'Did you ever in all your life see such a sweet, innocent little girl as I found?'

When we at last got out of that flat Jim untied the setter without a word, and he did not say a word until we were back in our digs, him sitting on his bed, and me on mine looking at the rain flecking the window, thinking of one wet Sunday, a couple of years back, when I was on the river with that pretty girl Fan Looney.

'Well?' he said at last. 'What are you thinking about?'

'Me?' I said, looking away from the rain on the window. 'Nothing!'

'Damn it,' he snarled, 'you must be thinking about something.'

'Very well,' I laughed. 'In that case tell me what was I thinking?'

'How the hell do I know what you were thinking?'

'Then I don't know what I was thinking either.'

'So you admit you were thinking?'

'T.J.,' I pleaded. 'Come off it.'

'And you were looking at me!' he growled.

'I was not looking at you, I'm sick of looking at you, do you think I'm in love with you?'

'Oh! So you were thinking about love?'

'Are you going slightly daft?'

'I got over that stage years ago. But *I'll* tell *you* what *I* was thinking. I was thinking, why is it in the name of all that's holy that fellows see things in girls that simply aren't there? And that's what you were thinking, too, whether you know it or not.'

'Tell me,' I said, to pacify him. 'Why *do* we see things in girls that aren't there?'

He whispered across to me:

'Because they aren't there.'

I began to think that maybe he really was going a bit daft. I started looking again at the drops of rain on the pane.

'Well?' he said, after another while. 'Why don't you say it straight out?'

'Say what straight out?'

'What you're thinking.'

'I'm not thinking! Unless,' I said, on an inspiration-like, 'maybe I was thinking, why do girls see things in fellows that aren't there?'

'You're a flaming liar! You were thinking no such a thing! You were thinking when will I start seeing things in some girl that aren't there. And that's why you were looking at me.'

I laughed very loudly at that, because it had crossed my mind that it was a funny thing that he had never married.

'And,' he said, very solemn-like, 'I'll tell you another thing I was thinking. It won't be long before I see you starting to see things in some girl that aren't there. If you haven't started doing it already.'

At that I peeled off and went to bed. So did he. I stayed awake for hours listening to the rain, and I could tell he wasn't asleep either.

4

After that night we could not be kept away from Olly and Janey. Once a week, at least, we would tie Babs to the railings, ring the bell, wipe our feet, sit on the settee, accept our glass of stout, and, as T.J. put it, wait for Olly to start unveiling. He was right – it was just like the quick-change-artist act in an old-time Music Hall. Enter Olly as Cork's Casanova, the historian of the river and all its wily ways. Loud guffaws. Black curtains. Enter Professor Oliver Carson as the warm admirer of Little Tich, George Robey, Lord Beaverbrook, Chief Scout Baron Baden-Powell, Marie Stopes, Stanley Baldwin and Eamonn de Valera. Black-out. Bright lights. Drum-rolls. Enter Olly in a check suit, straw hat, white bowler and malacca: 'Did I ever tell you the one about the absent-minded Professor who took his dog down to the garage to be oiled and greased?' Guffaws. Black curtains. Enter the Confirmed Pacifist: 'Let me ask you a question, sir. If you was to say to me, "What would you do if you saw your poor, dumb sister being raped by a German?" what would I answer you? I would answer you, "I ain't got no dumb sister! That's my wife!" Hahaha!' Oliver! Black curtains. Enter Olly, very serious, as John Calvin, announcing the doctrine of the salvation of the elect; which, so far as I could make out, included everybody in the world except the foreman of the works and the population of Germany. To that particular shebang Janey Anne could only respond with small, gasping noises.

Every night T.J. would come away either in a daze of silence, or asking the same question in a variety of ways: What did I think of *that* performance? I answered him once and only once. I said that I thought Olly was being very honest with her, that he was laying his soul open at her feet, and that it was very noble of him. I thought T.J. would strike me with the setter.

'Honest?' he roared at me. 'Noble? Do you want to drive me mad? Well, that's the end of it. I'm finished with him. If that's what you think he's doing I'm never going to put my head inside that madhouse again. For the first time in my life I'm actually beginning to sympathize with that eedjut of a woman. I'm honestly beginning to conclude that the unfortunate woman is too bewildered at finding herself married to that roaring lunatic that she'll either sink an axe in his head or end up raving in a padded cell.'

The week after that Olly unveiled in a way that dumb-founded the three of us. He revealed that he was a Freemason, that his father was a Freemason, and that not only had he been a member of a Sheffield Lodge but that the first thing he did when he landed in Cork was to join the local Lodge. I looked over at Janey Anne, and by the fright in her face I saw that, like us, this was the first she had heard of it. As if I was sitting inside in her head I could feel the rats running around in her brain. Secret society, condemned by the Church, enemies of the Vatican, Grand Orient, goats, devils, Carbonaries, Black Magic, passwords, handgrips, tip-the-wink, never-know-who-you're-talking-to, red fire, dark rooms, the-Lord-save-us-or-we-perish – all this time, unbeknownst to her, in her own house, from her Olly whose jokes she laughed at, whose life she thought was an open book to her, whom she had by this seen night after night padding around on his stubby legs in his nightshirt, now looking at her as mild as milk saying:

'Very fine body of men. Very philantropophic. Philantropophic to everybody. Without respect to class or creed.'

T.J. got me out as fast as he decently could. As we untied Babs we could hear the voices rising inside the window of the little parlour. When we taxed Olly the next day about never telling us he was a Mason he said, shortly, that he did not want to upset us.

'But what about Janey Anne?' T.J. asked.

'Well, I've told her, haven't I?'

'You didn't tell beforehand,' I charged him.

'She wouldn't have had me.'

At that T.J. said one of those daft things he was always saying:

'She'd have had you double-quick. A brand from the burning, Olly. A brand from the burning.'

We did not go down so often to the flat after that. The atmosphere, if I might make so bold as to borrow the vivid image, had changed. For one thing the Troubles were starting, and Olly was English and she was Irish. For another thing they could not talk about anything now without her dragging the Masons into it. A sign of it was that Olly had got hold of a little-toy Union Jack, the sort you might put up in front of your motor-car if you were daft enough; and she had brought a little toy papal-flag, yellow and white; and they had stuck the two flags into vases on each side of the mantelpiece, so that all they had to do then was to look at one flag or the other and off they were, hammer and tongs. If we walked into the middle of one of these arguments they barely took time off to greet us, and as Olly drew the two bottles of stout he would hardly look at what he was doing.

'England,' he would say to her, hauling at the cork, 'is my! Country! Right! Or! Wrong!'

'Then why didn't you fight for your country during the war?' from Janey Anne, never afraid to hit below the belt.

'I 'ave my convictions,' he said. 'And I stand by 'em.'

'Ha!' she said. 'Locked up in your bedroom drawer in tissue-paper, your little green and gold apron, with your sash, and your trowel and your secret book of the devil's rules!'

When she talked that way, T.J. said afterwards, she looked like Bluebeard's wife talking about the locked chamber.

'Are we discussing the Empire or the Freemasons?' Olly asked politely.

'How any men,' she sailed on, 'can be so ignorant, so misled, so benighted, so superstitious as to be riding a goat around a room...'

'Janey Anne,' Olly protested, 'we don't go riding no goats around no rooms. You're not allowed to keep a goat in a room. The RSPCA would be after you like a shot.'

'Ye call up the devil!'

'Janey Anne! Do you really and truly think I'm the kind of man who...'

'Then why don't you tell me what goes on there?'

Very quietly he explained all over again that Freemasonry is a purely philanthropic society.

'Good works. Helping poor boys who are afflicted in any way. Orphans. Polios. Bastards. All the same to us. Each for all. All for each. Assisting one another in our private or commercial difficulties. Naturally these are things we don't wish to be discussed in public. You can see that, darlingkins, can't you?'

She looked at him, doubtfully, tight-mouthed, teeth buried, eyes big as plates, and started muttering about secret societies condemned by the Pope.

'Janey Anne! Don't you trust your own Ollykins?'

We could see her wavering. Then she cracked her beak on a hard, hempseed 'No!'

'I think it's wicked, and sinful and evil. I don't know why I ever married a man who keeps secrets from his wife. A man with a double life. Not like other men I've known. Carol Costigan wouldn't have deceived me like this. Johnny Hartigan wouldn't have done it. Georgie Conlon wouldn't have done it. But you . . . Come to mumsy, my own Charlie-Barlie,' she says picking up the old mongrel and putting her nose down to his nose. 'You wouldn't deceive me like that, would you?'

'No,' says Olly sourly. 'Not unless he went riding a goat around a room.'

'Oliver!'

'Or started wearing a little green apron like a nancyboy. Go on, kiss him, do!'

'Don't you dare say one word against a woman's best friend! You Mason! You!'

T.J. would always leave the flat whistling after one of these hot nights; or saying something cheerful like, 'It's on the rocks! We'll all be back on the river next June.'

## 5

Just before Christmas Olly came up to me in the works one Monday morning red with pride and excitement.

'Know what's happened? I've been made Master of my Lodge. Elected last Friday night.'

'Here?'

'Here in Cork. Wot an 'onour! My old man'll be tickled to death.'

'What about Janey Anne?'

'Delighted. She'll be at the Banquet. She's gone into town to buy a frock. She's thinking of blue.'

When I told T.J. he said he did not believe it. I assured him that Olly himself told me. He said he meant about Janey being delighted. After supper he said we must go down to the flat at once. Olly was not at home but she brought us in, gave us the two bottles of stout, so far forgot herself as to bring out two more, and started in to tell us all about it, as excited as a girl going to her first dance.

'Of *course* I'm going to the Banquet! It really is a great honour for Oliver. And as his wife I shall be the First Lady.'

'But what about the Church?' T.J. goaded.

'Well,' she said primly, 'at first, when he asked me would I sit beside him in the place of honour at the Banquet I didn't know what to say. So I went around on Saturday morning to Saint Anne's to consult Father Butts. It was he married us. He said he would have to think about it and to come back that night. When I went back that night he asked me why I wanted to go to the Banquet. I said I wanted to stand by my marriage vows to love, honour and obey. He said he must think some more about it and to come back on Sunday afternoon. So I went back on Sunday afternoon and he said: "Where will this Banquet be held?" I said, "In the Imperial Hotel." He said, "Very well, Mrs Carson, you may attend the Banquet. The place is neutral. And the intention is to avoid domestic friction. But, after this, you must try to wean him away from his ungodly ways." I thought he was very understanding. Even when I asked him should I tell Oliver that I had consulted him he said, "It would be tactless and unnecessary." I was thinking of blue.'

'Your taste is perfect,' T.J. said. 'And you are very loyal.'

On our way home I told him I was surprised at his paying her the compliment of being loyal. He explained to me that he did not mean that she was being loyal to Olly.

## 6

I think it was in the end of January that Olly came over to us one morning waving a telegram. It was a radiogram for Janey that her father had sent down to them the night before. It said: *Arriving Cork Thursday night for three days stop hospitality welcome if available stop three cheers and what-ho Carol.*

'It's from her old boy-friend Carol Costigan. A radio-officer with P. and O. Wonderful man. Salt of the earth. Janey wants the two of you to come to supper on Thursday night and view my defeated rival.' He began to laugh like a zany. 'The joke of the whole thing is Janey's like a cat on hot bricks. She never told him she's married. He's going to get a right land when he sees me.'

We went down, we tied Babs to the railings, rang, were let in by Olly, who gave us a rather watery wink, wiped our feet and went into the parlour. The first person I saw was Mrs Charles Costigan, a luscious blonde. Then I saw Mr Salt-of-the Earth Costigan. He was about the size of a jockey, false teeth, hair going thin, and he had a bulge under each eye like a blue moon in its last quarter. Mrs Costigan turned out to be Yorkshire, and a non-stop talker, with all of Olly's sense of humour, who roared at his roughest jokes, told a few blue ones of her own, and lowered her liquor like a man – whiskey, in honour of the double marriage. I will say this for Janey Anne, that she carried the whole thing off like a good sport: loud jokes and laughter about secret marriages, and 'I-only-had-to-turn-my-back', and 'We-both-seem-to-like-the-English-don't-we?' But Olly was not taking it so well. He kept looking at Costigan, and then glancing over at Janey Anne, and it was as plain as a pikestaff that he was wondering what she had ever seen in the fellow. All the same, the man was his guest, so after the supper was over he had no option when Costigan said, probably because he saw there was no more liquor coming up, 'Say, chaps. Why don't we leave the girls alone for a bit to get acquainted and drop around the corner for a little bit of manly pow-wow and a night-cap? What-ho?'

We went down the road to the old *Internationale*, just where the houses stop and the river is wide open. It was a lovely calm night, with a tingle of frost in the air. The buses were like stars, and the stars were like buses. A ship went slowly chugging down the river on the high tide. For an hour it was just like the good old days, boozing there together, swopping yarns – if Olly was being a bit quiet, for him – so that I was disappointed when T.J. said it was getting late and we must push off for home. On the way I said:

'Did you remark how quiet Olly was? I think he's feeling sorry for poor Janey. That fellow Costigan was a terrible let down for her opposite us all.'

T.J. snorted at me.

'Simple Simon,' he said.

'What do you mean, Simple Simon?'

'Don't you know a Woolworth's wedding-ring when you see it?'

The following morning Olly stepped into line with us and came right out with it.

'I told that fellow this morning that if he and his floosy aren't out of my house when I come back tonight I'll throw the pair of 'em out on their necks in the middle of the road.'

'How did you find out?' T.J. asked.

'He had the cool, brazen brass to tell me. He had the gall to think that I'm his kind of a man. I didn't sleep a wink. I could hear Janey crying all night. Do you know what? Her pillow was as wet this morning as if you'd thrown a bucket of water on it.'

At that T.J. stopped dead, and doubled over, pawing the ground, and all the fellows passing by looking at him and smiling to see him laughing. Olly dragged him up and around by the shoulder, and I thought he was going to hit him.

'What the 'ell are you laughing at?' he bellowed, and all the fellows stopped to look.

'Jealous!' Jim wails, between his laughs. 'Jealous!'

'Janey! Of that floosy? For that rat?' he roared. T.J. quietened. He stared at Olly as if he had been struck dumb. He shook him off.

'Did I say *she* was jealous?' he sneered, and walked away.

7

We never visited the flat again. We did not talk to Olly for the best part of two months. I did not see much of T.J. either, outside the digs, and not very much in them – I had seen a streak of cruelty in him that I did not like. Besides, that winter I was in the IRA and I was doing a special night course three times a week at the Tech, and I may as well also mention that once or twice I tried courting Fan Looney. And if I must tell the whole truth of it she would have nothing to do with me. She said she had heard too much about my goings-on from Janey Anne. In the end it was Olly who talked to us. He came and sat down beside us one day in the canteen. He was his old, cheery self.

'Boys!' he said right off the reel, 'my Janey Anne is one of the great women of all time. As Father Butts said to me last night when I was seeing him off at the door, "Your wife, Mr Carson, is a credit to Faith and Fatherland." I never before realized wot comfort a troubled soul can get out of religion. It's made me think, let me tell you that. It made me ponder very seriously on a lot o' things.'

'Coming over?' asks T.J. 'And, if so, what about the Freemasons?'

'As a matter o' fack,' says Olly, obviously dying to talk about it, 'Father Butts is very understanding about that particular question. He opened my eyes to a lot of things I never knew about the Masons. And he opened Janey Anne's eyes too. He lent us a very interesting book on the subjeck there last month. The two of us are reading it every night over the fire. It's these bleeding Continentals that gave us a bad name. The fack is English Freemasonry is away out on its own. British to the backbone! Not that I'm entirely convinced, mind you. But historically speaking...'

And off he went about the Scotch Rite, and some crowd called the Knights Templar, and the French Revolution came into it, and six Papal bulls, and only the siren stopped him.

'Hooked,' said T.J., as we walked back to the bench, 'booked and cooked to a cinder. He'll be dripping holy medals by Easter!'

Jim was wrong. That Easter, Olly got the 'flu and died as he had lived a true-born English Baptist. T.J. and me went down to the house for the funeral and she brought us in to see him in the coffin. When I saw what I saw the tears started rolling down my face. She had him laid out in the Franciscan habit, and at his head she had laid his little Papal flag that used to stand in the vase on her side of the mantelpiece. I never saw any woman look so happy.

'He was a bad, bad boy,' she smiled. 'But God will forgive him. As He will forgive ye, too. Praise and glory be to His name.'

That afternoon we walked away from the graveside as silent as the grave. It started to rain and we halted under a yew. The funeral was very largely attended, Catholics, Masons, Baptists, Boys' Brigade, all sorts and sizes of people, workers from the factory, every class and creed, scattered under yews all over the place sheltering from the rain.

'I suppose,' says T.J., after a while, 'we know what we're thinking?'

'T.J.!' says I, and I was wiping my face with my handkerchief. 'I'm not thinking anything at all, no more than that pile of ould yellow bones there. And I don't want to think, because all I want to do is to forget.'

'Well, I'll tell you what I'm thinking. That woman fattens on guilt like a cemetery worm.'

'Guilt? What has she to feel guilty about?'

'Nothing!' he shouted at me, forgetting where we were. 'That's why she loves it.'

'Daft!' I said and I threw the back of my hand to him and walked away down the path. He came raging after me, he shoved me up against a Celtic cross, he put his long nose into my face and he started haranguing me as if I was a public meeting, one hand on my chest, the other pointing like a politician's statue across the white headstones.

'Do we or do we not know what she did to that poor sucker lying there in his fancy dress under five feet of ground? Did she or did she not hypnotize him into thinking she was the incarnation of all goodness and virtue and that he was nothing but a Sheffield orang-outang?'

'Well, Olly, certainly, had a very high opinion of his wife.'

'And why? Why? Isn't this the question that's been tormenting you and me from the first day they laid eyes on one another?'

'Look,' I said, 'all I know is that the cold of his ould cross is going in through the small of my back.'

He held me gripped tighter than ever.

'I have decided,' he said, and his eyes were like two gimlets, 'that in what is commonly called love man creates woman after his own unlikeness. In love woman is man's image of what he is not. In love man is his own creator, midwife and gravedigger, awake, asleep, dreaming or hypnotized the way you are at this very moment into thinking what I damn well know you are thinking only you haven't the guts to say it.'

I threw him off, and graveyard or no graveyard I let a roar out of me:

'I'm thinking of nothing! And I'm proud to say I'm thinking of nothing! And I'll give you a sock in your greyhound's puss if you don't stop thinking for me. Aye, and tormenting me in the middle of my sorrow for my poor dead friend Olly Carson lying over there under a ton of wet earth and a pile of glass flowers.'

He leaned one hand against the Celtic cross and he sneered at me:

'You're thinking of your lousy soul and of your latter end.'

I can still hear the whistling of the blackbirds. I can see the sun on the raindrops of the yews, and the mourners fluffing themselves out, and the long black cloud moving like a black pot lid away over the city. I knew somehow that this was going to be the most wonderful night of my life and I began to cry rain down into the ould cross at the thought of it. At that the kindness broke out in him, and I was never more touched by anything he ever said to me as by what he said then. He put his arm around my shoulder and he said:

'Aly, boy,' says he, 'will you wipe your face, yoh slobbering eedjut? And stop disgracing me in the public graveyard? Come on out here to *The Last Post* and I'll stand you a pint of the best.' The pub was full. Of mourners. We leaned on the counter looking down into our two pints. Someone lit the gas-mantle. It was like the green sea. I started thinking to myself that no man can do without a friend. And I was thinking, wouldn't it be sort of nice, when all is said and done, to have somebody to look after me when I got old, and to lay me out when I'd be dead, with the tricolour over my coffin, and my IRA gun lying on top of it, and the band after the hearse playing *The Flowers of the Forest*, or the Dead March from *Saul*. I looked up at T.J. smoking his pipe and pondering on his pint, and I confessed it to him. I expected him to bawl me out. He looked at me a bit sadly, but kindly too, like some old priest after listening to you telling him your sins. He patted me on the shoulder, and he began at me, soft and warm, kind of pleased, I suppose, that I had confided in him:

'Al! There is no doubt whatever about it, you are a gom. And you always were a gom. And you always will be a gom. And it's a good job for you that you have somebody like me to advise you. A babe in arms, a poor, young fellow up from the country that knows nothing about the ways of the world or the wiles of women. If it wasn't for me looking after you you might have been hooked long ago by some vampire like that wan,' with a jerk of his head to the cemetery. 'Sucking your blood. Leeching you like a succubus. Turning you into a poppet. Let me tell you this one thing, and mark it once and for all. All every woman is waiting for is the day she can lay you out and be praying for you, and feeling good about you. They keep you out of their bed when you're alive, and they sleep with you when you're dead. The war of the sexes is declared by women on the weaker sex, and entered into by men because we are the weaker sex. And when we're beaten to the bed, that is to say when we think we have conquered our woman, what do we do but put her up on an altar and grovel before her, and work ourselves to a lather for her into an early grave?'

'But, T.J., what about love?'

'Love, my dear, poor boy, is a sedative disguised as a stimulant. It's a mirror where man sees himself as a monster, and woman as a thing of untarnished beauty. If it wasn't for that all men would otherwise, and normally fear all women. You fear women. I fear women. But because we need them we have to have them. And that's where they have us, in the great and final triumph of women over men, called – by them, not by us, and well-called – Happy Wedlock. Love is a prison staffed by female warders. Let me tell you . . .'

It went on for an hour, non-stop, pouring into me, pint after pint, like the sea into a cave. I did not understand one hundredth part of it. But I understood enough of it. I understood that he was advising me to look into the mirror of my own heart and there I would see Love smiling sweetly out at me. I went down to Fan Looney that night, and I told her all about it. When I was finished she said in her nice, sweet way that she always knew that Jim Mooney was no proper company for a nice young man like me, and if I had found him out she was very glad.

'Maybe,' I said, daringly, ''tis the way I found you? Have I a chance, Fan?'

She looked at me, and her eyes filled and her voice broke.

'Oh, Alphonsus!' she says. 'What are you after doing to me? I was a happy girl without a thought of anything in the world until you came talking to me and now you're after turning me into a grown woman. And,' she said, sobbing into my shoulder, 'now we'll have to start planning.'

'We will, Fan,' I said and I felt just as miserable as herself, and she made me feel an awful brute.

'You'll have to give up the drink,' she wailed.

'I will, I will,' I promised.

'And cut down on smoking,' she wept.

'Anything in the world you say, Fan! If you'll only stop crying.'

We are settled down now. We have five lovely children. Cherubs! I'm foreman of the works. And I can assure you I keep a sharp eye on the young fellows. After all, I know the ways of the world. T.J. got another job. For years I did not lay eyes on him until there last month when I was walking down the Marina one Sunday with Fan pushing little Sean in the gocart, and I had Deirdre on my shoulder. Suddenly I stopped dead. I saw the grey-haired man on the river, pulling along at his ease. In the prow with her nose up was a red setter, and it was that made me recognize him.

'Fan!' I said. 'That's T.J.'

She looked and she laughed sharp-like.

'The Rule of the River,' she said.

It was a lovely June morning, wind from the southwest, and the ebb with him. Very nice. He would come back on the tide. As late as he liked.

'Well?' Fan asked. 'What are you thinking?'

'Ach! Nothing!'

'You were smiling,' she said suspiciously.

'Was I?'

'Yes, you were!' she said and she gave me a dark look.

'I was just smiling sad-like. Thinking what a lonely poor divil he is.'

We walked on. I watched him slowly pull away from us. I could not get the old Barcarolle out of my head. *River girls, O river girls. How we love your dancing curls . . .*

I was careful not to smile.

# Charlie's Greek

It was twenty-odd years before I saw Rika Prevelakis again, encouraged to visit her by, of all people Charlie, for, of all things fun, in, of all places Athens. 'You will have no trouble in finding her,' he assured me. 'Everybody in the university knows her well.'

She did not look her forty-five years, though she had grown stout, motherly and quizzical. Her hair was still black but not so oily. Her skin looked so delicately soft and pink that I at once remembered our old Dublin joke: 'Charlie, does her face-powder taste of Turkish Delight?', and his cheerful wink in reply. Nothing really betrayed her age except those Swiss rings she wore, too tight on her plump fingers, the faint necklace of Venus on her throat, and the hard ball of her calf. I gathered that her husband, whom I did not meet, was an exporter of fruit, and judging by her charming house, with its modern paintings and pieces of modern sculpture, he was a highly successful one. She told me that her eldest son – she had three – was nineteen, a figure that startled me by taking me back directly to the year after her famous visit to Dublin. So she had made up her mind about Charlie as rapidly as that!

She was delighted to get first-hand news of him, asked many questions about him, and although she now clearly thought of him with a certain good-humoured self-mockery it was plain that she still remembered him with a warm and grateful affection.

'He made me come alive,' she said so simply that the hackneyed words sounded as fresh as truth.

We chatted for nearly an hour; at the end, just as I was leaving her, I said:

'I'd be interested to know how you would sum up Charlie at the end of it all?'

She laughed and put on a stage Anglo-Greek accent:

'My husband always say, and my husband ees a wise man, that whenever he ees asked hees opinion of any man he avoids the opeenion and sketches the leetle portrait.'

Wise man, indeed I thought as I walked away from her delightful house whose garden overlooked the winking blue of the Piraeus. 'Opeenions?' If I asked any dozen men who knew Charlie in his heyday I could guess the sort of juryman's anthology I would collect:

1. Charlie Carton? I'd trust him with my wife! For five minutes.

2. You know, I honestly and truly believe that he was the most outgoing, warmhearted, affectionate young fellow I ever met.

3. A cold, self-indulgent, self-centred, unprincipled hedonist!

4. A genuine lover of mankind, a born reformer and a natural revolutionary. Damn few people like him left in Ireland today.

5. What an orator! Brilliant! And so gay. A most amusing chap. A dreamer and a rebel. The essence of everything that is fine in the Irish nature.

6. Charlie Carton? That Big Mouth!

7. Would you not agree with me that he was rather a nice blend of Don Juan and Saint Francis? I mean, it was a toss of a coin which side of him would win out in the end. By the way, which has won out?

8. Had he any principles at all? I've seen him weep over a sick child in the slums one minute and the next minute deceive a woman, pitilessly.

9. No, I don't think I'd say that Charlie ever had many principles. A few? Perhaps? They certainly didn't lie too heavily on him. Do you remember what Aristide Briand said one time about principles? *Il faut toujours s'appuyer sur les principes; ils finissent par en céder.* Always lean hard on your principles – sooner or later they will give way. One thing about Charlie, though – he was a damn good sport. A real man's man. I liked him.

10. If you want my frank opinion of him he was a flaming bloody humbug.

11. I only knew him in his college days. He'd give you the shirt off his back. You have to forgive a lot to a youngster like that.

12. Soft. To the marrow of his bones. Mush. Incapable of tenderness because incapable of fierceness. Ask any woman. The only good thing they could all say for him would be that if he deceived them he damn soon undeceived them.

There was that night he loaned me his bed-sitter in London. The telephone rang every half-hour from midnight on. Always the same woman or girl.

'No,' I would reply. 'Mr Carton isn't here. I'm only a guest, occupying his room for the night.' Or: 'I assure you Charlie isn't here. For God's sake do you realize it's one o'clock in the morning, and I'm trying to sleep!' Each time she said the same forlorn thing: 'Well, just tell him I just rang up just to say goodbye.' After half an hour back she would come again, and again, and again, until, between fury and pity, I began to wonder whether he had not been expecting exactly this when he so generously offered me the loan of his room. In the end I appealed to the operator. In a tired, polite, English, three-o'clock-in-the-morning voice he said: 'I'm very sorry, sir, I've explained to the lady that Mr Carton isn't there. It does no good, poor thing. Besides, I'm obliged to put the calls through. And mark you, this is costing her a pretty penny – she's on long distance from Strasbourg.'

A Salvador Dali would have painted him with a woman looking out of each eye. His handsome boyish face would have delighted any painter of the high Renaissance in search of the epitome of the power and prime of youth; though it would have been a Florentine painter rather than a Venetian, because of his colourless skin, his buttercup hair, his teeth so small and perfect, his heavy-lidded eyes and because in spite of his bulk he suggested surface rather than roundness, depth or solidity. Neither his face nor his body ever made you conscious of his bones. Stripped for the boxing ring his body looked so soft, almost so feminine that nobody who had not already seen him box would have taken him for a stayer. But he was a stayer, and a frequent winner, obstinate, agile as a boy, a fender rather than a fighter, winning always on points of skill. He outboxed his men and outflirted his women. His boyishness was a fake. At forty-one he was still eager, laughing, garrulous, completely indifferent to appearance, uncombed, almost unkempt, genuinely feckless – he never gave a tuppenny damn about money or possessions and he was generally broke; which may have been the main reason why, even in his schooldays, women wanted to mother him and love him. It must have come as a shock to them to discover that his fecklessness was all-embracing, in every sense of the word. Their pretty boy was as hard as nails. I thought of him the first time I saw that well-known portrait of Lodovico Capponi by Bronzino in the Frick museum – an elegant young ephebe as you might think until you looked into his cool, grey X-ray eyes, and they make you jump like a drop of boiling water on your hand.

One of our jurymen remembers him as a natural revolutionary; another as a rebel. He was born in the wrong place and the wrong age to be either, to the full – in Ireland after the Troubles. How happy he would have been in the thick of them! If he had been shot then (though I have the feeling that he would have outboxed them too) he would now be one of our best-loved boy-heroes. He was born too soon for the war against the Nazis, and the Spanish Civil War was almost over when he was leaving school – together with the not-all-that-young school-mother who took him camping in a pup-tent all around England for the whole of that summer.

'She completed my education,' he used to say, with his usual happy grin. 'What happened to her? I don't know. She got sacked, of course. Oh, yes, she wrote to me. But,' with a graceful circle of his slender strong hand, 'we had completed the medallion of our love.'

That was the way he always talked, romantically; and behaved, ruthlessly. He used to say:

'I'm not really all that Irish, you know! The Cartons were always Cromwellian settlers. And you know how it is with these colonials. One moves on.'

'Would you,' I asked Rika Prevelakis, 'say he was ruthless?'

By way of reply she recalled their last encounter. I already knew (we all knew) something about it. She frankly filled in the details.

It happened at the time of his famous Monster Public Protest Meeting in Forty-one. He was then one of Ireland's active Communists (had we twelve?); in public calling himself a member of the Irish Labour Party which, as everybody knows, was and is about as left as my right foot; calling himself a socialist in private; and (his own confession) in his bed or his bath loudly declaring himself a Marxist. The date is vital. Forty-one was a tough time anywhere in these islands for anyone to be a Communist. The Russians were still holding to their non-aggression pact with Hitler. The many thousands of Irish in the British army felt they were there to fight Communism as well as Nazism. Dunkirk was over. So was the Battle of Britain. But when Spain invaded Tangier, which reminded us all of the existence of General Franco, and the Germans entered Athens, which reminded Charlie of Lord Byron, it seemed the perfect moment to appeal to Ireland about the rights of small nations. Accordingly, Charlie and his friends boldly announced a Monster Public Meeting 'in honour of Greece' for the night of May 4th. The timing could not have been more awkward for all concerned. Had they waited until June Russia would by then be fighting Germany. And four days before the meeting this old flame of Charlie's turned up in Dublin.

She was about twenty-five then; small, dark, reasonably pretty, and so enchanted to find Charlie up in arms in defence of her country that her prettiness bloomed out in a sort of fiery beauty. In every way but one she was a most appealing young woman, as all who met her agreed; and most of us did meet her because from the minute she arrived he was madly trying to fob her off on his friends. (With her, also, it appeared, he had completed the medallion of their love – anyway of his love.) Her one unappealing characteristic was that although she was highly educated – she was then teaching Greek and Greek history in London to Foreign Office chaps – and well informed about most things, shrewd, hard-headed and clear-eyed, she was pathetically unable to perceive that Charlie detested her in proportion as her pursuit of him and his flight from her made them both look ridiculous.

'It's awful!' he sweated. 'It's like a blooming honeymoon! She never lets up for one minute. Can we have breakfast together? What am I doing for lunch? Where am I going for dinner? What about tonight, tomorrow night, the day after tomorrow! Listen – be a sport for God's sake; take her out to lunch for me and lose her somewhere in the mountains.'

One immediate result during those days before the Meeting was that we all had her on the telephone:

'Can I speak to Mr Carton, please?'

'Hello! Is that Rika? I'm afraid Charlie isn't here. He's never here. He doesn't live here, you know.'

'But he must be there! He told me to ring this number if he didn't turn up!'

'Turn up where?'

'In Stephen's Green. At three o'clock. Beside the bust of James Clarence Mangan.'

In the soft Spring rain? Now four o'clock! With a drop on the tip of James Clarence Mangan's green nose? What a good idea for getting shut of a girl! But it was not good enough for Rika.

'Well, he just isn't here.'

'I will ring again.'

'It isn't any good. He never is here.'

'I will ring again. He told me to keep on trying. When he comes please tell him to wait until I ring again.'

We kept asking ourselves, and asking one another why he was so devious with her. Why, if only in sheer kindness of heart didn't he give her the straight uppercut? Was this the soft streak in him? She revealed that whenever he could not avoid meeting her he would sit by her side, hold her hand, gaze into her eyes and in his rich Irish voice recite poetry to her, Byron for preference:

> *Eternal spirit of the chainless Mind!*
> *Brightest in dungeons, Liberty, thou art,*
> *For there thy habitation is the heart –*
> *The heart which love of thee alone can bind . . .*

If she raged at him he would say, soothingly and softly, 'Let the doves settle, Rika! Let the doves settle on your looovely head!' Once, being still as tempestuous as (in his admiring phrase) the stormy Aegean she found him gripping her hand and asking, 'Do I hold the hand of Queen Maeve?' to which she unwisely replied, 'Who is Queen Maeve?' only to find herself at once bewildered, delighted, infuriated and irrecoverably lost in a golden-and-purple tapestry of Celtic myth and legend:

'Our past, Rika, is so old and rich, like your great past, out of which you have come to us, so filled with wonder and mystery that it surrounds us like the murmuring night-sea, crowded with the dim faces and the lost voices of our dead, whose whispering words we never cease to hear and can never hope to understand. In that dark night of the Irish memory there looms always our bull-goddess Queen Maeve, surrounded by the tossing heads of the eternal sea, her herd of white bulls, up to their bellies in the green pastures of the ocean, her spear aloft, her great eyes roolling . . .'

She was never to know how that story ended. Dazed and mesmerised, in the very heat, heart and height of it, she saw him leap up and cry: 'My comrades await me! The battle approaches. Meet me in Davy Byrne's back in an hour's time.'

And there he was pounding down the stairs with her shouting over the banisters, 'But if you aren't there?', and him shouting up from the bottom of the well 'Ring 707070!' She had waited for the length of four whiskeys in Davy Byrne's. She had then found that there is no such telephone number as 707070, and decided that she had misunderstood him: until she saw it the next day in a bookshop window. *I Did Penal Servitude*. By 707070.

By the morning of the Meeting she was beside herself. Up to then she had grudgingly accepted that his secret preparations for the Meeting were a reasonable explanation for his disappearances and non-appearances. But when the Meeting would be over and done with? She knew that that would be either the end or the beginning of everything. Early that morning, so early that the gulls were still screaming down on the garbage bins, she found herself awakened by a knocking on the door of her hotel bedroom. He was standing in the corridor carrying a suitcase, his collar up, his buttercup hair in his eyes, and his eyes staring. He laid the suitcase at her feet and said with a terrible earnestness:

'Rika, when, perhaps even before, the Meeting ends tonight the whole city will be a cauldron of excitement. There may be riots. Blood may flow in the streets. Unless I am in jail, or dead, I will come to this hotel at twelve o'clock tonight with a motor-car. I know the night porter. A grand young fellow from Kerry. One of us. Absolutely reliable. He will let me in by the back door. We will fly together into the mountains where a friend of mine has a lime-white cottage with a roof of golden thatch beside a dark lake where the ripples are for ever washing in the reeds and the wild water for ever lapping on the crags, and there at last we will be alone.'

'But,' she had asked, clutching her dressing-gown to her neck, 'how do I really know that I can really trust you to come?'

He had glared at her.

'Trust? It is I who trust you. This case,' down-pointing, 'contains everything I possess – papers, books, letters, plans, maps. Enough to ruin me for life! Is this hand I grasp the hand of a weakling or the hand of Queen Maeve?'

('Idiot that I was,' she sighed, 'I said "Queen Maeve".')

'At midnight! Be ready! Be waiting! My Grecian bride!'

(Throwing out her arms like a pope she cried: 'And he was gone!')

She went to the Monster Meeting. ('I *attended* it,' she said mockingly.) The evening was a trifle damp. Charlie had said that College Green would be thronged from end to end. Rika found a gathering of about three hundred people most of whom looked like evening strollers, invited by a loudspeaker – and gently shepherded by an Inspector and six guards – off the main thoroughfare of College

Green into a piazzetta called Foster Place. This broad brief cul-de-sac, mainly occupied by banks, is used during the day as a parking space, and commonly used by night for smaller public gatherings such as this. She soon observed that the organizers of the Meeting (old campaigners), having placed their decoy speaker at the farther or inner end of the cul-de-sac, then drew up a convertible motor-car at the other or open end for their main speakers, with the evident intention of leaving themselves a ready line of retreat into College Green if things turned nasty. Across the backs of the convertible's seats they had laid the kind of shallow packing-case which is used for transporting such flat objects as sheets of glass, wall-boards or pictures, a platform just wide enough to support and display one speaker at a time.

The pilot-speaker – a young Trinity College student named Phil Clune, who was later to become chief financial adviser to one of the new African nations – was both careful and lucky enough not to provoke his audience to anything more serious than a few sarcastic interruptions on the lines of 'Lord Byron was a dirty scut!', or 'And what did Greece do for us when we wor fightin' the Black and Tans?', or, in bland disregard for Phil's age, 'And where wor you in Nineteen Sixteen?' She found it all deflating and confusing until the crowd had to turn right around to face the main speakers. Then things began to warm up a bit while still remaining confusing, especially when what she called 'a butchy-looking woman with cropped grey hair like Gertrude Stein' started to speak of the Greek church as a citadel of truth, liberty and outstanding moral courage. This produced shouts of 'What Greek church?', and 'We don't recognize no Greek Church', which made her feel that it was her duty to explain to those near her what the Greek church really was; the main effect of which was to break up the opposition into small growling groups arguing among themselves about which Greek church recognized Rome and which recognized Constantinople. These arguments subsided when the butchy woman started talking about 'the deplorable silence of the Prisoner of the Vatican', whom she referred to, rather over-familiarly, as 'Papa Pacelli'. The result was such angry cries as, 'His Holiness the Pope to you, ma'am!' and, 'Hey! Are you from Belfast?'

At this point, if Rika had known her Dublin properly she would have realized that it would only be a matter of minutes before somebody would start singing *Faith of Our Fathers*, and then it would be high time for all prudent men and women to start edging off to the shelter of the nearest bank-doorway. Instead she started elbowing to the front where she saw Charlie insistently plucking at the tail of Gertrude Stein's skirt and madly whispering something to her that made her quickly wind up whatever she was saying about the Red Dean of Saint Paul's and lumber down off the packing-case.

Charlie at once leaped to the rostrum, his arms spread, his yellow hair blowing in the wet wind, his splendid voice ringing out:

> '"*Eternal spirit of the chainless mind!*
> *Brightest in dungeons, Liberty, thou art,*
> *For there thy habitation is the heart –*
> *The heart which love of thee alone can bind . . .*"

'My friends! I give you a clarion-call that I believe no man or woman listening to me can fail to answer. Up the Republic!'

The crowd did not say a word in answer to this clarion call – which was probably exactly what he wanted since they at once fell silent to listen, though possibly more dominated by his fine orator's voice and his burly lithe boxer's body than by the actual words he said:

('Oh!' she recalled. 'He looked superb. I fell in love with him all over again. Say what you like about him, he had presence. He had guts.')

'My friends!' he shouted. 'We are an old and ancient race whose past is so old and so rich, so filled with wonder and mystery that it surrounds us like the murmuring night-sea that defends our green shores, like the whispering Aegean whose antique memories for ever ripple among the reeds and lap upon the crags of ancient Greece. That darkness of Ireland's primordial memories is crowded tonight with the dim faces and the murmuring voices of our beloved and rebellious dead, whose words we never cease to hear and every syllable of which we fully and clearly understand – whether it be Queen Maeve of Connaught among her herds of milk-white bulls, the tossing foam of the sea, her great spear aloft, her thunderous voice calling to us to remember our birthright, or the quiet, sad figure of Cathleen the daughter of Houlihan passing through the shadows like an uncrowned queen.'

(Rika shrugged. 'Yes! He had only been practising on me. But I felt it made me his colleague! And I was proud of it!')

'My friends!' Charlie was bellowing. 'What do those voices say to us tonight? They say to us: "As we are free and as we will remain free, so must all mankind be free and for ever so remain."'

At which point he whipped a small tricolour from his left-hand inside pocket and waved it over his head – a gesture that actually produced a few approving cheers.

'But, my friends, I said "*all* mankind!"'

At which he whipped from his right-hand inside pocket the blue and white flag of Greece.

'This is the flag of fighting Greece! Tonight we fight under two flags in Freedom's name. Long live Liberty!'

He got a few more cheers. He now produced from his left-hand outside pocket the black swastika on a red ground.

'Does this flag stand for that Liberty? For your liberty, or for the liberty of your children? What can you say, what think, what feel? I will tell you what I think of it.'

And like a conjurer he produced half a dozen matches from his vest pocket, struck them alight on the seat of his trousers, and the Nazi emblem burst into flames. ('I had it well soaked in petrol!' he explained to us afterwards.)

'A sign!' he roared, as the emblem flamed and fell. 'A sign as black as treachery and as red as blood. And only in blood can all its cruelties be avenged!'

At this the Inspector and his six guards began to edge forward. After all, Ireland was officially a neutral country, even if we were more neutral against Germany than for it, and he had issued stern warnings before the meeting began that no word should be said that night contrary to Irish neutrality. But Charlie's next words made him pause, indecisively:

'I mean, my friends, the blood coursing through your veins, pulsing in your hearts with pity for the children in our slums, our unemployed wailing for bread, our aged sick neglected and dying all about us, the thousands of our young men, aye and our young maidens, mounting the gangways day and night to emigrate to foreign shores. Your warm Irish blood can remind you only of the triple cry of Liberty, Equality and Fraternity that led so many of our young men in every age to die for the Republic. That blood is the Rights of Man! That blood is the colour of universal brotherhood!'

Reaching behind him he received, unfurled and waved, blazing in the electric light of the street lamps, the red flag.

At one and the same moment a collective howl of rage burst from the crowd, a female voice began to sing *Faith of Our Fathers*, the Inspector and the guards breasted towards the car, the mob surged forwards, the car rocked and Charlie, to prevent himself from being thrown down among the lions, grasped the lamp-post beside him, and clambered up it like a monkey, still waving the red flag, still shouting 'Long live Liberty!'

(I could see it all in Rika's eyes, immense as two coloured television screens.)

'You know, those Irish policemen were marvellous! They got in a circle around the car and the lamp-post. One of them climbed up and pulled Charlie down by the legs, and the Inspector said, "Run, you bastard!" And, my God, how he ran! Some of the crowd ran after him, but he was too fast for them. I kept clawing at the Inspector and shouting, "I am a Greek girl!" He caught me and threw me head first into the car, my legs up in the air, just as the car started and ran away with me, the butchy woman, four or five men, and the red flag streaming behind them. They stopped in a long, quiet street, pulled me out and dumped me on the pavement, and drove away off down that long street into the fog.

'My face was bleeding. My stockings were torn. I was a sight. When I got up I saw I was opposite the Abbey Theatre and I will always remember the play they were playing that night. It was called *The Whiteheaded boy*. When I saw it I thought of Charlie. My God! I said to myself. He may want to hide in my hotel, and I ran all the way to it. I cleaned myself up to look my best for him when he would come at twelve o'clock. I packed my bags though I was shaking so much I could hardly do it, and then I threw myself on the bed and I cried for my whiteheaded boy. I cried that he knew I had seen him run, that he had been shamed into running for his life, that he was homeless and an outcast. Then suddenly I saw his suitcase and I thought, my God, the police may come here searching for him and find all his papers, and letters, and plans. I managed to lug it to the window-sill – it was very heavy – and I stood it up there outside the window and I drew the blind and the curtains, and I lay down again to cry and to wait.'

'I woke up at half-past one. I ran down to consult with the night porter, Charlie's friend. He was a nice, sweet boy, about seventeen or eighteen. He told me he had never heard of Charlie Carton. I knew then that Charlie would never come. But what was I to do with the suitcase? I decided to take this boy into my confidence. I told him that Charlie was a patriot and a hunted man. I shall never forget what he said to me. He said, "Miss, if he's for Ireland, I'll do anything for him." I cried when he said that, it was so warm, so Greek. When I told him about the suitcase that I must protect with my life, he got a bunch of keys and a screwdriver and we went upstairs together to see what we should do with this terrible suitcase. Between us, this boy and me, we dragged it in from the windowsill – it was by this time soaked with the rain – and we laid it on the ground and we worked on it and at last we managed to open it.'

(I shook my head. Not because I did not know what was in it – Charlie had told me – but in pity for her. Rika looked out of her window down at the waters of the port.)

'I suppose,' she said, 'in everybody's life there is one moment of shame that he never forgets. This was my moment – when that boy opened that suitcase, that nice boy who would have done anything for Ireland. It contained two bags of sand. Nothing else.' She laughed merrily. 'He really was a rascal! I told the boy, "This is probably dynamite." All he said was, "Yes, miss." I stayed in my room until the morning broke. Then I took the boat for London.'

I think if Charlie were with us at that moment I would have struck him. I said:

'Some people would be less kind about him than you. They would say he was a poseur, a sham, an actor.'

'Oh, no! He was much more than that! Much more! He was actor, dramatist, producer and play all in one. And we were his audience. He was always trying to play out some play of life that was real to him for as long as he imagined it, though it was always only real in the way a child's soap bubble is real. A dream full of swirling colours, in the end floating away, exploding silently.'

'Wasn't that a bit hard on the people who had to be his co-actors?'

'You mean people like me? Very hard. If we were foolish enough to think that any of his plays would last. Not hard if we knew that at any moment he would ring down the curtain and start another romantic play in some other theatre, in some other city, in some other country. Even then, of course, it was hard on his fellow-actors whom he left behind out of a job. He was inexpressibly selfish because he was *so* hopelessly romantic. Always dashing away. An artist whose only art was his life. Not a very good artist, I grant you, but, still, an artist.'

'Some people would say he was just a Don Juan.'

'I hope not! That most unhappy race of men. Always chasing shadows. Always hoping. Never sure. He is married.'

Was it a statement or a question?

'How did you know?'

She smiled:

'We all marry. If it comes to that Don Juans – and Donna Juanitas too – are of all people the most certain to marry, in order to be sure at least once before they die, or become impotent. To feel sure that their search was . . . Oh, well, it's too difficult. It took me a long time to work it out. Until I did I hated him more than I have hated anyone else in my whole life. And,' she grinned, 'I'm very good at hating. When I realized that he just had to be what he is I no longer cared.'

'Have you ever written to him?'

She looked at me coldly.

'I am a happily married woman, with three sons. I am a professor. I have an adoring husband. I have a lovely home. Why should I write to him?'

'He has not forgotten you.'

She smiled a gratified smile and we shook hands.

'Give him my affectionate greetings. And all my sympathy.'

I glanced at her, startled until I saw that she did not mean it derisively. Her last question was to ask what he was doing now. I told her: a salesman for sanitary equipment. She was still laughing as she closed the door.

As I walked down through the narrow streets about the port I wondered for a long time what I would say if somebody asked me for my opinion of her. Like all experienced women, sensible, practical, and absolutely without illusions, despising above all those fantasies of which even the oldest men are never entirely free? Or would even she sometimes remember, with a tiny, secret, happy smile, certain earlier days when she had been a little otherwise?

I was amused when I told Charlie of our meeting in Athens, and he at once asked, eagerly, if she remembered him.

'Indelibly!'

'And is she still beautiful?'

'More so than ever!'

I watched his blue X-ray eyes narrow with penetration, widen with the lovely image they received, and then, ever so slowly, relinquish another dream. He had little bags under his eyes. His hair was thin as dust. He said, 'Oh, well! We had completed the medallion of our love!' – and made a graceful circle with his slender hand.

# Billy Billee

'Charms, omens and dreams . . . ' He came on the phrase while ruffling through some sixty-year-old papers. It was in his first penny Catechism, salmon-pink, ear-crumpled, tattered. '*Question:* What else is forbidden by the first commandment? *Answer:* All dealings with the devil, all superstitious practices, such as consulting fortune-tellers or trusting in charms, omens and dreams.' He grunted. He said aloud, 'Oh, yes! Oh, yes, indeed!' He lit his pipe. He gazed out over the harbour. What was her name? He sniff-grinned. Presently the old man was scribbling on the back pages of the Catechism. It finally came out as, and he gave it the title of, *The Ballad of Billy Billee.*

> *Dear Blackie, dear Lottie, Billy Billee,*
> *Star of my morning's simplicity,*
> *Whispering low that love's sorcery*
> *Is hidden in charms, omens and dreams,*
> *That love, ever true to her faithful few,*
> *Like me and like you, gives us our due*
> *Fullness of bliss, eventually.*
> *Did you lie? Once again, my old query!*
> *Did you really dance that night for me?*
> *That November night when I thrilled to see*
> *You leap on the stage of an earlier age*
> *To the whistles and wolf-calls*
> *Of the boys in the front stalls*
> *Immediately under Box B, and me.*

Wearing his best Sunday suit, short trousers, with bare knees, a red bow tie in his celluloid Eton collar, fawn-edged, hot palms clung to the purple carton of Rowntree's Cream-filled Chocolates that, to crown his night, she had put for him on the velvet ledge of Box B. His face felt underlit by the blaze of the footlights.

*Barely fourteen, the first time I'd seen*
*The frilly high kick, the round of a knee,*
*The entrechat flick, splits done to a T,*
*Full of pride as a bride 'till I damn near died*
*When, tier upon tier, they started to cheer,*
*You made it so clear, every wink, every leer,*
*You were dancing for me, for me, in Box B.*

Not even barely fourteen. Thirteen and ten months. And she? Thirty-five, Thirty-six? Thirty-seven? Her red, toy-soldier cheeks hopping, her breasts jumping, her shoulders powder-white, her strong legs tightly cross-gartered. Had she ever been slimmer? Or in those days did men like their women plump? They certainly did not two years later when the stalls were half-filled at every matinée by wounded soldiers in hospital cream-and-blue, smilingly lifting their crutches to the applause of the audience as they faltered to their seats. Their ideal was the teenager, hair shingled, her eyes vast and unrevealing, a slim illusion of innocence.

*Your Bolero brought the gallery*
*Up on their feet in a roar like the sea*
*For you, for me, crouched like a flea,*
*Caught by a spotlight, held by your glare,*
*Your whirligigs, your stamping rages,*
*Cursing like blazes, wishing to Jaysus*
*I was dead in the bed of the old River Lee.*

And he really was praying: 'O dear, kind Jesus, please make them believe I'm her byechild. Brought over from London specially to see mamma dancing on the stage of the Cork Opera House.' (Only the week before she had put him in Box B to see *East Lynne*.)

Not that her figure was news to him. He knew all about it from certain damp afternoons when she showed him photographs of herself on her world-wide tours with The Dainty Delamare Dancers.

'That's me in Singapore, dearie. What fun that was! That's me in Toronto. Look at that snow! Seventy-two inches it was! Me in Auckland. Here's me in Jo'burg. Me and Molly Marples in Bombay. O how I love you! Roll on you rolling rivah! Where the dawn comes up like thundah outa Chiner 'cross the biy.'

She absently stroked his bare knee.

'Across wot biy, Mrs Black?' (In her company he used always talk the way she talked.)

'The Biy o' Chiner! Doncherknow no geography, Jacky dearie?'

She was their star lodger. She had stayed with them for three out of the four years that Jimmy J. Black spent in Cork as manager of the Opera House.

It was upstairs, in their sitting-room, that she used to show him those albums of her youth, one plump hand about his shoulder and the other turning the pages, her armpits exuding a scent that he knew was called Phul Nana because she once bedewed his crumpled handkerchief and his hair with it. Much to the annoyance of his mother who said that he must have been secretly creeping into her sitting-room, which was true, or else that she was 'up to no good' – a remark that inflamed him with enchanting possibilities.

'Up to no good?' Or just that she wanted somebody to talk to? Even if it was only a kid of thirteen, about her days of glory.

> *So long ago, yet I still want to know,*
> *After we parted where did you go,*
> *With what Jimmy or Jack, Tommy or Joe,*
> *To what house on the hill, what toff for a thrill,*
> *What military swell, tight as a kite,*
> *Laughing like hell, well out of sight –*
> *At the back, maybe, of Box A below?*

Face it! Give her thirty-seven. Hot as hell. Common as Get Out. A lecherous, treacherous old bitch. Only a boy would have thought her any better. English, of course. Maiden name, Carlotta Tottle. Born in Highgate, London. Father, a barber. Mother, a dresser in the Palace Music Hall, on King's Road. Pomade, patchouli and poverty.

(Across the bay the lighthouse gleamed, and was gone.)

What a throaty voice she had that day!

'You do know 'Ighget, Jacky dearie, or don't you? I mean, you must at least 'ave 'eard of 'Ighget?'

'No! Ah, no, Mrs Black, I don't know about Ighget at all, at all.'

'Not even 'eard of 'Ihget? My Gawd! Where 'ave you been all these years? 'Ighget's near 'Ampstead. Come on, Jacky! Surely you 'ave 'eard of 'Ampstead 'Eath?'

'Oh yes, Mrs Black, I do know about Ampstead Eath. I've read *The Woman in White*, and that begins at midnight on Ampstead Eath. Remember, Mrs Black?'

'Call me Lottie.'

'As a matter of fact, Mrs Black, Lottie, I know an awful lot about London. I've read all about Sherlock Holmes and I know all about Baker's Street, and the great detective Nelson Lee, and Sexton Blake, and Pedro and Tinker, and I've read Fergus Hume's *The Mystery of a Hansom Cab*. And I know about Paris, too, *The Three Musketeers*, and *The Hunchback of Notre Dame*, and *The Murders in the Rue Morgue*, and *The Scarlet Pimpernel*. And Rome. That's in *Fabiola* by Cardinal John Henry Nicholas Patrick Stephen Wiseman. He was called Patrick because his father was from Waterford. Lots of English cardinals were Irish, you know. That's why we always say that Ireland is the brightest jewel in the crown of Rome. I got *Fabiola* for a present at my First Communion. I read it four times.'

'Fancy that now!' she had laughed – she always made two chins when she laughed. She stroked his head. Then she breathed out a deep sigh.

'See wot comes of reading books. Now, before Jimmy J. brought me to Ireland I'd never read any book at all about this plice. If anyone had told me that one day I'd be living in Cork I wouldn't 'ave as much as known what country they meant. At your age I was dreaming of the wide, wide world.'

At which she looked glumly out of the window at the empty, Sunday afternoon square. There the only noise was a sparrow squeaking in the damp gardens of the Cork School of Art, whose tall, red railings swept around to the front of the Opera House.

It was his clearest image of her, leaning her elbows on the window-sill between the blowing lace curtains, her round, rosy face in her hands, gazing down into the square, or up the lean length of Academy Street at whose distant end she could see a trickle of traffic passing silently along Patrick Street. On fine days she used to spend hours that way. Like a wax statue. Sometimes talking, dreamily. Sometimes, then, her hand would touch his bare knee. A padded hand, not young.

> *Whenever my hand knocks out my dottle,*
> *Cowslip-freckled all over with mottle,*
> *Whenever I pluck the strings of my throttle,*

> *I understand your hand on my knee*
> *As you talked of Rio or Singapore,*
> *And why, with a sigh, more and more,*
> *As I do now, you groped for the bottle.*

When they were in their cups the rows she and Black used to have! Shouting and throwing things at one another, making so much noise that one night his father had to go upstairs and beg them to pipe down for God's sake and the honour of his house.

Black could not complain if she took to the bottle. A convivial fellow who belonged to two boozing clubs and never came home before two in the morning. A fine figure of a man, though! Tall, straight, florid. At his best standing every night in the brilliant front of the Opera House, in his white tie, tails and high choker, ready to click his fingers to an usher, wink at a club crony, bow over a city merchant and his wife, hover about a bunch of English officers down from the barracks. A solid Londoner, mounting guard, like them, over his far-flung outpost of the Empire.

That was her finest hour, too, in a feather boa and a picture-hat two feet wide, in her regular place in Box B, second-up, right-hand side, drinking in the smells of canvas-glue, grease-paint, stale dust, old ropes, faded scent.

One night after a Rugby Final the University students started a small riot in the Pit, and Jimmy came before the curtain. (The Bay of Naples in blue, Vesuvius in scarlet eruption, acres and acres of purple bougainvillaea.) They booed him. He threatened to call in the police if they didn't stop it. They booed louder. He retired in disdain and defeat.

'Oooh!' Lottie said afterwards. 'He looked so brive. Standing up there behind the footlights. Ficing them all.'

Sun-bronzed, gun in hand, topee over his left eye?

But Jimmy was smart. When the students started writing furious letters to *The Cork Examiner* he invited the whole team and their followers to be the free guests of the Opera House the next Monday night, and before the play began he came out again before the billowing Bay of Naples and made such a fine, manly, chummy speech about fair play and goodwill between fellow-sportsmen that they cheered him to the roof and sang *For He's a Jolly Good Fellow* . . .

'I tell you straight! I nearly cried up there in my box, I was so proud of my man!'

Jimmy J. must have made lots of good friends during his four years in Cork city; not one of them ever visited her. You could see it by the bareness of her mantelpiece. Every other coming-and-going lodger, actor and actresses all, used to crowd their mantelpiece with photographs in silver frames and leather frames, smiling relatives and friends, always signed. She had only two pictures to show: one of Jimmy, in his choker; the other of herself – brief frock, bare shoulders, fat, gartered legs, standing against a photographer's woodland scene, ferns to her right, ferns to her left, her plump arms poised as if she were about to rise with a whir out of the heather.

(Directly outside his window a seagull squawked. Alone. He listened. Not a sound.)

He had grown up in Cork, and never known until he left it how utterly alone he had been there, and how little he even still knew about what older people did there. The place was full of rich merchants. Did they have a good time? Did they entertain? Did they throw dinner-parties? Did they have dinner at all? Or did they just have high tea when they returned home at night to their big houses on the hills? Did they have bridge-parties? Travel? Whatever they did they would not have Lottie Black from King's Road, the barber's daughter, among their guests. She was as much outside it all as he was. Two of a kind.

They had no children. Neither of them ever read a book. They read the grey morning paper, the pink *Evening Echo*, the weekly, red-covered *Answers*, the green-covered *Tit Bits*, Horatio Bottomley's yellow-covered *John Bull*, and the black-and-white *London Life*. It was that one that lured him every week into her room to peep at its sepia Art Supplement – always a naked woman, with a figure as plump as her own. After which he might take a deep smell of her Phul Nana, with its label showing a harem-girl dancing in diaphanous trousers. Their whole apartment reeked of Phul Nana. Their lavatory stank of it.

The day she came back unexpectedly to her room and caught him looking at *London Life* . . . When he saw that she saw what he had been looking at he started to bolt.

'Don't run awiy, Jacky,' she ordered, going to the mirror to remove her gloves and her hat, fluff up her hair, and look at him, impaled in the glass, staring at her across the room.

'So soon?' she laughed. 'You know you'll be a 'andsome fellow when you grow up. I shouldn't be surprised if.'

She stopped, turned and surveyed him. Then she sat in her chintz-covered armchair by the open window and with one finger beckoned him over to her. He came and stood by her shoulder and she put her arm around his waist. Her throat whispered it, her eyes looking into his, six inches away:

'I suppose you'd like to see a real woman like that, wouldn't you?'

He hardly had the breath to breathe, let alone to answer, as she undid the top buttons of her blouse, and always looking at him led his hand firmly inside it to the hot blubber of her breast.

'Oooh!' she said. 'Your hand is so bloody cold!'

And threw his hand away, buttoned her blouse and glared into the square. Then she said:

'After I first married Jimmy I used to often wonder wouldn't it be nice if . . .'

She stopped. She looked back at him for a long while. Then she said gently, 'Poor little bastard!' Then she patted his bottom. Then she said furiously, 'Run off to your bloody mama!' He did not dare return for weeks.

She discovered God during her second year with them, one soft, spring night when every place of entertainment in the city was as dark as her boot for Holy Week, the last in Lent. The Opera House was shut; the music-hall; every cinema; our one *Palais-de-Dance*. The two clubs drew their blinds. Men slipped into the pubs by back alleys. Only the pigeons in the square dared to court openly: the male pigeon puffing himself into a muff of feather, displaying his fantail, following the female around with a piteous *luggudygoo, luggudygoo*, snubbed always by a scornful *so what, so what*? Only the black of the ash trees dared to burgeon. At night the square and streets were like a wake-house until a quarter to eight when the patter of footsteps that usually hastened eastward beneath their windows to the Opera House now hastened westward to the parish church of Saints Peter and Paul.

That Wednesday night his mother and he were getting ready to go out to the chapel when they suddenly saw her standing in the doorway of the kitchen, so pale and frightened that she at once reminded him of Lady Macbeth in the sleep-walking scene. His mother, her arms

hooped over her head in the act of shoving her black hatpins into her
black straw hat, cried out at her:

'Lord save us, Mrs Black, I thought you were a ghost!'

'I wish to Gawd in 'eaven I was a man!'

'But, Mrs Black, that's flying in the face of God's holy will!'

'Then wot is God's 'oly will! I've been walking the streets of Cork
until my feet are dropping off me. Everything shut tight as a tick. Jimmy
in his club soaking it up. Wot about me? I awsk you, is it Gawd's 'oly
will for me to become a roaring, bloody secret, soaking, stinking
alcoholic?'

'Why don't you come out with us to the Devotions?'

'Wotcher mean?'

'I mean,' his mother said piously, 'that we must all pray for the sins
of the world. For Jesus in the garden of Gethsemane. Every one of his
apostles abandoning Him. And the priests praying on the two sides of
the empty altar. Until only the one blessed, holy, white candle is left
alight in the whole church.'

'And then,' he had joined in, 'when that last candle is taken away
behind the altar the electric lights go out and we all clap our hands in
the darkness.'

'For the night of Calvary,' from his mother. 'For the end of the
world.'

'The end of the world! Wot end? Wot world?'

'Every Wednesday, Thursday and Friday of Holy Week,' his mother
said flatly.

He sat between them in the church. His mother loaned her one of her
rosaries, which, on seeing other old ladies do so, she kissed repeatedly.
She went with them on the following nights. He went with her alone
to the morning devotions on Holy Thursday, where she loved the
flower-drowned Altar of Repose. She stood for a long while before the
great statue of Calvary, which included Mary Magdalen and the
Madonna, and afterwards she had long, pious talks with his mother and
father about it all.

> *When you said every Magdalen everywhere*
> *Kneels at the foot of Calvary's stair*
> *Singing the song of all girls who bear*
> *The fruit of their ignorant Spring in the Fall,*
> *Whom did you see, rich with maternity,*

*Pushing a pram for all eternity –*
*A planet afloat in the heavenly air?*

Summer is a thin time for churches and cities. He and his mother and father went off on their usual summer holidays to the County Limerick, to watch its crops grow brown and its shallow lakes sink lower still. When they came back they found that she had pinned or pasted on the wallpaper of her apartment, pages upon pages cut from art magazines showing plump, vast-limbed nudes: naked Andromeda chained to her rock, Rubens' half-naked Sabine women, Titian's Profane Love. Every week another naked woman smiled from the wall. They curled there in the heat of an Indian summer that filled the square with boys playing football, little girls playing with skipping-ropes, big girls singing, arm-in-arm, three abreast, around the Opera House, shawled women coming out from the lanes to give their babies to the cool of the night.

By September, her nudes clung like snowflakes to her mantelpiece, her washbasin, billowed from her mirrors. They pursued Black into the bedroom. A line of them hung over their double-bed. They adorned the walls of the bathroom.

Every day his mother said disgustedly that her house was not that kind of a house. She announced one afternoon that either the pictures must go or the Blacks must go, and stamped upstairs to give out her ultimatum. She came down as soft as a dewdrop.

'We can only pray for her,' she said. 'That man,' she cried, with womanly passion, 'should be horsewhipped. All he thinks of from morning to night is drink. Is he a man at all? Ah,' she sighed, looking across at the statue of the Virgin in the kitchen-corner, 'may the mother of sorrows look down on the poor mothers of the world.'

Day after day he used to spy on her from a far corner of the square, gazing up at her window where she sat gazing glumly down at the mothers with their babies, and the children playing; or, at dusk, listening to the arm-in-arm girls singing their love-songs from one lamp-post to the next. Then, in the damp of October, the pictures began to slide to the floor, where their slavey, Bridie McCarthy, used to collect them and bring them, with much lewd smirking and winking, to his mother, who would at once seize them and poke them into the red fires of the kitchen range. Not until they were all gone did he dare to start revisiting her in her room. She let him hold her hand.

Then she discovered Magic. One morning, just after breakfast, she appeared in the kitchen, radiant, gurgling with laughter, to tell his mother what had happened the night before. That week there was a conjurer in the Opera House called Chung Ling Soo. He did all the usual tricks, including The Lady Sawn in Half – a shapely, blonde young woman who also stayed with them and who always laughed merrily when his mother said to her each morning, between relief and disappointment, 'So ye're alive still?' Chung Ling Soo also threw cards, magically produced out of the air, down to the people in the stalls, entitling them to have their fortunes told during the interval by a chiromancer sitting in oriental robes in a little coloured tent in the foyer. Billy had got one of these cards, and had her fortune told.

'I let down my veil and I took off my ring so he wouldn't know anything about me. The things he said to me! O, very clever, you know! O, very clever, those orientals! He said "You've got bed-trouble! The third finger of your left hand is lonely. You will cross deep water in the space of Three. You will meet a fair man under the Crown. You will walk with him under the Star between Trees and Water. He will have great Hearts for you. You will touch Gold. You will have three children."'

She burst into peals of laughter.

That was when she first began to show him those albums of her tours, her arm about his shoulder, her plump fingers touching his knee, her eyes wandering down over the square or up the lean street. It was then, too, that she started going to the Turkish Baths on the South Mall to get her weight down; and to Professor Angiolini's Dancing Studio in Cook Street. She was less and less often in the house, especially on weekends, when, so she said, she was able to use the stage of the Opera House for rehearsing. Finally she announced that, for a charity concert, she was going to dance again.

(The fog-horn grunted like a pig across the misting water of the bay. He laid down his pipe and began to scribble some more figures on the pink cover of the Catechism. She danced on the night of November 10th, 1912.)

> *You danced for a dream, for a gleam in your eye*
> *That no one could spy, not even I,*
> *Perched so close, perched so high*
> *That I once saw you spit in the wings.*

> *At the end I raced down the long corridor,*
> *You winked one eye through your dressing-room door,*
> *And laughed. I turned. I wished I could die.*

The next day when he came hurrying home from school she was gone. The only sign of her was one small, lace-edged handkerchief in the fireplace. It smelled of Phul Nana and whiskey. He kept it a long time. Then he stuffed it into a mousehole in his attic bedroom where – he presumed he might now suppose – the mice dreamed on it and had lots of fat little babies.

Come the next July, just as they were all about to go off again on their holidays, Jimmy Black told his father that she had died and was buried in Bombay.

'Very hot,' he said stiffly. 'Very hot in Bombay.'

It was later rumoured around Cork that she had died in childbirth.

> *Not even a child to dandle.*
> *Charms, Omens and Dreams –*
> *That's a game that's hard to handle,*
> *Though – say it, say it –*
> *You who led me on to play it,*
> *A dream you found well worth the candle?*

# Before the Daystar

When you come out into the Place Pigalle from its dark side-streets your first impression is of its brightness, then crowds, then noise, and then you become one more aimless wanderer around the jammed pavements. Tonight there was a sharp sense of liveliness, even gaiety, almost like the end of a feast-day, although the streets were cold and damp and a cobweb of pink mist hung suspended over the roofs. It was Christmas Eve, about ten minutes short of midnight.

In a corner of the overcrowded terrace of *Le Rêve* five young people, three young men and two young women, sat crushed about a small table behind the fogged glass partitions, talking loudly to make themselves heard above the gabble. The youth who was doing most of the talking looked like a light-weight boxer. He wore a black polonecked sweater; his blue-black hair, harsh as metal, peaked over his forehead like a wound-up watch-spring; his smile was a lighthouse flash. The others interrupted him only to spur him on. Their Scherazade? Their pet liar? Indulged. Bantered. Approved.

In a pause in his flow of talk the fair-mousy, pretty girl at his side tilted her scarlet tarboosh so as to tickle his cheek with its blue, silk tassel, and said, 'Happy now, Andy? This is better than Dublin, isn't it? Or isn't it?'

He gave her his white grin, gripped her frail arm and squeezed it.

'As happy, Jenny, as a lamb with two mothers.'

He turned swiftly to the fat youth at his other side. 'Jaysus, Fatso, I wonder what'd we be all doing this minit if we were back in Dublin?'

Fatso raised a finger for silence, groped inside his mustard-and-cress overcoat and slowly, very slowly, drew a vast, silver half-hunter from the well of his fob-pocket. He clicked it open with the air of an ancient out of an ancient world, considered its convex face, smooth, shiny and milk-white as his own; and pronounced in a slow Abbey Theatre brogue.

'I would be afther thinking, dearly beloved, that at this minit we would all be up in the Lamb Doyle's, or in The Goat, or The Cross Guns, or The Purty Kitchen where George the Fourth had his first glass of Guinness, being thrun out on our ears for the fourth time in succession. Althernatively, Andy, you would be snoring in your little white cot in your little white home in Templeogue.'

'Would I now? Well, then, let me tell you, Mister Laurence-O-bloody-well-Toole, I'd be doing no such a thing. I'd be being hauled off by my ma by the short hairs to Midnight Mass. That is, after the usual couple of preliminary breast-wallopings with the Dominican fathers up in Blackhorse Lane.'

He paused to turn to Biddy.

'Our privileged heathen,' he mocked.

Champagne-blonde, older than Jenny, not pretty, her splendid pigeon's bust straining her white sweater.

'Yes?' she queried, in an English voice so tiny that the first time they met her they had asked her if she had the pip.

'I mean Confession,' he explained, politely flicking two imaginary crumbs, one-two, from her bosoms. 'The annual clear-out. Old Father Berengarius. A mile of hardy sinners queuing up before me. The ould chapel as cold as a vault, and the wind under the slates moaning like a hundred banshees. He's as deaf as a post. Very convenient for yours truly. Doesn't hear a blooming word you say. Did I ever tell ye the night he disgraced me ma?'

He received their quizzical attention.

'There she was, late on Saturday night, inside in the confession box, asking him, if you please, was it a sin for her to believe in spirits and ghosts, and the mile of hardy boys outside all grumbling, and growling and rearing to get in and get out before the pubs closed on them. "Having commerce with ghosts", was what she called it. "What are ye saying to me?" says he, and his hand to his ear. "Is it a sin, Father," says she at the top of her voice, "to have commerce with ghosts?" "Speak up," says he in a roar that you could hear down at O'Connell Bridge. "To have commerce with ghosts, Father," she squawks, and the buckos outside all leaning sideways to hear the pair of them. "You have been having commerce with goats!" he roars at her. "At your age?"'

Once more they gave him the soft accolade of their laughter. Modestly rejecting the honour he turned aside and as suddenly turned back. Crook-necked he gestured to the dark street behind their corner café.

'Will yez look, boys! The foxy-headed whore is back again. Trying to click a GI she is this time. They're brazen tonight. Out in the open. He's twice her height. He'll make pancakes of her.'

They all swayed. The nearest of them to the glass partition was Mackinnon. He peered out under his black Homburg hat, low over the boils on his forehead. She was a small, skinny woman in a sheepskin jacket, a white beret, a white satin bottom as taut as two mushrooms.

'She must be frozen,' said Jenny pityingly.

'Behold the fruits of French logic,' Biddy piped. 'They close the brothels and every woman in Paris gets pneumonia. That foolish man will be streaming at the nose tomorrow morning.'

'I consider it most unseemly,' said Mackinnon. 'On Christmas Eve!'

Andy pointed his index finger at him, pulled the trigger, said, 'Bang, you're dead!' They laughed. They knew their Mac. A tongue of gall. He had never said an original word in his life. He worked at the Irish embassy. He would go far. They called him Mac the Knife.

'Mac!' Andy said, 'I wish you to understand that I am on the side of all rebels, exiles, outcasts and sinners. What Genet called The Saints of the Underworld.'

Biddy calmed his clenched fist with one scarlet-netted palm.

'Easy, Andy! And it was not Genet. Pasolini. And I do trust, dear boy, that you are not going to go all romantic on me tonight. I mean, talking about Dublin. And your mamma. And Midnight Mass. And Confession. And Dominican fathers. And, now, French hoahs.'

He was too fascinated by the comedy in the street to heed her. She enlisted Jenny's help.

'Jenny, is our broth of a boy about to get plawstered on us yet once again?'

'Haven't you observed?' Jenny sniffed, 'whenever he takes to the bottle in a big way it always means the one thing? Some new crisis with his precious Deirdre.'

'Deirdre?' she whispered. 'But that little Irish fool doesn't mean a thing to him. Deirdre is merely the girl he sleeps with.'

At this Jenny laughed so bitterly that Biddy peered one-eyed at her.

'I trust, my dear, that you are not getting soft on him? I mean, as one old harridan to another, you must be hitting twenty. And,' she whispered out of the side of her mouth, 'he is only a poo-o-oodle!'

Jenny considered him seriously. In Paris less than six months, as Dubliny as the first day they met him, light-headed, light-hearted, feckless, a liar, much too fond of his liquor. Nobody was ever going to travel very far on his roundabout. Certainly not Deirdre. As if he felt her looking at him he grinned at her and turned back to the street. She said loftily to Biddy, 'I assure you!'

'There is no need to protest, dawrling. We're all gone about Andy. That irresistible Irish charm. He's even gone about himself. It's his disease.'

Under the table Jenny felt his hand creeping slowly over her knee.

'Andy, why didn't you bring Deirdre tonight?'

His hand withdrew. He sighed, 'Poor little Deirdre.' He burst into a sudden passion. 'Jenny! Do you know what I am? I'm a sink!'

'Tell us, Andy,' she said sympathetically, 'why are you a sink?'

'No! You tell me! Examine me! Have no mercy on me! Tell me what's wrong with me.'

Mac the Knife tapped his arm. His speckled forehead became suffused with venom. He assumed a stage-Cockney's wheeze.

'I'll tell you, chum, wot's wrong with you. You're 'omesick for dear, old, dirty Dublin. Your wrists long for the chains. Your back aches for the lash. Cheer up, chum, this time next year you'll be back there for keeps, with no Pigalle, and no cafés, and no night-clubs, and you'll have your eye on a good job, and be wearing more holy medals than a Lourdes veteran, and you'll be running off like a good little boy to Midnight Mass, and Aurora Mass, and Third Mass, and Fourth Mass, and . . .'

Andy leaped up. His chair fell. All over the terrace heads turned lazily towards them. A waiter paused in his stride.

'Do you want a sock in the kisser?' he roared.

The two girls dragged him down.

'Andy!' Jenny chided and stroked his arm as if he was a cross dog. 'Aa-a-ndy!'

He retrieved his chair. He sat down glowering. Then he leaned over, seized Mac's hand and shook it warmly, rapidly, hurtingly.

'Mac! My old pal from schoolboys' happy days! As one unconverted and thoroughly corrupted Irish crook to another leave us be honest for one brief moment of our all too long and useless lives. Leave us admit that we've both been emancipated by La Belle France. We've killed Mother Ireland. We're free!' His grin fell dead on the table. His visor sank slowly over his toddy. 'We're emancipated. And disbloodywellillusioned.'

'I knew it,' Biddy piped to the striped awning. 'The Celtic Goat of Pure Romance. I saw it coming. I felt it in my bones. And I warn everybody present that I shall not be able to bear much more of it.'

Andy's head shot up.

'Anyway I gave up all that Holy Joe stuff years ago. I was a converted atheist at the age of seven. I was thrown out of school at fourteen for denying the existence of God. I proved it by logarithms.'

'You don't say so?' Mac jeered.

Andy shot him again on a quick draw, turned to Jenny, put his arm about her narrow waist and confided into her ear for all to hear.

'Jenny, my love, I'll tell you why I'm a sink. This morning Deirdre said to me. "Don't go out from me tonight, love! Don't leave me on Christmas Eve," says she. "Okay," says I, "come along with me." "You'll only get tight again, shéri," shays she. "Don't abandon your own loving, little Deirdre," shays she. "Spend it alone with me," shays she. But I did leave her! And I *am* going to get tight! And to hell with her! God Almighty, does she want to turn me into a monk? Imagine a fellow not having a couple of jars with his pals on a Christmas Eve! The trouble with Deirdre is she's not emancipated. There's one for you, Mac, who'll be back in Dublin in six months. In five years she'll have a squawl of kids around her saying the Rosary every night. Still and all I did ditch her. And there's no getting away from it. I'm a lousy sink!'

She stroked his cheek with one long finger.

'I don't think you're a lousy sink, Andy. I think you're a sweet sink. You just can't hold your liquor, any more than you can hold your conscience.'

He tightened his arm about her waist.

'Jenny! You understand me better than anybody else in the entire, global world. You're the grandest girl in all creation!'

'Better than Deirdre?'

He banged the table and shouted.

'I'm worse than a sink. I'm a flamin', flittherin', filthy, finished-off sink!'

'Jesus help me,' Biddy moaned, and began wearily to powder her nose.

Jenny whispered something into the whorls of his ear, he let his head sink on her shoulder, her blue tassel fell over his eye, he put his arm around her again. Mackinnon twirled a palm of antique boredom at Larry Doyle, who beamed pleadingly at him as if begging indulgence for all young lovers. Suddenly Andy flung up his head with a wild jerk.

'Boys and girls! I have a smashing idea! Why don't we all tumble into a taxi and go off to Midnight Mass in the Irish Church?'

'Here it comes,' said Biddy, brightly snapping her compact. 'Back to our vomit. Cassandra the daughter of Priam, that's me. Often heard, rarely heeded, always right. Never let it be said that I am a spoilsport,' she begged them all, gathering up her handbag and a four-foot-long, peacock-blue umbrella. 'Which is this church you mentioned, Charlie? Church of Ireland? Papish? Celtic synagogue? I'm with you all the way even to the Mosque. Or would it do if I led you to some good, old, solid ten-by-twenty Nonconformist tin chapel somewhere?'

Mackinnon rose, took off his black hat, held it to his chest and spoke with Castilian pride.

'*Mademoiselle, vous oubliez que je suis Catholique.*'

She made a soft noise like a duck getting sick, they all laughed, and while Andy was paying the bill they scrambled out on to the pavement. It was jammed by the crowd outside *Le Jardin d'Eve* looking at lighted photographs of naked women with breasts like udders. Biddy said in annoyance to Jenny. 'I notice they always leave him to pay the bill.'

'The boy is a fool. He loves to play the milord.'

'Tell me, does he always get religion when he starts thinking of Deirdre?'

'You've known him as long as I have. Are you getting soft on him now?'

Biddy shrugged.

'I wouldn't mind having a bash at old Andy.'

'He's not your sort. He is what you said. A poodle. A puppy. He's just a kid. Let him alone.'

The kid rushed out and hooked the pair of them into the crowd. They saw the redheaded whore, her eyes circling slowly about her like a slow waltz, glance at and dismiss Mac and Larry. Andy laughed, 'Business bad tonight.' It occurred miserably to Jenny that her eyeballs would be circling under her green eyelids even in her sleep. Larry called out, 'The Irish Church is miles away, can't we go somewhere else?' The crowd bumped them. The doorman of *Le Jardin d'Eve* barked at them to come and see the most nude women in the whole world. 'Ask him,' Andy suggested, and Larry approached him. While Larry and he were comparing silver half-hunter with gold half-hunter Biddy said he was like Georges Brassens' daddy. Jenny said he was like her own daddy. The barker closed his watch, directed them to the Rue des Martyrs, called after them '*Vite, mes enfants! C'est tard!*' Then, behind them his voice soared, '*Les plus nues du monde . . .*'

They turned from the lights, and the crowds, and the rumbling beat of Pigalle's heart into the narrow street whose prolonged silence gleamed distantly with coloured windows. By the time they were filing into the church the congregation were shuffling erect for the Gospel. Biddy halted inside the door. Mac and Larry stayed with her. Andy probed along the aisle and found two empty places in the front row directly facing a small Christmas manger with the Infant, the Virgin, Saint Joseph, the cow, the ass, the shepherds and the coloured kings huddled about a crib under an amber light and a bald electric star. Whoever had arranged the *crèche* had perched a stuffed robin redbreast on the edge of the cot. Andy nudged her, nodded at it, and winked conspiratorially.

She was back, one frosty morning, four years ago, at home, awakened by a thud on her bedroom window: it was a robin lying stunned on the window-sill. In her nightgown by the open window she had held it, throbbing between her palms, staring at the one big eye staring up at her, and for that one sleepy moment all life was as simple as a captured bird. She opened her palms, the robin flew off into the frosty air, and the morning star gleamed above the hills and the murmuring beach. *In splendoribus sanctorum.* The priest was intoning the psalm. In the brightness of the saints, she remembered from other midnight masses. *Ex utero anti luciferam* . . . From the womb before the day-star, I begot Thee. Did he remember? She touched the hand beside her and they looked at one another. Thereafter, silently from her white shore her bright moment ebbed. It fell as softly as a leaf from a book, a rose petal. Her window empty, her beach dry, she saw, leaning against a pillar beside them, the woman in the sheepskin coat. When the sanctus tinkled everybody else but she knelt. When everyone raised their heads she was still standing there, staring blankly in front of her. Andy was gone. There was no sign of him down the aisle, nor could she see the other three.

Crossly, she made her way back to the doorway, and out to the street. It was so dark that at first she saw nothing; then she made out the four figures on the opposite side of the street clumped like a bunch of gangsters, smoking cigarettes. She crossed over.

'Why did you come out?'

Biddy slowly smoothened her netted fingers and said sullenly, 'It wasn't my show, dawrling.' Larry Doyle looked uncomfortably at Mac the Knife who made a half-moon with his hangdog mouth, performed a high, dissociating shrug, and looked at Andy who let out a zany guffaw and then said sulkily, angrily, 'We should never have gone!

'It was you who proposed it!'

'We shouldn't have done it!'

'I thought they were doing it very nicely?'

He appealed to them, boxer-crouched.

'When you don't believe in a thing what is it but tomfoolery?' He stood back, his claws to his chest. 'I don't believe in anything. It's all kid stuff. I felt indecent inside there.' He shot out his left. 'And that bloody redhead in there finished me off. God Almighty, people have to be honest, don't they? They have to come clean, don't they? When I saw that wan in there I felt, Jaysus, what am I but another dirty bloody hypocrite?'

Jenny slapped his face, stepped back in dread, ran a few yards downhill, he after her, turned, a lean hare, ran faster and faster until he caught her, whirling her against a black wall under a street lamp, gasping, her palms spread against him. They panted.

'What's wrong, girleen?'

'What's wrong is that you *are* a hypocrite. First Deirdre. Then that street-walker. Who are you going to blame yourself on next? Me? Biddy? Why don't you go back to Dublin and rot there? It's what you want, isn't it?'

She turned to the wall and burst into tears. He waited while she sobbed. When she was quiet she turned and asked him for his handkerchief, wiped her eyes, said, 'May I blow?', and blew.

'Why should I want to go back to Dublin? I'm happy here, with you, and Biddy, and all the gang.'

'Are you?' she challenged. She gave him back his handkerchief. 'I think, Andy,' she said quietly, 'you'd better go back now to Deirdre. You know she'll be waiting up for you all night.'

He made a noise of disgust.

'She's not the answer.'

'And what is?'

He took her arm and led her back to the group. Sacerdotally, Larry blessed them with a sweeping arm, '*Benedicat vos. Pax vobiscum.*' Mackinnon said, with immense bonhomie. 'A Happy Christmas to the happy pair!' Biddy said, coldly, 'And what does one do now?' Larry threw his arms around Jenny, and intoned.

> *My beloved, drink the cup that cheers*
> *Today of past regrets and future fears,*
> *For, ah, tomorrow we may be*
> *With yesterday's seven thousand years.*

Nobody commented. The woman was standing alone on the step of the porch looking across at them. As they looked at her Andy walked over and spoke with her. Then the two walked off slowly, out of sight.

Mac gave a beck of his head to Larry, said to the girls, '*Le Rêve*', and the two of them went off, hunched together, nose to nose, back to Pigalle. Jenny whirled and stared downhill towards the pink glow over Paris. For a while, Biddy considered her rigid back. Then she contemplated her long slim legs. Then she regarded her left thumb, wiggling it double-jointedly. Then she looked up at the sky and said, 'Andy once told me he spent an entire night discussing the works of Guy de Maupassant with a hoah in Marseille. He said they were still at it when the sun rose behind the Château d'If. Odd! Even in Marseille the sun does not rise in the west. I shouldn't worry about him if I were you, Jenny. He will be back in *Le Rêve* in half an hour as chaste as the dawn and without as much as a franc in his pocket. He'll tell us that she has a grandmother in Provence, or a child in hospital, or that she reads Pascal every night. The party's over. The night is bitter cold. And I am sick at heart. We'll get a taxi and I'll drop you at your door.'

'I want to walk,' Jenny said sourly.

Biddy's fledgling's voice took on an edge.

'In this cold? To Saint Germain? Do you want to die for him, like Mimi?'

'What is he up to? Always expiating for something or other? What's the point of it? Why doesn't he grow up? If he does give that woman all his money he'll only leave Deirdre penniless for a month, and borrow from us, and then borrow from his mamma to pay us back.'

'Unlike us he is young and innocent. It is what makes him so appealing. In his bothered way he's different.'

'Or is it just that all Irish men are different? Look at the other two. My God! What are we *doing* with them?'

Biddy hooted.

'Dear child, you obviously have no idea what Englishmen are like. I know! I've put dozens of them through my little white hands. Full to the gullet of guilt, black silences, sudden glooms, damp despairs, floods of tears and then that awful, manny, British laughter and "Let's have another one, old girl". Paris has been absolute bliss after London. Every Frenchman a swine. It's been such a relief. It's his only trouble – he thinks he's a sink and he isn't. It takes centuries to produce a really first-class sink. Still he shows promise. The right woman could do a lot for him. Not Deirdre, a silly little Dublin chit, just as stupid as himself. Let's get a cab. I'll pay for it and drop you right at your door.'

'I still want to walk,' Jenny said stolidly.

'It's savage. My ears are dangling by a thread. A cab, for God's sake!'

'Are you trying to get rid of me?'

Biddy regarded her with admiration, and shrugged.

'Biddy! What do we see in him?'

'Ignorance? Hopelessness? Eagerness? Terror? Charm?'

'But he is such a fraud!'

'And as you said, such a fool!'

'But, you say, innocent?'

'As a rose!' Biddy sighed.

'Let's go back to *Le Réve* and see if he does come back.'

'He will come back. His type always comes back. One of the lads.'

He came, wildly excited, bustling in, penniless, full to the gullet of lies and boastings – or, if they were not lies, of fantasies, and if they were not boastings, of dreams.

'All our lives,' he pronounced, 'we dream of love, and love eludes us. We have fled, Mac, from the sow that eats its own farrow. And all the time we dream of our childhood and are never free of it. O exiles of Erin, love ye one another. My bloody foot! Two single tickets to Dublin, that's the right ticket. But where shall we find her? Every mis-match Irishman a born matchmaker, and good at it. Saving others who cannot save himself. Sitting in a Dublin pool of drink and dreaming of the Arc de Triomphe. I told her I'd follow any woman to the ends of the earth but not to the end of the world. Nobody would take a fellow up on that! Gimme the Queensberry Rules and be God I'll not complain. I want a loving, lovely, innocent wife!'

'With squads of babies?' Jenny asked and felt his hand start to rove over her knee.

'Squads and squads of them!'

'All chawnting the Rosary?' Biddy piped mockingly, and pressed his other hand.

Their mockery could not halt him. The girls looked at one another with big eyes, shook their heads and made wry mouths of self-astonishment. Mac's eyes kept closing and half opening from sleep and drink. 'What are we waiting for?' he asked dully. Larry Doyle looked at his turnip-watch and sighed, 'It's gone two o'clock.' The terrace was empty. The pink haze fell as glistening rain on the street. Nobody stirred. Even their talker was silent.

After a while he spoke, looking around at them sullenly.

'I'm going to take a plane to Dublin in the morning. Who'll lend me the money?'

# £1000 for Rosebud

Rosebud met him one summer afternoon in London while she was lying flat on her face on the pavement of St James's Street outside Prunier's restaurant, during an air-raid. 'Suited him down to the ground,' she used to say long afterwards, with a laugh, 'I didn't stand a chance.' When the bomb fell somewhere in Green Park she looked sideways and saw a handsome young fellow in the RAF lying beside her, head on elbow, pensively admiring her. He might well admire her – hair like a wheat-field in September, two big frightened eyes of cornflower-blue, aged, he rightly guessed, about nineteen, and nicely fat. Plump girls were at a premium in London during those years of food rationing. She was happy to let him lead her off to the Ritz for a drink, downstairs in the crowded bar; all present, he assured her, being either spies or counterspies, heroes or whores. He told her that he was in Intelligence, with the effective rank of Wing Commander, and that his father owned a racing stable in Ireland. His name was Mick Donnelly. He had the mouth of a boy, the jaw of a man, and wicked brown eyes. She told him she was Rose Powis, straight off a farm in Wiltshire. Within an hour they were madly in love, within a week she had slept with him, a month later he married her, and the next day he left her, for Sicily and the Italian campaign, promising that when the war was over he would transplant his Rosebud to the finest house in Mayfair where they would live like a king and a queen.

She believed every word he said, and she knew that nothing he could ever do or say all her life long could hurt or surprise her. Within two months of his return, demobbed and jobless, he had surprised her so often and so variously – even though she was by then twenty-two, and those three years in London had taught her a lot – that she never mentioned him afterwards to any old, wartime chum without ending up, 'Say what you like about Clarence, life is never dull with him.'

The 'Clarence' had been her lightest shock.

'You see, Rosebud,' he explained to her, 'it was all mummy's fault.

She christened me Clarence Michael, after the Duke of Clarence, and then, God knows why, always called me Mikey. I hated it but it stuck. Furthermore, the proper spelling of our name is not Donnelly but Dunally. So, from this on I am Captain Clarence Dunally. Much better style! More dash to it! And much more in keeping with the kind of appointment I want, and,' sternly, 'mean to get.'

She had been Mrs Mick Donnelly. Now she was Mrs Clarence Dunally. She thought it great fun. She was game for anything – so long as it was not mean, or calculating, or nasty. Reared on a farm, educated by a war, total and timeless at every moment, she had the simple appetites of a kid-goat and was as innocent of morals as a child. In other circumstances, depending on what wind blew into her eager sails, she could have been anybody, done anything, died in the swamps of Ravenna wearing a red shirt, stabbed Marat in his bath, been a Manon or a Margherita, Lady Macbeth or Lucy Lockit, Judith or Saint Joan.

'Fine!' she said. 'Clarence! And what's my name?' she asked with fond assurance.

'You,' he said throatily, 'will always be my Rosebud, let's go to bed.'

It also surprised her a little, but it did not trouble her, as long as the funds lasted, that he showed no sign either of getting a job or of much wanting to get one. She was merely sad for him when he broke the news to her that his dad's racing stable had gone bankrupt during the war so that, as he put it, he had 'no very large prospects for the future'. She was further surprised, but more angered, for his sake, when he explained that owing to certain, low army intrigues, too complicated for her to follow, he would not enjoy the pension due to a Wing Commander. Only one thing he did really shook her – the place where he took her to live.

On his return to London and civilian life they had gone straight into Claridge's for three gloriously spendthrift nights, and then into a lodging-house in Paddington. They were still there two months later. What with the bombing, and no houses being built, and mobs of extra people in London, they soon found that they would be lucky to get houseroom anywhere. At last, nagged just a tiny bit by her, Clarence solved the problem overnight. He rented a small houseboat, called *Evangeline*, permanently moored to the towpath above Walton-on-Thames.

'Do us for a few months,' he said. 'Just to get over a bad patch. Just long enough to give me time to explore the ground at my ease.'

One glance at *Evangeline* made her eyebrows soar and her heart sink. She felt her first hint of fear. She saw an ancient, waterlogged wreck; everything metal on it was rusty, the glass in the tiny portholes was broken; its woodwork had fed generations of woodlice. It had, obviously, stood, lain or leaned there for so many years that nothing now kept it from keeling over in the mud but its gangplank, its hawsers and its long-settled condition. She foresaw fog, smelled rats, noted that it was a mile from the nearest shop, guessed that it must be twenty from Mayfair, and on dark nights every step of that overgrown towpath would be a menace. She threw her arms about his neck and said, 'Clarence, how clever of you! We'll make it simply lovely. Let's get cracking at it right away!'

It was October and raining. They worked on *Evangeline* like galley-slaves all through that autumn and into the fogs of winter. They caulked the yawning timbers, replaced what they could afford of the rotted woodwork, painted the superstructure in pink and every inch inside in white. Rosebud lined the scuppers with Henry Jacoby geraniums in toffee-tins and hopefully set an Albertine rose in a tub to grow across a trellis above the companion-way.

One afternoon in November, when they had almost finished the job, that is, done about as much to the junk as they could do, a lone passer-by along the towpath paused to watch them, said, 'Looking ahead to the summer? It will be fun,' and winked. They thanked him and said yes, it would be nice for weekends in the summer. When he had passed on they looked at one another shamefacedly. They had come to know from the various words dropped by tradesmen and others that that was about what the river had always rated in those parts, a raffish wink. Clarence said nothing. He had already noted that Rosebud could never mention the name *Evangeline* without an embarrassed flutter of her eyelids. She had already observed that whenever he gave his address to a stranger he let his hands rise and fall feebly like a dying duck, though if the man said encouragingly, as he usually did (with or without a wink), 'Lucky to have anything these days!', Clarence would always gallantly agree, and always add, 'It's not exactly Mayfair, of course.'

That night – they were below, finishing their dinner of sausages and mash, and their one bottle of beer – she said, probing him, 'Clarence, if this isn't exactly Mayfair, what *is* it?'

'It's County,' he said bravely, and then hit his fist a wallop on the deckbeam two feet over his head. 'Rosebud, we've got to get out of it. We're mad to be living in this Chinese sampan. Into the Rialto! Into Mecca! I said Mayfair, and I mean Mayfair! Some people might even settle for a mews off Pont Street, or a mews in Kinnerton Street. They might even settle for NW1 – all those super Nash terraces. But not me! If I could only lay my hand on a thousand quid, if I . . .'

'Here, here, hold on! What's a supernash terrace?'

'Nash? Great English architect. Don't you know? Haven't you heard? Sir Henry Nash. Wonderful houses. Pure seventeenth century.'

'Seventeenth century? That was the time of Queen Elizabeth. They must be as rotten as this junk. And what's wrong with a nice little house in Hampton, or Kingston, or Richmond, or even in Walton-on-Thames?'

He looked at her as coldly as if she were a stranger.

'Did you say Walton-on- . . .? Rosebud, I see I've got to take your education in hand.'

He had placed, she had seen them but never looked into them, three books on a small bulkhead shelf. He shoved aside the plates, the beer-bottle and the bits of holly branches she had stuck in a milk-bottle, took down the three books and lobbed them on the table. Then he stared at her, like a dentist gazing speculatively at a really hopeless tooth.

'Where can I begin? This is *Who's Who*. Observe! A plain statement. No question-mark. Everybody, I mean everybody, is there – who counts. This one is *The Home Lawyer*. I've won a dozen court-martials out of that.'

She ruffled it. It was, in due course, to become her favourite book of the three, so much so that whenever she laid it on the table it opened of its own accord, as softly as a sea-anemone, at the chapter headed 'Divorce'.

'This one is the map of the known world. *The A.1 Atlas of London and Outer Suburbs. Latest, revised edition*. Three and six. This tells us where everybody out of *Who's Who*, who lives in London, lives. Now!'

He opened it. Like a field-marshal he spread his hands above the web of black streets and began.

'Operation Rosebud! Here,' drawing a swift line about Mayfair, 'is our objective. The heart of W1. But don't let that fox you. Soho is also W1. And a damned shame it was to put it there. Good Lord, if it comes to that Tottenham Court Road – and we all know what that means – is W1. But this,' finger on the M of Mayfair, 'is the citadel we shall enter and conquer. There are alternatives? NW1? You've got some really posh places up there. Clarence Gate. Or York Gate. Down here, SW1. Pretty good. Backs on Belgravia. Which, you observe, backs on Buck Palace itself. SW3? Tricky, but not bad. I've been tempted in my time by Cheyne Walk, even Brompton Square. Time was when I wouldn't have sniffed even at Egerton Gardens. Though, God knows, the way the world is going nowadays you never know who might be cowering in some godawful square off dim places like the Fulham Road. Would you believe it, Rosebud, I know a depressed peer who's actually reduced to a boarding house in Bayswater. And a pal of mine told me the other day, it made my hair stand on end, that he knows a retired general who is actually living on a barge beside the gasworks on the Grand Union Canal at Hanwell! Could you ever believe such a thing would happen?'

'If you say so, Clarence!'

'The moral is plain!' he snapped. 'Never give up a major objective for a lesser. I have set my face against that pitfall. Because if you once let yourself think that you might put up with less than the best you'll end up by taking less than the less. And in the end, less than the less than the less! No! A garret in Mayfair, Rosebud, even a simple garret will do us for a first foothold. I know so much. I can teach you so much. If we could only lay our mittens on a thousand quid and a garret in Mayfair I know, I simply know, that with your beauty and my brains we'd be on top of the social tree in six months.'

'But, tell me, Clarence, supposing we did get a garret in Mayfair, what would we do there?'

'Haha! Second stage of Operation Rosebud. It wouldn't really matter a damn what we did, ye know! Infiltrate. First get in. Once in – spread. I could start by making leatherbelts for Fortnum and Mason like that fellow Roskolski who began with five quid in a back-lane off Bruton Street and now has a swank shop in Bond Street. And how did he do it? He got to know the right people! You could sew old school ties for Burlington Arcade like that Polish Countess who came there as a kitchen-maid and now has that posh boutique in Pont Street. Clients, friends, backers! That's the ticket. I could even be a taxi-driver and some day pick up Lord Who's Who, the fellow that started Marks and Spencers on a borrowed five hundred quid. "Where do you live?" he'd say. "Oh," I'd say, casually-like, bowling him over on the spot, "I've got a little hole in Mayfair. Why don't you drop around some night, my lord, and have a good Russian vodka? I could tell you things about London that not even you know." Into my lap in the click of a finger! But supposing I said, "I've got a little hole in Pimlico?" do you think he'd bite? See what I mean? Be around. Have your ear to the ground. Be in the way of luck. Be where the pickings are. Plant your knowledge where it's going to bear juicy fruit. But how in hell can we possibly hope to get to know anybody from a base like this? I tell you, Rosebud, I'd commit the most foul, fiendish, hellborn, stygian, diabolical, unforgivable crime this minute for even a coal-hole on the uttermost edge of Mayfair.'

She laughed fondly at him, patted his head, told him he wouldn't hurt a flea, and went off with the dishes to the galley.

'Little do you know me, my lass!' he called after her. 'Little do you know!'

Rubbing the greasy dishes with her rosy fingers and throwing the scrap out of the porthole into the flowing river she wondered. Three months on the houseboat as a wife had taught her more than her three years in London as a grass-widow. She had foreseen the rats frisking under the floorboards, the fog lying thick as wool on the river. She had not foreseen the savage damp, or how lonely the drip off the poplars could sound on the deck when he was in town, the discreet pawnshops of Kingston and Richmond, or that Clarence was full as a honeycomb of secret places where no woman would ever go. She was often reminded of him by their cat, Rodolphe, squatting by the stove with eyes half-closed in veiled aloofness. On such lonely days and dripping nights she had sometimes got the feeling that *Evangeline*, stuck in the mud, moored by the edge of the flowing river, was an image of her own life in those three years since she left the farm at Tisbury for the blackout, the bombs, the excitement of London. Which was why, on many such nights, silent except for more instructions about Operation Rosebud, more nervy plottings and wonderings about how could they get to Mayfair and where the hell could they get a thousand quid, and the life they were going to have when they got out of this junk on the Upper Amazon, she would silence him with, 'Darling, do you really love me?' and he would simply utter her rosy name from the depths of his throat and she would say, from the depths of hers, 'Let's go to bed,' and, for a while, they would hear only the water muttering past their ears, and, for a long, wild, heavenly while, nothing at all. (She was not a girl to make any bones about that. 'He was *marvellous* in bed!') Then, after he had fallen into a contented sleep, she would lie awake gazing fondly sideways at him who, for all his boastings about all he knew, looked then as helpless as a boy.

All he knew... They were such odd things, and so interesting, and always so mixed up with 'our future', and with 'maintaining us in the manner to which we are accustomed' – not 'his' future, or the manner 'to which "I" am accustomed' – that she could listen to him happily for hours of it.

One night it would be all about food and drink.

'Drink is very important. Vodka, for example, must always be served in paper-thin, ice-cold glasses. And whatever the hell it is always call it Soviet vodka. No real gentleman would drink anything else. Major Grey's Chùtney? Sound stuff – but never ask for it, too many people know about it. Gentlemen's Relish is definitely eaten by gentlemen. But Riley's Royal Fishpaste is most certainly not eaten by royalty. Then there's sauces. Very tricky. I once heard about a fellow at a bank luncheon who asked the head-waiter in a loud voice for some stuff called Kutie Katie's Curry. I believe you could have heard a pin drop. Draw a veil! Painful story! Poor slob had to emigrate to Australia.'

Another night it would be clothes.

'A law of life! No matter what depths a fellow may be driven to he must never, simply never, wear a made-up tie. If you're rich you can dress in rags. If you're hard-up – use the best tailor in Savile Row. Last button of the weskit left undone? No, madam! Only grammar-school boys, Africans, – Abyssinians – poor old Haile Selassie always does it – Indians, Italians and Americans trying to be English do that any more. No weskit! Weskits are gone! Absolutely out of date. So are watches with chains. Better have no watch at all. Or a signet-fob on a black ribbon. Did you know that Edward the Seventh creased his pants down the sides?'

Conversation.

'I suppose you think good chat drips from the tongue? No, madam! You make it up the night before. Little casual odds and ends. Such as, "I wonder how many of Edward the Seventh's bastards could I name off-hand?" Or, "How many people know that if Oscar Wilde hadn't rejected the filthy advances of the Marquis of Queensberry he'd never have been hounded by that old sod?" Or somebody happens to say "Trilby". Ha, ha! That's my cue. "Did you know that her real name was Billy O' Farrell? Father a parson in Trinity College, Dublin. Had her by a barmaid in Paris." Oh, we'll keep them gaping, Rosebud! We'll dazzle 'em!'

'We?' Love would gush in her. 'Do you really love me, Clarence?' And the sleeping boyish face on the unwashed pillow-slip of the double-berth, and she, as the winter dragged on, and he still jobless, feeling fear for him or, as the first signs of spring came, jealousy, of certain unknowns, creeping slowly over her love like the lichen scaling the tree trunks on the bank.

Her mamma's letters from Tisbury always ended, 'What's Clarence doing these days?' She never answered the question. She could only have said, 'He goes to town every morning' – having kissed her tenderly, taken his bowler hat, and his rolled umbrella, said, 'Into the breach once more dear friends', stalking then across the gangway, back erect, gamp on shoulder like a gun, along the tow-path for the train to Mecca. If she asked him on his return – she soon ceased to ask – what he had done during the day he would talk volubly about it.

He had met an old pal at the Army and Navy Club. 'A grand chap! He swears he's got a real opening for me. It appears that the latest idea in textiles is plastic lavatory basins. Let me tell you all about them. You see, the great thing about these gadgets is that if you wanted to you could roll 'em up and put them in your pocket. They're made in . . .'

Or he had run into Tommy Lancing at the Union Jack Club.

'Let me tell you, Rosebud, about Tommy Lancing. My bosom friend. Saved his life once outside Catania. He's sitting pretty now, importing furs. He's mad about racing. He persuaded me to put ten bob, ten whole bob, on a horse running at Kempton Park, an absolutely wizard tip he got at the Cavalry Club.'

And that would be a day when he would then either plank down on the table ten single pound notes, or sadly produce Tommy Lancing's carbon copy – careful man – of an IOU for ten shillings. She never asked him how he got entry into those clubs. She was too eager to know what it was like inside such grand places.

On bad days he might have just dropped into the Distressed Gentlefolks' Aid Association, or visited an old chum in the Star and

Garter Home for Disabled Soldiers and Sailors, on Richmond Hill. Once
– they were at rock-bottom that week – he had called in, 'just for idle
curiosity', to the Army and Navy Labour and Window Cleaning Corps.
Her heart leaked for him that night. Now and again, through his
'contacts' he would get a real job, never held for long. ('Bum lot!
Pointless! Leads nowhere.') Once it was with the Society for Improving
the Condition of the Labouring Classes; once with the Junior Imperial
League; once with the Irish Church Missions and Scripture Readers
Society, a job he held for two whole weeks. She always asked him what
he had for lunch, to which he would always say, 'Beer and a sandwich,'
and he would ask what was there for dinner. She would reply, 'The
usual – mash and bangers,' or, 'There's a bit of cold meat left,' and
produce an excuse for a meal, with branches or wild flowers from the
tow-path stuck into the milk-bottle. After it they would always go
down to *The Bunch of Grapes* for a half-pint of mild-and-bitter
apiece.

The jealousy began over what he called his art gallery, five framed
photographs of female nudes fastened to the wall of the cabin. She had
never bothered her head about them until the night she heard him hail
her from the deck with a joyous cry of 'Lolly!' and come clattering
below to throw fifty quid in tenners on the table under her widening
eyes.

'Who?' she asked in excitement.

'Haha! I have friends.'

An old chum! Spike Halloran of the Royal Irish. 'Let me tell you about
good old Spike . . .'

They had drinks in *The Bunch of Grapes* that night, and went out the
next night to celebrate in style. 'As befits our station in life.' They went
into Richmond for steaks and wine at Shortt's, and afterwards around
to *The Three Crows* on the Green to booze up. There they ran into a
young fellow named Milo Doyle – blue eyes, a complexion like a girl,
a creamy brogue, a Customs officer somewhere – a simple chap who
enchanted Rosebud by seriously believing Clarence's joke that he was
Sir Clarence Dunally, and gave Clarence even greater delight by being
so obviously taken by Rosebud who, as he well knew, would not have
given the trout's eye to a duke. Afterwards when he teased her about
the lad, in their double-bunk, she had just laughed and said, 'Nice boys
like him shouldn't be left out alone in London.'

'Nicer than me?' he had asked throatily.

'Lots of men are nicer than you, darling. But nobody is so attractive.'

After that they heard no noises in the boat for a long while. Then, as he slept and she lay awake, jealousy burst in her like an aneurysm of rage. Her eyes, wandering around the cabin, had halted where there had always been those five photographs. Now there were only four. For a long time she again heard nothing, neither the occasional rat awake, nor the gurgle of the water, nor the distant sound of the railway. She waited until he left the next morning, unscrewed two of the photographs and carefully took them apart. On the back of the first she read the inscription, 'Belinda – altogether yours'; and on the back of the second, 'Coco to Clarence, with luff.' The other two pictures were also of Belinda and Coco. Staring at their bare haunches she remembered that during their earliest days together he had a camera and had coaxed her into letting him photograph her in the nude. She also remembered certain coy references to a Lady Belinda. She had laughed – she had never taken men's boastings about women seriously. She knew now that a picture like that would be easily worth fifty quid to a real Lady Belinda.

She held her fire – she had too often heard her mamma say, 'I'm not going to dig my grave with my teeth, or my tongue' – until a month later when they were broke again. Coco disappeared and another fifty quid came – he came back with it quite late that night. She had been simmering all day and now she let him have it. She called him names and words she had never known she knew. She finally leaped on him and scrawled his face with her nails.

'What am I married to? A pimp, or a blackmailer, or both? How long has this been going on? How long have you known these women?'

'Hi! Hi! Hi!' was all he could shout, fighting her off, pursued by her from saloon to cabin and back again. 'What's all this about? You gone daft?'

She hit him on the head with the beer-bottle, she threw *Who's Who* at him, she tore his *A.1 Atlas* down the spine, flung it on the floor and kicked it. To his horror she grabbed his ten fivers, tore them across and showered them at him. Then, glaring and panting, she was sitting on the berth, spitting at him when she had the spit, he standing in the farthest corner of the saloon by the companion-way, ready to dash for the deck, dabbing his bleeding face with his handkerchief.

'You second-lieutenant! You were never a captain, you were never a Wing Commander, you were never anything, you ground-force garbage emptier, with your bowler hat, and your rolled gamp, and your two splits behind over your duck's bottom! You toy drum-major! You vain, vapid, muttonheaded, silly, bone-lazy, bloody ass!'

'But, Rosebud,' he said gently, 'I did it for you. Honestly!'

At which appalling statement, patently true, she had to bustle out to the WC and sit there weeping on the can for sheer love of him. When she came back all she said was, 'You do it again, Clarence, and I'm quitting. And for keeps.' She asked no more questions. Unasked, he told her that he took all those silly pictures for fun, during the war, when everybody was a bit crazy, and kept them for fun, and for memories, and anyway, it all happened before he met his own, his only, his dear. 'My darling, loved Rosebud.' Bit by bit he melted her. Then he got throaty. She forgave him. Locked in one another's arms they did not hear a sound until the morning.

The next night he made her come out to dinner on, his own words, 'the wicked lolly'. She only went because he had run into that young Irish fellow Milo Doyle and, for her sake, asked him to join them. They had by then met him several times and become quite friendly with him. He had visited them on the boat, they had met him for drinks at Hammersmith, he had taken them to supper in a little Italian place off the Brompton Road. She liked him, Clarence's pal, a pleasant young fellow, neither handsome nor unhandsome, quiet, a bit dull really, the son of an Irish farmer, always sighing for 'Ioreland'. This night he was in high fettle – he was about to be transferred from Dover to Holyhead. He even sang them an Irish song called, 'One step nearer home!' Clarence was at his deludhering best as the fellow exile. 'Go on,' Clarence kept prodding him, 'tell us more about good old County Roscommon.' She liked him a lot then, talking excitedly about County Roscommon and his boyhood there. She exchanged Wiltshire and her childhood. She even pretended to flirt with him because he blushed so easily. It was a good night.

'All the same, Clarence, it wasn't worth it. Poor but honest – that's me.'

The next morning, as he was sitting up in their berth drinking his morning cuppa, she sitting sideways on it, leaning across his legs, drinking hers, she knew by the way his eyes were half-closed that he was moving around inside his own secret mind. Presently he said:

'Wasn't that interesting, what Milo was saying last night about gold watches?'

'What about them?' she asked, and felt her heart going bang-bang.

'Silly! Or were you too busy flirting with him to notice? Gold watches smuggled out of Ireland. Every one of 'em worth in London, depending on its value, anything from five to ten quid in sheer profit?'

'Clarence! Stop it! For God's sake, if you're thinking...'

'Somebody's got to think or we'll never get out of this madhouse!'

From there the argument began. It went on hammer and tongs for an hour. He must have known he had won when she said, 'And anyway, where would you get the money to buy them?' He leaped from the bunk, in his red-and-white spotted pyjamas, seized his striped trousers, emptied the pockets on the blankets and counted his cash. There were forty-five pounds odd, in coins and in notes – now mended across with stamp-selvage.

'See! We've got forty-five. Another fifty-five and we've a hundred quid in capital!'

He began to wash, shave and dress, whistling, fresh as a daisy, pursued by more hopeless pleadings and warnings, even while he was stalking across the gangplank, and vanishing, rolled gamp on shoulder, his bowler hat on his ear, two splits behind, down the towpath for the Rialto.

It came as no surprise to her when he returned that evening triumphant. ('If he had put only one-tenth of the persistence...')

'Got it! Fifty-five quid! Tommy Lancing! And it's God's truth this time. The three bottoms are still there on the wall. And there's his carbon of my IOU.'

'You will do this once, Clarence.'

'I'll try it once.'

'If it works you will try it twice.'

'Possibly.'

'You will try it three times, and then you will either be caught or I won't be able to stand it one second longer. But whether you're caught or whether you're not you'll give me whatever rotten money you make, every single penny of it and I'll open a bank account for it in my name. Not that I want to be associated with this swindle, but I can at least try to protect myself and you, and I can stop you from wasting your precious lolly on your usual swank and nonsense.'

He agreed, sulkily. He made his haul. And it was a washout. There had been no hitch in Dublin – no country is much interested in what goes out of it. There had been no hitch in Holyhead. In the Customs hall he had easily picked out Milo along the line of counters, planked his hide suitcase in front of him, said, 'What cheer, Milo!' and opened it with a frank sweep of his honest arm.

'Hello, Clarence! You've been over?'

'Just been vetting a horse for a hunting friend,' Sir Clarence said. 'No dice. Spavined brute. Hoho! Can't trust these Irish. What, what?'

Milo had patted his shirts perfunctorily, chalked his bag, said, 'Give my regards to herself', and Clarence had walked on to the train with his five watches – all he had been able to afford – strapped around his waist under his shirt. It took him a week to sell them, and, when he had deducted his expenses, about £10, he found that all he made was twenty-three quid odd. For half a day he was filled with gloom. At this rate it would take him years to achieve a coalhouse in Pimlico. She did not tease him – she was too happy that it was all over. She even felt sorry for him. By that night he had rallied. The answer was simple: they must go into this thing in a much bigger way. He had about £113. Where would he get another hundred quid?

'What can we sell, Rosebud?'

She laughed at him affectionately. He jumped up.

'I've got it! We'll sell *Evangeline*.'

'Are you out of your mind? It's not ours to sell. We only rent the junk.'

'We can sell it to somebody who wants a houseboat for the summer. Offer them an option for a hundred quid down and the rest on possession. Three months to go until June, they'll never cop on. In June we pay them back the option and if the worst came to the worst we'd be no worse off than we are already. Bob's-your-uncle!'

She closed her eyes in agony and gave him up.

'Surely,' Milo said to her afterwards, 'at the moment you should have known.'

'Known? Known what? Known Clarence? I knew him from the first day he led me to that houseboat. Our home. You saw her when we'd worked at her. Hoo, hoo! If you'd seen her that day! It was October, and raining. That night! Don't remind me of it. I looked around me and I said to myself, "So this is the sort of bloke I'm married to." Oh, I knew Clarence! You never did. He'd charm the birds off the trees. He'd sell radiators in hell. And aren't you forgetting something? That love is perfect and the loved one can do no wrong.'

'I meant, "known yourself".'

'And who does, smartie? But there was something I did get to know. Going away like that he left me alone for the first time in my life. Really alone, for days at a time locked up in that bloody submarine.'

She had been alone in London when he was off with the Eighth Army, but she was working then and had friends. The dank tow-path, the locked-down houseboat, the fogs, the total silence, the rain, the jet-black nights relieved only by the distant glow of London on the underbelly of the sky were very different. Forcing herself to go alone one night into Walton-on-Thames, wandering alone in her white mackintosh around its streets, she saw it for the first time as it really was. The pub lights appealed, the Palais de Danse was neon-red, the cinema lights blazing white, she felt that in every other little villa-house – red roof, tiny garden, bow-windows, empty garage, people were playing bridge or listening to the Light Programme. To hell with Mayfair! She wanted a home, and kids, a pram, going shopping, hearing the *Daily Mail* flop on the hall every morning, the milkman jangle the bottles, Clarence yawning and saying, 'I better get up, I suppose, and get off to the office.'

On his second visit to Ireland he took with him a round two-hundred quid. On the resale he made fifty. His third haul, she noted with satisfaction, brought her bank total up to £310. A couple of days after his return he got a letter, one sentence: 'The chief officer here asked me on Monday after you left were you a pal of mine.' There was no signature and no address but the postmark said Holyhead. He did not hesitate a second. Tommy Lancing was clamouring for the repayment of his loan. That morning Rosie had put pussy-willows in the milk-bottle. April.

'They've copped on to me. Now you must go.'

'No!'

'Rosebud!' – appealingly.

'No! And that's flat.'

'Rosebud!' – threateningly.

'No! And now I've said "No" three times and that's three times too many. I won't do it. I like the money just as much as you do but this I won't do.'

'Rosebud, you damned fool, do you realize that on two more runs, just two more runs, we'll have five hundred of that thousand quid we've been wanting all our lives. We'll be within sight of a home where we always wanted to have a home.'

'Lives? A home? What do you know about lives? I want a decent home, a real home, kids, a pram, a...'

'I want you to have a real life.'

'And I want it! I'd do a lot for it. But not this. I won't do it. You know damn well either one of us will get caught or that poor boy Milo will get into trouble. He'll get the sack. Do you want that to happen? I couldn't live with it.'

'For me, Rosebud? For us? Say just one, just one more run!'

Once more the hammer and tongs began again. She gave in. She had her own dream.

The evening she came back from Dublin and Holyhead she threw the watches on the bed and sat down and stared at him like death.

'For Christ's sake, Rosebud! What happened?'

'Nothing.'

'Then what's wrong?'

'When he chalked my bag he looked at me and he blushed.'

Clarence snatched up the watches. He held them over her head. He clutched them to his chest. He laughed triumphantly.

'Splendid! Perfect! It's in the bag. He'd do anything for you.'

She said quietly that he well might, and that was precisely why this (she screamed it) was the bloody end.

He approached her, hooped, white, trembling, his eyes peering, his hands shaking.

'Then I'm going to do it the next time. And this time if I'm going to chance it I'm going to chance it big. I must get another hundred quid. Another two hundred quid! We'd be over the line, we'd be in the big push. It's your life that's at stake, our lives.'

She caught his glance over her head at the three photographs. She said, 'No!'

They squabbled for two days. Then it was she who got the letter, from Dublin.

Dear Mrs Dunnally,

I am so happy in myself that I must tell you my great news. I've done it at last. I'm back in Ireland. A while ago there I applied for a post with the Irish Customs. Last week they called me for an interview, and the Wednesday you passed through Holyhead, you brought me luck, I went home and there was the letter waiting for me telling me I had been successful. I am in Dublin now stationed at Dunleary Pier. I had to tell you because I knew you would be particularly pleased by my news. Please give my regards to Clarence. I remembered you both at Mass this morning.

Yours sincerely,
Milo Doyle.

She gave the letter to him and went to the porthole. A swallow skimmed the water. She heard him utter a deep and fervent 'Damnation!' After that he was silent for so long that she turned to look at him. His eyes half closed, he was slowly winding the letter about his forefinger. She sat down, and watched him and waited. He tossed the paper tube on the table and glanced over at her. His voice was very soft and very slow.

'So there is a Customs in Dublin . . . Does that suggest something to you? No? It does to me. It means there must be things worth smuggling *in* there. Eh?'

She did not stir. She sat looking at him like a brass idol. He did not say anything until, bowler-hatted, his rolled umbrella in his fist, he was ready to leave the boat. She had not stirred.

'I have to do it. Within a month that fellow will be coming around about the boat.'

She did not answer. He went to the bulkhead, ripped the three photographs from it, slipped them into his pocket and clattered up the companion-way.

She spent the morning and early afternoon cleaning and polishing the boat. She took the brown-paper coverings from her geraniums and pruned them down – there could hardly be any more frosts. She let the Albertine look after itself. She washed herself from head to foot, packed a suitcase, ate a sandwich, drank a beer, wrote 'Goodbye' on the back of Milo's letter and propped it against the bottle of beer. Then she looked about her carefully for the last time, and left. She put the key where they always did under a stone on the bank.

At the ticket office of the Southern Railway she bought her ticket for London. She was turning around to pick up her suitcase when she found him beside her holding it. He took her by the arm and led her firmly to the waiting-room, sat her down, sat beside her and laid the three photographs on her lap.

'I couldn't do it. I did better. I spilled the whole thing to Tommy Lancing. God, what a rocket I got from him! Why the hell hadn't I told him before? Was I a pal or was I not? He rumbled it in one second. Fur coats! That's the real McCoy for Ireland. As you know, he imports them. He's putting five hundred quid into it. He takes a third and we take the rest.' He laid a fat envelope on top of the pictures in her lap. 'There's five hundred Johnny-o-Goblins in that. Now, are you with us?'

She took the lot from her lap and gave them back to him.

'I'm going home to Mum and Dad.'

'Don't do that! Believe me or not, God's truth, I'd be lost without you. I want you. I couldn't live without you.' Furious, she made to get up; he held her down. 'Why don't you just go to London for a couple of days and think it over? Get away from me. We've been too much on top of one another. Go to Bournemouth. Forget me for a while. You could go to Dublin.'

She looked at him.

'Why Dublin?'

'Anywhere, but, for God's sake, not home. Give me a break, lass. Just two or three days. If you come back I'll never raise the question again. We'll go on just as we did before all this began,' and he lobbed the pictures and the five hundred pounds back into her lap and strode out the door. By the time she had thrown the stuff after him he was gone.

She sat beside her suitcase for as long as it took two trains to pull in and out. Then she got up, took the package, and went out on the platform to wait for the next train. She spent the night in a cheap hotel near Waterloo. If there had been a telephone on the boat she would have phoned him. She even thought of going straight back to him. The next day, not thinking, not planning, not deciding, just going, she found herself on a plane for Dublin.

That night, sitting among the Saturday night crowd in Mooney's in Dunleary, over a couple of Guinness, she told Milo about the watches.

'I know I shouldn't have come, Milo, but I've no one to talk to about it all. And I've got to talk to somebody. Well, should I leave him?'

He pondered on it, or on something.

'Does he love you, Rosie?'

'He says he loves me, he says he's doing it all for me. He calls it Operation Rosebud. He doesn't call it Operation Clarence. But I wonder.'

'That's the crux. After all, a fellow has to give proof of his love. Show a woman what he'd do for her. I don't mean he has to go out and kill tigers, or, like the old knights long ago, go out carrying his lady's handkerchief and come back with the Golden Fleece or something. That old houseboat he put you into! I suppose you might think my ideas about love are very dull, and ordinary and, as you might say, homespun. But from the first day I started earning money I started putting a bit aside every week against the day when I might meet a girl and want to marry her. I could see it – the red roof, and the bit of garden, and how we'd have a television.' He laughed at himself. 'And – it's not very romantic I suppose – we'd have a washing-machine. And a pram in the garage. *Very* dull!'

'You're making fun of me. You're mocking me.'

'*Me?* Mocking *you?* Rosie!'

She could not stop herself; she put her hand across the formica table, clasped his hand and pressed it.

'You're a good man, Milo.'

She wrote to Clarence that she was not going back to the *Evangeline* ever again, she did not know if they could ever make a life together, but if they ever did it would have to be in a real home, and she described to him how nice Walton-on-Thames was. If he sent her the address of the man who had taken the option on the boat she would send him a cheque for £100. And he must get a job. She signed it, 'Love, Rosebud', and enclosed a five-pound note. He recognized the address of Milo's lodgings. He wired. 'Send me a tenner. Leaving junk. Will write soon. Have a lovely time. Longing for you. Clarence.' When his letter came, a week later, it was headed '13a Antrobus Street, SW1, Near Buckingham Palace.' It ran:

My Rosebud!
    I've done it at last. SW1 . . .

(It was, indeed, technically in SW1, although the street turned out to be in Pimlico, and on the wrong side of the railway lines radiating out from Victoria Station.)

... And I've got a job. It's not much but it will do for a while. I've
left the junk for keeps and as nobody but you know where I am we
needn't pay back that option money ... London is absolute heaven,
people, people, people. I'm dying for you to see it, and to touch you
and give you a thousand smacking kisses and great hugs.

Your own, wicked old Clarence.

The next morning she was outside 13a Antrobus Street, and there was
Clarence at the door going off to work in his dungarees, jacket,
neckerchief and cap – he was window-cleaning – with a grin as wide
as a church door and a hug like a bear.

The room was terrible. She worked on it in a frenzy all day to astonish
him when he came back, with half-a-dozen bottles of beer in a bag, and
a mouthful of jokes, and then she was sitting beside him in a pub, or
arm-in-arm out in the streets, with the crowds, and the traffic and the
good old smells of London, until the cosy night opened its arms to them
both, and she was utterly certain of him and herself as the noises
gradually vanished into their own breathing and his little murmuring
words of love.

On the third day, at lunchtime, he said,

'Rosebud! I'm really on to something good at last! I met a man
today...'

'Clarence. If you could only get a decent job!'

His brows sank.

'What do you mean, decent job? Do you mean five quid a week? What
do you want to do with me? Make me a commissionaire outside
Harrod's in a guardsman's coat, with a bandsman's epaulettes, and big
brass buttons, tipping me cap to nobs in swank cars? A car-salesman
selling dud cars in Paddington? An auctioneer's assistant in a green
apron holding up antique chamberpots? Let's face it! I'm not trained for
anything. I'm thirty. I can't start at the bottom at thirty. I'm making
for the top!'

'But before the war...'

'Before the frigging war I lived in Ireland, I was a young fellow about
town, I lived off my people, I hung around Dublin. The only job I ever
had was for six months before the war and do you know what that was?
In a drapery store selling yards of flowered muslin for women's frocks.
Do you expect me to go back to that?'

'But other men...'

'Rosebud! One run. Just one run with two fur coats, another two hundred quid, within yards of the winning-post. One more...'

'One more, and one more! I won't do it. I'd be caught. You don't care if I'm caught.'

'You can't be caught, not with Milo there.'

'He wouldn't know. I couldn't tell him. He'd kill me if he found out.'

Clarence peered at her.

'You soft on Milo?' he asked gently.

She stared at him sullenly.

'I like him. So what?'

'Nothing. I was just thinking. An idea. Look! Just one more little run, Rosebud? And this time I mean it. Honest to God, just this once and it's in the bag.'

'Clarence, don't send me back. I beg and implore you, don't send me back.'

'I ask so little.'

She argued no longer. She said sadly, 'You think more of your thousand quid than you do of me.'

'Untrue! I love you, I want you always and I'll never let you down, and if you love me you'll never let me down. Do you love me, Rosebud?'

'I don't think it's me that's the trouble there,' she said, and let it go, and took her mac and her head-scarf and went to the pictures.

It may have been then that she made her decision, or later, wandering about stuffy, smelly streets that had suddenly become hateful to her, thinking of the cool rain of Dublin, a shadow of a mist, so light that the earth was dry under every bush, so faint that you saw it only against dark tree-caves or in hollow archways, or on the windows of Rosita's Fish and Chip Shop where she had eaten with Milo, hearing the evening bells, looking out and up at the long, grey, tented daylight. In early May she went back to Dublin, laden.

All the way across she had wondered, 'What will I feel? Will he suspect? Will I blush when he chalks my bags?' She stood tense on the deck as the morning light slowly touched the mountains, the green hills, the wet houses, the town's church-spires and, at last, they were bumping the black pier with its fenders made of hairy ropes. When she saw him, pink, fresh, so young, absorbed in his job, she was so far from feeling anything but pleasure in his sudden flash of delight – 'Three bags? I see you brought everything!' – that it was she who blushed, forgot all about her contraband and was about to open up her suitcases when he chalked them with a cheerful grin and a 'See you later!' Within hours she was wondering what on earth she had ever seen in Pimlico or why she had ever left Dublin.

They were together all day, and still together late that night at the pier's end, looking at the late Irish sunset – it was nearly eleven o'clock – still red low over distant Dublin.

'Milo,' she said suddenly, 'I'm not going back to London.'

For a second she thought he was going to kiss her: then she realized that he was the sort of fellow to whom a kiss is as good as a promise. Without intent, or the desire that waits on it, she leaned her head on his shoulder in a posture that obliged him to put an arm about her waist.

'You're married to him.'

Slowly she released his arm and stood erect. She turned from the last red-black line over the city and looked eastward across the sea. As she looked creeping horror entered her. Only last week, in that crowded pub outside Victoria Station, talking over their beer with some fellows about marriage and divorce, Clarence had said, 'Funny thing, there's no divorce in Ireland. But any man or woman who was married in a registry-office in England can remarry in Ireland. Catholics don't count that as a real marriage. So, Rosebud here,' he laughed, 'could chuck me any day she liked and marry an Irish Catholic!'

He had looked at her, smiling softly, with half-closing eyes.

'Let's go back,' she said sombrely to Milo, and all the way along the slim lamplit pier she was silent. Why had he brought that up? She halted and gripped Milo's arm, staring at nothing.

'Are you all right, Rosie?'

Could it be possible? Operation Rosebud? Was the bastard thinking that if she married him it would be awfully convenient . . .

'I'm just feeling tired, Milo.'

'Sit down here. You've been having a hard time of it.'

She sat on the bench, still holding his arm. Two could play at that game.

'What you need, Rosie, is a long, long rest.'

'With you around I mean to take a long rest.' She leaned towards him. 'Kiss me, Milo.'

He did so, chastely, on her cheek. She did not press him further. She just said, 'Milo, I'm sure there are lots of men just as attractive as you. But few can be nicer.'

The furs were locked in her wardrobe. Every morning, after Milo went out to work, she took a cab at the pier and drove into Dublin with them. Within a week her bank-book showed a total touching the last quarter of the thousand. After that she dawdled on happily, blind to thought – every day Milo and she seemed to have so much to do, to see, to talk about. She mentioned to him this strange idea that an Irish Catholic could, if he wanted to, marry a woman who was already married legally in England. He had never heard of such a thing. She said, 'It must be a crazy idea I picked up all wrong.' When she wrote to Clarence about the furs he wrote back, 'Wonderful woman! Have a nice time, ducks! I can wait. But don't keep me hanging too long. I'm only human. And I'm mad about my Rosebud. Every day I clean a window I say, "Soon one day I'll be watching some other poor bugger cleaning ours."'

She heard no more from him until, as if he was inside her head, as if he knew every movement of her body, she got a letter headed Tisbury, Wiltshire, in his handwriting. 'Dad is ill. The doctor talks about heart. Do come and see us, even if it's only for a day...' Wavering, she kept it for two days. Then she tore it up, savagely. That night, in Rosita's, she said:

'I've made up my mind, Milo. It's not very ladylike of me to say it, but it's say it or go back. If I stay would you marry me?'

He whispered his answer:

'As a matter of fact I found that I could. I remembered what you said and I inquired about it. There is nothing against it in principle. There have been several cases like it.'

'Well?'

'There's only one thing I'm not sure of.'

'Which is?'

'I'm not sure that you love me.'

'Oh, you great fathead! Milo, you said it yourself – there's only one proof of love, what you'd do for love. Don't you know I'd do anything for you? Anything! Just anything to make you sure?'

She made him sure that night. She was astonished by his wild passion, of which afterwards he was both touchingly ashamed and youthfully proud.

She delayed writing to Clarence. Then she invented an illness and sent him a tenner. When his letters became impatient she replied to them lovingly, sending more money, and telling him that she was now all in favour of his scheme, exploring everywhere for better markets. By late June he was getting angry. She tried to pacify him by telling him that since it would be far better to sell the coats to private customers she had already fixed one and nearly fixed another, that she wanted to bring three or even four coats, that he would be wise to wait. She sent him twenty pounds. When June ended he ordered her to return within three days or he would come over himself. She did not reply. He wired her: 'Am crossing by tomorrow's mailboat.' When she wired back she wrote at first only, 'You may come,' then, with a last vestige of old feeling, chiefly pity, she added, 'But take no chances,' signing it, 'Rose Powis.'

Her time was up. The next morning she went to a doctor; that afternoon she told Milo everything. If she had been confessing to one of his priests she could not have bared herself more completely. She even told him all about the photographs, and the furs she had smuggled. The disgust on his face when she spoke of the nude pictures terrified her. At the furs his rage was as wild as his love had been. From Clarence she would not have minded the words he spat at her; from his mouth they were horrible because he believed them, and from him they were just. When at last he had exhausted himself and was sitting, sobbing into his hands, on the edge of the old, velvet armchair of the sitting-room of their lodging-house, she sat in the farthest corner of the room and stared at him hopelessly. The rest was as quiet as mice talking.

'I did it only for you, Milo. Honestly.'

He raised his head.

'Honestly? That! From you?'

'I loved you. I still love you. I want you always. I'll never let you down, and if you love me you'll never let me down. I'd be lost now without you. I wanted you. I wanted your baby.'

'How do I know it is mine?'

'I know! I'm four weeks gone, and I'm as regular as clockwork.'

'I don't believe you.'

'All right! If you won't have me, I will just have to go back to Clarence. I'll palm it off on him. He'll be mad. But he'll never know. Is that what you want?'

'If you could fool him you could fool me.'

'I wouldn't. There's just that difference, Milo. I love you.'

'Love!

There was a long silence during which they sat and stared at one another.

'Why don't you chance it, Milo? We could be very happy. We could make a go of it.'

He kept staring at her. She got up.

'It's not such a big chance to take,' she said sullenly. 'Well? Finish me off! Do I stay with you? Or do I go back to him?'

'You could do that? Ha! Maybe you love him, too!'

'No, Milo! I don't think that any more.'

'Think! Do you *know*? Do you know anything? Which of us do you love?'

'Isn't that up to you?'

That was their longest silence. The room darkened slowly. She saw seagulls wheeling against a blue-black sky above the mailboat's masts. She went to the door. He stood up.

'Would you swear to God in heaven that it is my child?'

'No! I don't hold with that lark. And I'm not going on my knees to you. If you don't believe me, you don't love me, and I don't want you if you don't love me, and if you don't love me it wouldn't make any bloody difference to you anyway. Let it go, Milo! You've had your fun. Besides, it's not your baby. Or mine! It's ours!'

She opened the door. He banged it to.

'Suppose I did chance it?'

'Why should you?'

'I suppose because I thought you loved me.'

'Why am I in no doubt? Why is it always the man who can't trust?'

He fell, weeping, on her chest.

'I believe you, Rose! Don't let me down!'

She threw her arms about him and gave out a deep triumphant sigh, like a ship sloping into harbour with furling sails. She drew back and looked at him fondly.

'Milo, I won't let you down. You'll see. We will make a go of it! Oh, Milo!' she laughed, and he with her. 'Isn't it just like that picture we saw last week at the Pav!'

She stood back from him, rummaged in the bag on her arm, found the bank-book and gave it to him. He threw it on the floor as if it was a snake. The thunder crashed.

'Why do you give me that thing?'

'Throw it into the sea. Do what you like with it. All I'm worth now is what I'm standing up in. You have me as you see me.'

'It's the way I want to see you,' he laughed, 'Or even in less.'

They stood clasped together, their eyes closed, indifferent to the sudden downpour of rain and the rumble of the thunderstorm as it wandered away to sea, where, miles out, under the vast storm-cloud stretched all across the horizon, a small brush of smoke indicated the mailboat beating its way into the west wind towards their sheltering shore. He sought her mouth.

'My darling!' he muttered throatily through her lips. 'Let's go to bed.'

She seized his hand and they fled, cautiously, through the dusky corridor to her room. They were lost in love for so long that they did not even hear the soft hoot of the mailboat making its careful entry to the pier.

# A Sweet Colleen

The stink and smell and dust of this bloody station! And the rudeness
of that fellow in the ticket office. What a fool to come by bus, and an
hour too early. She was exhausted from lugging this old leather suitcase
of Aunt Edie's. She let a parcel fall. A porter came over to her.

'Can I help you, miss?'

'Oh, please do! The Irish Mail.'

'Got a seat reserved?'

'O Lord, I forgot!'

Nice voice, nice kid, nice legs and the real Rossetti neck.

'This way, miss.'

When he had lobbed her case up on the rack of an empty carriage and
she was fumbling for a coin in her purse, he said:

'Forget it.'

She looked up at him. He had the most beautiful eyes she ever saw,
pure cerulean, with long lashes. His temples were grey. Plump apple
cheeks like an old lady.

'I'm Irish, too,' he smiled. 'That's a heavy bag.'

He removed his porter's cap to pad his forehead with a blue
handkerchief. He could be forty. He chucked down his waistcoat, put
away the handkerchief in his back pocket. But she noted that he still
held his peaked cap in his hand. He was so tall that he was able to lean
on one foot with his other hand grasping the rack above him.

'Been on a holiday?' he asked.

'I work in London.'

'Over long?'

'Three months.'

'First time?'

'Yes.'

'I could guess. Like it?'

Was this a bit unusual? But the platform was empty, there was no rush yet and Daddy used always say that once you got on the Irish Mail you were in the friendly climate already.

'I have a nice, quiet job. It's all right. I work in the National Gallery.'

'I'll be blowed!' he laughed, but quietly. 'I worked there for three and a half years. I used to be one of the warders.'

She could imagine him in the gallery in uniform, and knew at once that he had been in the War, and she would take a small bet that he had been a sergeant.

'And what do you do in the Gallery?'

'I work in the bookstall.'

He laughed happily, as if recalling the good old bookstall.

'I'd better drop into the Gallery one of these days and count the pictures. There were a couple there I used to like. The Rokeby Venus.'

She smiled discreetly. He said:

'Actually my favourite painter is Dante Gabriel Rossetti.'

She saw that he would have liked to go on chatting and gave him full marks for not doing it. He stepped back on to the platform, put on his cap, half an inch sideways, swept the grey wing of his hair back over his ear, closed the door and said through the window:

'Give my love to O'Connell Street. And take good care of yourself. You ought to. A girl as pretty as you.'

He went off laughing. Funny little fluting voice she has. He suddenly wheeled and came back to the window.

'Tell old Rutchie I was asking for him. My name is Tom Dalton.' He laughed back mockingly over his shoulder. 'Tell him give my love to Pom Pom.'

Rutchie? She wondered a bit at a Gallery warder becoming a railway porter. Maybe there was more money in railways. The journey sent him out of her head: the sleepless discomfort, the changing to the mailboat at Holyhead in the small hours, meeting her sisters, Dublin, everything.

Then one afternoon about a month later she heard herself being asked for the postcard of the Rossetti *Damozel*, looked up and saw the beautiful blue eyes smiling at her.

'Hello,' he said politely. 'Forgotten me? Tom Dalton. Euston Station. The Irish Mail. Did you have a pleasant holiday?'

'I remember you,' she said, and caught herself blushing and glancing

along the counter out of the corner of her eye to see if Lorna Alleyn was
listening.

'How is Dublin?'

'Just the same old Dublin,' she laughed, responding to his genial
smile. His own teeth; staining; he smoked too much; and a pipe, the
way Daddy used to. 'Have you been home this summer?'

'Why, girl, it's fifteen years since I saw Dublin. I wish you'd tell me
some time what it's like nowadays. You wouldn't care to join me for
lunch? No harm in asking, I hope?'

Her eye wandered to a waiting customer and she excused herself.
When she came back to his end of the counter he was still there, leafing
the cards. He was wearing a well-cut, grey suit and soft, brown hat with
a snap-brim. She wondered what his story might be.

'No?' he asked lightly, yet with such a note of pleading also that she
hated to refuse him.

'I'm sorry, I'm not free for lunch.'

'Why not come out and have a bit of dinner with me tonight at a nice
little Greek café?'

In her embarrassment she laughed.

'Aren't you working now?'

'I can get a pal to stand in for me. Give him five bob. We often do
it on night-shifts.'

'Oh, all right! Thank you. It is very kind of you.'

'Fine. I'll see you outside when you knock off. Now I'm going in to
see my favourite picture. He held up the postcard. 'She's very like
you.'

During the afternoon she went into the gallery herself to have a look
at that picture. She was standing on one leg looking at it, searching for
some mirror-likeness when she became aware that two men who had
been talking quietly in a corner of the room were parting, and that one
of them was approaching her. He was sallow, middle aged, very dark
eyed, soldierly, not bad looking. He said amiably:

'Excuse me, you are at the bookstall, aren't you?'

He spoke as softly as befitted the place and the heavy, June
afternoon.

'Yes.'

'I noticed you a couple of times. It is pleasant to find that one can
go from postcards to pictures as well as from pictures to postcards. I'm
in the curator's office. My name is Rucellai. Guido Rucellai.'

'What name did you say?'

'Rucellai.'

'Oh? Did you know a warder named Tom Dalton who used to work here?'

'The mad Irishman?'

'In what way was he mad? By the way I am Irish.'

He raised an apologetic hand and eyebrow. His teeth were white as paper. A strong, hooked nose.

'There is no real harm in being considered a little mad, you know. My English friends consider me a mad Italian. I have several Polish friends and I think them all quite mad. Only the English are never mad. Do you like Rossetti? Of course he was not really English. His father was an Italian. Very nice drawing there.'

'Somebody said that she appears to be a little like me.'

He looked to and fro between her and the picture, so often that she felt herself blushing.

'Nonsense. You are High Renaissance. Parmigianino?' he suggested, looked her all over. 'No, it must be a Florentine. Domenico called Veneziano? No! Pollaiuolo? Or why not Botticelli? The sloping shoulders, the distant look, the firm legs. That's it. As a matter of fact there is a girl very like you in the Villa Lemmi frescoes.'

'Why was Tom Dalton considered mad?'

'Do you know him very well?'

'I do not know him at all. I just met him by chance last month at Euston Station. He is a railway porter now.'

'Hm! He may be more suited to a railway station than an art gallery. I think I may have said that he is mad because he got so excited and cross with me one day. He told me, an Italian – consider my position here – that he hates all Italians. I had to reprimand him. I found out later that he married an Italian girl during or just after the war, and it turned out badly.'

'Oh, well! I must go.'

'Come again, Miss Plunkett?'

'You know my name?'

'I inquired,' he smiled. 'I don't know your first name.'

'Barbara.'

'Come again, Barbara' – and he bowed from the neck sedately. A bit superior? Or was he soapy?

Dalton took her first to a pub called The Cat and Cage off Oxford Street, at the Marble Arch end. It was a quiet street, among flats, mews, office buildings and the backs of hotels. Evening sparrows chirruped in the runnels. One might expect to find near at hand a flower shop, small but elegant houses, a church, an expensive boutique.

'This is a nobby district,' he told her. Watching her looking around at the mahogany and the cut-glass mirrors, he could tell that she had never been in a pub before. There were less than a dozen customers there. 'Anyway it once was a nobby district. We are in what Sidney Smith called the parallelogram – that is the whole district between Oxford Street south to Piccadilly, and from Park Lane over to Regent Street. Cream of the cream when England was an empire and Ireland was her pup.'

'Who is Sidney Smith? A friend of yours?'

'He's dead long ago, a famous English writer.'

'Do you read a lot?'

'It passes the time. What's your poison?'

She did not know what he could afford so she asked him to decide. He brought her a dry sherry and a pint of mild-and-bitter for himself.

'Sherry is always safe,' he advised her gently. 'It is a ladylike drink. And take it dryish, never sweet. Never take Martinis. Two of them could knock you out so you wouldn't know what you were saying or doing. Besides, they are expensive and no lady feels happy if she feels she is drinking beyond the means of her consort. I hope you don't mind my bringing you here for an *apéritif*. I thought it might interest you. Nowadays it is quite a respectable thing to do. Of course, there are some pubs I wouldn't bring you into.'

'It is a lovely pub. It is the nicest pub I have ever been in. Thank you for bringing me to this pub.'

He asked her what he might call her; and if he might call her Barbara; and would she call him Tom; he felt as if she were his own daughter; and did she mind if he smoked his pipe?

'I love a pipe. Daddy always smoked a pipe. It makes me feel quite at home.'

He laughed, a little mockingly, but she plainly did not see his joke. She was as slim as a sapling in the moon of March, with the *Damozel's* waving hair, and eyes blue as speedwell. *The wonder was not yet quite gone from that still look of hers.* No lipstick yet. A bit on the skinny side, in spite of the strong legs.

'How old are you, Barbara?'

'Nineteen and a bit more' – adding one to her eighteen.

'I've got an idea. The next time you go to Dublin I'll get you a "P" Ticket. "P" stands for Privileged. If I say you're my daughter I can get you a ticket for next to nothing.'

'You are awfully kind, Tom,' she said, considering him. 'Are you sure that would be all right? I mean wouldn't they want me to prove my identity and so on? I would not want to get you into trouble.'

He looked hard at her.

'You're not being snobby, are you? Not wanting to say you are a porter's daughter? There are no questions asked, you know. You just present your ticket like everybody else. We're all one in this on the railways. Each for all and all for each as you might say.' He patted her knee paternally a couple of times. 'It's all right, I've upset you now I can see. You're not a bit snobby. What was the journey like this time?'

'Fine. Except for having to change for the mailboat; get out at two in the morning just when you are almost beginning to fall asleep.'

'How I know these night trains! During the war – ooh!'

As he talked on she was pleased to find that he had, indeed, been a sergeant, fought in the desert and right up through Italy. And, as Rucellai said, he had married an Italian girl and it had not worked; in fact he had only lived with her for a year and then sent her back with her child to her people in Italy. He told her this quite calmly, as if it was something he had put well behind him.

'Last time I saw her she was a little bit of a thing. She'll be fifteen now. I've seen her photograph, quite pretty. It was a pity, but what's the use? I couldn't bring up a child on my own in London, and her mother was a wash-out. Her old *nonna* will look after her. If I could have married again . . . But being a Catholic!'

She said he must be lonely, but he waved it away.

'Tell me about dear old dirty Dublin,' he said, with one eye over the rim of his tankard. 'Where do you live there?'

Well . . . She lived with her mamma and her three sisters up in the hills behind Rathfarnham. It was a dear old house, supposed to be eighteenth century, all curls, and corners, and humpty-dumpty roofs. Daddy was dead. He had been a retired army captain. She did not specify British Army, but he knew it. He asked her where exactly in

Rathfarnham, or beyond it, she lived; he wanted to know; he really would like to know.

'Up near Rockbrook. It's lovely there. We can see Dublin miles away below us, on the bay. At night you can see the line of yellow lights strung out along the edge of the water beyond Clontarf. And all the little lights of the city. It's really lovely, Tom! It's like a stage, with footlights. We've always lived there. It's a bit far out, but Donna and Lulu and I went in every day for two years to Alexandra College. Of course since Daddy died we've been hard up and I knew that, sooner or later, I'd have to take a job. I wanted to be an air hostess with Aer Lingus but Mamma was dead against it. She always said, "It's no use, Babs, our sort never earned their living." She thinks what I am doing now is not work, not real work. She lives in a dream. I think she always hoped I'd marry an earl or something.'

She laughed gaily at the folly of their lives. He chuckled.

'All Ireland lives in a dream, bless its heart. I believe I know your house. I used often go up around Rockbrook on Sundays when I was in the cycling-club with a lot of boys and girls out of the factory – Jacobs'. We'd cycle all around through Glencree, on up the Old Long Hill or up the Sally Gap. And so that's where you always lived?'

'Always and always.'

From Oxford Street they could hear, through the open doors, the swishing of tyres. That night below Monte Cassino, looking out of that *cantina*, the bombing up in the hills, he had a letch for Oxford Street; a pipe-dream Oxford Street, with no blitz or black-out and the girls all wearing light cotton frocks.

'What used you do all day up in Rockbrook?'

'I used to love drawing horses. I could sit drawing horses all day long. I'm really quite good at drawing horses. I think that's why I looked for a job in the Gallery. When they asked me what was I good at I said, "Horses", so they gave me the job. You see, it did help. We used to ride a bit when we were able to afford it. Played tennis a bit. The old tennis lawn was full of bumps. We went to a dance once or twice. Nothing much, really. Or went down to town to meet somebody for a coffee. Really, the time just passed. But I did like drawing horses. Bears, too, but I was not so good at bears.'

He put down his tankard. He felt his heart beating. Smoking too much? He looked around the pub. In one corner a small man in a bowler hat was feeling a fat woman's knee and she was shaking in her fat with laughter at whatever he was saying to her.

'Barbara! Have you got any friends here?'

'Not real friends. I have Aunt Edie, of course, but she lives in Hampton Court. She is one of those State widows or whatever they call them. Her husband was governor of the Bahamas. She has arthritis, so she never comes out.'

'Where do you live?'

'In Oakley Street I have a room there.'

'Are you sure you're able to look after yourself in London?'

She opened her speedwell eyes.

'What on earth can you mean? I've been looking after myself all my life. Mamma is sweet but she does not know whether she is coming or going. I've often cooked for the five of us. So there!'

'What can you cook?'

'I can cook a steak. I can cook bacon and eggs. I used to be good at cooking a ragout, but I'm forgetting recently what I used to put into it. I was thinking of it only the other day when I saw onions selling in a shop. Tom! What does go into a stew? Do you put onions in yours? Oh, I can cook when I put my mind to it, I do assure you. You must come to my place one night and I will show you!'

He laid down his pipe. His hand fondled his heart-side.

'I am going to have another beer. Another sherry?'

'Will it make me tight?'

'I don't think so.'

He had intended to take her to a Greek place he knew between Oxford Street and Soho Square; instead he took her to Bertorelli's in Charlotte Street. He ordered for them both, including a half of Chianti.

'It is Italian but it is good. Now and again, for a blow-out on payday, I come down here from my hill fortress.'

She felt sad that he lived on the Harrow Road because she had passed that way once and got an impression of an Irishy quarter with flats over cafés, a bit toughy: he probably could not afford anything better, supporting his wife and daughter in Italy. For no reason she saw him in his room on a Sunday evening, when London can be rather dreary, sitting in his room reading Sidney Smith, looking out at the noisy street. Oakley Street, anyway, was at least quiet. Maybe this was what made him become a railway porter? He could make friends that way.

'Don't you ever want to go back to Ireland, Tom?'

'You ask me that? You know how it is being a misfit in Ireland.'

'True, I do know, don't I?'

They considered one another silently in the noisy, cheerful, crowded hither-and-thither of the restaurant until he wandered out of that island of silence into a winding, wandering discussion about what it is to be an exile and about friendship as an island in an island – 'You know, like Robinson Crusoe and the footprint.

'The Irish are like Jews. It's in our blood. We never belong, not really. Being Catholics, too, cuts us off. We are exiles in the bloody world. Shaw said somewhere, I think it's in *John Bull's Other Island*, that the Irish are hardheaded and realistic. I don't believe a word of it. What makes us get on in the world whenever we do it is the outcast feeling, never knowing when some blow is going to fall. You and me, though, we don't give a damn about the world, do we? Do you?'

'Not really. No! I don't think I do.'

'All we ever want is a couple of drinks and a friend to pass the night.'

That, she was to find, was always his style of talk. He was on now to love and marriage, talking non-stop, even when they went out into the summer-lit evening and took a bus to the Park and were strolling across it, threading their way through the last couples strewn like forgotten dolls on the grass, enjoying the coolness after the hot day. He was telling her about the odd characters he had met in the army, and out of it; 'opening your blue eyes', as he said with his little mocking smile, 'to the ways of the world'; just to show her the queer, dark things that are in men, especially men you would never suspect, and how all but a few confuse their lives in love and marriage. All she said was, 'Yes!' or 'Oh, yes, indeed.' Nobody had ever talked to her like this ever before.

She saw his big hands, pallid in the evening light, and wondered mildly, though only for a second, and for the last time, if she was wise to be with him, alone. They sat, and he talked now about Italy, while the sky over the farthest roofs became masked with silver-grey, the grass grew dusky, the trees grew heavy and dark, and the water darkened, and then, across the park, lights came out in the streets and the booming traffic dulled.

'You loved Italy, really, didn't you, Tom?'

'But not Italians. I don't trust them. And I advise you, if you ever run into any of them here, don't you trust them either. We never trusted them in the army. All the men ever think about is their looks. Combing their hair all day long. Pfu! And all the girls think about is men. I knew lots of men besides me who fell for Italian girls, and it never worked for any of them that I knew.'

She was on the point of mentioning Rucellai. She shied off it.

'Tom, tell me about your wife.'

'She was pretty. I met her in 'forty-three one night in a village called San Vittore. Just below Monte Cassino. Oh, maybe she wasn't all that pretty, maybe I was like a lot of other chaps who fell for Italian girls, maybe we weren't so much in love with the girls as dying for a taste of home. Besides I was only twenty-two when I went into the army, straight from Ireland where twenty-two is equal to about seventeen or eighteen here. I'd had four years of the war. I saw her only twice, then we pushed on to join up with the Yanks from Anzio. It was months before we entered Rome. You know what I mean – absence. I got three days' leave to meet her in Naples. A girl like you couldn't even imagine what Naples was like that time. God! It was filth! She was young, and sweet, and lovely, and O Lord God, innocent as the moon, and I asked her to marry me. I had to wait until 'forty-six. I was thirty and that was the first time I slept with a girl, believe it or not. She gave me a baby.'

Her white throat was the only thing he could see clearly. Like the whisper of leaves, that was her voice. She would have breasts like little white apples. He jumped up.

'I'll see you home,' he said, and led her, arm-in-arm, through the Park, talking incessantly, as if he had not talked to anybody for months, walking the whole way to her door. She politely invited him in for a cup of coffee. He did not seem to hear. There were five bell-pushes on the door-jamb and he was examining them. He laid his finger on one of the tabs and, in a dark, heavy voice, he asked, 'Antonelli. Who is he?'

'I believe he is a musician.' She opened the door. 'He plays the oboe. Listen, I think he is playing now. My landlord says he is a nice man.'

'How do you know he is nice?' he said angrily. 'You think every man you meet is nice. Is he young?'

'Oh, no! About your age, I should think. He is quite an elderly man.'

He gave a sharp laugh, looked abruptly at his watch, said:

'I'll give you a ring some time.'

'Thank you for a delightful evening. I enjoyed it immensely. You were really very kind to ask me, and nobody has ever talked to me before like you. Not even Daddy. And we were great pals.'

He jerked out another laugh, and ran down the steps, waving backwards. She watched him almost race across the street. He seemed a little put out. Perhaps she should have pressed him to come in for a coffee. She closed the door. The hall was stuffy. No letter. Upstairs the oboe had stopped. She regretted the end of the day. The Irish are so nice.

He did ring her again about a week later, and they met again at The Cat and Cage; but not for dinner, because – or so he said – he was on a night-shift. She hoped it was not because he was short of money, and she noted that he was not smoking. She happened to utter the wish that she were going home for the long August weekend, now a month away.

'Go!' he said. 'I'll get you the ticket. Cost you hardly anything.'

He did get her the 'P' ticket, then met her, all smiles, at Euston Station and put her into a First Class carriage, to which – she already felt him an old friend – she did not demur.

'You've squared this up, too, Tom?'

'All the way,' he grinned. 'It gives you a better chance to snatch a sleep before they turf you out at two in the morning in Holyhead.'

Of unkindness she had had no experience, though she knew indifference, yet his attentions made her think, when she was home, that he must be one of the kindest men alive. She had done nothing for him to deserve his kindness; merely met him, twice, at a pub, brought him twice to her room for coffee and a chat, sent him two postcards to cheer him up; so that she was furious when her mamma laughed over the railway porter who got her daughter free travel on British Railways, saying, hootingly, 'There you are! It shows you the depths to which the Socialists have dragged poor old England. Corruption from top to bottom.'

She was so furious at this mean-spirited way of looking at his kindness that she did not bother to explain. All she said even to her sisters was that she had a secret man in her life, but they refused to take it as a joke, probing and probing until they got it out of her that she was talking about a railway porter, at which they said:

'You and your jokes! Now, if you said a Member of Parliament, or a movie actor, or a stockbroker...'

Bored, she listened to them babbling by the hour on the telephone to their boys. She was ashamed for them when she heard them telling Mamma cover-up lies about their meetings with boys in town. (As she said, afterwards, to Tom, 'They seemed such kids to me. And dreadful snobs.')

She never mentioned Rucellai, whom she had now met several times, in the Gallery restaurant, over elevenses, and at tea, and who had twice taken her to lunch outside. She loved listening to him talking about Italy and his experiences during the war when he had known and worked with all the famous partisan leaders, Ada Gobetti in Torino, Dante Livio Bianco in Piedmont, Filippe Beltrame in Val d'Ossela, Bisagno in Liguria – at first mere names to her, then growing, as he talked of them, into real men. What she most liked to hear him talk about was his boyhood and youth outside Turin – the hill villages, the vineyards, the small fields, the screens of reeds, the river in its deep valley, the tiny, far-away passing train, small things that glowed in his mind like bits of an old world slipping away into a legend that had once been his life.

'It is my myth,' he once said, between a smile and a sigh.

Lying on the dandelions of the ragged lawn on her stomach, with one of her daddy's war-histories between her elbows, open at *The Italian Campaign, 1944*, she looked out over Dublin at the clouds moving in a white mass slowly towards England. She sent a postcard to Signor Rucellai, at the Gallery; and another to Mr Thomas Dalton, at his address in the Harrow Road. Apart from their first meeting, that day in the Gallery looking at the Rossetti drawing, she had not mentioned Tom to him. But he had spoken of him.

'Odd your meeting Dalton. Oh, I have no doubt he is a decent chap, as the English say, but he wouldn't know anything about Italy or the Italians because he never knew any of these things. He only saw the war from the sergeant's viewpoint. It is all over now and I am a kind of clerk, if you like, and he is a railway porter, but we are made by our experiences. Twenty-two years ago when I came over here first to help Don Sturzo to explain these things to the stupid British all this was high politics. The things we do pass but the lessons of the things – that is the important matter, that is the real experience.'

Twenty-two years ago? He looks so young, with his dark hair, and his straight back, and his clear eyes. If there was a war tomorrow he could be in the thick of it again. But not poor, nice old Tom!

When she stepped down to the platform off the Irish Mail in the early morning she saw him in his porter's cap and vest. He was limping. He saw her and waved to her. She looked like a child, tousled after her sleepless night. Passengers off night trains always reminded him of soldiers or children, waking up like puppets coming alive.

'I knew you'd be on it,' he said gleefully, 'I got your postcard.'

'Tom, you're limping!'

'Pfu! Just a touch of sciatica.'

'Oh, Tom, you've not been taking care of yourself.'

'Now you're here I will' – taking her bag. 'Have a nice holiday?'

'Not really. It was a failure, really. Really and truly. I must be getting old. Or losing touch. I'm very glad to be back. That is the real truth.'

He chuckled down in his throat.

'Come back to England, mavourneen, mavourneen. I'll tell you this – I'm damn glad to have you back, Barbara.'

It touched her that one person more or less in London could make any difference to such a lonely man. His limp was bad as he led her to a taxi – she had to be at her post in the Gallery that morning. As he closed the door of the taxi he said, 'Tonight we'll have a drink at The Cat and Cage and you must tell me all about it. But right afterwards you go right to bed, my dear, and make up for your lost sleep. Tomorrow night I'll show you a new restaurant I've found. Spanish. Tops. Have a good breakfast.'

She wiggled her fingers to him as she drove out into the morning sunlight of the station yard. A red milk-car by the kerb on Euston Road welcomed her home.

As he watched her go a mate said to him, 'Oye, Paddy! You're picking 'em young.'

'That,' he said with dignity, 'is my little girl, Barbara.'

'Sorry, chum. Didn't know you had a daughter. Got any more as pretty as her?'

'My one and only,' he said, and limped away.

For economy's sake she let breakfast wait until elevenses in the Gallery. Rucellai was there.

'Welcome,' he said. 'I am glad to see you.'

'Do you really mean that?'

'I never say things I do not mean. London has been making *la festa*, and making me feel a stranger. I stayed in my lodgings all Sunday, reading. I felt a little jealous of you, able to go home and be happy. But all my life I have been unhappy.'

'But you know, Rucellai, I wasn't happy.' (Neither then nor at any time did she call him Guido. He preferred to be called Rucellai because it was not his real name: it was his Partisan name. He had, he said, bade farewell to his youthful reality, and he once startled her by saying that she would, soon, bid farewell to hers.) 'I was miserable. Is that awful of me? I ought not to feel that way about my own home.'

At once he lit up, both excited and pleased.

'Exactly the same thing happened to me after the war when I went back to Turin. For years I'd been dreaming of going back home. It was no longer my Torino. All my friends were either scattered, or killed, or married, or interested only in making money. Heroes had become men. I was an exile in my own country. I am also an exile here. You are experiencing the same thing now. And here you, too, you are also an exile, in this Anglo-Saxon city with its queen, and its court, and its rich clubs. What does one do about it? We must talk of this,' he urged. 'Will you dine with me tonight?'

Alas! She was exhausted by the journey, already half asleep on her feet. He need not be surprised if she were found curled up under the counter of the bookstall, snoring.

'Very well,' he ordered, 'tomorrow night we dine. We will go to La Speranza. One of the best Italian restaurants in London.'

He rose, bowed, left her. She would have to tell Tom that she had forgotten that tomorrow night she must go and visit Aunt Edie in Hampton Court, with messages from Mamma. And so she did, fixing to eat with him two nights after. Later, looking at herself in the washroom mirror, she remembered Lulu and Donna deceiving Mamma about their meetings with boys because they thought they were in love.

'Am I,' she asked her mirror, her comb suspended, 'in love?'

She laughed it away. How old was he? Forty? More? It was just that he was interesting to talk to; as she again found him the next night, sitting beside him in the expensive-looking pale cream and green restaurant, with all the waiters dressed like gentlemen at a dance, and all the other diners obviously rotten with money. She said, 'I hope this

is not too expensive a restaurant, Rucellai? No lady feels happy, you
know, if she is dining beyond the means of her consort.'

He had some profound thoughts (his words) about this.

'Money,' he said, 'does not necessarily make people happy. Happiness comes from the heart. Happiness is freedom. Freedom, to me, is not
having bonds. You have no bonds. I have no bonds. This is one of the
great merits of being an exile. No ties of relatives. Here I am just me.
You are just you. It is a great thing to be oneself. I have never been
attracted by an Englishwoman because I could not feel that I possessed
her completely. Only the beloved should exist for the beloved. This
country which you and I inhabit is a good place for us because it is the
land of loneliness.'

Trying to understand his strange and interesting philosophy she
asked:

'Are you lonely, Rucellai?'

'I,' he said proudly, 'am always lonely. I am a dreamer of dreams. I
am a sad, bad man. *Tristuccio.*'

'But you have been a man who did great things too. A man of action.
Those days of the Partisans were not just dreams.'

'My dreams came true – briefly. I was in love in those great days with
my country. The land of loneliness – and this is a profound thought –
is the land of love where love is unrequited.'

'Poor Rucellai!'

'Do you not,' he asked her seriously, 'ever feel this loneliness?'

'Oh, yes!' she agreed. 'I am often lonely on Sunday afternoons.'

'Tonight,' he smiled at her, 'I will not be lonely. Nor you. Tonight
our country of dreams will have a population of two.'

'Will you never go back to Italy?' she asked hastily, fearing that she
understood him.

'What should I do in Torino at my age? One day I will go back, as
all Italians do, but only when they can *far figura*, cut a dash, as you
say, with a lemon-coloured car and a pretty wife. If I went back now
I would be competing with men twenty years younger than me, men
who have been keeping their eyes on jobs ever since they went up to
the university, flattering their professors, carrying his briefcase,
opening the door of his car for him, taking his daughter out, with
discretion, agreeing with all his rotten political ideas. No! *Sta bene
qui.*'

'What does that mean?'

'I'm fine here.'

'You must help me to learn Italian. Whatever else you lose you cannot lose that.'

'I should not want to. I love Italy, there is no country like Italy, but I do not admire her as I used to. I have seen her naked and ashamed. You must come to my flat for lessons. I will give you a lesson every night. But now we must hurry.'

Every night?

He had tickets for a concert of Italian music, mostly of the seventeenth and eighteenth century, Cimarosa, Lully and Tartini. During the *largo* of the Cimarosa Concerto in G he laid his hand on hers and they smiled at one another over the dreamy flutes and the muted strings humming like bees. 'All the tears and gaiety of the south,' he whispered. During the Lully he laid his hand tenderly on her knee. In an interval she delicately pointed to his temple and dared to say that she saw one grey hair.

'Do you mind?' he asked. 'I could dye it if you wish.'

'No. I think, really and truly, I prefer older men. They are more interesting. Usually.'

He made her blush by asking her if she had had great experience of older men. During the Tartini she held his hand, tightly. After the concert she invited him to have coffee with her in her room. As he helped her doff her coat he kissed her, and asked her if she were a Catholic. When she said, 'No! Daddy was a Presbyterian,' he said that he would instruct her, and began to unbutton her blouse, and her heart began to wallop.

'There! The sloping Botticelli shoulders. The wide-eyed look of the air and the sea and the earth.'

'Rucellai,' she whispered, while he was removing her blouse, 'I never let anybody do this before.'

He laughed. 'You prefer to do it yourself?' His arms were around her, groping for the fasteners of her brassiere. She grabbed it to her bosom.

'Rucellai! I'm, really and truly, not that sort of girl. Really and truly I'm not!'

'You have not had lovers?' he demanded, glaring at her.

'Lots!' she said, terrified. 'Dozens!'

'Tell me the truth!' he bullied.

'No!' she squeaked. 'Never!' She paled. 'I mean not really and truly.'

'Which is it in the name of Jesu?' he shouted.

She clasped her arms in front of her and burst into tears of misery and shame.

'Donna e madonna!' he shouted, fell on his knees, clasped her about her thighs and gazed up at her in joy. 'A virgin!' Rising, he gently slipped down one strap, kissed the slope of her breast with reverence, and replaced her blouse. 'We shall be married in the New Year. And we shall live in a flat in Wigmore Street. And drive a yellow M.G. It has been my dream for years.'

He gazed at her voraciously, threw his hand up in the air, and moaned, 'See what England has done to me! I am behaving like a milord. Italian and religion tomorrow night,' and dashed for the door.

O gosh! Tom!

'Not tomorrow night! I have to go to my dear Aunt Edie to Hampton Court Palace with a pair of chickens from Mamma.'

He paused at the door. He said in the cool lofty voice of an old Wykhamist, 'Hampton Court Palace? Really? You have an aunt in the Palace? Can you find your own way to the Palace? Will you be returning late from the Palace? After dark? I'm sure Aunt Edie would disapprove strongly. As do I!'

'I've done it a dozen times. And it will not be late, nor after dark.'

He shook his head dolefully.

'You don't know how attractive you are, or how innocent you are. All those coloureds! I have often thought that young ladies in London should all carry police whistles. I shall buy you one.'

He looked as if he was about to hurl himself on her. Instead he hurled himself down the stairs, thump-thump. Just as it was beginning to soak into her mind, which felt like a flower-bed after a Newfoundland had lolloped over it, that he had talked about marriage, her doorbell rang. Her white blouse flying she ran to the window, lifted it and looked down at the pavement. He started waving, and using his palms as a megaphone he shouted up:

'Cover yourself! No bra! Button up!'

'What is it?' she shouted down, clutching her collar to her neck.

'Those chickens!' he shouted. 'They'll go bad. The heat.'

'The what? I can't hear.'

'The chickens!' he boomed.

'What chickens?' she shouted down.

'For Aunt Edie!' he shouted back.

A window lifted across the street and a man shouted:

'Would you please be quiet, you silly oaf!'

'They are waiting for me at Fortnum and Mason's,' she shouted, astounded at her powers of invention.

He waved and sent her up an immense shrug, threw one arm into the air to the man across the street, uttering some Italian vocable which may have been meaningless but which sounded insulting, and to which the man in the window replied with two uplifted fingers and an English vocable which she knew had no meaning but sounded just as rude, and so – he replying to the man, the man to him, he back to the man, the man to his back – he went away. Then the man, who, she observed, was young and stark naked, waved to her, whereupon she slapped down the window, flicked the curtains together, and threw herself on the bed staring at the mottled ceiling.

'But I couldn't,' she said, and on her fingers started to make calculations.

If he is now twenty years older than his competitors who would be, say, twenty-one, he is forty-one, in which case – forty-one from 1962, one from two, four from six, leaves 1921, and that means when the war broke out, 1939, one from nine leaves eight, two from three leaves one – he was only eighteen then and could not have taken part in high politics with Don Furso and is A Liar! No! He said he came here twenty-two years ago, which is 1940, and was only nineteen, and is still A Liar! Or else he is much older. My God! How old is he? He could be forty-five! Twenty-seven years older than me. Oh! If I had only somebody to talk to! He could have a wife in Italy, too! If only old Tom didn't hate all Italians! I could trust Tom. If he knows anything really about anything. But I know all he would say is that Rucellai is a treacherous Italian. O gosh.

At which she thought how awfully awkward it would be if the two of them ever met, and got up and looked with wide eyes in her mirror at her Botticelli shoulders.

Tom took her to his Spanish restaurant and talked about Socialism, and an American philosopher named George Henry, and loaned her a slightly worn paper-back copy of Shaw's *Intelligent Woman's Guide to Socialism and Capitalism*, which had the mark of a tea-cup on the cover. She took him to Oakley Street for coffee. There, in the hall, she found waiting for her a portable gramophone and a record of the Cimarosa Concerto in G. She deftly hid the card accompanying them – it bore the message, 'Music, Religion, Language and Love, this is Our Lonely Land' – and said to Tom, 'Oh, look at what I bought at lunchtime. I wanted you to hear a record that might remind you of happier days. It contains all the sorrow and gaiety of the South.'

As she played it for him she sat curled on the floor, thinking, while he tapped his foot to the *rondo* and the *allegro*, that he was very like old Sullivan who used to help Daddy in the garden, and to whom she often confided her troubles; which, in turn, reminded her of old Sulky the white Persian into whose belly she used to cry whenever she was sad. When it was over she said, 'Are you a Catholic still, Tom?'

'Yes.'

'Are all Catholics very strict?'

'Some of them are. In Ireland most of 'em are. In Italy they take it in their stride.'

'Are *you* strict?'

The way she was sitting ... He looked out the window. 'Not as much as I ought to be.'

'Tom, what do Catholic girls in Ireland do about men?'

He chuckled his throat-smile.

'They do their best. Why are you asking?'

'What does "do their best" mean?'

He shuffled in his chair, and coughed a bit, and rubbed his heart, and said, 'Ye're wearing yeer skirts very short this year.' She pulled her skirt over her knees. 'Listen! Didn't you ever have any boy-friends? You know what I mean.'

He got up and went over to sit on the edge of the bed. She slewed around after him. He looked out of the window again.

'Oh, yes!' she said scornfully. 'I have had lots of boys, of course, and am quite familiar with what is known as the facts of life if that is what *you* mean. I know all about babies and what they call sleeping together. What I am interested in is if Catholics are all that strict what do they do when they fall in love?'

'They marry. Why are you asking me these questions?' He got up and went back to his chair. 'Sit on the bed, you'll get cold on that floor. What are you after?'

'It is Lorna Alleyn. She works at the bookstall. She is in love with a Catholic and she is not sure that he is not married. She does not know what to do about him. You would condemn her, wouldn't you, for going on with him?'

'I condemn nobody,' he said glumly. 'Everybody's case is different. We're all human.'

She sighed. They were silent for so long that she got up and said, 'I will put on that lovely *largo* again.'

It floated softly over them, part-dance, part-dream, part-dirge. She stood by the window looking up at the ashen and pink sky. Suddenly she found him by her side, his arm around her shoulder.

'Barbara! I want to be honest with you. I want you to know why I left the Gallery. I got mixed up with a loose woman. She used come after me at all sorts of times. She followed me into the Gallery. You know that fellow Rutchie in the Gallery? You must have seen him. He came over here during the war. He was down and out, like all those refugees. He got a job as a clerk in the railways, then he got a job as a clerk in the Gallery. He was over us warders. He caught her bothering me one day, and he threw her out. I had to leave. She follows me still. I'm terrified she'll find out I'm at Euston and come after me there. Every night going home I never dare get off the bus at my own door for fear she'd be waiting for me, wanting money.'

The pulse of the *largo* burst into the race of the *rondo*, into dancers, blue sea, blazing sun. They stood back from one another.

'Poor Tom! You never did have any luck with women, did you!'

'Not until I met you.'

'Oh, me? I'm only a girl. I'm only a kid. Why do you let yourself be persecuted like this, Tom? Why don't you clear out of London? Get a job somewhere else?'

He looked at her. He looked down into the street. He tapped the window with his forefinger. So sweet, so good, so innocent.

'So that is what you would advise. Is it?'

'You would be so much happier. It is better than staying here and being tormented.'

He looked at her. So cruel.

'You would advise that?'

'Yes, I would,' she said in a firm, practical tone. 'Have peace, Tom. Have peace.'

'In Birmingham? Liverpool?' He gave his sour, throaty chuckle. 'I'll think about it.'

'Poor Tom!'

'Don't give me pity!'

The music stopped. He grabbed his hat from the table and went out so fast that she could only wave to him over the banisters and, for fear of disturbing the house, whisper, 'Give me a ring, Tom, won't you, some time?'

She returned to her room and her window. Across the street the young man of last night was leaning on his elbows on the window-sill, smoking a big, crooked pipe, looking idly into the empty street, his shirt off – perhaps more.

She leaned her left temple against the window-pane and glared at the darkening sky over the chimney pots. If Rucellai were here now she would lever the truth out of him. But, first, she would praise him for not betraying Tom Dalton's secret to her. She would certainly ask him, please, really and truly, how old he was. But she could not mention Tom – he would never understand. He was sweet to give her the gramophone. She put on the *largo* again, first swathing the black box in her bath-towel so that the music could be barely heard in her room. She undressed, and lay down to sleep, letting the record play itself out. Was this the real Rucellai? Dreaming of Italy, and yellow MG's. He would never go back. He would never have a flat in Wigmore Street. And I am never going to ask him any questions, ever, about anything at all.

In October he gave her an engagement ring (telling her never to wear it at the Gallery: their secret for another while) and put her into a tiny top-storey flat in Wigmore Street: two tiny rooms, with a bed in one and a table and a chair in the other.

'It is all yours,' he said. 'I shall not intrude. Not very much.'

'Am I,' she thought as she looked about the almost bare room, 'a kept woman?'

'Now,' he said happily, 'you can tell Mamma.'

'But she will never allow it. I am only twenty!'

'You mean I am too old?' he asked angrily. 'Or is it too poor? I have always been poor. Because I fought for my country. Do you know that when the war ended I had to take a job as a clerk in the railways? Me! A Rucellai! Are you ashamed of me?'

'I will tell her at Christmas when I go home! Really and truly!'

Every week after that they went shopping for furniture; this week an armchair, next a rug, then a picture, then he could not resist a set of six Regency silver dessert-spoons, then he persuaded her that they would need this small silver salver 'for visiting-cards when our friends call on us.' She had to rebel to get a mirror. 'I am your mirror,' he throated like a wood pigeon. 'Besides we have so little money.' They met every evening, for dinner, or a film, or a concert, and afterwards there was a little Italian lesson, and a little Religion, and a little love, never going beyond, or stopping short of, a lowered strap and a kiss on the slope of her breast, usually followed by a roar from him like a lion from whom a joint of beef has been snatched, a rush and a banged door.

One night she moaned to him, 'But, Rucellai, why do you insist on tormenting yourself?'

'I am a man of deep feelings!'

'I have deep feelings, too!'

'Am I a brute?'

'I want to give you peace,' she whispered, sad for him. 'Besides you get me all upset! I don't know what you want from me!'

'Innocence,' he said, drawing himself upright, 'is a precious jewel. I never knew,' he groaned, just before he banged the door, 'how expensive it could be.'

He fled, and with a sigh she slowly unzipped her skirt and removed her blouse. The door crashed open and his eyeballs stared at her.

'I do not understand you,' she wailed.

His whole frame seemed to dissolve like a polar bear sitting down.

'I have sought you too long,' he said feebly, 'to lose you now,' and very slowly, and quietly, he closed the door, and flung it open again to growl, 'Lock it! Tight!'

She got a postcard from Tom Dalton, forwarded from Oakley Street. It was a coloured picture of Rossetti's *Annunciation* in the Tate Gallery. It was from Cardiff. 'I am among the dark Celts. I do this for you. One step nearer home? Tom.' She burned it. Then she got another, a postcard, in colour, of a railway engine. 'You do not reply. Where are you? I need you. Pray for me.' She burned this in the tiny grate, knelt and said an *Ave Maria* for him in Italian. That was November. The first week in December she got a telegram, at the gallery, from Naples. 'PLEASE MEET ME IN THE GREEN LION AT EUSTON TONIGHT AT EIGHT NEED YOU BADLY LOVE TOM.'

She had arranged to go with Rucellai to a concert that night, and went to his office to explain about Tom. She said, blushing to the roots of her hair, 'An old gentleman friend of Mamma's is suddenly come to town. I really must meet him tonight. Do you mind if I don't go to the concert?'

'Who is this man?' he asked irritably.

'A friend of Mamma. Old General Butterly.'

'Why didn't she write beforehand?'

'She thinks I have nothing to do at night, any night.'

'If you had told her about us months ago this deception need never have happened.'

'What deception? Whose deception?'

'Yours, ours, mine, to everybody, about everything, about me. How old is this man?'

'He is as old as a general.'

'I don't like old men taking you out. I know all about old men.'

'I'll be back after the concert. I'll be back by ten o'clock. I will tell Mamma at Christmas. Really and truly.'

'I wish we had got married last summer. You are too simple, too innocent. What are you going to talk to this general about?'

'I don't know, the war I suppose, he's always talking about the Dardanelles.'

'But that was the 1914 war! He must be ninety.'

'He's awfully old, very, very old, really and truly. He is much older than you.'

'I shall expect you,' he said severely, 'at ten-thirty. We have to do the Conjunctive Pronouns and the Tenth Commandment. You will then be ready to go for final instruction to my dear friend Father De La Poer at Farm Street. And not a minute too soon!'

He took up his pen. She almost said: 'Yes, Daddy.'

It was a dripping night. From beside the door of The Green Lion he saw her approach under the hazy light of a street lamp and knew her at once by the slim neck and the strong legs. She was wearing a tight-belted white raincoat and a little red beret on the back of her poll, her hands dug into the two big patch-pockets of her coat, her head bent against the rain. She knew him by the slouch of his back. He was wearing an old army raincape and a cap. When he took her two hands she saw that he was grey-faced, worn, tired and lined.

'The same old Barbara!' he said warmly.

'The same old Tom,' and she laughed to make it sound true.

'I've a surprise for you,' he said quickly, 'I'm just back from Naples. My wife . . .'

'Your wife?'

It came out in a rush:

'My wife was killed last week when a house collapsed in Naples. I'm not married any longer! I'm free! In the summer I'm going to bring back my little Gemma. She's about your age. You'd get on fine with her. I've got lots of plans. I have it all worked out in my head. You and everything.'

He led her into the pub; very different to The Cat and Cage – crowded, noisy, damp, smelly. No sooner had he set her on a bench by a plastic table than he jumped up and limped over to the counter for drinks. She got a disturbing feeling that he was glad to move away from her. She hoped he was not returning to live in London. As he moved back slowly, cap on poll, still in his waterproof cape, his head down, watching the glasses in his shaky hands, she saw that he was drinking whiskey and realized that he had been drinking before they met. When he sat down he clutched her hand. By the way his eyes kept sliding away from her as he talked she felt that he was afraid of something.

'It's this way, Barbara – I've been thinking about security. We all need security. I've thought it all out, all the way from Naples. I've never had a home. Gemma needs a home. I'm going over to Dublin tonight to look for a . . .'

He stopped dead and stared at her.

'You look terribly tired, Tom. Tell me everything.'

'I'm worn out. All this week in Naples – discussions. arguments, fighting day and night, the priest and the lawyer, her father and mother, brothers and sisters, grandmothers and grandfathers, uncles, cousins, aunts, all of them rubbing together in that coal-hole in a wall in a lane that they call a house, crushing around me like a lot of bloody damp dogs yapping at me. It was them, seeing them all together there, one family, all in a bunch, that made me see how much I need a home and a wife.'

She laughed. 'A wife? Good for you, Tom! Never say die!'

He waved her laughter away from him, roughly.

'I didn't know what they were saying, and all I could say – I was saying it all the time – was "I want a *mollyeh*", that's Italian for a wife, "I want a *casa*". Did you know the Italians have no word for a home? Only a *casa*. Like a bloody packing-case, and that's about all they have.

I can marry! I'm free! And I want that little girl of mine, to bring her up like you. That's where you're going to be so marvellous, Barbara. Look at you! Exactly the way I thought of you, the way I was dreaming of you there in the middle of them all, and all the way home in the train and the boat. Good, and lovely, and pure and innocent. No stinking Italian scent about *you*, no paint, no powder, no gewgaws. You will, won't you, Barbara? You'll be my little Barbara always? Say it, Barbara, say it!'

Inside in her she felt a big, choking breath that she could not breathe out. She heard her mamma saying it, and Donna and Lulu: 'My dear! How utterly squaliferous!' And, to her horror, she heard the words go ballooning out of her mouth, just the way Mamma would say it. 'I am afraid, Tom, we are a trifle intoxicated, aren't we? Don't you think it would be advisable for us to continue our chat on a more propitious occasion?'

'Stop that! Don't be snotty with me! I've had an awful time. All those bastards fighting me! But I'll get my rights. I'll get what I want, everything I've been dreaming of for months and months. I'll best them!'

'Sssh! Tom!'

His voice had risen. Two men at the near counter were looking over at them. He clutched her hand more tightly.

'Bloody Italians, they'd sell their souls to best you. But not me! Not me, thinking of you, Barbara! To Dublin, tonight! I have the "P" tickets. First-class. Once we get to Dublin and get a nice little house . . .'

She dragged her hand away, she half rose, he grabbed at her and knocked over his glass so that it spilled over the table, and his knees, and broke on the floor. She looked around for help. More people were looking at them now. A barman in a white apron was approaching.

'I must telephone,' she said.

She slipped into the booth and dialled the first letters of Rucellai's lodgings, and stopped. He wouldn't be in. And if she told him he would never trust her again. Through the misty glass she saw him feebly wiping the table, with his hands, and mopping his knees, and the barman upbraiding him. She dialled the complete number. A foreign woman's voice replied, 'No, Signor Rucellai is gone out.' She came back to the table and sat down helplessly.

'He isn't in.'

'Who?'

'I was trying to get Rucellai.'

He all but shouted the name: 'Rucellai?'

'I thought he might help.'

'Help who?'

'You, me, all of us.'

He was really shouting now. 'Why should you call that bloody skirt-chaser? What's he got to do with it? Is he butting in on me again? If that bastard butts in on me again...'

'Don't you dare talk about Rucellai like that.'

'Why the hell shouldn't I talk about him like that?'

'Rucellai is a gentleman.'

'Oh? So Mr Bloody Rucellai is a frigging gentleman? How long have you known Mr Bloody Gentleman Rucellai?'

'It's none of your damn business!'

(I'm arguing with a drunk. In a common pub.)

'It's very much my business. I found you first.' He sobbed it. He shouted again, 'If he's buttin' in again on me ...' His grey face went white, completely white. 'What's between you and him?'

Like a woman putting down a trump card, she slapped her splayed fingers on the wet table, staring at him, waiting for him. He stared at her. Then slowly he lowered his eyes, and saw the ring. 'I'm marrying Rucellai.'

He looked up slowly and whispered it, evilly, 'You little bitch!'

'And you!' she cried, getting up, shaking all over. 'You dirty old ram!'

He scrambled up, his chair fell, this time her glass. The barman came back and grabbed his arm. 'Now then, out with you, both of you!' He struck at the barman. The whole pub was watching them, their glasses held immobile. The other barman rushed out and the two concentrated on hauling him, cursing at them, his heels dragging on the tiles, out through the cut-glass doors. One of them returned for his old suitcase and a brown-paper parcel and threw them out after him on the wet pavement.

With her palms to her cheeks she stood for a moment looking around at the indifferent crowd, and then she ran. She halted at the glass doors, looking between the two barmen at the street where, through the hazy rain, he staggered from one lamp-lit pool to the next, dragging his suitcase. One of the barmen glanced at her, and said coldly, 'Hop it!' She went out and stood with her back to the window of a closed shop and watched him move slowly towards the station. He would be all right in there. His old station. The friendly climate.

She followed him at a careful distance, hanging back under the porticos, now bustling with passengers. She watched him pass through the railings where an engine stood in a cloud of hissing steam, and pass out of sight behind it to the Irish Mail. She bought a platform ticket from the machine and went as far as the train's hither end, watching him move slowly along it, his cap falling, his paper parcel, and at last clamber into a carriage. She waited there for a long time, against the brick wall, out of the way of the travellers filing noisily into the train. She kept her eyes fixed on that one carriage until, at last, the porters slammed the last door, the guard lifted and waved his lamp, and all the lighted windows began to curve away, flickering like falling cards, out into the wet dark. Then her head sank, and she wept for him. She walked all the way down to the Strand and westward as far as Charing Cross. Her hair was a tangle, her shoes and stockings were sopping. She got a bus to Oxford Circus and walked home. When she got into the little flat she leaned her back against the door, and it seemed as if it was only then that she let out the pent-up breath of terror. She felt safe, cruel and bitchy, and filled with a deep longing for love.

She was still trembling as she lit the fire and drew a hot bath. She put her Secret of Venus in the bath. In her old blue dressing-gown, that she had had ever since she left Dublin, tied about her neck, she made coffee and sandwiches, and squatted with them before the fire. Full of guilt she heard her mamma's voice, 'London, my dear Babs, I warn you, is no place for little girls.' Resolutely she shook her head. 'I am not a little girl!' Feeling the warmth of the fire and the food steal over her she began to paint her toenails; made up her lips with a pale lipstick; tried on a pair of coral earrings that Rucellai had given her, turning her head now to the right, now to the left, straightening her Rossetti neck, holding back her Botticelli shoulders.

Maybe all he had meant was that she should cross with him to Dublin to ease the way for him? As he had done for her? But how long did he think . . . ? He must be crazy to think . . . The rain glistened in the street lights on the window. She looked at her watch where she had laid it on the mantelpiece. He would have a bad crossing. She put on the Cimarosa record and squatted again before the fire, and with the little gold scent-spray that Rucellai had given her she lightly dewed her hair, her shoulders and above her knees, which, Lorna Alleyn had said with

an unlikeable covert smile, was the way you should do it. The wind
sweeping down Wigmore Street rattled the windows. She saw the old
*Hibernia*, all its lights ringed with mist, waiting at its moorings in
Holyhead Harbour. She put on her Italian slippers and curled up in the
armchair to do her fingernails. An hour later she was awakened by his
insistent rapping on her door.

His black raincoat was shining, his black umbrella trickled, his black
Homburg hat dripped on the mat. He looked big, grave , and – his
pet-word whenever he felt melancholy – *tristuzzo*. She took his things
and as she was stacking the umbrella upright in the kitchen sink, with
his hat on top of it, she called out, 'Rucellai! I hope you aren't cross
with me? I came back early specially for you.'

He was standing with one hand on the mantelpiece, one leg, held to
the fire, already steaming, staring into the fire.

'Oh, my poor Rucellai! Your shoes are wet. Let me take them off. Sit
down, darling.' As she untied them she said again. 'You're not cross
with me? You don't think I am a naughty girl? Did you have a lovely
night? You are sure you are not cross with me?'

'I did not think of you at all,' he said sombrely to the fire.

'Your socks are damp too! Let me take them off.'

She got a cushion and laid it near the fire, and laid a towel on it and
tenderly laid each bare foot on the towel near the heat. She sat back
on her hunkers and stroked his instep.

'I felt quite lonely,' she said to him as he looked down at her, looking
up at him.

'I have never seen you look so beautiful, and so innocent.'

She laughed. 'You said that last night.'

'But you don't know how beautiful, and how good you are!'

'Let me make you some coffee.'

'Play me some music. It will calm my soul.'

She put on a Lully ballet suite that he often asked for and sat with
her arm across his thigh looking at the fire.

'Nymphs and shepherdesses,' he murmured and stroked her hair.
'Enchantress. Wafted on a seashell as a gift from the Spring.'

'You said that last night, too.'

He clasped her to his side.

'Barbara! Promise me you will always be my little Barbara. Promise
me you will never change. Say it!'

'I will always be me. And you, Rucellai? Promise you will never change.'

'I shall never change!'

She felt his fingers gently undo the silk knot of her dressing-gown for his usual ritual kiss. Drawing back her head to see better, she waited for the look in his eyes. The dressing-gown fell to her waist. She saw his eyes widen and then close with what, afterwards, she could only think of was despair. Three wild and rushing minutes later, during which he dragged on his socks and shoes, and ran for his coat, hat and umbrella, she found herself staring, defeated and ashamed, into the fire.

He was not at the Gallery the next day, nor the next after. On the third day she rang his lodgings and was told that he had left. On the fourth day she went to his office in the Gallery where she found a strange young man. 'I was looking for Mr Rucellai,' she said, wild-eyed.

'He has gone to Italy, I believe. Perhaps,' he said, smiling agreeably, 'I can be of service?' She said, 'Oh!' and, not taking in his question, she added, 'Thank you.' He said 'Not at all. Do come again.' She went away. Two days later she found a letter from him in her letterbox. The postmark said TORINO.

Dear beautiful, good Barbara,

I have fled from you because I am unworthy of you. I have betrayed you too often in the grossest ways. I am torn asunder by the hounds of Artemis for gazing at her beauty. My Hercules has been too strong for me. (Pollaiuolo. Formerly in the Uffizi Gallery, Florence.) Do not try to seek me out. I am a monster. The flat is all yours. The rent is paid to December 31st. I shall never live in Wigmore Street. I shall never have an MG. I shall never see your loveliness again.

Your despairing,

Rucellai

POSCRITTO. Corrupt as I may be your sweet innocence has corrupted me more than ever before. As the great Lord Acton said – All innocence corrupts, but absolute innocence corrupts absolutely.

Over and over she said aloud, 'It is extraordinary!' For days she kept saying it. Sometimes she said, 'It is really and truly extraordinary.'

Once she found herself saying it, standing in Trafalgar Square, and said to herself. 'I must stop it, I'm talking like old Aunt Edie!' An hour later she found herself holding a postcard out to a customer, her eyes on the window, thinking that it was really and truly the most extraordinary thing that had ever happened to her in her whole life. Only the customer saying with a smile, 'Please, may I have my card?' brought her back to where she was.

In the end she had to talk to somebody about it all, so she confided one day in Lorna Alleyn at the bookstall. She even showed her Rucellai's letter. Lorna, a dark, goat-toothed wench of whom it would be kind to say that she was largely endowed in every way, and frank to say that she was very fat, read the letter in wide-eyed glee. When she had read it she hooted with wicked laughter.

'Oh, gosh! "Dear, beautiful, good Barbara . . . " That's a tall order! To be beautiful is good, Babs. To be good is, I suppose, good too. But to be beautiful and good? Fatal! You will always attract the wrong kind of a man.' Then her black eyes narrowed and she said angrily, 'You kept all this to yourself very cleverly! You never uttered a word about Rucellai. You *are* a minx. And a silly, bloody little fool. I could have told you!'

'I did not want to hear!' she said proudly. 'In love the beloved has no faults.'

Lorna lifted dismayed paws.

'Beautiful. Good. Innocent. You poor kid!'

'But,' Barbara wailed, coming at last to the point, 'I am just like any other girl.'

'Of that, my dear, I have no least doubt, only you don't look it!'

'Then, what's wrong with me?'

Lorna went back to her postcards, banging and boxing them from Antonio da Messina to Zurbaran.

'Men!' she said furiously.

# Appendix

## These Tales
### (Preface to *The Heat of the Sun*)

To these offerings I have given the subtitle *Stories and Tales* to point a distinction that has been in my mind when writing them, and which I think may be worth explaining.

As I see it a Short Story, if it is a good story, is like a child's kite, a small wonder, a brief, bright moment. It has its limitations; there are things it can do and cannot do but, if it is good, it moves in the same element as the largest work of art – up there, airborne. The main thing a writer of a short story wants to do is to get it off the ground as quickly as possible, hold it up there, taut and tense, playing it like a fish. The reader will never know how much time was spent on getting it airborne, how often it flopped, stumbled and dragged along the ground in all those first efforts, those discarded first drafts, those false beginnings, that were cut out once it was up – so much dismissed, forgotten but necessary labour. The limits of the Short Story are apparent. It may not wander far; it has to keep close to its base-point, within the bounds of place, time and character; it will only carry a few characters, three at least, at best not more than three; there is not time, or space, for elaborate characterization – we are flying a kite not a passenger-balloon or an aeroplane; and there is often no plot, nothing much more than a situation, and only just enough of that to release a moment or two of drama, enough to let the wilful kite swirl, change colour, catching the winds of mood. A short story is concentrated stuff. It is called a short story because it is short. An essentialist art. Maupassant and Chekhov invented it between them.

A Tale is quite different. Like a small plane it is much more free, carries a bit more cargo, roves farther, has time and space for more complex characterization, more changes of mood, more incidents and scenes, even more plot. Because it is more relaxed the reader may find the Tale easier reading, and he may even take more pleasure in it, but it is likely to give the writer-craftsman rather less pleasure, since what he always most enjoys is the fascination of what is most difficult. It has its own problems, however, for the writer, whose toughest task is to orchestrate his Tale into a single, satisfying shape of flight. For me, the greatest master of the Tale was Prosper Mérimée, even though he did not bother much about shape or form, not because he lacked the skill but because he nourished a certain, coy horror of seeming too much of an Artist. Hemingway was something of an American-style Mérimée, though never quite so tough, and no good with women. Compare any of his women with the Carmen of Mérimée.

The possibilities of both the Short Story and the Tale become evident when we compare them with that plane-carrier, the Novel, which can carry as heavy a load as the writer wishes, for as long and over as many seas. Yet the Novel, too, justifies itself only in the same moments of packed crisis as the Story and the Tale. These are the keychapters of its long voyage, when its planes go swoosh into the air. After they have returned to roost the slow, majestic pace begins again – until the next moment of dramatic crisis. It is such moments that the writer of the Short Story isolates.

I set out to write Tales in *A Sweet Colleen*, *£1000 for Rosebud* and *In the Bosom of the Country*. I was writing short stories when I wrote *The Heat of the Sun* and *Charlie's Greek*. Whichever is which, and the reader will easily distinguish, all I hope is that, now and again, the Story or the Tale 'levitates a little', like that endearing character The Flying Monk in Norman Douglas's *Old Calabria*. Any story, tale or novel that does not levitate a little is, as far as I am concerned, a grounded albatross. A prince of the air, all he can do on the earth is waddle a little because of his wings.